DYING IN THE TWILIGHT OF SUMMER

Seth O'Connell

authorHOUSE®

AuthorHouse™
1663 Liberty Drive, Suite 200
Bloomington, IN 47403
www.authorhouse.com
Phone: 1-800-839-8640

First published by AuthorHouse 1/9/2009

ISBN: 978-1-4389-4050-2 (sc)
ISBN: 978-1-4389-4051-9 (hc)

Library of Congress Control Number: 2008912082

Printed in the United States of America
Bloomington, Indiana

This book is printed on acid-free paper.

For my grandparents,
without their love, nothing was possible

In the late days of August, the sunshine can seem never-ending. The summer, warm and lazy, is gently slowing down. The fresh evening air is cool and calm. The land is green, filled with life, and time passes gracefully. Students, preparing for school, are filled with anticipation for the upcoming school year. The future gives hope of new beginnings and goals of greatness. Young boys, dreaming of becoming men, rush head first toward their desires. They vow not to get stuck as their parents have done. This small town, these dead end jobs, those wasted dreams are impossible in the last days before fall.

Little does anyone know that the summer is coming to an end. The cold days of winter are rapidly approaching, and everything that seems so alive and bright is dying. Dying the same way it did last year and every year before. Life is a cycle. Time is a continuous drip into a bucket. We try to fix the drip, but we are unable. The more we try to stop the drip the worse it becomes. With time, we grow accustomed to the sound of the drip and forget about it. Eventually, the drip fills the bucket, and the bucket overflows. But in August, everything still seems possible.

August 5th, 1996

"Can you believe that Dugal pulled me?" Andrew asked, making it clear by his tone what answer he wanted. Before his companion could answer, he quickly piled on more evidence to his rhetorical inquisition. "I mean seriously, a two run lead with one out in the eighth inning, and he pulls out his best pitcher. Can you believe it?"

"Your pitch count was at a hundred and twenty-five though." Eric, his squat, burly companion, said calmly without taking his eyes off the road ahead.

"But I was cruising man. They hadn't hit a ball out of the infield since the fifth." Andrew cried dramatically moving his entire body to face the driver. "I walk one guy and I get the rope. I mean shit man, the least that fat ass owes me is a chance to get through that inning. I mean if it wasn't for me we wouldn't even be going to State." He added, speaking continuously faster, as was his habit when trying to get others to join his side.

"I mean us...the pitching staff, I mean." This last sentence he said slowly, wishing he could some how take back the arrogant comment he had let slip off his tongue.

Eric reached over and changed the song on the stereo then turned the volume up a few notches.

"Yea, everything was pretty crazy." He commented over the now blaring vocals, trying to ease the pressure that would surely build on Andrew if there was silence.

Eric knew his friend did not mean to be cocky. He was merely fired up as usual and speaking his mind. Besides, all apologies aside, Eric knew damn well what was common knowledge to every baseball fan in Lodge Pole County, and that was that Andrew was absolutely correct. He was the messiah here to deliver the Wranglers to the promise land.

"The point is that everything worked out ok, and the Wranglers are going to the state tournament!" Shane exclaimed suddenly moving to the center of the backseat and leaning forward between his companions, his hands on the head-rests. His face beamed with a mischievous smile, looking back and forth at his two friends.

"Hell yea!" Andrew replied, hunkering down in his seat and pumping his arm in and out. He laughed his contagious laugh and slapped Eric enthusiastically on the right shoulder. "After a twelve year hiatus, the Wranglers are back for blood!"

The three shared in heartfelt laughter, and Eric cranked the volume up even higher. Eric's car, a 1990 Chevy Lumina, glided smoothly down the road. There weren't many high school students that took better care of their car than him. They drove down the winding highway out of town, all the windows rolled down, passing cars that were driving the speed limit.

The boys joked and reminisced on different games of the season. Each of them recalled certain moments most pertaining to themselves, good or bad, a great deal clearer than the other two. Finally, Eric slowed the car down and turned off onto a small dirt clearing just before a two lane, concrete bridge. The turnaround was about ten vehicles in size and dead ended into a large limestone cliff jutting out over the lake.

"I don't wanna jump the cliffs today. Let's jump off the bridge." Andrew suggested as the boys climbed out of the car. The sound of the doors shutting echoed off the barren rocks beside them.

It was late afternoon, but it was still very hot and dry. The sun seemed overbearing, and there wasn't a single cloud in the sky. A slight, dry breeze only teased with the idea of cooling anything. It mostly stirred up dust and made the weather even more unbearable.

"Yea right man, you can get like a hundred dollar fine if you get caught doing that. Besides, there's rebar under the bridge." Eric warned as he leaned his pale sleeves arm on top of the car, shading his eyes from the sun and addressing Andrew over the car. His arms looked like mini powder kegs, no definition only steady bulk from the elbow to the shoulder socket.

"That's bull shit. I've jumped off that bridge twenty times, and I know of at least ten other people who have done it. I have never once heard of anyone getting hurt." Andrew replied, squinting his eyes and wrinkling his forehead. He frowned at his friend for a short second then turned toward the bridge. "There's no way anyone will call the cops either. I bet less than five cars will drive by in the time it would take to jump off the bridge three times."

"If no one's gonna see you do it why do you want to do it anyway?" Eric asked, poking at his friend's weakness for hotdogging.

"Real funny, asshole. I am serious let's do this."

I don't know. It just seems easier to go over to the cliffs." Eric said, desperately trying to win the battle quickly.

He knew that Shane was fearless and probably didn't care what they did, but once Andrew started walking toward the bridge he would definitely follow. This would force Eric to do the same. It wasn't even that Eric was that scared of the jumping off the bridge just that he had grown accustomed to jumping off the cliffs. He was comfortable with them. He had jumped off them fifty times and knew that he would not be injured. The bridge however was unknown territory, and he had heard stories of it being too shallow and rebar jutting out sharply from the support columns.

These same rumors of uncertainty that made Eric fearful to jump off the bridge drove Andrew to want to do it all the more. Andrew had always been reckless. It was almost as if some primitive need for adrenaline drove him to continuously push the envelope ever further. He was never where he wanted to be but always headed there. Those close to him had simply grown accustom to it and would be shocked if he acted in any other way.

"Well, let's do something already. I didn't come to the lake to fry in the sun. I gotta get wet." Shane complained, laying his forearms across the trunk of the Chevy, and lowering his face onto his arms dramatically.

Shane was an instigator deep down inside. He wanted to jump off the bridge, not because he cared but simply to see if Eric would actually do it. As if this had settled the dispute, Andrew pulled his sleeveless t-shirt off, crumpled it into a ball, and tossed it in the still open passenger window then threw his arm around Eric's shoulders, who, looking confused, still hadn't realized he lost the debate. Andrew began guiding him in the direction of the guardrail where a small hill of scorched grass and weeds led pedestrians to the bridge. Andrew's tan arm clashed with Eric's pale freckled skin. Shane followed jogging excitedly around his friends, whistling and making goofy gestures with his arms.

As the boys walked onto the cement of the bridge, Andrew remained stuck on the morning's game.

"I mean it would have been different if Dugal pulled me and brought in Bard, but instead he brings in Jack...JACK THE CROSS EYED FISHERMAN!" This last name he said with clear frustration in his voice. Since no one responded to this, he continued, "Where the hell is Bard anyhow?" He looked around when he said this, as if expecting his friend to magically appear at the sound of his name.

"He had to go take some test at the school. He's trying to get into some class where he would get college credits or something."

"Are you serious?!? What a toolbox! We win the biggest game of the year, and he's too good to come hang out with his friends."

"Today was the only day he could take it I guess."

"I swear that guy always puts school in front of us."

Eric didn't answer this simply shrugging. He knew that Andrew didn't mean what he said. He was only talking to hear his voice as usual. Andrew had a way of always overdoing things, for he wanted everyone to share in his opinion, regardless of how trivial that opinion was. He is the kind of kid that would argue with someone for hours about which fast food joint had the best fries even if nobody cared or even disagreed with him.

"Ok boys. Here goes!"

Shane's voice drew the attention of both his friends. They turned around in time to see him climb onto the four foot guard rail of the bridge and jump off before he had time to lose his nerve. Eric leaned over the side and watched him drop. Shane flailed his arms in irregular patterns and let out a scream, as he dropped the fifty or so feet into the dark waters below.

Andrew, laughing hysterically, climbed up on the ten inch wide wall and stood looking over into the water below. Shane's head resurfaced, and he coughed on some water before joining in the laughter. He paddled backwards out of the shadow of the bridge but continued to look up to where his friends perched.

"Come on pussies!"

His yell was deafened by the enormous concrete structure above him, so it sounded very distant. Still laughing, Andrew balanced on one foot and stuck the other out over the water at a forty-five degree angle. He balanced there for a few moments until he had stopped laughing. Then he glanced over his left shoulder at Eric, smiling brightly. He gave a wink and turned his entire body around to face the bridge with his back to the edge. Squinting his eyes, his face became serious as he gazed out across the opposite side of the bridge and down the canyon beyond. Town was just visible from his perch. Still staring at who knows what, he bent his knees as if he meant to sit down on an unseen stool and in one smooth motion jumped pushing with his muscular legs outward more than up.

Eric watched with an open mouth as his friend's body tightened into a perfect back-flip and then straightened out in time to cut through the water at a perpendicular and perfect line. Before Andrew had time to resurface, Shane and Eric's eyes met and both their shocked expressions said one clear thought...

'Wow.'

"Shit," Eric whispered to himself, climbing methodically up onto the cement rail. His heart pounded against his chest, "Here goes nothing."

August 15th, 1996

Darin Bard sat on the far bench, listening to his coach's voice. His shirt-less back cooled by the primer white cinder block wall he leaned against. Every now and then he would reach one or both arms up and grab the shelf above his head that lined the entire locker room. He listened to his coach's voice, but he could not hear or comprehend what was being said. Every time the coach's eyes stopped on him, Darin feared he might realize he wasn't listening and he would hold eye contact with a solemn look until Dugal continued his scanning of the room.

He wanted to listen, but he could not. His left toe bounced up and down rapidly his heel not making contact with the floor. He pursed his lips together and glanced around the room. Even in the dimly lit room, he could see that his teammates all had the same intense look in their eyes, the same stern demeanor.

The locker room smelt of damp basement and sweat. The only sounds were that of Dugal's deep drawl and an aluminum bat that was being gently tapped repeatedly against the bench between someone's legs. The echoing sound of Dugal's hands clapping together just once and a few loud enthusiastic grunts in response awoke Darin as if from a dream. The heavy-set coach walked out of the locker room, and the players began moving around, putting on their uniforms and joking with each other quietly.

Darin looked down at his lap and clenched his fists a few times. The veins in his already glistening forearms bulged through his tight skin.

At six foot three, Darin was the perfect specimen of an athletic build. He wasn't skinny, but he was far from the bulked out bowling ball Eric was. He didn't have a defined six pack or bulging biceps, but it was clear that his torso was all muscle, and his long arms were nothing to laugh at. Darin had blond hair, cropped short in the back and sides. His German features were strong and handsome, defined most clearly by his firm, square jaw. He had blue-grey eyes that every girl at Great Pines High dreamed would fall on them in good favor. His thin lips were of little notice and drew even greater attention to his perfect teeth and dimples.

He looked around the little room again as he pulled up his stirrup socks and removed his pants from the hook to his left. He couldn't help but wonder if everyone else in the room realized how monumental this game really was. Since Coach Dugal had left the room, nobody looked nervous or even seemed to care that this was the biggest game in the history of Great Pines. Of course, Darin being the serious young man that he was considered every game from a more strict point of view than his teammates. This wasn't just another game though. This was the State Championship game. The first State Championship game the Wranglers had played in since 1962. Darin realized how much more than just another game this was, and he would be damned if he let anything come between him and the title.

"How you feeling big guy?" Darin repeated, putting his hand down firmly on Andrew's shoulder, pinching down in a sort of mock massage.

"Ready to shove nine up some cougars' asses." Andrew replied, taking off his headphones and looking up at his friend from his seat on the bench.

"That's what I like to hear." Darin returned his friend's smile and they struck each other's knuckles together fist to fist. He turned around and walked up the front steps of the dugout. His cleats sounded unnatural against the concrete floor.

Stepping out onto the field, Darin took a long look around. The sun was shining, and it was a gorgeous day for baseball. A few puffy white clouds floated low in the sky, and the American flag staggered enough to catch the attention of wondering eyes. It was a dry, late summer day. The grass was a brilliant green. The dirt of the field, already damp and grated perfectly, awaited the teams to take infield.

Darin closed his eyes, bowed his head, and crossed himself. He did it more out of superstitious habit than religious belief. He was from a Catholic family like most others in the small town, but Darin was a realist. He believed only in facts that could be proven or seen. He still wondered about God, but his beliefs dwindled smaller each year that he attended school.

Turning, he looked over his shoulder one last time at his friend sitting under the overhang of the dugout. Andrew was jamming out and air drumming frantically, every now and then repeating a word or two from the song blaring from his head phones in a high pitched scream. A scowl came across Darin's face.

'The fate of our team...no of our town lies on this kid's scrawny shoulders but to him this is just another day.' he thought.

He turned back around and stared out over the field. He couldn't stop thinking about Andrew. How can he never think even ten minutes into the future? How can a person with so many gifts not give a damn? He wondered if he pitied his friend for his simplicity or if deep down inside he was jealous that he never had to stress the way Darin always did. He wondered how nice it must be to go to sleep every night with a completely clear conscience, not giving a second's thought to what had to be done the follow day, week, or month.

"Hey are you gonna stand there much longer? If you are I will warm up with someone else, but I think that would be bad luck."

Shane yelling at him suddenly pulled him out of his trance. He looked over and saw him staring at him with a questioning smile throwing the ball into his mitt from about eight inches away, over and over. Darin didn't return his friend's smile but jogged out to the right field line.

"Were you planning which at bat you were gonna go yard?" Shane joked with him as he ran out beside him.

"Something like that." was all Darin replied without looking back, still maintaining the same straight face.

The team seemed loose, usually a good sign for a team that is playing in a big game. A team that seems too ready can often get in their own heads or over do the simple fundamentals that make up a baseball game. In the game of baseball, momentum creeps up differently than in football or basketball. A player can't afford to lose his cool, and therefore it is not as useful to get all pumped up as in other contact sports. Mistakes will happen, but these mistakes can't be mental in a big game. A physical mistake must be forgotten or it will feed on the player and spread like a virus to the rest of the team. The best sign is when the team acts the same as it would for any other game, all the extra concentration lurking below the skin.

The team's mood was light through stretching and warm-ups. Conversations were carried; there was some goofing and laughter. It wasn't until taking infield that the difference in intensity could be felt and heard by everyone in the stadium. The team looked sharp with everyone quick to compliment each other, and the zip on the throws showed that everyone was fired up. Crisp would be a good adjective.

When their opponents took their turn at infield, the Wranglers couldn't help but notice the size and speed the team displayed. Everyone stood on the top step of the dugout. Not a word was spoken. Their heads moved with each throw from release to catch. They were well aware that the Cougars were the defending State Champs. They knew that the Cougars had only lost five games all summer. They knew that the team led the conference in home runs and the entire state in batting.

The Wranglers knew all these things but still held their heads high, for they also knew that in order to beat them the Cougars had to beat Andrew Main. This gave the Wranglers a confidence deep down in the pit of every player's stomach, a faith that no matter what happened Andrew would keep the game close. No matter how inhuman these giants looked taking infield, the Wranglers showed no intimidation. The entire team watched their opponents' every move, but the high whistling and the loud snaps and pops of leather, cracking like a bullwhip when handled by an expert, coming from the right field bullpen were the sounds that inspired them to think nothing but thoughts of glorious victory.

The Wranglers took the field to start the game and were greeted with an eruption of cheers from the large hometown crowd. Shane ran to his position at third base, butterflies bouncing around in his stomach like dice in a cup. He jumped up and stretched his arms in and out a few times, looking into the grandstands and trying his hardest not to float away from the earth. He took a grounder from first base and grunted as he whizzed it across the infield on a line. He walked back to his position smoothing the moist dirt back and forth with his foot.

When he turned back to the diamond, he was greeted by a big child-like, toothy grin from his pitcher as we walked out to the mound. It was a smile he had seen a thousand times. He smiled back and gave him a hand gesture with his index and pinky fingers pointed up. The bull's horns. Andrew stuck out his tongue and shook his head violently back and forth. His thin upper body seemed to be swimming in the baggy number twenty-one jersey that he insisted on wearing.

Andrew threw a few warm up pitches from the windup. He threw all four seam fast balls, but everyone on both teams and in the stands knew he was throwing maybe seventy-five percent. After Eric screamed 'coming down' in his deep monotone, Andrew let the last pitch really go, and the scouts sitting behind the backstop began making strategic moves to get the best positions and prepare their radar guns.

Shane stood a few feet off the mound and waited for the ball to come back from around the horn. Andrew fumbled with his jersey, bobbing his head to some unknown rhythm in his head.

"Well I guess its go time huh?" Shane asked his friend as he placed the ball with his bare hand into Andrew's glove.

Shane scanned the crowd one last time before turning back to his lifelong best friend. Andrew was staring so hard into his eyes Shane was sure he could see his soul.

"Show these pussies how we do things around here, alright?" He said, suddenly determined.

This time Andrew smirked a little, but still looked right in his friend's eyes. Shane couldn't help but notice that his dark blue eyes didn't reveal even the slightest glimpse of nerve, fear, or anxiety. Those eyes didn't reveal anything for that matter. In fact, he had the same carefree gleam that had talked Shane into doing at least a hundred hare-brained, often illegal activities over the years they had spent growing up and growing wild.

Shane gave a short laugh and jogged back to his spot. Somehow, without even the slightest twitch of movement, Andrew's eyes had signed a promise to Shane that in less than three hours he would be hoisting a State Championship trophy over his head.

Andrew struck out the side on eleven pitches.

August 20th, 1996

"What about Mrs. Root, is she supposed to be tough?" Eric asked, tapping the end of his pencil against his forehead.

"Yea, I heard she's a real witch. I guess she doesn't like athletes either." Andrew answered his friend without taking his eyes off the television.

He sat on the love seat with his head leaned back over the top of the cushion, his legs crossed at the ankle with his feet up on the coffee table. His hands were behind his head supporting it with his fingers interlaced together. He was wearing short running shorts and thick, coarse hair hid his white legs that looked as if they had never experienced the sun's rays. He had no shirt on, as was the norm whenever possible. He would usually take his shirt off as soon as he entered the house in the summer, even before removing his shoes or socks. The contrast between his tan upper body and chalk white legs gave the appearance that the two belonged to separate people.

Andrew stood six feet tall, but due to his poor posture, he never appeared taller than five foot ten. His upper body was very thin making his long tentacle-like arms seem even longer. He had enormous hands and long thin fingers. Everything from the waist up seemed very disproportionate, for he had moderately thick thighs and a decent butt which made his upper body appear skinnier still. His light brown hair was never noticeable because he had it buzzed marine style every ten days or so. Andrew's face had very rough features. He had a crooked boxer's nose and his skin was tight and weathered like a person who had been abused by working out in the elements far too long. His small mouth was home to a full set of strong, slightly fanged teeth, but his most noticeable facial features were his eyes which were a dark, brilliant blue and quick to gain and hold eye contact and fascination.

It was impossible not to feel the imposing power those eyes held. Andrew was well aware of this ability and often wielded it for persuasive purposes. Currently, those eyes were locked on Jon Smoltz as he prepared to throw a pitch on TV. He was dialed in with concentration.

"Damn, I should have done this stuff a long time ago. Now, I'm not gonna get any of the good classes or easy teachers. I hate this stuff." Eric whined, slamming the catalog and pencil he was holding down on the table and rubbing his thick, rough hands up and down his face.

"I can't believe how dirty Smoltzy is." Andrew said, not paying any attention to his friend's words. "I mean he hits spots like a thumber, but he throws his breaking ball in the nineties."

"Hey, when are you planning to do all your schedule stuff?" Eric asked trying to keep the conversation focused on his concerns.

"It's like he never throws a ball on the middle third of the plate, and he never gives in to guys." Andrew exclaimed, suddenly sitting up attentively, inching his head ever closer to the television.

"I'm serious dude, you better go see Coach Parriman, or you're never gonna graduate on time." Eric took the paternal tone that Andrew recognized as being reserved only for his close friends and family. Andrew turned, giving his friend a look of pity and nodded his head in agreement.

"Don't worry about it. I got it taken care of." He stated.

These were two phrases he was famous or perhaps infamous for stating even in rather fickle spots, especially in fickle spots. His voice was calm, but the tone clearly stated to back off.

"We start two-a-days on Monday, and I'll have coach check out my classes." He turned back to the game, and his face regained its childlike glee.

"More like you'll make him do it all for you." Eric said under his breath picking his pencil up and scribbling on the catalog.

Coach Parriman was the head football coach, and like many adults who gave the skinny, wise-ass a fair shot, he had developed a particular soft spot in his heart for Andrew.

"What's up?" Andrew challenged, his brow lowering, his lips slightly parted, but without taking his eyes from the television.

"Nothing."

Although Andrew had amazing leadership qualities combined with a natural skill for manipulating people and never caring what anybody thought, Eric had always taken an older brother role with his friend at least as far as school and money were concerned.

Andrew's mother had died in a car accident when he was only eight. His father, supposedly a bohemian deadbeat, had left her before he was even born. It was rumored around town that he was in prison somewhere, serving a long sentence.

Andrew had lived with Eric's family in the valley since his mother's death. Knowing that this was not his family, Andrew did not ask for much, but he was happy to take what was offered and always showed gratitude. Being an orphan had gotten Andrew out of trouble a number of times growing up. Adults were more sympathetic to him. Eric, who was often with him on such occasions, wasn't as lucky. This meant that the two were impacted very differently by their childhood together and was partly to blame for Eric always taking responsibility, at least in some part, for his friend's crazy exploits. This difference in treatment also played a part in leading Eric to become very father-like to all his teammates and friends.

Eric stood about five foot nine and weighed over two hundred pounds. He had always been stocky and was even quite pudgy in his childhood, but he had a great passion for weightlifting and an iron work ethic that led to him bulking up even more through high school. He had short arms and legs and a wide chest already covered in patches of reddish brown hair. He had a flat head tied onto his stout exterior by a thick, veined neck. Eric's face was square, with his eyes being the only large feature. He had a small, short nose, small ears, and a little mouth often covered by a reddish brown goatee. He wore his curly, brown hair long only cutting it when his parents or coaches made him.

He was the perfect build for a fullback, which is what he played in football, and he had been playing catcher since he was ten. His grandfather on his mother's side was second generation from Ireland and responsible for his pale freckled skin and the red shade to his hair.

"So where do you think we should go for the camping trip this year?" Eric asked, squeezing his right bicep with his left hand and flexing it in and out, his eyes moving to the TV.

"Oh yeah," Andrew clapped his fist into his other hand, pushing down with the open palm to pop his knuckles. "I was gonna tell you I heard about this huge waterfall on the other side of the lake. I think we should check it out, and if it's cool camp there."

He got up and began to pace the room out of habit as he spoke. His thoughts, absorbed by the trip, had completely abandoned the game. "Yeah, I think this spot is gonna be tight. We'll go check it out tomorrow morning. We'll bring the .22's up there and do some shooting and find the best spot to set up."

Eric couldn't help noticing the implied 'will' and not 'should.' This usually meant that the discussion of it being a possibility was already over, and it was only a matter of deciding when it would be done. Eric had been there when a friend told Andrew about the waterfall and didn't think it sounded like a bad spot.

"I'll steal us some beers from Gordon's on our way out of town."

Eric glanced up sheepishly at his friend and in a meek voice of submission didn't argue.

"Sounds good."

He said this, while thinking at the same time that it definitely didn't sound good but, in fact, sounded like trouble. Eric always enjoyed drinking as much, if not more, than any of his friends. Ever since the State Championship though Andrew, who had always been a light weight, had been drinking much heavier, and the heavier he drank the more unpredictable he became.

At the celebration party after the game, he had borrowed a teammate's pickup, saying he was running back to town to pick up some more girls. He ended up driving the truck off the road a few miles from the cabin where they were partying. Fortunately, he was alright, and the truck suffered only a couple minor scratches.

A couple nights later, after drinking for a couple hours, he bragged that he could throw a rock threw the window of a passing car. Before anyone could talk him out of it, he wound up and let a stone fly forty yards, cracking the windshield of a dark SUV traveling down a hill street perpendicular to the boys' position. Once more, his luck held out, and he was never caught, but with football season rapidly approaching everyone worried about him getting in trouble and being kicked off the team.

Shane, who didn't go out for football that year, only made things worse. He had started smoking weed, which only encouraged Andrew to do it too. The two of them seemed to be speeding down a dead end road. It was all too common in this small town, and Eric wanted to say something, only he lacked the courage to confront his friend, afraid that he would only push him away and eventually out of reach. He looked up at his friend's joyous face, but when their eyes met he gave in, returned his smile, and turned back the TV.

August 28th, 1996

The night was a typical, late August evening. The sun beating down on the earth without mercy all afternoon, until finally as the landscape had given up, sizzling and dying, the sun retreated on schedule behind the pine covered hills. The day's heat began to return to the atmosphere above like the last straggling soldiers of a battle, realizing too late that their artillery cover had long since abandoned them.

The night was crisp, with a cool, gentle breeze relieving the tattered valleys. The night time temperatures wouldn't dip below fifty degrees, yet the sheer heat of the day would make this a rather drastic change calling for sweatshirts or light jackets. The stars were bright and clear, paying homage to a gorgeous, orange half-moon.

In the hills around the lake, the squirrels and birds called it a day. Everything was quiet except for the campsite of high school teens, causing their voices to feel much more powerful than reality. This phenomenon was realized subconsciously, giving them all a feeling of the freedom and immortal pleasure only felt by the young. In the still evening, they felt alive. They felt free, unbound, and uncommitted to any destination in life. Their voices grew animated and took on carefree, mischievous tones.

Kids stood crowded around a large bonfire of pallets; others existed only as silhouettes in the darkness, but the sounds of canvas rustling, zippers working, and young girls softly giggling provided evidence of their existence beyond the light of the fire. Coolers strung out between the fire and the various tents and vehicles with the lids open were continuously being pillaged for beer, chips, or hotdogs. The attention of those around the fire was at that moment concentrated on one loud, slurred voice in particular, speaking from the far side of the large crackling flames.

"Alright you cowards, I'll go first, but I better not be the only one with big enough balls to do it." Andrew's voice called, challenging a couple boys standing in his perimeter.

He glanced at the faces around him, a huge toothy smile covering his face ear to ear. In the fire light, he appeared almost sober though he had already drunk eight or more beers.

Without receiving a response, he looked straight ahead got down like a track sprinter and ran headfirst into the flames. He jumped upon entering the fire and landed on a pallet near the far side that was still relatively unburned. The pallet slid from its position, causing him to lose his footing for a moment. He moved his other foot quickly forward to stop his momentum, lunging as he stepped onto the ground on the other side. After regaining his balance, he raised his arms in the air triumphantly clenching his fists. His eyes were wide; his face covered with a look challenging anyone it landed on.

"Yeah, baby." He exclaimed, turning back to the others and wiping his hands on the reinforced thighs of his tan work jeans.

"What's up now?" He had the crazy look that he showed when excited or angry.

Cheers were going through the crowd.

"Somebody beer me."

He walked over to the tailgate of a pickup that had been backed up to the edge of the fire and sat down between two brown haired girls.

Darin had watched this display from a spot where he sat with some friends about ten yards back from the fire. He frowned, shaking his head, but his eyes never left Andrew. He had decided a few days before that he was going to talk to Andrew about his behavior but was waiting for the right time. It was beginning to dawn on him that the right time might come too late, so he had better speak up soon.

Around two a.m., the action had died down considerably. Most everyone was either with a girl, passed out, or trying to find a spot to sleep. The breeze of the early evening picked up to become a stiff, cold wind. The trees in the valley gave some protection, but occasionally the approaching fall could muster enough force to whistle down the valley, whipping tent flaps and anything else not tied down. A few kids still sat around the fire, which had been reduced to mostly a large bed of coals, only a few strong flames still burning.

Shane stood leaning against an old Jeep pickup with Eric and another friend. He was listening to his friends talk about the new plays added to the offense for the upcoming season, trying to figure out how he could light a joint without putting his beer down. Just as he got his spliff cherried, he saw Darin walking over toward them. Trying to put the joint down inconspicuously, he began to cough.

Darin didn't notice, seeming to look right through him. His face showed that he had something heavy weighing on his mind. He leaned against the hood of the truck without putting his weight down and stared out into the darkness beyond.

"What's up QB?" Shane asked lightly.

"Nothing, I'm pretty tired," Darin replied, finally noticing his friend. Catching a sudden whiff of the pot, he glanced down at Shane's hand, flaring his nostrils slightly.

"Why do you smoke that stuff?" He asked with the stern look of a teacher scolding a young student.

"It helps my glaucoma." Shane piped quickly then raised the joint back to his mouth for a long drag. Figuring a lecture was coming anyways, he saw no point in hiding it any longer. Besides, he didn't really want to have to relight it.

"I'm serious. It's terrible for you, and it makes you worthless." Darin lectured mightily, ignoring Shane's joke.

"I don't know. I like to get high. Why do you hate anything fun and have to be so damn serious all the time? Everyone is different. Not everyone wants to run for president." Shane looked at his friend, decided it wasn't worth taking the argument any further, and changed the subject. "Ready for the big game? How many touchdowns you gonna throw in the opener?"

"I think the team is ready. We've been looking good in practice." Darin answered, quickly morphing into a politician.

As if this reminded him of something important, he suddenly shot his eyes passed Shane and looked for Eric. Eric caught this last comment and took a few steps to get closer to Shane's side. He held a bottle of beer in his big right hand and had a crooked, drunken smile glued on his red face. The guy was long gone.

"This guy... this guy here is a machine out there...he's gonna be danger...er...deadly there this season." Eric slurred.

His drooping eyes and staggering movements made it quiet obvious staying on his feet was proving difficult for him.

"Gonna win State. Two times...one year. Baseball and the foosball."

Shane couldn't hold back any longer, breaking out in a slow, stoned laugh, glancing back and forth between his two friends. His dark eyes and Cree features gave his face a haunting look in the deep-cut shadows.

"You're a moron, you know that?" He asked Eric through his hoarse laughter. He slugged him in the shoulder with a quick right. Darin couldn't help but crack. He smiled first, but then gave a couple short laughs before stopping when he regained his stern purpose.

"It's going to take a lot of hard work and some luck if we want to have a shot at the playoffs. Everyone's going to have to keep their noses clean, and stay sober."

He shot a quick look down to the brown bottle in Eric's hand, returning his cold eyes to meet his friend's. Eric looked lost for a second, but the big grin returned to his face quickly. Without even looking around he flung the bottle over his right shoulder and leaned on the truck door. He didn't say a word just looked around smiling. Shane, loosened up from his buzz, came to his aid.

"You're only young once. You gotta live life, have fun while you can. These are the best days of our lives."

"Don't you want to accomplish things in your life though?" Darin interrupted. "Maybe even get out of this town someday?"

Darin realized by his friend's faces that he was wasting his words on them. They were in no mood or frame of mind to be lectured.

He sighed and prepared to return the conversation to football when a girl moaning caught his attention. Shane and Eric heard it too and were already walking quickly in the direction of some cars parked beyond the light of the fire behind a small row of tents. A minute later the moans had grown to screams. It would have sounded like someone was being murdered if it wasn't for the sexual phrases being screamed by the female voice.

The boys narrowed the source of the sounds to a white civic parked between two pickups. While they stood in awe listening to the cries of passion, Shane snuck up to the car, keeping low to the ground, and glanced into the steamed up rear passenger window. He was laughing when he walked back to his friends.

He told them it was Andrew getting at it with a blond sophomore named Jenny. The boys all remembered how Jenny had been on Andrew's jock throughout the summer even though he had shown little notice of her. Shane joked about how quickly a girl can gain worth in direct proportion to the number of beers a guy drank.

The boy's returned to the dying fire discussing football, the upcoming school year, and reminiscing on the summer. As the conversation thinned, Andrew appeared at the fire. His hat was missing and his hair was all disheveled. Eric cracked a joke about the girl's high pitched cries, making the few stragglers left all laugh. Andrew filled them in on the story then the conversations gained momentum again changing from one frivolous topic to the next as only good friends can do without it becoming awkward. Finally, the topic turned to future plans, and Darin, seeing his chance, directed his questions at Andrew.

"I don't know. I always figured I'd end up working for Eric's old man maybe being a carpenter, but after baseball this year I'm not sure. I guess I'd like to go to college up at State, play some ball. I guess. Maybe if I got a scholarship that would be pretty cool."

The entire time he spoke he stared at the last burning coals where the fire had been. Sunrise was less than an hour away now, and it was already light enough to see the details of the boys' faces.

Although the banter continued a little while longer, Andrew did not say another word. He continued to stare into the ash of the fire pit with a blank, smoke-sooted face, occasionally looking up to whoever was talking, but he wasn't listening.

He kept thinking about Darin's questions. It seemed strange to him that he couldn't remember the last time he had even thought about what he would do after high school. Finally around six in the morning, everyone got up to find a place to sleep for at least a couple hours until the morning heat made it too uncomfortable.

Andrew climbed into the bed of a friend's pickup, but he didn't even lie down. He sat with his back up against the cab, staring out at the pine trees with his head cocked slightly to one side. For the first time ever, he couldn't stop thinking about the future. The sun crept over the horizon, and birds sang the first sounds of the morning's arrival. Somewhere in the distance, squirrels chirped angrily at the intruding campers, but Andrew still sat thinking. Where did the smoke go after the flame had died out?

August 9th, 1997

Eric lay sprawled out across the sofa looking like a yard sale. He still had his uniform on, minus the cleats. His face was smeared with dirt and sweat. He was completely ecstatic. All he wanted was for this moment to last forever. The Wranglers had won a 2-0 game over the West Valley Mavericks, winning their forty-second game, breaking the state's single season wins record.

He heard the front door open and excited voices echoing down the entrance hallway. Then footsteps approached the living room. Shane and Andrew came in looking as exhausted and sublime as Eric. No one waited for anyone else to talk. The first couple minutes were basically loud overlapping shouts, useless words for a stranger to the day's events. It didn't matter what was said. The emotions were clear from their tones and body language. They slapped each other high fives, wrestled around, and it wasn't until Shane went to the bathroom that Eric finally found the chance to have a word with his long time roommate.

"Talk about having a birthday. You were absolutely filthy out there today, bro."

He looked at Andrew the way a kid looks at his idol with all the awe of seeing him in person for the first time. "Everywhere I put my glove you hit the spot. The curve ball was falling off the table man. A couple times

I think I was more scared than the batter of that thing. A no hitter! A no hitter! I can't believe I just caught that game bro!"

His dirty face blushed with excitement.

Andrew smiled but said nothing. Eric had to remind himself to breathe when he felt himself getting dizzy from talking so much. Shane came back in the room. He pushed Andrew from behind onto the couch.

"Man you're lucky I picked up them RBIs in the seventh or all that work would have been for nothing. We'd still be out there sweating our balls off. Speaking of which, can I take a shower here?"

Shane took off his jersey and flexed his arms downward forming a circle in front of his chest. He wore a goofy face and tightened the veins in his neck. Shane's body was the typical high school infielder's. He never set foot in a weight room, claiming it would mess with his 'cannon'. He was about five foot nine, lean, with a little pooch of a stomach. His arms were hairless and seemed to be the same size from shoulder to wrist. His father was Native American, giving him his brilliant copper skin. He had very dark, nearly black eyes, a broad nose, and a pointy head that was used constantly in his friend's harassment. Shane had a sharp tongue, a great sense of humor, and an uncanny quick wit.

No one wanted to be in an insult match against him, for he would hold nothing back and remembered everything embarrassing that had ever happened to any of his friends in their entire lives. His father had been sent to prison when he was young. He never mentioned missing or even remembering his dad, but he would often threaten people when he was offended, claiming his father was out of prison and would stab or shoot them. These things were taken in jest to his friends, but it was very frightening to people who didn't know him well.

"Alright boys, if ESPN calls for an interview get a number and I'll call them back when I've freshened up."

He skipped gingerly back up the stairs.

Andrew grabbed the remote control off the coffee table and sat down in the recliner across from Eric. Eric continued to stare at him with wide affectionate eyes.

"So, do you think we could go back to back?"

"I know we will." Andrew answered confidently. "We are so much better this year, especially in big games and clutch situations."

He scratched his head nonchalantly while speaking.

A million things were running through Eric's brain all at once. He struggled frantically to keep his imagination from such big dreams just yet. He finally decided what he wanted to say, choosing his words almost cautiously.

"Are you gonna sign if you get drafted?"

"Yep." Andrew shouted with a mock laugh. He looked to Eric for a reaction with wide eyes and an exaggerated frown.

The fact that he answered so quickly, pointed to the probability that today's game already had him thinking about that very real possibility. He opened his mouth as if to say more but then decided not to, flipping through the channels arbitrarily. His forehead wrinkled, and he seemed puzzled for a moment but then appeared to regain himself. He smiled again, turning to Eric, "What about you? You gonna go play ball up at State?"

"I think so. I mean I think it would be pretty fun... Yeah, I'd like to if they offer me a scholarship."

He smiled sheepishly, rubbing his hands together.

Eric had only recently been approached by an assistant coach from the college. The idea of going to college to play baseball was still very new to him. His original plan was to attend the vocational school in Great Pines, studying auto mechanics as he was already very good at working with cars, and it was something he had always loved.

Eric always struggled with school, particularly math. He eventually scared himself away from it, barely passing the bare minimum to graduate high school. He swore he would never open a math book ever again. The new prospect of going to a major college brought this math fear festering back into his mind.

"What about Darin? I heard he's gonna go play football at some little academic school out east?"

"Yeah, I heard that too." Eric said pulling his dirty socks off, starting to smell them but deciding better. "I guess he wants to get into real estate or something."

"I saw that Elizabeth was at the game again today."

Andrew switched subjects like an experienced rounder deals an ace fluently from the bottom of the deck. He spoke with a ginger tone that showed little interest then turning to look at his friend he added, "Are they still going out or what?"

"No, he told me they broke up because he didn't want to have a long distance relationship."

Darin had been dating Elizabeth since the end of football season. She had been the first serious girlfriend he, or anyone in the group, ever had. The football team had fallen off at the end of the season, losing two of their last three games and failing to earn a playoff spot.

After the season, Darin distanced himself from his friends, spending a lot of time with her. His friends, particularly Shane, felt that he blamed the football season on them. Shane spoke his opinions to Eric and Andrew a number of times. While Eric always disagreed, feeling he just really liked his girlfriend, Andrew never commented on the subject and rarely spoke of Darin until the arrival of baseball season.

Andrew had known Darin his entire life. Darin wasn't always the stern, motivated machine that he had become in high school. He used to get in trouble and start fights. Andrew remembered times in middle school when the two of them would sneak out of Darin's bedroom window and walk around town looking for mischief into the early hours before dawn.

Darin's father was a local dentist who ran a well respected practice and made a very good income. His mother was a rich house wife with too much time on her hands. She became used to their high society lifestyle. She worried about her son running around with trouble makers, not because Darin might get in trouble, but she worried that it would look negatively on her to her snobby friends. She didn't like Shane and Andrew in particular, for they had no father figures to give importance to their last names. She seemed to blame this directly on the boys.

Eventually, she got her way. Though Darin remained good friends with Andrew and spent quite a bit of time with Shane during baseball season, he was not allowed to spend the night at Shane or Eric's houses and as high school progressed they rarely ever spent time at Darin's.

Andrew never blamed any of this on Darin. He still considered Darin one of his closest friends and was always there if Darin needed anything. It was Darin who seemed to change his opinions toward Andrew. Darin was popular at school and one of the best athletes in the state, but he was always jealous at how easy making friends and playing sports was for Andrew. It seemed like he was always working hard to earn the things he wanted while for Andrew everything happened naturally without any effort.

"Alright Birthday boy, what do you wanna do to celebrate the big one nine?" Shane spoke in a gruff humorous voice laboring to force the words out in a frog like croak, walking down the stairs to reenter the living room. Andrew, finding a baseball game on, set down the remote and turned with a big smile to look over the back of the recliner.

"I don't know. I guess we could always get a bottle of whisky and see where it leads us."

He sniffed his nose, giving a short chuckle then turned with questioning eyes toward Eric.

Eric, still feeling bulletproof, shrugged his shoulders, "Sounds good to me. We are in season, but it's your birthday. I gotta go shower though. I stink something terrible." He said, sniffing at his own armpit.

He stood up with a grunt and began laboring across the room. He slapped Andrew on the shoulder as he walked passed. His voice could be heard over the creaking stairs repeating 'no hitter' a couple times to himself. When he had gotten up the stairs, Andrew addressed Shane.

"Hey you should call your cousin up and see if you can get any pain killers tonight." He said in almost a whisper.

His face looked ashamed, his eyes almost pleading with the question.

"Alright, I guess I could do that. Don't tell anyone we're with tonight, not even Eric. Everyone will say I'm the bad influence and shit."

"I won't say a word. This is the last time I'm gonna try em anyways. I'm done after tonight," his face begged Shane to agree with him, but before Shane could respond he continued to reassure himself, "It's just for my birthday I wanna get real messed up and then no more."

He paused for a second trying to think of what to say next. Evidently, he couldn't think of anything to add, so he turned to the TV, pushing the recliner back to lay out. The announcer was saying something about how immortal youth is reserved only for pro baseball players, for as long as a man can put on the uniform, walk out on the field, and play, he never has to grow up.

August 10th, 1997

"What in the hell are we gonna do? This is bad. This is really bad guys."

Eric paced back and forth across his room, rolling his eyes and rubbing his hand over his mouth nervously. His lips were dry and chapped. There were small milky white pouches of saliva on either corner of his lips. "We have practice in three hours. Dugal is gonna kill someone...he's gonna kill me. He's gonna blame this shit on me. I know it already."

He sat down on the edge of his bed and buried his face in his hands swearing pathetically. He was nearly in tears.

"Calm down man. You're not helping anything by freaking out. Alright? Calm down bro." Shane spoke quickly, taking charge like an experienced general speaking to a private falling apart after finding himself under fire for the first time.

Shane had always handled trouble better than any one else in the group, partly because he was used to it. "Just shut up, so I can hear myself think," he continued.

Eric wasn't listening. In his mind, it was all over. He couldn't stop picturing his coach swinging those big fists at him, his parents banishing him from the house forever, and the police locking him up and throwing away the key. The son of good church going Catholics, he rode a rollercoaster between happiness and sorrow, wearing his emotions on his sleeve.

He continued muttering to himself, rocking back and forth on the bed. All three boys looked like hobos, and the room smelled like a packed gymnasium.

"Do you guys really think it's that bad?" Andrew asked from the near side of the bed facing the door to the room.

He was deathly pale; his blood shot eyes telling a million tales of torture. He held his left hand at his waist, supporting his wrist with his thigh. He was holding a bag of ice over it with his right hand. There were small fresh burns on his right wrist and a small gash with dried blood on his forearm.

It was nearly six in the morning and the boys had been sitting in Eric's room for over an hour now. The night before, they had all gone over to a younger girl's house to drink because her parents were gone. They had all gotten pretty tanked and around three in the morning decided to walk to Denny's for a bite to eat. This is when things went down hill quickly.

About three blocks away from the restaurant, an old beat up, primer-grey Nova drove by, and some one yelled something at the boys from the passenger window. The boys were quick to return the insults, flipping the bird and cussing at the vehicle. The car skidded to a stop. Four rough looking boys in their early twenties piled out. As the occupants of the vehicle moved toward the boys, none of them even flinched. These were tough, small town boys, and pride always came before logic.

Seven drunken males proved to be too much testosterone on this particular night, and the boys from the Nova got the fight they were looking for. A couple of minor scrapes and less than five minutes later the boys in their white tank tops ran back to the Nova, realizing they had miscalculated their targets. Eric gave chase for about ten steps, but tired from fighting and winded from yelling, decided insulting their mothers would have to suffice for the evening. He came walking back to his friends. They were all still pretty pumped up but soon settled down enough to have a good laugh over the entire event.

Andrew seemed to be grimacing and kept squeezing his pitching hand slowly. Shane asked him if he was alright. He said he was fine but his hand hurt a little. It wasn't until an hour or so later when they all got back to Eric's car at the girl's house that they saw how much his knuckles had swollen.

Eric started to panic. The entire ride home he cycled between asking Andrew if it felt broken and Shane if it looked broken. The more time passed the more of a wreck Eric became.

Stress is contagious, and it wasn't long before the dark storm cloud that is despair began raining on all three of them. Now, they sat in Eric's room panicking more with every minute as if the walls of the room were closing in to crush them. Eric had called Darin when they got to his house. He was the only one they could think of with a calm enough head to handle the situation. Besides that, he was sober. The boys had all been drinking heavily and hadn't slept all night. They needed an outside party to come tell them things would be alright, even if it wasn't true.

"I don't think it's broken. I can still make a fist." Andrew said, clutching for the last breaths of optimism in the room.

Erik looked down at the hand. It was swollen up like a beach ball and now it was taking on a dark blue color that wasn't present during the ride home.

"I don't know. It looks pretty bad," he said in a soft, sad voice.

The last tiny bit of hope in the room was shot out of the sky with this comment. The air in the room suddenly became incredibly thick. The boys sat quietly for a few minutes not looking in each other's directions. Each one tried his hardest to think of anything else. They were tired. They were sore. It all seemed pretty bleak. The door opened. Eric and Shane both stood up quickly, but Andrew didn't move. He stared down at his hand.

Darin entered the room with the sullen look of a detective that has seen it all yet still hates to be woken up. The new comer stared directly in the eyes of all three boys one by one. Each stare got a good few seconds, but to them it felt like an hour under a heat lamp. Still, no one spoke. Finally, he stood directly over Andrew. He sighed.

"Let's see it." He said calmly. Pity could be detected in his tone.

Andrew held up his hand, casting his glance toward the floor to his right.

"Shit." Darin examined it for a moment but said nothing more.

It was bad. Hiding it would be out of the question. He paced the room in the same path Eric had done early, but he paced with much more deliberation in his step, glancing occasionally up toward the ceiling deep in thought. After a few minutes of this had passed, he began giving his instructions to Shane and Eric. He decided that Andrew would call in sick to practice today, and they would keep the matter quiet until they could find out how badly it effected his throwing. Andrew would try to get some rest and continue to ice his hand. After practice, they could take him out to the park to throw a little. When Shane and Eric had left the room, Darin bit his lip, staring at Andrew.

"You couldn't wait till after the season? Had to go out partying, huh? You're so selfish. Can't you ever think of anyone other than yourself?" His voice spoke quietly, but the punch was direct, cruel, and prosecuting.

Andrew looked directly in his eyes without saying a word or breaking eye contact.

Finally, Darin gave in, looking away first.

"You were given so much in life, but that's not enough for you," he began to preach, but this time Andrew interrupted him.

"I was given so much? Why? Cuz I can throw a baseball? Did you ever think that maybe that's not the most important thing in everyone's life?" Andrew spoke with an anger he rarely used with his friends, though he kept his voice quiet.

This fire spread rapidly the more he spoke. "I was given everything, except parents...family." Then, he calmed himself with a deep breath. "You ever thought what it's like to spend Christmas without your mom, or to be the only kid in your class to have never owned a car. It must be nice to sit up in your big house, driving your nice cars, getting everything you ever want just by asking. You tell me I've been given everything because I've won a couple baseball games. You never had some asshole in white lab coat tell you that he was sorry but your mother's dead."

"Big deal! It's a damn game! Just once, one time I want to come home after a baseball game to have my mom there to hug me...tell me she loves me, that she made my favorite dinner," he paused for a moment looking at the carpet, "Hell, I'd happily lose every game I ever pitched to have my dad watch me one time and tell me he's proud of me...but I've been given everything...Did you ever think maybe not everyone wants the same things as you? I don't wanna go from sixteen straight to thirty-five. I don't wanna trade in my life to play sports. Sports are supposed to be fun games we play...not jobs. I don't want to plan out every detail of my life before I even have a chance to live it."

He stood up and walked to the closet to pull a shirt off the hanger. Turning back to Darin, his face became sad and his features beaten. "Most of all, I can't and would never give up on my friends just because they don't fit in with my parent's plans for me."

He walked out into the hall heading toward the upstairs bathroom, leaving Darin alone in the room. Darin walked over to the window, sat down on the bed, and began to realize how different things looked through his friend's eyes.

August 19th, 1997

It was a windy afternoon. The temperature was hovering in the high forties, and the dark clouds blocked out the sky entirely. It was ten minutes to one, but somehow already felt like late evening. Both teams had finished taking infield and awaited the announcement of the starting lineups. Despite the weather, there was a very good crowd buzzing with excitement already.

Dugal stood out behind the home bullpen mound watching Andrew warm up. His heavy body was clearly restless, uneasy. He stood with his hands on his hips, his massive feet shifting his weight back and forth trying to find a comfortable stance to balance his big body. Every couple pitches he would ask Andrew the same questions,

"How's that feel?"

"Any problems with this grip... that release?"

Andrew would reply with the same short response, "Feels good", even if that answer didn't make sense to the question asked. Andrew had thrown four innings of relief since his injury nearly ten days earlier, but this was the first time he would start. He had thrown well in his two playoff appearances but nothing close to a hundred percent.

In the four innings he had thrown, he had given up three runs on four hits, but it was the walks that had everyone worried. He had averaged less than two walks per nine innings all season, but since the injury had walked five including back to back walks in his latest inning. A double-play ball had kept the scare to only one run, but this was a very different situation.

Darin had stepped up his play, pitching eight strong innings in the semi-final to get them to the championship game, but the bullpen had been stretched a great deal in the early games of the tournament. They needed to get at least six out of Andrew, and this wasn't the same caliber of opponent he had pitched against in his first two return outings. They were facing the Bulldogs, a team that had earned their spot at State by winning nine of their last ten games. They were swinging very hot sticks, scoring an average of eight runs per game in the tournament.

Everyone who loves baseball knows that the only team to fear worse than a very good team is a mediocre team of scrappers that heats up at the right time.

Andrew threw a couple more change ups and finished his pregame with two fast balls from the full windup. While the home team was being announced, Dougal pulled Andrew aside giving him a few words of encouragement in his deep drawl which cracked when he was nervous or angry. Andrew would recall later that he had never heard his coach's voice crack more than it did during those few sentences, but at the time he didn't think of this or anything else. He listened to the crowd roar, the flag whipping in the wind in center field, the chattering from both dugouts, and the announcer's distorted voice on the old PA.

He heard only the sounds of baseball and jogged out to the mound without even going back to the dugout. This is where the wild animal inside him felt most comfortable, most free. Smiling at his infielders, he walked the final steps to the bump, his bump, winking at Eric before the big man pulled his mask down and began to crouch.

He could see Eric looked nervous, but this was typical of Eric. He threw his warm ups effortlessly as he had a million times before. Every set of eyeballs in the entire stadium studied his every throw for some clue as to how much his hand still affected him. He ducked the throw down, got the ball back from Shane who was cracking a joke, and fumbled with his jersey.

Everything seemed exactly the same to him. He had done this so many times it all came naturally. Even while he told himself this, he could feel the stinging pain in his hand clutching the ball. He took a deep breath, climbed on the mound, and zeroed in on Eric's glove. He tried to focus on his target but suddenly couldn't get his mind off his hand.

He looked at the batter's face. The kid was a typical short, spunky looking lead off. He was trying to stare Andrew down with a see-through grimace. Andrew stared at him as he tried to get comfortable in the box. Their eyes locked, and Andrew saw something deep down inside the boy's soul as only he is able to do. It was small almost invisible, yet it was there. Fear.

He remembered instantly who he was. Suddenly, he forgot his hand. He smiled. He found his target, wound up, and let fly.

Everything was silent. He could almost see the ball in slow motion leave his hand, traveling toward the plate, and into the glove.

"Strike one."

The umpire's call shook him from his stupor. The crowd cheered. Andrew's smile returned along with his confidence. His hand hurt like hell. Pain was temporary. It could be controlled, blocked out.

The batter would fly out to center field three pitches later on a 1-2 change up. The following batter struck out on a 2-2 fast ball, and the third would ground out to Shane on the first pitch. Andrew would never forget a single batter, count, or pitch of that inning for the rest of his life. He discovered something enlightening looking into that lead off batter's eyes, a discovery that would affect his philosophy for the rest of his life. He realized that it was natural to not know and even to be afraid of that unknown. It was a haunting though powerful discovery.

He cruised through the next few innings. The next thing he knew he found himself pitching in the seventh inning with a 2-0 lead. He was facing the bottom of the order, but the six, seven, and eight hitters for some reason always seemed a difficult task late in the game. Whether it's a loss of concentration or a rule of the baseball gods, it seems like when a pitcher is cruising into the sixth or seventh innings, it's never the heart of the order that blows the game up. It's always the bottom half that sneaks in silently, the same way that an unbeatable army with superior firepower, positioning, and defenses is destroyed by a disease brought in by one of their own officers. It spreads unchecked at first, by the time anyone sees the problem all that can be done is damage control.

Andrew got behind in the count to the sixth hitter before the kid parachuted a 2-1 pitch over the first baseman's head. It was an inside fast ball. It succeeded in sawing him off at the hands, yet somehow, someway he fought it off like a chip shot in front of the charging right fielder. The next guy fouled off two 3-2 pitches before walking to bring up the eight hitter with two on and nobody out.

In baseball, it's amazing how quickly things can get out of hand. It doesn't take a hail marry, a forty yard scamper breaking three tackles, a beautiful three pointer from way beyond the arc, or even an alley-oop. It doesn't take anything flashy. Sometimes, the offense doesn't even have to produce, only let the defense make a mistake. The non baseball fan might not even see it coming then in a flash the tides have turned.

Andrew jumped ahead of the next kid with a perfectly spotted fast ball on the outer half of the plate. He placed the next fast ball even prettier, just off the black but still getting the call.

Up 0-2, he tried to get the hitter to chase on a high fastball. The batter didn't bite, but the runners both broke.

It was a double steal. Andrew hadn't been keeping a close enough eye on them, and they both got great jumps. Eric came up out of the crouch like a cannon, yet he made no throw. The runners were both safe. Andrew realized, now, he needed to adjust his strategy. He was now pitching for a strikeout.

He broke off one of the dirtiest curves he had thrown the entire game in the dirt, right where he wanted it. The batter swung and missed, but the ball got by Eric. It deflected off his shin guard and rolled toward the third base bag. The runner on third started home but decided against it. By the time Eric got back to home plate, the bases were loaded with nobody out, and the Bulldogs came unglued. The yelling was so loud Andrew never even heard Eric apologize. He might not have heard him anyway.

Andrew knew the game of baseball better than anyone there that night. He knew exactly what happens in these situations. He knew what he needed to do.

He turned around walked back to the hill and went to a place only he could go. He took a few deep breaths, telling himself there was nothing hurt. Eric yelled to throw home on a comebacker. The crowd was rumbling. Small towners were tossing insults like confetti at a wedding.

The nine hitter stepped into the box. Andrew was only thinking one thing, and it sure as hell wasn't double play ball. He was pitching for the strike out. Dugal came out on the top step of the dugout and moved the infield in. Andrew went from the full windup. He kicked his leg high and delivered, grunting as he threw a fast ball as hard as he could. The ball was up though. The batter caught up to it enough to hit a weak fly ball to right field. The runner tagged. The right fielder came up firing. The kid had some speed. There was a play at the plate.

"SAFE!" barked the umpire, throwing his arms out with all the drama of a Broadway star. The runners advanced on the throw home. It was a 2-1 ball game with runners on second and third.

The lead off batter stepped into the box. Andrew started him off with a bender that literally fell off the edge of the planet. He watched the kid's knees buckle as the ball came in around the middle of the thigh. Andrew was in the driver's seat now. He could throw another one of those out of the strike zone or challenge the guy above the letters with a heater. He knew he had him guessing. He wound up and threw another bender. The pitch felt real good on release, but at the last second the kid turned and bunted it to Andrew's left.

Overthrowing the pitch for extra break, Andrew ended his delivery awkwardly, and he wasn't in proper fielding position. He charged it with all his might, picked it up bare hand, and tried to shovel pass it to Eric while falling to the grass. The throw was up the line a little. Eric missed the tag. The game was tied.

From the visitor's stands there was an eruption. When Andrew got back to the mound he saw Dugal marching toward him from the corner of his eye.

"How you doing out here skinny?" Dougal was smiling, but Andrew could see right threw the thin disguise. He was pale. His eyes looked like a junky that has gone too long without a high.

"I should have made a better pitch."

Dugal looked around into the stands before his eyes fell back on Andrew.

"Shit happens. We can get those runs back. We are alright, but we gotta end it here. Take the wind out of their sails, you hear?"

The words rolled off his tongue as if he had sat at home practicing what to say in this exact moment his entire life, over doing his already deep drawl. Andrew looked him in the eye nodding.

"Alright this guy's been trying to take you the other way all night. Let's tie him up inside, you hear?"

Andrew nodded again. Dougal slapped him on the shoulder, clapped his hands, and started slowly back to the dugout. He moved like a snail, but no one was watching him anyway.

After Eric had started back to the plate, Andrew stood off the mound fumbling with his jersey. He looked down at the ground for a second and tried to block everything out.

'God, if you let us win this game, I don't care if the rest of my career... no my entire life goes to shits. I will be forever grateful and never ask for anything more.' He prayed to himself quietly. He looked back up before whispering, "Amen."

He climbed the hill, looked in for his sign, and pitched. A fast ball inside caught a little bit too much of the fat part of the plate, but the kid rolled over it grounding it to Shane. Shane came up, checked the runners back, and tossed it over to first.

The momentum started to stagger toward an unseen neutral corner. The next hitter was the three hole in the order and a guy that was having a great tournament. Unfortunately, the kid seemed to have a terrible time hitting lefties. Andrew being one of the dirtiest around always found great success against him. The kid was big, strong and over anxious. He swung at a bad pitch to put himself behind in the count before just missing an inside fastball and popping a moon scraping high foul ball to the first baseman. Inning over.

Both teams would go three up and three down in their next at bat, bringing the Wranglers up in the bottom of the eighth. Shane, doing what he does best, picked up a lead off walk. The next batter, a slow runner named Jake, bunted him over, and Eric came up with one out and a runner in scoring position. He got behind in the count before grounding a 2-2 change up weakly to the second baseman. It was enough to advance Shane to third. Darin stepped to the plate with two outs.

The pitcher came inside with the first pitch but missed for a ball. His next pitch, Darin fouled straight back. He was right on it. On a 1-1 curve ball, Darin took for strike two. The pitcher tried to go up out of the zone for the punch out, but Darin laid off and the count went even again. This time, with two outs, both dugouts did their own variation of the deuces luck prayer.

The pitcher set and delivered. It was a fast ball on the outside corner. Darin went with it chopping the top half the other way. It was a bouncing ball between short and third. It bounced beyond the third baseman's reach, but the shortstop snagged it deep in the hole. He set his feet, turned and came up throwing. It was an amazing play.

For a split second the world stopped completely. Parent's held their breath, and girlfriend's closed their eyes. Old men's jaws caught gnats.

The ball traveled. Darin ran. It was a close play. The ball slapped the leather of the first baseman's glove.

"He's safe." The young umpire shouted. The call had two instantaneous effects on those present.

Depending on what color shirt you were wearing, it either broke your back or provided you total salvation. Either way, everyone cried out. The Bulldog's coach came out to argue, but everyone including himself knew it would change nothing. This was simply one of the strange formalities of the game.

After a short discussion, he made a call to the pen to bring in a long haired, right-hander. He was an off speed specialist that kept the ball down. The simple act of bringing him in seemed to quell the Wrangler's momentum. He induced the first batter he faced to ground weakly to second on the first pitch ending the inning.

When Andrew jogged back to the mound, the crowd was amazed. Everyone knew this kid's story. Even his enemies on this day were impressed. After finishing his warm-up pitches, he reminded God of his promise once more while he fumbled with his jersey.

"This is all I want God. We are eternally even after this last goose egg and you can turn your ear to others in need forever."

He squeezed his hand a few times and realized it didn't even hurt a little. He shrugged his shoulders a few times. He glanced around once at all the poised faces behind him eager with anticipation. There was no smile on his face. The man became something more.

He started his windup. He threw the ball harder than he ever had in his entire life. The plate felt almost too close to him. The scouts stood in awe. They almost couldn't believe their radar guns.

He threw twelve pitches.
He threw all fast balls.
Once again, he struck out the side.

August 20th, 1997

A brilliant sun was setting over the horizon, casting shadows down into the valleys where the creeks barely trickled, nearly dry now in these late months long since the spring run off. The barren peaks, vying for their fifteen minutes alone in the last red rays of the sun, stood still against time, reining proudly over the endless miles of conifers as far as the eye could see. The river churned ever onward off the rocks, majestically singing. Every few minutes, a Crow could be heard cawing at nothing and for no particular reason other than to be heard.

Cars drove on what remained of an old rutted out path into the large meadow a short hike from the popular waterfall. Grass had long since covered what remained of the old road. Only the distance cleared between trees on either side gave hint to its former existence. The cars parked first in an organized row near what remained of last summer's old fire pit, but it wasn't long before the lots plan was lost, leaving people to park wherever they could find room.

Friends and teammates high-fived, girls giggled and flirted batting their eyes in confidence and the red and blue plastic coolers came out and squeaked open. A few guys threw three pallets into the fire pit, stacking the remaining wood down the hill a little toward the river. The fire burned and the liquor poured. All around were the sounds of youthful exuberance.

Eric sat at an old picnic table someone had brought up in a pickup, playing drinking games with Shane and a couple other baseball players. Everywhere the conversations were the same:

"Can you believe it back to back?" and "So what are you gonna do next year?"

The greatest moment in these young men's short lives was still fresh in their minds, so the future naturally could only hold further achievements of success and greatness. Most spoke of college or plans to travel. One of the guys turned to Shane and asked about his plans.

"Well, Hollywood's been knocking down my door with movie offers, but I think I might take NASA up on their job offer." He said swigging from a plastic cup.

He laughed with everyone else, but he stopped short. The truth was he had no plans for next year. He never even thought about the possibility of high school ever ending. He had been offered the chance to play baseball at a couple small schools but had no means to pay for school or interest to sit in a desk ever again for that matter. He was an Indian, and Indians didn't like to leave their homes. To him, this land was still sacred even if it no longer belonged to the people.

'Oh well, tonight I'm not going to worry. I'm just gonna celebrate, enjoy the moment.' He thought to himself. He smirked, glancing his eyes up at the table without raising his head.

He bounced a quarter off the table into a pitcher sitting alone in the middle of a circle of red, plastic cups. Everyone grabbed a cup chugging quickly. Beer dripped down their chins onto their shirts as they gulped the golden liquid down as quickly as possible. Shane slapped his cup down hard on the table cracking a split down one side of it.

"Ha ha, who's your daddy, girls? Huh? Who's your daddy?"

He threw his head back laughing.

Darin walked up to the table. He stood behind one of the chairs with his left hand shoved in the front pocket of his jeans. He held a green, forty ounce bottle in his right hand, and he caught Shane's attention. They shot each other looks of approval.

"Well, well, well, if it isn't Mr. Rogers himself drinking a little ripple." Shane joked, raising an eyebrow questioningly.

"Yeah, I guess it's not everyday a team wins back to back championships. If you can't beat them join them," He blushed sheepishly. "Besides, I figure it couldn't get better than this. Life only goes downhill from here."

He raised his bottle in a toast, and everyone listening to him cheered. He watched the game taking place for a couple minutes then looked around a couple times.

"Where the hell is Andrew at anyways? I haven't seen him since we first got here."

"I don't know. I'm sure he's around." Shane answered, clearly concentrating on the action at the table.

"I think he went up to the waterfall." Eric entered the conversation, after missing his shot with the quarter.

"Who's he up there with?"

"I'm not sure. I think," Eric stopped in mid thought as someone sank the quarter in his cup. "You son of a bitch! I swear you've been going after me the whole game!"

He looked at the shooter throwing his hands up.

"I think you're trying to get me drunk. I hope you know I don't kiss on the first date." With a flash of his eyes and a quick smile, Eric picked up his cup, bottoming it in one big gulp.

Darin turned around looking toward the fire for a second before heading toward the path that led up river toward the falls. He disappeared into the trees before walking up a short hill. At the top of the hill the lake could be seen in the distance. He peered out into the distance and caught his breath. The lake, barely visible in the evening light, was calm as glass.

The path turned hard to the left, crossing the river on a makeshift bridge made from an old board. The board dug into a huge stump that had fallen into the river years before and had become part of the landscape. He could still hear voices from back at the fire, but he couldn't make out what was being said except for the occasionally blurted profanity. He pushed his way threw some deep brush that blocked the path before seeing the canyon wall that led up to the waterfall. It was still a couple hundred yards, but after getting up to the wall he could hear the falls.

A couple of girls' voices could also be heard. When he was in sight of the falls he could feel the cool mist on his face and arms. The sun had disappeared now, but it was a bright summer evening and he could make out three people sitting at the base of the pool where the falls ended.

It was two girls and a kid named Brian. Brian was a junior first baseman who hadn't played much all year. He stood in his boxers. His hair was wet, and he was playfully poking at one of the girls. The girls both had their shirts off and wore only their bras and very short jean shorts. As Darin drew closer, he could see their shorts were wet. They must have been in the pool recently, for they still had goose bumps on their legs.

He recognized one girl as Lacy Wood. She was one of Elizabeth's best friends. She was a slim, good looking blonde. She wore her hair past the shoulder and always straight. Darin couldn't help but notice her small firm breasts breathing in and out in her pink bra as she giggled playfully with Brian. He didn't remember the other girl's name, but he knew she ran with the same crowd. She had long, wavy brown hair. She was very curvy with a nice plump bottom and large breasts. She was the first to notice Darin, calling out hello in her peppy cheerleader voice. Darin gave a little wave and walked up grinning sheepishly to show off his dimples.

"Hey brother."

This call surprised Darin, so he stopped in his tracks. It wasn't until then that he noticed two figures sitting on the rocks above the falls. He glanced up straining in the evening light to make out their faces. He recognized Andrew's voice, but he could only tell that he was sitting with a girl. He couldn't tell who it was. Andrew stood up waving. He was wearing plain blue board shorts and had his shirt off. The girl beside him was wearing a white tank top, the only thing making her visible. Darin squinted his eyes. His smile vanished.

It was Elizabeth. He thought for a moment his mind must be playing tricks on him. He kept staring, but she made no gestures. She sat still on a mossy rock just out of the water's spray.

Now, he was certain of it. It was definitely her. He glanced around embarrassed as if this was all a big joke on him. Brian was saying something to him, but he wasn't listening. He felt his ears burning hot. He looked back to Andrew, who was watching him closely too.

"Come check out the view up here, bro." He called flatly over the roar of the falls.

Darin couldn't even respond. A million thoughts filled his head all at once fighting to gain dominant ground.

'Andrew and Elizabeth? It couldn't be. No, it was. It definitely was. But for how long? And how had he not known?'

Rage began to overtake him. He looked up again to where Andrew stood. Andrew was now standing in the shallow edge of the river, motioning Darin up with his hands.

"You can climb up from right over there."

He pointed to the right side of the rock face beyond the waterfall's path.

Darin didn't look or even move. He didn't answer either. He simply stood there. Finally, everyone realized what was going on. It became very quiet. Brian and the girls looked back and forth from Andrew to Darin waiting to see what would happen next. A full minute passed. Andrew looked around for a moment.

"What do you think bro? Could a guy jump from here and live?"

He spoke in a clear serious voice. Darin didn't answer. Brian stood up, moving toward the bottom of the falls.

"Hey, don't try that shit, man. That's not even funny. That pool's not even four feet deep." The fear could be heard in the quiver of his young voice.

Neither Andrew nor Darin moved. The other three observers continued asking Andrew and Elizabeth to climb down. Elizabeth stood up moving toward Andrew. She asked him to help her climb down. Andrew stepped out onto the edge of the canyon wall. The water came just below his knee.

"You know I love you like a brother," was the last thing that anyone heard.

He jumped out and went into a dive. The girls screamed in horror. Brian scrambled frantically toward the pool.

Andrew splashed into the pool in a perfect shallow dive. The sound of the water crashing seemed to instantly amplify, drowning out the girls' screams. The next few seconds seemed like an hour had passed. When Andrew came up on the far edge of the pool, there was blood on his face and chest. Brian helped him climb out of the pool.

Darin turned away. He coughed slightly as he fought his emotions back, and he felt a single solitary tear slide down the side of his cheek as he walked back down the path.

August 31st, 1997

The screen door creaked painfully as Eric pushed it open from the inside with his foot. He struggled down the stairs waddling awkwardly toward the car parked in front of the garage. He was carrying the TV from his bedroom using his chin to balance it close to his chest. He set it down on the edge of the backseat of the Lumina then situated it, so it wasn't leaning against the driver's seat. He looked around at the other objects filling the back of the car like a compact garage sale. He couldn't help but think he was forgetting a lot of stuff. After all, this was the first time he was really leaving home. He moved some things around with his large hands. Tiny clouds of dust rose and danced as the seats were disturbed. He wore a puzzled look on his face, as if this act of reorganization would somehow help him realize the things he was forgetting.

It was a dry, scorching hot day. Sweat was already beading on his face and back from his labor. However hot it was outside, the stale air inside the car was ten or more degrees higher even with all four doors open. He heard Andrew breathing heavily behind him. He pulled his head out of the car to find his friend carrying a big black garbage bag. Andrew carried the bag by two pull strings that looked on the verge of snapping under the weight of the bag. The bag itself blocked his legs from forward progress, forcing him to waddle bull legged to the trunk. Finally, he dropped the bag two or three steps short of its destination. Sweat dangled off his brow. He looked at Eric panting heavily.

"What the hell you got in this bag anyway?" He wiped his forehead with his forearm. Before Eric had a chance to guess, Andrew smiled at him, "I bet it's your porn collection huh? Damn, this much porn can't be called a collection. It's more like a porn museum."

They both laughed, but something uncomfortable could be detected. It may have been a small subtle difference, but when you've spent everyday with a person for over nine years it stuck out as obvious as a vegetarian at an NRA meeting. For the last two days, this unusual sense of discomfort had been everywhere. Even when no one spoke, the silence felt different than before.

Eric had signed a letter of intent to play baseball at State University. He was excited for the opportunity. He never realized leaving home would arrive this fast or be this difficult. He was only going to be five hours from home. He could easily make that drive any weekend. It wasn't being home-sick or even being someplace new that bothered him. It was this strange thought he had stuck in his head for the past three nights. He realized that no matter what happened in his life, good or bad, things would never be the same. No matter how hard he tried to convince himself otherwise, he felt the inevitable hand of change plucking away like the guitar songs in an old western film.

He told himself that his friends would never change. He thought of older kids he'd known that graduated high school and either went away for a few years before coming back to town or just stuck around never leaving. None of them seemed any different to him, yet something deep inside his gut told him everything was changing, and it was changing forever.

Maybe it was normal. Maybe everyone felt this way the first fall out of high school, or it might be that their baseball team had been such a successful, tight group that it bothered him to see them separated. Perhaps, it was the new rift that seemed to have grown between Darin and Andrew the last couple weeks. Eric couldn't put his finger on it, but he knew it was something. It was the loneliest of heartaches and he couldn't shake it.

He smiled at his friend a long time that afternoon standing by his old Chevy. His parents came out and each worried in their own way. Eric's father repeatedly reminded him to check his oil, tire pressure, and anything else he could think of to avoid saying goodbye. All the while, his mother was reminding him to call as soon as he got there or if he needed anything or for no reason at all. Her big eyes, nearly identical to Eric's, were emotional and moist.

"Well," he paused hoping the right words would come to him, but they didn't so he continued.

"I guess that's probably everything. I should probably get on the road. Uh, I was gonna say goodbye to Shane, but I guess he's not gonna make it."

He hugged each of his parents a long moment then he turned to Andrew and stuck his hands down in his pockets glancing around.

"You know Shane. He probably just didn't want you to see him cry." Andrew said. They all laughed at this, and it felt like a good genuine laugh to the boys.

"Uh yeah, well... I guess I'll see him anytime I come home anyways. It's no big deal." He pouted his lip out nodding his head to convince himself of what he was saying. "I went to say goodbye to Darin this morning."

He looked at Andrew cautiously trying to read him before going on.

Andrew held his poker face steady.

"You know you should talk to him before you guys both leave. It'd be pretty dumb to leave things this way after all you two have been through together. There's no point in holding a grudge. I mean..."

Andrew closed the trunk hard, making Eric lose his train of thought.

"I'm not mad at Bard." He looked with tired eyes at something behind Eric's left shoulder.

"I never was."

With that he moved in close to his friend and grabbed him in a hug, squeezing Eric's arms into his own body.

"I'm gonna miss you bro. Take care of yourself, keep in contact with me, and for the love of everything holy don't let yourself drop below the Mendoza Line and don't get all fat on light beer up there either." He smiled and slapped his friend lightly on the cheek. "Drive that ball the other way." He said in his best Coach Dugal impression.

"I'll see you at Christmas."

"Yeah, same to you, and good luck at winter ball."

Then as if he remembered something important, fighting back the tears, he added, "Don't ever believe for a second you don't belong there.

You got drafted just the same as any of them big city, groomed from birth, Prima Donnas. Kick ass for us little people."

Tears filled both their eyes.

They hugged again to avoid seeing each other's faces. Eric's dad could handle no more and moved swiftly back into the house. Then without looking back Andrew slipped toward the house too. At the porch he threw a lazy goodbye wave over his shoulder with his left hand, but he never turned around. Eric watched the screen door close before climbing behind the wheel. He turned the key, and after a little sputtering the engine rumbled to life. His mother leaned in the window and kissed him long on the cheek. He said goodbye one last time to her then looked at a picture of Andrew and him as little kids he had in his visor. It brought a smile through the tears.

'We are both going to be big baseball stars,' he thought confidently. Backing out of the driveway, he glanced back at the house one last time saying a quick prayer to himself before turning toward the highway.

August 3rd, 1998

Darin sat down on the carpet in the middle of the large living room placing his legs in the shape of a four with one leg straight out and the other foot touching his knee. He leaned out over his extended knee grabbing his toe. Sweat beaded off his brow. His hair had grown long over the summer. It was usually thick and bushy, but right now sweat kept it matted against his forehead. He had just finished working out, and his pulse hadn't returned to normal yet.

The room was decorated with contemporary art and furniture that showed his mother's determination to boast the family's income with its imported modern style. The couches were expensive but stiff. The only comfortable seat in the entire room was the black leather lazy boy that sat in the far corner nearest the dining room. It was always the seat people were drawn to if left alone in the room; though, Darin's mother complained that it was tacky and didn't fit the room's mood. It was true that it did stand out, but it also made any red-blooded American who set foot in the house feel less uncomfortable in the art gallery like experiment in decor. The room had a spacious opening between the couches and a forty-six inch big screen along the back wall. When Andrew used to come over, he habitually mentioned that this space was perfect size for a game of knee football, but no one in the house ever took advantage of this fact.

Darin finished stretching his legs and was doing some sit-ups when he heard a knock at the door. He sat up starting toward the door, but halfway there he called out a winded "come in." The big oak door opened to reveal Eric's beaming face. He was wearing a pair of board shorts and a Wrangler's baseball tank top. He had a farmer tan, but his arms weren't a whole lot darker than his bright white shoulders and chest. His wide, freckled face was smudged with streaks of black.

"Are you ready or what?" he looked Darin up and down, a confused expression on his face.

"Oh the lake, that's right. I totally forgot about our plans. Hold on, it will take me two seconds to get ready, k?" He held his index finger up taking a couple steps backwards toward the stairs.

"Alright, but hurry up man. The sun is beating down. It's supposed to be ninety-five today, and I'm not getting another day off till next week. I need to get drunk."

He stepped inside as Darin disappeared up the stairs. There was an instant relief stepping out of the sun into the well air-conditioned home. He was standing with his hands behind his back waiting with the door still open when Darin's mom came around the corner. She gave a startled little sigh when she noticed him standing there.

"Oh, hello Eric. It has been a long time since I have seen you around. How are you? How was school this year? Darin told me you were playing baseball at the University." She spoke in a kind voice, but everything about her screamed contempt.

"Hello Mrs. Bard. Good. Yes, school is good." Eric blushed shyly.

Darin's mom had always made him very nervous. He knew that she didn't particularly like Darin hanging around with him because of his friends, but he didn't actually care until she was present.

"What are you studying?"

She looked at him with wide questioning eyes.

"Oh, I....I'm still undeclared, just kinda studying everything."

He avoided her piercing gaze, but he could feel himself getting very uncomfortable.

The truth was Eric had ended the spring semester very poorly. He was barely able to stay eligible for baseball. Luckily, she didn't seem to care much for continuing on the subject.

"Honey, could you shut the door please." She interrupted.

Eric feeling relieved to be doing something rather than speaking closed the door gently, turning back in time to catch a glimpse of her leaving the room the same way she had come in. He sighed heavily, itching his belly which had grown soft in the past few months.

Darin came down the stairs a moment later.

He was wearing a designer tank top and an expensive pair of bright orange board shorts with white flowers on them. Darin's new taste for high priced clothing had become apparent since his return from school, and Eric didn't think twice about what he was wearing. He turned to the door volunteering to drive at the same time. Walking out to the car, Darin made a few comments on the fact that the old Lumina was still running.

"All I do is change the oil every three thousand miles. I guess they must just tighten the bolts down a little better on a Chevy."

Eric proudly defended his car. His face took on a beaming glow that always appeared when Eric spoke of his car or his family.

They drove in silence for the first few minutes. The radio played, Darin looked out the window, and Eric watched the road. On the outskirts of town, before turning onto the lake road, Eric broke the silence. They made small talk asking each other about school experiences, similarities, or differences. The conversation was loose. Both boys seemed genuinely interested in hearing the other speak.

"So is there a ton of coons going to school out there?" Eric asked.

He was leaned back in his seat with one hand gripping the top of the wheel. His window was down, and the hot air whistled in as they cruised down the road about fifty miles an hour. The heat seemed to almost steam off the shiny dashboard which evidently had been cleaned recently.

"No not really. Not at school at least. There's a ton of Asians though, more than you could ever imagine. I bet my school probably has as many Asians as white kids."

"Seriously? Can they understand English or do they have translators?" Eric asked squinting his eyes trying to paint a mental picture while Darin spoke.

"Yea they speak English. I mean they are American born mostly I think, but you do hear a lot of them speaking Chinese or whatever to each other all over campus."

He adjusted his tank top for a few seconds. The air conditioner didn't work, and the car was uncomfortably hot.

"That's crazy man. I wonder why there's none at State?"

"Too far from a big city," he put his arm out the window trying to deflect the air toward his face.

"I think the winters here are too cold too." he added.

Eric nodded, gave a little grin, and then turned back to the road. They drove on in silence a little longer. A radio edited version of Sublime's 'What I Got' played quietly in the background. Finally, Darin adjusted himself to face Eric better. He started to speak unsure of how to bring up the subject he wanted to ask about.

"So...Uh...Have you talked to Andrew at all?"

His eyes looked longingly at the driver.

"I've been meaning to ask you." He added apologetically at the end.

"No, he doesn't have a phone, and he hasn't called me since I've been home."

Darin could see immediately that Eric was very hurt by the situation. He cleared his throat before continuing, "I guess he's still in Arizona. Shane took a bus to visit him in February or March. He said he looked good. Said he was even skinnier than before."

He smiled at his friend then he turned back to the road. His face went neutral. He held the wheel with both hands sitting up rigidly.

"How was he?"

"Shane told me he was playing really good I guess. He told him the coaches expect him to move up to Triple A by next year." Eric said.

Darin could tell there was more to it. He tried to carefully inquire further.

"Did he say anything about how he was doing?" He asked calmly, putting heavy influence on the second he.

"Yeah... I guess he's living with a couple other baseball players. Shane said he was down there for five nights, and there were hot girls at the house the entire time, day or night. He, uh, he also said Andrew was really partying."

He glanced nervously at Darin from the corner of his eye.

"Well, Andrew always could party." Darin said with a chuckle.

He was relieved to hear his friend was doing alright. Being away for so long had given Darin a lot of time to think about home. He couldn't help feeling bad about the way things had left off with Andrew.

"Yeah, I guess so."

Eric didn't laugh or even crack a smile, and Darin spotted this immediately. Alarm bells started ring in his head.

"Is there something you're not telling me?"

Again Eric glanced at him nervously from the corner of his eye.

"I don't know. I mean it's probably nothing. It's just that...that ever since Shane came back from that trip he's been different."

Darin didn't take his gaze off his friend only waited patiently for him to continue.

"He's been doing some drugs. I guess even a little cocaine, man."

Darin had heard the rumors that their friend had been dealing with amphetamines lately. Quite frankly, it didn't even surprise him. Cocaine seemed to be everywhere at Darin's school, and he knew it was only a matter of time before someone close to him began using it back home. However, it wasn't until that moment that he had made a connection with Andrew and the drugs.

"Andrew would never get caught up in that shit though." He half stated, half asked, but then repeated it in a demanding question.

"Shane said they were doing it one night down there."

Eric's face clenched with fear. He felt like an informant ratting out his best friend to the feds.

"That's bad. That shit is bad news."

Darin glanced around.

All he wanted to do was get out of that car. He couldn't stand sitting. He needed to pace or run. He always handled situations better on his feet. Eric didn't respond. He kept his helpless eyes on the road.

Eric was still the father figure. He couldn't help always feeling everything was his fault some how. They drove the rest of the way without much conversation. Both of them wanted to let the other know that whatever came to be wasn't his fault but neither of them knew how to say it.

They drove to a spot at the lake popular for college kids home from school. The hot weather had attracted people to the lake like flies to garbage, and they had to park a good ten minute walk from the water, high above the sand dunes. The sounds of laughter and hearing familiar voices eased Darin's tension. It wasn't long before he was having a good time catching up with old friends. They met up with a couple of their real close buddies sitting on the beach. One of whom was telling a tall tale.

Like all stories of college exploits, the story had probably truly happened, at least some of it. Telling it over and over though the story naturally fabricated so readily and easily that the teller actually begins to fancy the exaggerations have become facts. Everyone knows they can't prove otherwise. Besides, everyone loves to hear a good story, so nobody argues. It's a win-win.

The story being told at that moment was about the kid's first threesome with two girls, and it was getting a little hard to swallow. Darin was only half listening. His mind wondered with the heat of the day.

He caught a girl checking him out over her glasses from down the beach. She sat with two other girls on beach towels sunning. She saw him catch her glance and immediately looked away. Darin got up without a word and walked toward her. Eric thinking something was wrong stood up. He was about to ask Darin where he was going then he noticed Elizabeth. He smiled, hoping for the best as he always did for any of his friends, and sat back down to catch the climax of the story. He held a plastic fountain cup of coke which he had mixed with Captain Morgan's Rum.

He didn't move from that spot for the next couple hours. More kids shared stories, and Eric was having a wonderful time. After a while, the numbers started to dwindle down. His friends slowly said their goodbyes. He was buzzed up real good. Words came and went. Once in a while, he grew confused and maintained only his smile. Late in the afternoon, all that remained were him and two other guys from high school who had been more acquaintances than old friends before today. All three had been drinking in the hot sun all day though, so they were in great company. Eric's speech had become slurred nonsense, but his companions nodded understandingly, laughing or exclaiming at the right times, so he kept on telling story after story.

Finally, Darin returned to find his inebriated friend. It took him several minutes to get his attention and even longer getting him to willingly leave. Eric stumbled up the hill behind his friend. His face and arms glowed bright red against his white tank top. When they arrived at the car, Eric was huffing and puffing pretty heavily. He leaned his head against the door of the car.

"Zo...you wanna dwive, buddy?" He asked smiling at his friend.

Darin laughed heartily.

"Unless you expect us to walk back? I sure as hell ain't letting you drive."

Eric closed his eyes, but he was still smiling. Darin took the keys from him and turned to walk around the car. He heard Eric gagging. He shook his head. He couldn't help but laugh, watching his friend puking in front of the old car. It was classic high school all over again. People driving bye honked and laughed at the sight.

"You done? I don't want to smell that shit, so don't puke in the car."

Eric bobbed his entire body in agreement. He climbed slowly in the car, barely getting the door closed behind him.

"You are really gonna regret some decisions tomorrow morning, my friend." Darin commented as he grimaced at Eric's new skin tone before starting the car. His burn would definitely blister.

He backed it up to get on the road back to town. He drove slowly, knowing from experience that the bumpy road could wreak havoc on a drunken stomach. They had only driven a couple minutes when Eric started jabbering. Nothing he said made much sense. Eventually, he remembered Darin's absence.

"Zo, how's old Lizard doin?" He murmured, his eyes closed and his head rocking freely off the head rest with every bump in the road.

Darin looked over at him cautiously. Realizing that this was as good a chance as any to get things off his chest, he spoke honestly.

"She's doing really well. She's taking classes here at the junior college. She scored herself a full time job at the bank, so she's in the night class program," he paused, but Eric didn't respond, so he continued.

"I asked her out to dinner tomorrow night."

"I guess I never got over her."

"I just, I just never felt those types of feelings for any other girl. You know what I mean?"

"Oh yeah..." Eric agreed then began giving advice, but he was trailing off and slurring so bad Darin had no idea what he said.

"I never told anyone this before, but Elizabeth came over the night before I left for school," Darin said.

He spoke like a man trying to confess himself free of sins before he had time to lose courage. "She told me that Andrew and her had sex that night after the championship game up at Jack's cabin. She told me that he was way drunker than she was. She said he freaked out in the morning when he realized what had happened. She tried to tell him that we were done, but he said it still wasn't something he could ever do. He told her I was like flesh and blood," his eyes filled with tears.

He started choking on his words.

"They were spending a lot of time together after we broke up. She said they were together everyday, and he would talk to her on the phone till three in the morning. He never touched her again though other than that one time. She said they never even hugged let alone kissed after that night at the cabin. I guess that night camping she told him she was in love with him. She didn't know if it was true or not. She just said the words. He told her it had been a mistake...that he would die before he'd hurt me. I guess that is when I found them at the falls."

Darin had to wipe his eyes to see the road. He coughed a few times, crying harder. He had longed to speak of this to someone, anyone, for a long time. Bottled up, these thoughts had grown dark. He looked over at his friend wiping his eyes frantically. He wanted to know what Eric would make of all this. He knew if there was anyone that would understand and never make fun of a friend pouring his heart out it was Eric, but his friend didn't say a word.

He was passed out.

August 16th, 1998

Darin was sitting down to dinner when the phone rang. He didn't plan to answer it, but he looked at the caller ID anyways. It was Eric, so he picked it up. Eric told him that Weller, a former teammate of theirs, was having a party that night. Weller was a year younger then them and had just graduated, but Eric assured Darin that there would be a lot college kids back for the summer at the party. He said a lot of their old friends would be there.

Darin was reluctant at first, but it had been a while since he had been to a large social gathering. Besides, Eric could be very persistent. He told Darin that if it wasn't fun they could leave early. Although Darin knew it would be fun for Eric basically no matter what because he was sure to be wasted, he didn't see any other excuse and finally agreed to go. He hung up the phone, immediately wondering if Elizabeth would be there. Since he had spoken with her that first day at the lake, they had been talking on the phone regularly, and he had taken her out a few times. They had gone to dinner twice, watched a movie at his house, and he visited her house once. However, they had not been out around people from high school together. Darin couldn't help but wonder if there would be a lot of drama caused by the former couple's new situation.

After dinner, he showered but still couldn't clear his head. He spent a great deal of time getting ready, trying to be sure everything would look perfect. Scenarios ran wild through his imagination and nothing looked right in the mirror. He wore an expensive pair of jeans, a blue and white dress shirt, his nicest shoes, and gelled his hair meticulously.

He sat in his room trying to visualize how he would be received at the party. He figured the younger guys would look up to him, probably ask him about football. He pictured all the girls talking about him, wondering if he was seeing anyone, hoping he'd notice them. High school all over again. Everyone would see the way he was talking with Elizabeth, and it would become the main attraction of the entire party. He practiced how he would answer questions about the two in his head.

Around a quarter till nine, he heard a knock at the door. The knock was distinct. It was four quick hard knocks, very serious, very deep. He moved quickly down the stairs opening the door with his right hand while quickly touching up his hair in the wall mirror. Finally turning his attention to the open doorway, he was surprised to find Shane standing on his porch wearing a baggy t-shirt and a pair of black jean shorts. He had grown taller in the year since Darin had last seen him. His thick, coarse hair was shaggy with an unkempt bird's nest appearance, and his complexion had cleared up. He looked at Darin smiling with his crooked teeth showing.

"What's up QB?"

"How's it going Shaner?" It took Darin a moment to get himself together before he answered.

"Pretty good," he looked Darin up and down very deliberately for a few seconds. "Damn, you're looking pretty cute. You better be careful tonight, or all the guys are gonna be all over you." He challenged.

Darin ignored the comment, glancing down at his own clothing, but Shane reached out his hand to give him five. Darin slapped his hand as they started toward the car. Shane called out "shotgun", opening the door to get in the front seat. Darin climbed in behind him on the same side of the vehicle. When they had pulled away from the curb, Eric glanced over the seat.

"Hey buddy, you made the right choice. I think this party is gonna be huge. Weller lives up on the mountain behind the old junkyard. He has no neighbors, so its not gonna get broke up."

Darin felt his gel crystallized hair again as he addressed the front seat, "Are you gonna drink tonight?"

Eric and Shane both looked back with surprised looks on their face. Then they looked at each other. Eric started laughing, "I've already been drinking brother." Darin was confused.

"Oh, well then who's driving us home?"

"Don't worry. I'll sober up by the time we leave. I'm gonna stop drinking as soon as we aren't having fun."

This worried Darin still more. He looked out the window wondering if he had made the right decision by coming out. Something caught his eye. He turned forward to see Shane reaching toward him. He was holding a brown forty ounce bottle.

"Here you go bud. I hope forties are still your drink of choice?"

Darin took the bottle, placing it between his legs. He sat there for a few minutes wondering what he had gotten himself into. He watched Shane taking pulls off a bottle of some sort of hard alcohol and chasing it down with Coke from a plastic bottle. He couldn't help thinking of Andrew. He longed to talk to his old friend right now. Andrew's calm demeanor always balanced out Darin's constant paranoia. They were like yin and yang. No matter what terrible scenario Darin warned of, Andrew would ease the tension. It was one of his great skills, his ability to convince others that everything would work out alright.

When they were younger, Andrew always used to tell Darin that there was no point in ever worrying about making bad decisions. He always advised his friends to trust their intuitions. He said it didn't matter whether or not free will existed. If it didn't exist, then it was your destiny to do the exact things that happen, good or bad. It would not matter.

If free will did exist then it still didn't matter because you would make the decisions that were based upon who you were. Your will would already be predetermined by your environment and experience. Thus you would make your choice good or bad based on everything you had learned about the world around you up until that point. Regardless of your actions, there would be consequences. It is a law of physics: for every action there is an equal and opposite reaction. He said no one person's will could cause future damage because it would be impossible to act against one's own will in the first place. It made no sense to Darin at the time, but he couldn't help considering it whenever he felt anxious before going out.

One of Andrew's key tools in convincing others had always been using spiritual or other philosophical speech that no one could disprove. Darin had never been religious, but something about Andrew had always made him at least a little curious in the existence of a higher power. Darin had always been very scientific. He believed in things he could see, measure, or prove. Andrew was the exact opposite. He showed little or no interest in anything known to man. His greatest interests had always been in the unknown, particularly in matters that required faith without evidence. He said, 'a man's reality is created by the perception of his own mind.' Then, he would get drunk somewhere and pass out naked on a picnic table. Suddenly, Darin couldn't help laughing. He didn't even realize he was doing it until he heard Shane's voice.

"What the hell is so funny?" He asked. Darin stopped, but a smile remained on his face.

"Nothing, I was just thinking about a funny story." He replied nonchalantly.

Shane looked ironically at him. He seemed to be waiting for Darin to explain the story, but then lost interest quickly when he didn't. He turned back around, taking another long pull off his bottle and wincing to swallow it. Darin watched him still smiling. He looked at the bottle resting between his legs. Deciding what the hell, he cracked open the bottle, raised it to his lips, and took a long slow drink. It was an instant release. He could feel the pressure of his entire life ease as the cold liquid flowed down his throat. He smiled.

"So Shane, I heard you went and visited Andrew. How's he doing?"

He had been burning to hear about Andrew first hand the entire summer.

"He's doing awesome man. I was telling Eric you guys couldn't believe the way girls jock him down there."

Shane grew animated. Andrew was one of his favorite subjects. The fact both their fathers were deadbeats created a common bond. Shane loved this shared trait, seeing Andrew achieve so much always made his future seem potentially brighter as well. Everyone that knew Andrew felt this way. It was like simply standing close to him made anything seem possible, as if he had so much confidence and charisma it seeped into those around him.

'Reality created through perception.'

In Shane's case, it was even stronger. He could truly feed off Andrew. His mother once told Andrew that if it wasn't for his friendship, Shane would have never made it through high school let alone baseball.

"How does he get around?"

Shane laughed and grew even more animated.

"That's one of the funniest parts. The first thing he did when he got his signing bonus was buy a car," Shane could barely tell the story he was laughing so hard.

"Not just any car either. He bought a real prize. He went out and bought himself a 1988 Lincoln."

Shane paused to take a pull off his bottle, but he was still laughing and it made him choke then cough. After a few minutes, he finally poised himself.

"So get this, he pays eight hundred bucks cash for this beautiful maroon boat right? He's driving it around feeling pretty cool. After all, it's his first car. On the *second day*, he gets in a hit in run. The *second day*!"

He can no longer contain himself. He stops talking to laugh. This time the others join him. Everyone is laughing hysterically. Shane is a talented and hilarious story teller. It takes several minutes before Eric ventures to ask another question.

"So, what happened man? Where was the accident?"

His eyes already wet from laughter.

"I don't know. He said he was driving on a hill. He came up to a light kinda quick, and he said he just didn't stop all the way. He said he barely bumped the lady in front of him." Shane's hands are flying frantically animating the story. "He said she looks at him in the mirror and pulls into the parking lot on the right, but he just drove on."

A fresh batch of laughter rolls out through the car. They are still giggling and commenting on the story when they arrive at the party. As they are stepping out of the car, Shane's voice could be heard, "You guys truthfully got to hear him tell the story though. I swear to God you will piss your pants."

The party was already going full swing when they arrived. They could hear music and laughter walking up to the house. The house was a very large, dark-stained log home. It was surrounded by pine trees on both sides, and an eight foot cedar fence kept them from seeing into the back yard. A deck ran around three sides of the home above the fence, and the boys could see people on either side of the house crowded around the railing.

Eric was right about the party. They knew a lot of the people present most of whom were either graduated seniors or their own age. Several people asked Darin about college and football, but he was disappointed that he didn't seem to draw the kind of attention that he had expected. Even when he found Elizabeth, they spoke only briefly a couple times before one of them was caught up in another conversation. He was surprised but not a single person asked him about her or even seemed to notice that they spoke at all. He didn't dwell on it long though.

The more awkward he felt the more he drank. Being a lightweight, it wasn't long before he was feeling buzzed. He played drinking games, talked about old glories, and spent most of his time with Shane.

Eric on the other hand was nowhere to be seen. His sole concern all night was a girl named Claire. He had met Claire at a party earlier in the summer. Claire had graduated in May from the school across town. He had failed to get her number, but he hadn't stopped thinking about her. He had expected her to be at the party, and as soon as he saw her he would let nothing hinder his pursuit.

It was after two in the morning when things finally started winding down. The majority of people were leaving or trying to find a ride. Shane was looking for Eric. He found him outside sitting in a porch swing with Claire. The couple was startled when they noticed Shane. Eric's face looked like a child's after being caught with his hand in the cookie jar. Shane didn't mean to intrude on his friend, but he was pretty drunk, so he didn't really put two and two together.

"You ready to go bro?" He asked flatly. Eric sat up. He had been so caught up with Claire that he had forgotten all about his friends.

"Where we going?" he asked.

He spoke in a voice that was somewhere between the voice he usually spoke in and the softer, more enunciated version he used when trying to sweet talk girls. Shane, who usually would have been all over him for this mistake, didn't notice.

"I don't know, but everyone's leaving, and I am starving."

He hunched over holding his stomach dramatically for extra effect.

"You wanna go to Denny's?"

This time Eric had cleared his throat before speaking in his deep regular bark.

"Yeah, man. Let's go."

Shane deserved an award for his body language.

"Alright, alright, just give me two minutes."

Eric made a glance toward Claire, hoping that Shane would catch his hint.

"Just try and hurry up man." Shane whined, walking away feeling he had triumphed.

He went back in the house to find Darin alone in a small sitting room next to the kitchen. He was in an arm chair slouched over. Shane smiled knowing how drunk Darin must be. A bunch of the guys had all decided to really go after Darin during the drinking games, for they never knew if they would get another chance to sauce him up.

"Hey muscles, get up bro."

Darin peeked through a bloodshot eye tilting his head slowly toward the opposite shoulder. A big smile took over his face, and he smacked his lips loudly a couple times.

"Leave me alone. I'm just taking a short nap. I'll drink more in a couple minutes. Just let me sleep for ten minutes."

This made Shane laugh.

"We are going to Denny's. Come on."

The mention of food seemed to strike a nerve in Darin. He sat up, blinking his eyes a few times to wake himself.

"Are we really?" He asked inquisitively, hoping his friend wasn't leading him on. "Cuz I am so very hungry. I bet I could eat a small child right now."

"I feel the same way. We're just waiting on lover boy."

Shane made a quick glance over his right shoulder toward the porch. Darin's look made it clear he didn't understand, so Shane filled him in on the situation.

"How bout one more shot while we wait?" Shane asked grabbing his friend around the shoulder. He was already leading him toward the kitchen when he spoke.

When they had downed another shot of vodka each, and Darin officially appeared to be on the verge of vomiting, they went out to the porch to get Eric. This time, they stood their ground until Eric finally gave in. He couldn't decide how to say his goodbye to Claire with two of his friends standing by watching his every move. The way he saw it he had two options. He could either say a real goodbye and kiss her, facing nothing worse then a couple comments on the ride home before his friends would forget about it, or he could risk all the ground he had gained tonight by trying to play it cool, though he would still likely face some teasing. Of course to Eric the answer was obvious, he stood up nonchalantly dropped an 'I'll call you sometime' and blew her a short kiss and a wink as he pushed his friends toward the porch steps in front of them. Eric was beaming all the way out to the car, and he climbed in and started it only to wait several minutes for a dispute over front seat, before Shane was awarded the position through a paper-rock-scissors playoff. He put it into reverse and backed out of the driveway. Like clockwork, when he shifted the car from reverse to drive the teasing began. It was the usual drunken friend comments:

'You missed out on the party.'

'When's the wedding.'

And of course the infamous:

'Bros before hoes.'

The comments weren't mean. They were only jokes.

Besides, someone could have stuck a knife in Eric's leg, and it wouldn't have mattered on that night. He was infatuated. Eric wasn't a guy who went crazy over girls, so for him this was all a new experience. He felt butterflies. He filled his friends in on his evening, but they wouldn't accept that all that had happened was kissing. They egged him for every juicy detail.

Despite their behavior, Shane and Darin could see Eric's excitement, and they were both very happy for him. Shane did most of the talking, Darin sat in the back listening, his head still spinning from all the alcohol. Every once in a while, he would laugh or add in a few comments to whatever the conversation called for. He was mostly thinking about the night.

He always reflected on everything. It was something he could never help. Even his football coaches at college told him if he had one weakness it was that he thought too much. Sometimes he couldn't sleep for days on end even when he was exhausted because he couldn't stop his brain from running.

Right now he was thinking about Elizabeth. She had left the party early. She said she had to work the next day. Darin wondered how things had gone between them that night. He also couldn't help thinking about how little attention he had drawn in the gossip. He wondered if he was becoming a 'High School Henry.'

A Henry was a term used to describe athletes who were very important in high school, but failed to add anything to their legacy. Darin was very self conscious. Being forgotten was one of his biggest fears. He knew as long as he succeeded at college ball he would never be forgotten. This was a huge motivating factor for him.

He was still on this when Shane said something that made him laugh. Suddenly, he stopped worrying. He thought about how great it had been to hang out with his friends. He knew that even these seldom times were rapidly disappearing forever. He had to remember and cherish these moments. He smiled. After all, it was a good night. He had fun, spent time with his friends, and got to forget about everything at least for one night.

He heard his stomach rumble. He was hungry. Pancakes became the primary focus on his mind. He looked into the darkness in front of him at the silhouettes of two of the closest friends he would ever have. He wanted to tell them thanks. He wanted to explain to them how much they meant to him, but before he got the chance lights suddenly caught his attention in the mirrors. His heart jumped. The lights flashing behind them were red and blue.

"Oh shit man. Everyone put your seatbelts on."

"Shit."

"Stay cool."

"Grab my shit out of the glove box."

"We are screwed."

It was an instant reality check, a reminder of how painfully real the world was. The entire night disappeared instantly. Panic grabbed them by the throat and slowly squeezed. The more they panicked the more bleak the outlook appeared. They all watched the officer walk through his spotlight beam slowly, methodically up to Eric's window.

"How are you doing this morning?"

He leaned down to get level with the window, but he still held a downward gaze. The flashlight he carried blinded the boys one by one as he glanced first around the front seat then sharply toward Darin in the back. The spotlight lit up his face while the boys remained in the dark looking into the light. This made them feel even guiltier. The officer was of middle height and build. He had dark features, dark eyes, and brown hair that peaked out from the sides of his patrol cap. He appeared to be in his late thirties, but he held his age well and had the look of man who takes his physical fitness seriously. He stared at Eric coldly.

"Driver's license and registration please."

Eric handed him his information while remaining silent. He tried to hold eye contact, yet he felt himself wavering.

"Where are you boys headed this morning?" The officer asked shining his flashlight down at Eric's driver's license.

"Uh, we were just headed home."

Eric fought to maintain a steady voice.

"Where you boys coming from?" To add pressure to this question, the officer shined his flashlight into the car again.

"We were at a friend's."

Eric could feel the light shining right through him. His seat seemed to get a hundred degrees warmer. He hated this situation, but he was trying to stay quick on his feet. The officer looked down at the information for a moment before returning his hard stare into the car.

"Are any of the passengers over the age of twenty one?"

"No sir."

"Have you been drinking tonight?"

"No sir."

"None of you have been drinking tonight?" He leaned his head closer to the window, directing the question at Darin and Shane.

"Nope," Shane answered quickly.

He was the one most in control of his emotions.

"Ok, the reason I pulled you over tonight is for speeding. I got you traveling 35 in a 25 right back there by the park. I am going to give you a citation for speeding this morning Mr. Shay. I am also going to ask each of you to take a Breathalyzer for me this morning. The reason I am doing this is because I definitely smell alcohol inside the vehicle and everyone inside the vehicle is under the legal drinking age. Do you understand all this Mr. Shay?"

"Yes sir."

"Alright, I am going to go run this right now, so just hold on tight. I'll be right back."

He turned and walked back to his car. Darin placed his forehead against the back of the driver's head rest. He felt sick to his stomach.

"We are so screwed man. What the hell are we gonna do?" Darin asked, his panicked voice climbing several decibels.

"*We* are gonna get possessions. Its Eric I'm worried about," Shane seemed very calm considering all that was happening around him. "Have you been drinking bro?"

"I haven't drank anything in at least a couple of hours. Shit. I am completely sober. I'm serious. I'm fine to drive, but I might still blow I don't know."

He knocked his head softly off the steering wheel in disgust.

"I'm so screwed right now. I don't know what I'm gonna do guys." Darin whined.

He seemed to be getting worse with every passing moment. He spoke in whimpering bursts. He could feel everything caving in around him. He could see his football career, his future disappearing.

"Settle down. It's a possession of alcohol. It's not the end of the world. It's like five hundred bucks though. Not that you have to worry about that, your parents will pay that shit for you. Everything will be back to normal in your perfect little life in no time at all."

Shane was clearly venting some frustration out on Darin for being so self-centered. Darin's stress mixed with Shane's words proved volatile.

"I've never been in trouble before. I know its all in a day's work for you, but for me it's not acceptable. My dad's gonna kill me." Darin shouted.

"Oh yeah, my mom's happy when I get in trouble. I mean after all I'm an Indian that's all we're good for right?"

"You selfish son of a bitch, you act like you're the only one in trouble. Everything's always got to be about you huh, rich boy?"

He gathered his breath to go on, but they both shouted at the same time making it impossible to hear anything.

Finally, Eric took control of the situation. It was rare that gentle Eric ever yelled, but when he lost his cool it was noticeable. He was big, strong, and very scary when he was angry.

"Both of you shut up. Arguing ain't gonna do shit. We are already screwed. There is no reason to blame anyone. This is all my fault. I should have been paying attention, but I am asking you both to keep your voices down. Panicking in front of some asshole cop will only make his day."

He spoke in a warning tone that both his friends heeded. Everyone sat back and thought to themselves. The car was silent. Breaths were held as the cop walked back up to the window. Darin couldn't hear his footsteps, but he imagined he could as he watched the shadow bounce and move in the bright backdrop of the searchlight. Each of them felt a cold hatred for this robot- like-man and his high and mighty demeanor, but Eric's solitary, lonely sigh was the only sound that was heard.

AUGUST 24TH, 1998

Eric pulled over to the curb, cutting the engine. He climbed out of his car, slamming the door behind him, and started toward Shane's apartment. Shane lived with his mother and younger sister in a run down apartment building on the east side of town. The apartment stood out because it was the only multi-story building in the entire neighborhood. The structure, painted white at some point in the past, had long since faded to a puke colored yellow. It was surrounded on either side by long single story apartments in similar states of disgust and kitty corner from an equally appealing trailer park. Across the street was the Old Chief Motel, which looked like it was straight off one of those true crime shows on cable, it was also the place Andrew and Eric had seen their first adult fist fight.

Eric still remembered the day. They were in the sixth grade, and had been playing catch with a football out in the street when they heard two voices arguing with some very choice words. Andrew ran around to the parking lot. Eric followed close behind. They watched the two men, both of whom were grizzled and looked to be in dire need of a shower, push each other until the skinnier of the two, a homely white guy with long, stringy grey hair and a full matching beard, struck the other in the side of the head with a frantic hook. The other man, a Native of medium build with a beer gut, deep wrinkled face, and equally long hair that was black but beginning to take on a silver tint, took the blow before tackling the white guy at the waist.

They rolled around punching and grabbing. Neither one seemed able to find an advantage or get back to his feet. Until finally, the white guy staggered up and was able to strike the other man on his exposed back with a downward swinging motion. The boys were probably seventy yards or more away, yet they both could see the man was holding something in his hand. The native let out a painful moan before rolling into a defensive position a few feet from his attacker. The white guy hesitated as if he wanted to strike the man again but decided against it. He jogged slowly to the far side of the motel and disappeared into an alley running north away from the trailer park.

The boys stood motionless. Eric was scared to death. He told Andrew several times they should run, but Andrew didn't pay any attention. He stood still. After a couple minutes, he started slowly toward the man still laid out on the concrete moaning softly. About twenty steps from the man, Andrew called out asking if the injured man needed help. The man was startled by the sound of a voice, yet he didn't answer. Instead, he struggled to his feet holding his right shoulder with his left hand. Andrew asked a second time if he needed any help. The man looked at him, told him no, and walked in the direction the other man had fled without another word. When he reached the alley, however, he turned the opposite direction, disappearing into the trailer park.

Every time Eric told the story, he pointed out how stupid Andrew had been, but Andrew usually ignored him. On the rare occasion he did answer, he would reply that the man had been stabbed and that regardless of who he was, what he had done, or his appearance, he was in pain. He would say that he offered help because he would want someone to offer him help in a similar situation.

It had always puzzled Eric. He looked over at the old motel, remembering the day as if it had happened yesterday. He suddenly realized how much he missed his friend's daily presence in his life.

Shane's apartment was on the ground floor of the building. Walking up to the apartment, the top of the door stood about knee high, for there were four concrete stairs that led down to it. Frequently, Shane used this bunker-like entrance to scare the daylights out of visitors. Eric had learned to enter from the side away from the street to be sure this trick wasn't played on him any longer.

There was nobody there today. Instead, an old warn out straw mat greeted the stocky youth. Eric climbed down the steps and knocked a few short raps on the door. He heard Shane's mother shout 'come in' over the voices from the television. Before he could even poke his head in the door, the smell of cigarette smoke burned his eyes.

Upon entering the apartment, the kitchen was immediately to the left and the small living room was on the right forming a single rectangular space about twenty or twenty-five feet by eight feet. Directly in front of the entrance was a bathroom, with a hallway leading left to the two small rooms or right to the master bedroom. Shane's mom sat on a small sofa on the wall next to the hallway entrance. She met Eric's glance with a smile, standing up slowly to give him a hug. They exchanged casualties, before Eric asked if Shane was in his bedroom. Her smile disappeared, leaving a smug look in its place.

"Yeah, he's sittin in there on his ars as usual. I told him he needs to go find a damn job."

She picked at her front teeth with a long pink polished nail.

"He's been out of school for a year, but he hasn't held a job for more than three weeks. This last job he had over here at the grocery store," she pointed toward the wall which Eric had entered through, "He worked two days. He didn't even go pick up his check."

She reached out grabbing a purse off the lamp table beside the sofa. She dug through it quickly grabbing a pack of cigarettes and pulling one out.

"I told him if he don't pay the ticket you boys got the other day, they're gonna throw his scrawny ars in jail."

She spoke through tight lips clenching the cigarette in her mouth. She paused momentarily to light it.

"I worry he's gonna turn out like his dad."

She shook her head a moment and sighed, but then, she offered up a smile, "So, how have you been? You're sure getting big aren't you now?"

"Yea," Eric laughed, stretching and eyeing the TV as he went on, "I am real sorry about what happened. It was all my fault. I guess I just..." but she cut him off there.

"Oh bullshit! Shaner told me the whole story." She shouted ashing her cigarette with a quick flick. "The cops in this town have nothing better to do then harass kids because they are on some sort of fucking power trip."

Eric was accustomed to Shane's mother's language, so he smiled and left it at that. As he turned toward the hallway, she said, "Tell him to get off his lazy ars or I'll throw that damn video game out the window."

Shane's bedroom was on the end of the hall. The door was cracked open, and Eric could see a dim light flashing inside. The only window in the room, which had a black garbage sack taped over it, was on the left wall behind the head of Shane's bed, limiting the only light in the room to the flashing glow of the TV screen. The room was a small, eight by eight square, with a small door-less closet. Shane sat on the end of the bed hunched back with the remote in his right hand.

He looked up at Eric uninterested when he entered the room, before returning his attention to the TV. Eric could distinctly smell pot though it was mixed pretty well with the smell of incense. The fact that there was little space to sit down in the small room led him to lean against the wall next to the door.

"What were you doing yesterday? I called you like five times to see if you wanted to go play some basketball over at the school." Eric asked, trying to make his position on the wall look less uncomfortable than it was.

"Uh, I was...I think I was probably sleeping. I can't remember. What time did you call?" He moved over onto the far side of the bed when he asked the question to make room for Eric to sit down beside him without blocking the view of the TV.

"I called at like eleven, but I called a couple more times before three."

Eric graciously took the seat trying to take up as little room as he could with his big body.

"We wound up just shooting around and playing a quick game of twenty-one."

"Who's we?" With the question, Shane finally looked at Eric.

"Me and Darin." Eric said fragilely.

"Darin and I." Shane corrected him sharply.

"What?"

"You said me and Darin. It's Darin and I."

"Alright, thanks professor. I forget you're such a scholar sometimes." He stated sarcastically, making a sour face.

They both looked at each other for a moment then broke out laughing.

"How is old Bard? I haven't talked to him since the whole MIP. How did his parents take the golden child's possession?" He asked, his face showing true interest for the first time.

"I guess he's gonna plead not guilty."

"What? He blew the highest out of all of us. How could he fight it?" Shane shifted around crossing his legs and fidgeting with intrigue.

"Yeah, his parents got a sweet lawyer though man." Eric said shrugging his shoulders. His body language made it clear that the news had surprised him too.

"Wow. It must be great being rich." Shane whistled.

He sat still for a second looking up at the ceiling lost in thought. Eric turned back to the TV. A beer commercial was showing cowboys choosing a particular brand of beer in front of some city slickers in a bar. When the cowboys left, the city guys ordered the same brand.

"Well, I guess if he's immune to the law we should take him out drinking tonight, but this time he's driving."

"Fat chance. I think his mom was madder that he was with us that night than the fact that he got in trouble. I'm scared to cross paths with her ever again. He left for school this morning anyways."

"Already?"

"Yeah, I guess he doesn't start school for a couple more weeks, but he's got football practice tomorrow or the next day."

"Is he gonna start this year?"

"I don't know. I think the starter from last year was only a junior, but I'm not positive."

Shane started to ask another question, but the sound of his mother's voice stopped him in mid sentence. He fell silent craning his long neck toward the door. His mother yelled again. He couldn't hear all that she said, but he knew there were only a few reasons she yelled at him. She was telling him someone was here to see him. Suddenly, Shane took on a new personality. He seemed jumpy or nervous. He got up, rummaged through his closet for a minute, and put something in the front pocket of his jeans. Eric couldn't see what it was in the dimly lit room. He wasn't sure what was going on, but he'd known Shane long enough to tell that something was going on.

"Who's here?" he asked.

"I'm not sure. I think its David Gardapee." He trailed off when he spoke the name, almost trying to sneak it by his friend.

"Who?"

"Why the hell would Gardapee be coming to your house?" Eric asked with an ironic look of astonishment. He couldn't believe what he heard.

He didn't know a lot about the Gardapee brothers, but everything he had heard was bad.

David was the younger brother. He was probably two or three years older than Eric and Shane. Eric remembered him being a gifted athlete. He played basketball with amazing skill and ease. He had been on varsity as a sophomore, but he dropped out the next year. The two brothers still dominated the court at City Park though. Eric had played against them a couple of times.

The older brother, Jonathan, was a carbon copy of his little brother, just older and carrying more negative weight on him. Jonathan had a very similar fate to his brother, though he never played varsity ball. He was predicted to be one of the better players in the state. He once scored thirty five points in a game his freshman year, but he got in trouble and had to sit out his sophomore year. More troubles followed, and he dropped out before the end of his sophomore year. The only thing Eric knew about them was that they were good at basketball, and they had more tattoos than anyone else he had ever seen. He heard they had both done some time for stealing cars or something, but he couldn't remember the rumors.

"We have been hanging out a little lately. Just shooting hoop or smoking a bowl once in a while." Shane spoke quickly, avoiding Eric's questioning eyes.

"Man, these aren't the kind of guys you want to be hanging out with bro." Eric preached.

"Relax man. It's nothing. It's just that Andrew's gone and your not here during the school year. I just made some new friends." He tried to take a defiant tone but failed.

"Shane, these guys aren't friends. They're convicts." He screamed in a whisper afraid to be overheard.

"Ok Darin. What are you my mom now? I gotta go. I'll call you tomorrow. We should go paint balling once before you leave for school."

Shane picked up a black backpack off the floor beside his bed and moved past Eric. Eric followed him down the hall. In the living room, he caught the look of terror on Shane's mom's face. He opened his mouth but the words wouldn't come.

In the doorway stood a tall thin native dressed in jean shorts and a tight wife beater. His skin was rough, tan, and covered from shoulder to wrist in tattoos with more visible on his chest. He had long black hair pulled back tight in a ponytail. His tight face was smooth except for a mustache. It appeared that he grew very little other facial hair.

He nodded his head when he saw Shane without saying a word. His eyes locked on Eric for a moment in what Eric took as a cold look of hatred, but he turned around quickly walking up the stairs out of sight. Eric said goodbye to Shane's mom who seemed shaken by the visitor then followed Shane out the door, shutting it behind him. The boys were crawling into an old Corolla when he reached the street. He stared at the car as it groaned away from the curb then walked to his own vehicle with a blank look on his face.

He wished he had been more firm. He wished he could defy Shane from climbing in the car, but he knew it wouldn't work. He would be leaving for college at the end of the month. Shane would have to make his own choices.

Eric started his car. He wondered if things would be different if he hadn't gone away to college, or if Andrew were here to speak with Shane. He pulled away from the curb, playing the scene over and over in his head. He couldn't help imagining his friend fighting to stay afloat in dark waters, and he couldn't help blaming himself for leaving him to drown.

August 27th, 1998

Andrew sat in the stiff wooden chair looking around the office. There wasn't a whole lot to see. The small room was very plain. The white washed, cinder block walls had a couple photos of past players with a name or a small caption. Some were posing with a smile while others were swinging or throwing. There was a grey filing cabinet in the back corner and what appeared to be America's original fax machine resting on a small wooden table on the other side of the desk.

Andrew chewed his gum loudly snapping it and blowing bubbles. He was still wearing his uniform. He finished what was expected to be his last start of the season about half hour earlier. Before, he had time to shower or change he had been told to report to Payton's office.

Mark Payton was the manager of the Stallions, the rookie league team where Andrew had been assigned after spring training. He was a short balding man whose passive demeanor showed he'd been around long enough to see everything. There was very little that surprised Coach Payton. He realized long ago that his team had been assembled to develop talent, not to win championships, and his coaching reflected this goal.

Coach Payton walked into the office with his flat feet slapping the concrete floor and shut the door behind him softly. He cleared his throat and scratched it constantly as old men sometimes do. He then sat down without paying much attention to his young ace pitcher.

Turning in his big creaky chair, he sorted some papers behind him with great concentration for a few moments. Andrew could usually tell when Coach Payton was intently focused because he often exhaled from the front of his throat as if he were about to cough. It could be mistaken for a raspy sort of humming. Eventually seeming to find what he was looking for, he turned back to his desk and began writing on a form he pulled from the jumbled stack.

The fact that he had not greeted Andrew did not come as a surprise to the lanky lefty. Earning a 5-1 record over the summer, he realized that Coach Payton spoke to players a lot more when he was upset with them than when he was pleased. Andrew couldn't remember the last time Payton said anything to him besides the occasional, 'good game, son.' Payton was old school; a man belonging to a time long since faded. He rarely wasted words.

Andrew spent most of his time with the pitching coach, Coach Scully, and the rest of the pitchers down in the bullpen. Scully had a similar 'learning is more important than winning' approach to the team as Payton, but their personalities were as different as night and day. Where Coach P only spoke when he either had to or felt cornered, Scully was a fifty-one year old adolescent. He spoke constantly, though rarely on the subject of baseball. He was always asking questions of all his pitchers or preaching the philosophy he had developed from a life filled entirely of the game. Scully had played in the minor leagues from the age of twenty-one until he finally retired at age thirty-two.

In those eleven years of 'bumming around baseball', as he liked to describe it, Scully had been called up to the Major Leagues twice. The first time, at twenty-four, he threw two-thirds of an inning for the Detroit Tigers. A young flame thrower similar to Andrew he forced the first batter to ground out to short, walked the next three, then struck a guy out before giving up a grand slam. He was sent back to the minors the next day. Three years later, he was called up before the All-Star break by the Padres, but after six games with the club he was returned to the minors without even getting up in the pen.

Though he rarely spoke of the second occurrence, he talked about his true outing in the 'Show' nearly every day. He would find ways to squeeze it into almost any conversation. He would say things like, "It's rare in this world that a man can say that the greatest moment of pure joy in his life was followed directly by an event so catastrophic that he would contemplate suicide mere moments later." He spoke of this in jest, but it was clear to anyone that spent enough time around him that he was serious.

Scully had been retired from baseball for three weeks, wondering what he was going to do for the rest of his life, when he was offered a position as a rookie league pitching coach, and he had been doing it ever since. He loved it. He never had to grow up. Half his year was spent teaching eighteen and nineteen year old kids how to sneak girls into a host house or properly execute a hot foot. The rest he wasted away in Florida with his brother and his family.

Once, when Andrew had asked him if he liked his job, he told him that baseball was the only job in the entire world that a man could stare at a girl in the stands for three hours and still be complimented for a good days work. It was partly due to his influence that Andrew longed to coach baseball someday.

Coach P's story was different. Coach P had been a pure scrapper. He had been a utility infielder and had worked his butt off his entire career. He had played in the Major Leagues five years for three different teams. He had never been a consistent starter, though he had started over fifty games over the course of his career. He was a student of the game. He wasn't there to become a star or make a bunch of money. He loved baseball. Coaching college baseball was his eventual plan, for he felt the players would have more passion to win. After all, there is a lot more at stake for a bunch of college kids that may have nothing in life to look forward to after those final four years on the diamond than for a bunch of cocky blue-chippers who have almost spent their entire signing bonus and are more concerned with renegotiating their contracts than sliding into third on a close play.

However, the connections from his playing days, and his reputation as a tough character earned him immediate positions in coaching pro ball after his retirement. He had always planned to keep moving up, maybe one day being a base or bench coach for a big club. It never worked out. He didn't complain, yet he longed for more. It wears on a guy. Eventually, he became the sad hound dog that his players saw him as.

Andrew watched anxiously as that hound sat before him hunched over his desk writing, his flabby cheeks hanging down past his chin. Andrew often wondered what could make two men with such similar lives so very different. He wanted to stand up, walk around the desk, put his arm around his old coach, and tell him everything would be alright. He was staring at the shiny bald head lost in thought when Coach P cleared his throat to speak.

"Well, you had a damn fine year, son."

He looked up out of his hollowed out sockets toward Andrew for the first time.

"Thanks Coach." Andrew replied chipper, a big smile covering his face as he tried not to blush.

The old coach cleared his throat again, glancing down at the form before returning his glance to Andrew.

"The organization has decided to move you up, son. They're sending you out to the AA club in Washington."

Andrew could barely contain his excitement. He gripped the arms of the chair tightly trying to remain poised.

"You're to fly out tomorrow. You're going to be getting at least one maybe two more starts this year up there," he continued, while he looked down checking a box on the form he seemed to have missed before.

"Congratulations son. Your itinerary and things will be ready at the hotel, so get everything packed up tonight."

Andrew stood up to leave the room, but then thought to shake his coach's hand first.

"Thanks for everything Coach. I really appreciate everything you've done for me. Thank you," he repeated barely able to connect words together.

He turned and walked swiftly out of the room. His feet barely touched the ground. He was so excited. He was moving up. Wonderful thoughts started to fill his head. He couldn't help but think that if he performed well, he might be pitching in the Show by next year. He had never been happier in his entire life. He grabbed his bag and walked directly out of the stadium without changing into street clothes. His mind was racing with possibilities of the future. He knew the time to fulfill his dreams was close at hand.

August 5th, 1999

Eric was startled from a dream when he heard his cell phone playing some classic piano melody on the night stand beside his bed. He sat up still groggy with sleep. Squinting his eyes, he read the time on his alarm-clock. It was ten minutes before nine. He couldn't imagine who could possibly be calling him. He reached for his phone, stretching his arms without moving his body. His hand came up empty several times, but he finally pulled the phone to him. He glanced quickly at the screen. He didn't recognize the number or area code. He pushed a button, raising the phone to his ear, " Hello?"

"Yes, this is Fred Caps, the voice of the morning with 103.9 KVAT FM calling for a Mr. Eric Shay."

The voice spoke very loud and frantic, making it difficult for Eric to pick up everything that was said.

"Uh, this is Eric speaking." He said sitting up.

He rubbed his head with the palm of his free hand.

"Whoooa, congratulations Eric, you have been chosen as our random call, rock quiz contestant for the week. Now, if you can answer the rock quiz question you will be winning a free all expenses paid trip for two to sunny Florida. Are you ready to play, Eric?"

Eric still wasn't fully awake, but his heart beat with excitement.

"Uh, yea, yes I'm ready."

He rolled over to sit on the edge of the bed placing his feet on the floor. He shook his head trying to clear it of sleep. He held his breath while the stimulated voice reeled.

"Alright, here we go. Name the band that sings the classic rock hit, 'Highway Star'."

Eric could hardly contain himself as he blurted out his answer, "Deep Purple."

"Congratulations, Mr. Shay, you've just won yourself a trip for two to Florida. All you have to do is come down to the station to pick up the itinerary by three p.m. this afternoon, and you and a guest will be on your way to beautiful, sunny Miami."

Eric suddenly stopped dancing around the room in his boxers.

"Wait. What? Where is the station at?"

"615 Waterfront Ave. in Boise."

Eric's heart sank when he heard this.

"Shit, there is no way I can do that."

He felt the frustration surging through his head.

"Well, tough luck Mr.," the voice seemed to be fighting back, yet he could no longer contain himself.

"Hello?" Eric was startled by this response.

It took him several moments of listening to the laughter before he realized he had been fooled.

"Real funny, asshole. You almost had me."

He could feel himself smiling though he was trying not to.

"*Almost?* I *almost* had you? I have never heard anyone fall harder," Eric now recognized the voice very well. "I bet you're dancing around your room, huh?" Andrew joked.

Eric had to admit he had been fooled, but he was so excited to hear from his friend that nothing else mattered.

"Ok, I admit you had me going for a minute there, but I was just playing along at the end."

"Yeah, I bet buddy." Andrew teased, then asked warmly, "How's things back in the homeland?"

"Pretty good, I guess. A bunch of us got completely wasted up at some girl's cabin behind Mt. Ash a couple nights ago. Besides that, I've just been working a lot."

"What about you? How's the big baseball star doing? My parents told me last time you called you were living in Spokane."

He strained trying not to ask too many questions at once, but it was difficult. There was so much catching up to do. Eric had only recently gotten a cell phone. His only contact with Andrew before that had been a couple phone calls during Christmas and news he received at school when Andrew called the house.

"Uh, things are pretty good. I've thrown a lot this year, and I'm living with a couple of pretty cool guys from the team," He paused for a moment. Eric thought he could hear him breath out a long sigh before he continued, "Actually, I'm gonna be coming home for a while."

Eric knew his friend well enough to realize something was bothering him.

"Really? That's great. Don't you have games though?" He asked, his senses telling him to tip toe.

"No, I'm getting some time off," Andrew responded coolly, though again there followed what seemed to be a desperate pause.

Both ends fell silent as Eric tried to word his next question, but Andrew came out with it before Eric found his next response.

"I hurt my shoulder in a game last week. The team doctor told me today that I'm gonna have to have surgery."

Though he didn't state it, Eric could clearly hear the next sentence being, 'I may never pitch again.'

It was all too sudden, too real. Eric felt like he had the wind knocked out of him. He sat down slowly, staring at a picture of Andrew, Shane, Darin and himself taken immediately following the second Championship. They were all dirty and were all smiles. Andrew stood between Darin and Shane with his arms around their shoulders. It was impossible to look at the picture without seeing his invincibility. There was a presence about him so powerful, even a camera could capture it.

"Surgery? Must be pretty serious, huh?" He choked out trying to remain neutral though he wanted to know everything.

"Nah, I don't think it's a big deal. I'll be throwing harder next year than I ever have before," Andrew spoke his preplanned speech like a politician describing his platform to the uneducated masses.

Eric didn't have enough information to draw any conclusions, but he also realized that if Andrew had both his legs amputated, he would still say he could beat anybody at anything. He didn't want to dwell on the news, so he tried to think of a new subject. Andrew beat him to it.

"So, your old man told me you and that girlfriend of yours are getting pretty serious."

"What? Get out of here with that. No, we aren't that serious."

This was one subject he truly didn't want to speak of. His answer was sharp.

"Whoa there buddy, you need to settle down. You're getting all sorts of wound up," Andrew couldn't help but chuckle picturing his best friend's flustered look.

"I hope the wife will let you out for at least one night while I'm home."

"Shut your mouth. I bet you twenty bucks that the great ball player can't even keep up anymore. They probably got you on a diet of lettuce and broccoli. Do you even remember what a shot of Jim Beam tastes like?"

Eric was rather proud of himself for his witty comeback. Quick riposte was a skill that he was well known amongst his friends to be lacking in.

"Unfortunately, I do, and it still tastes foul." They both laughed.

"But, I gotta run. The time on this card is almost up. I will see you soon, brother. Tell all the mothers that you see to lock their daughters up, cuz trouble's coming to town."

"Alright bro, I can't wait. Bye."

The smile seemed to be glued onto Eric's big face as he hung up the phone. He hadn't been this excited in a long time. Lately, it seemed like not a whole lot could go right for him. He had quit baseball before the season even started, and since baseball was the only thing keeping him in school, he decided to bag that too. He had moved back in with his parents toward the end of the winter. He found a job working in an oil lube garage, and he'd been spending the rest of his spare time with Claire, whom he had been dating since moving back home.

Eric hated working full time, and he knew he lacked the training to make any serious money. He worried about getting stuck in a job that he regretted but couldn't get out of. He still went out with Shane occasionally, but Shane seemed to be headed ever further in the wrong direction. He never had any money to do much. On the seldom chance that he did have money, he only wanted to spend it on drugs. Eric tried to talk to him, yet he could never seem to find the right words. He looked forward to the summer when all his old friends would return from college, but when it arrived things didn't change any.

It seemed like every year fewer guys from the old crowd returned home. Those that did usually worked, making the weekends the only time they might go out. Darin had come home in July, but Eric had only talked to him once. The message was clear that Darin still dwelled on the events from the past summer. The one bright spot in Eric's life was Claire.

After work, he would either pick her up, or she would come over to his house. They rented a lot of movies and had a lot of sex, but it eventually became routine and sort of boring. Both of them longed for excitement. Neither of them spoke of the problem. Perhaps, they didn't even realize what the problem was. It wasn't long before they bickered constantly about everything. It wasn't each other that they weren't happy with; it was their boredom. They were both too young to be giving up on dreams.

One day, Claire seemed particularly quiet. Eric asked her about it several times while they ate at a local pizzeria downtown. She said nothing was bothering her, but she continued to be self absorbed on the ride back to her house. They hadn't been in her room for ten minutes when Eric couldn't stand it anymore. He instigated a fight.

Claire didn't take the bait. She buried her face into his shoulder and began sobbing. Eric apologized for his comments, but she didn't stop. He hugged her close to him trying to comfort her.

"What's wrong baby?" He asked feeling like an asshole now for not realizing how serious it was earlier, for Claire was not a girl who cried often. He had to repeat similar questions several times before Claire lifted her face. She cried huge alligator tears, leaving her face completely soaked. The mascara around her eyes had run down her cheeks.

"I'm moving to Portland," was all she could squeeze out before her sobs choked her up again.

"What? Portland? When? Why?" Eric shouted hoping he had heard her incorrectly.

"I am moving at the end of August," The crying increased, but she tried to finish.

Eric could only hear the key words.

He clearly made out, "living with aunt.....classes at fashion school.... so sorry..."

Even if she were speaking clearly, it would have been difficult for Eric to pick up much. He felt like she was speaking from a mile away. He began to pop his knuckles without even realizing it. It was something he always did when he became really nervous. Claire noticed the behavior. It made her realize that she wasn't the only one struggling. She wiped her eyes with her sleeves, sniffing her runny nose.

"I'm so sorry I didn't tell you earlier. I have wanted to for a few days, but it is so hard."

Eric didn't look at her. He was staring at the floor with a scowl on his face. His eyebrows bent in an arch. Claire went on explaining. She felt that eventually he would have to say something. He didn't though. He just kept staring.

"I love you." She finally whispered.

It seemed to be the magic words. He turned to face her staring deep into her eyes. The scowl had disappeared. It was replaced by the look of a very scared little boy trapped in that big rough frame. He wanted to argue with her, scream at her. He wanted to hit her, tell her she couldn't go. Instead, he did nothing, only hung his head. The room grew very still. When he looked at her again he tried to smile. Tears filled his eyes.

"I love you, too. You're making the right decision," he paused while tears silently fell down her cheeks.

He pulled her tight to him. Over her sniffles, she heard his deep voice whisper, "I hate this town."

It had been three weeks since that night. Eric had sunk deeper into depression with each passing day. He still spent time with Claire. He spoke to her on the phone several times every day, but sometimes he would avoid her. It helped him feel more depressed. He started smoking weed with Shane. He also began drinking heavily and more frequently. He spoke little to anyone. Often, he would go to work, come home, drink a couple thirty-two ounce cans of beer in his room and go to bed at seven or eight o'clock.

Two days before Andrew's call, Claire had finally taken matters into her own hands. She sat Eric down in his room and fully explained her story for the first time. She told Eric that her decision had nothing to do with him. He had only made the decision that much more difficult. She told him that the program she was taking was only two years, and she would still be living in town during the summer months. This drew no response from her stocky boyfriend, so she told him if he wanted to date other girls she would understand, but it was her hope for them to stay together. This seemed to open Eric up, and they talked on the subject for hours. Afterwards, Eric felt a lot better about the situation, though he was obviously still heartbroken.

He was starting to get back into the swing of life when Andrew had called him that morning. It was like a gift from above. It only took speaking to his friend for two minutes before he felt like his old self again. He lay in bed after their conversation, thinking of how his own misfortune and Andrew's might be related. He couldn't help noticing the coincidence of timing. He didn't feel guilty because he knew pitchers bounced back from minor surgery all the time, and Andrew was a rock. For the first time, he started to think everything would work out fine.

He picked up his cell phone again. He had to tell Shane about Andrew's return.

'Who knows,' he thought, 'maybe the three of us being back together will solve all our problems. Maybe things would go back to the way they used to be.'

He dialed Shane's number and it began to ring, but his mind was still on the Andrew conversation. 'Hell, Andrew coming home might even get Darin back to normal', he thought and shivered with excitement.

August 20th, 1999

It was the middle of another gorgeous summer day, and Eric was driving home when his cell phone rang. He figured it was probably Claire. He had been at her house all morning helping her pack up her things.

'She must have thought of more things she left at my house', he thought.

He struggled to hold the wheel straight while he dug in the pocket of his jeans for his phone. It had been several months since he joined the cell phone carrying community, yet he still hadn't mastered the art of talking on it while he was driving. There was a tendency for him to become too absorbed in the information from the phone call, and the last thing he wanted was to damage the Lumina over some frivolous conversation, but he couldn't help answering when that stupid thing rang. It was addicting.

He remembered how excited he had been when his parents told him they would pay for a cell phone while he was away at school. It was a big deal to him, and he laughed at the thought that it really didn't seem all that long ago Darin and him were watching an episode of 'Saved By the Bell' and one of the star characters had a cell phone at school, and they had both laughed at the impossibility of high school students ever having cell phones. They must have been in the fifth or sixth grade.

Now, everyone had cell phones. He estimated at least three-fourths of the kids he graduated with had a cell phone by the end of senior year. When his relatives had come to visit for Christmas, he discovered his cousin, Martin, had a cell phone, and he was in eighth grade. It was getting almost ridiculous.

Although it had been such a short time since he started carrying a cell phone, he could barely imagine what his life had been like without it. It seemed he constantly needed it in tough spots. One of the exceptions to all the cell phone enthusiasm was Andrew. He still spoke against them with fierce passion. Eric could swear that a cell phone had mugged him in a dark alley once by the way he spoke out against the convenient technology. Andrew said that cellular phones seemed great and useful now because they were still a relatively new commodity.

He said it wouldn't be long, though, before people would become so dependant on them that it would be impossible to make it through the day without them. He said people would lose their freedom because they would have increasing difficulty to ignore calls. Employers would soon know they could reach employees at any time, and workers would have no excuse for not being available twenty-four hours a day. According to his conspiracy theory, cell phones would be followed by cell television. Face to face human communication would weaken further than it already has and people would grow cold to each other and lose compassion and understanding. Eric could only laugh.

Andrew had always spoken of things Eric felt no normal person would ever think of. He had been particularly out there since his latest return. Andrew had had only been home for a few days, yet everything he spoke of seemed philosophical or obscure to Shane and Eric. It wasn't that he had changed, for Andrew had always talked nonsense, but he seemed more engorged in his lofty philosophies than ever.

He also seemed to be more unpredictable than ever before. This type of behavior was shocking to Claire who was not used to someone with so much swagger. Eric could already hear her now telling him to be careful and to stay out of trouble on the phone. She worried about leaving Eric with Andrew while she was gone.

Upon looking at the call screen, though, he was shocked to see the call was from Darin. He answered, his voice expressing his surprise.

"Hey buddy, what are you doing?" Darin answered back.

From the tone of Darin's voice, it wasn't nearly as odd to him to be calling after a nearly two month hiatus.

"Nothing, man. I was just heading home from Claire's actually. I was over there helping her pack some of her things up." Eric answered, still skeptical but curious to the reason behind Darin's sudden call.

"Oh, I heard about her moving. I'm really sorry bro. Is everything ok?"

Eric couldn't help but notice the genuine sincerity in his friend's voice.

"Yea, it still hasn't really settled in. How did you know about it anyways?" Eric asked curiously.

"Andrew stopped by today. I laughed my ass off at that car he's driving. I didn't believe him when he told me it was his. Anyways, he told me about the whole situation. If there's anything you need man, don't hesitate to call me."

"Thanks man. I think it's gonna work out ok. God has a plan for us all."

He felt a little uncomfortable with the conversation. Darin was one of his best friends, but he hadn't been around during his relationship with Claire. It seemed odd that he would appear just when everything was at a rough spot in the road.

"Well, I wouldn't put too much faith in that mumbo jumbo, but keep your head up. And again, if you need anything, call me anytime, bro."

"Thanks, bro."

Eric was glad to hear from Darin. He was not the type to hold a grudge. Besides, it didn't seem to him that there was even a dispute. Communication had ended. That was it, plain and simple.

"So, what have you been up to?" Eric asked partly out of routine conversation etiquette but also because he had truly been wondering what Darin was up to.

"You know. This and that. I've been working out pretty crazy everyday. I am doing some work part time at the bank too. One of my dad's friends lined me up with a pretty cool job."

"Hey, I have to run some errands, but Andrew was thinking we should all go out tonight? What do you think?"

"Yea, I'm game."

"Alright, sweet. I'll call you guys in a while, so we can figure something out. Good to hear you are doing alright. It has been too long, brother."

"You too, bro," Eric said hanging up the phone.

He stayed away from replying to the last comment for the time being. There would be plenty of time for catching up. He placed the phone on the seat beside him with a huge smile on his face. Andrew was truly amazing, he thought. No other person in the world could possibly have the kind of magnetism that just pulls people toward him. Eric turned up his CD player and sang along to a classic Garth Brooks tune. He felt tickled all over the rest of the way home.

Eric, Shane, and Andrew were sitting together on the far side of the bar when Darin walked cautiously into the smoky room. He tried not to glance around too much, but his fear was clear as day to his friend's when they noticed him. It was around ten, but the bar was relatively empty. Two fellows played pool near the back and two rougher looking men, apparently shower and mirror impaired, appearing to be the bar regulars sat alongside an older woman fighting a losing battle with graceful aging.

Otherwise, the boys were alone in the establishment. The two drunks were trying their hardest from either side of the solitary female occupant to impress her with terribly delivered jokes and overwhelming heaps of cigarette smoke, so they didn't even notice Darin walk past them. One of the pool players leaned his cue against his chest and shot Darin an eye that made him even more cautious of his movements though he never looked directly toward the table, but then, the sound of his partner's shot broke his gaze, returning his attention to the game at hand.

Darin stared forward toward his destination, so he didn't even catch a glimpse of the bartender though he knew there was someone standing behind the bar. He could sense it. He was happy to see there was an empty stool between Shane and Andrew, so he didn't have to sit unguarded on one side. It was obvious this was his first time in a bar. Shane lifted his glass with a manufactured laugh as Darin tried to sit down inconspicuously.

"Glad you could make it." Andrew greeted his friend.

Although he had told Darin on the phone to meet them there at ten, it was apparent that Andrew had taken a head start on the drinking.

"Yea," he gave a nervous grin.

"You're sure they won't card us?" He asked softly while arching his head to mask his words.

"Positive, bro. You gotta relax though."

Andrew slapped his friend heartily on the back of his hooded sweatshirt.

"If you are all nervous and pissing your pants the guy's gonna be forced to ask for ID, but trust me. Just be cool. This guy is really cool, and he wants our business."

He gave that reassuring smile that could sell a ketchup popsicle to a woman in white gloves. That smile could convince the pope to exonerate the devil himself. It made Darin feel more secure and he hated that.

A moment later the bartender appeared in front of him. Darin looked up to see him for the first time. He was a big guy that stood around 6'2. He had a crew cut that had receded to a sharp widow's peak about a quarter of the way off his scalp. His hair was brown, and he had thick grey whiskers, but he looked like he had recently shaven. He was a heavy set guy that had a swagger to him that gave Darin the impression he used to stay in good shape. He was probably a former athlete. He was wiping the bar down with a wet towel when he asked bluntly, "What can I getcha?"

Darin was blank. The harder he tried to answer the more he clammed up. "Uhh…" was all he got out before Eric saved him.

"Another round of PBR, Jim." He said slapping his hand down on the bar.

The movement seemed to draw the attention away from Darin. He didn't know whether Eric had done it on purpose or not, but he was glad he did it.

"You got it," and Jim was gone again.

A couple of rounds later, the tension had disappeared. The conversation was pleasant, focusing mostly on catching everyone up on each other's recent happenings. This meant that the majority of the speaking was done by Andrew and Darin. They were comparing similarities and differences between life as a college quarterback and life as a pro ball player. Finally, Darin realized they were excluding Eric and Shane. He decided to steer the conversation toward them.

"Been getting any b-ball in this summer Shaner?" he asked while trying to pour beer from an aluminum can into the glass he was drinking from. He still hadn't gotten the hang of it, and his glass filled over with foam.

"Yeah, I've been trying to play as much as I can, but my damn job makes it hard."

He spoke with irony of his job. His voice made it apparent he was discouraged with working for the first time while at the same time his emphasis on 'my job' seemed to be a point of pride. Darin noted this.

"Oh really? Where are you working?" he asked.

"Over at the full service car wash on Main Street." He said with the same irony.

"Sweet, man, how do you like it?" Darin continued to draw him out with questions.

"It sucks. I get paid seven bucks an hour though, so I guess it'll do for now." He said bluntly, sipping from the glass in front of him.

"This is awesome man," Andrew interrupted. "All of us together again."

"Hell yeah, I've been missing the old days a lot lately." Shane chimed in, finally showing interest in his facial expression.

"Me too, man. I have been doing a ton of reminiscing," Eric said holding an empty glass in his thick, dry hand.

"I was beginning to think we would never all get together again. No matter what happens in life I hope we all stay close pals. That is all that matters to this guy."

"Pals huh?" Andrew asked looking at him with a quirky smile.

"Yea... Pals, you know best friends." Eric clarified, changing to his meek shy voice. He rotated the empty glass in his hands without thinking about it.

"I like that. It's a great four letter word to describe the four of us." Andrew kidded, but he wasn't poking fun at Eric.

"To pals!" he said raising his glass in toast.

The others joined him bringing their glasses together.

Shane called the bartender to order another round, but Darin told him this one was on him. He was feeling a euphoria he hadn't felt in a long time. He was popular at college. His football team already looked to him as a leader. Girls smiled invitingly at him, and he knew if it weren't for Elizabeth he could date any number of girls. Still, none of it made him feel the same as being in the presence of his three best friends. There was a feeling of belonging that filled a subconscious void he never realized was there until he was apart from them for so long. Anyone he met could learn how he acted, or learn to read his personality, but nobody else, not even Elizabeth, knew him inside and out like his childhood friends.

They knew who he really was. They didn't need to read his personality, for they were there for the environmental events that shaped that personality. They knew his parents. They knew his fears.

He wished this night would never end. He looked at his watch. It was nearly midnight. The boys had been so caught up in the glow of reunion they hadn't even noticed the bar was filling up.

"Man, I don't know how I'm gonna get up for church in the morning." Eric said rubbing at his lips with one hand. His eyes were already taking on the glassy look that signaled he was feeling buzzed.

"What the hell are you talking about? You've never been in a church in your life." Shane challenged.

Six eyes turned to Eric expecting a well delivered punch line.

"Yeah right, dude. I have always gone on Christmas Eve and Easter and shit," he defended,

"Andrew's even come before, huh?"

Andrew still wasn't sure how to read the topic, but he answered, "Yea, but that was like freshman year or something."

He started to laugh but stopped short. He already forgot what they were even talking about.

"Anyways, Claire and I decided we are gonna start going to church. We think it will help strengthen our wills during tough times being apart."

He spoke like a wolverine that felt cornered, defending before there was even a sign of danger.

"You mean she decided." Shane said.

Andrew laughed again spilling some beer on the front of his shirt.

"Come on. You know that whole religion thing is bull," Darin said, remembering Eric's comment earlier on the phone.

Now, the beers had him loosened up. He was ready to speak his opinion on the matter.

"I'm telling you evolution is a proven fact. Science all but proves the impossibility of Christianity. I think it's so stupid when people try and make themselves feel better by saying things happen by divinity."

"That's why you're going to hell, jackass."

Eric leaned toward him flaring his stub of a nose.

"I'm serious. There is zero evidence in it. Almost everything is refuted by reason...Answer me this, if there is a God, then why do good people still die while evil people live? How did a guy like Hitler get away with killing millions of Jews?"

"How is it that against gazillion to one odds humans have developed into what we are today?" Eric interrupted. An intellectual argument was not something he wanted to get into with Darin, especially while he was drunk.

"What are you talking about?"

"I mean how is it that in the vast nothingness of the universe life just happened here."

"I don't know. There are endless amounts of gases and elements mixing and changing. Something was bound to become a living cell sometime."

Darin drew a breath in ready to keep going, but Shane interrupted him.

"Who gives a shit? Both of you shut up. Look around you. We are in a bar where people can't even learn to pee in the bowl without missing the seat, and you guys are trying to go all CNN on us."

"Yea, why don't you guys agree to disagree? Eric can become a priest, and Darin you can burn down the Vatican," Andrew added rising from his stool.

"I guess this is what happens when guys settle for screwing just one girl. You both got too much time on your hands."

He finished with a belch and started toward the bathroom, shooting a quick glance at Shane who followed him. Darin turned back to his beer, dropping the subject but still organizing his next point lest Eric decide to push it. He could feel Eric looking at him.

"Do you ever wonder if Liz is the one?" Eric asked in a soft voice that Darin could barely hear in the noisy bar. Darin wrinkled his brow in response.

"You mean like the one I want to marry?" he asked stalling for time. "I don't know. We talk about it sometimes, but it's mostly just pillow talk I think. I guess. I'm not sure. Maybe...What about you? Do you think Claire could be the one?"

His face burned from being put on the spot.

"Yes. I hope so." Eric said flatly.

Darin was surprised not only by the conviction of his words, but at the speed of his response. Clearly, he had given this a lot of thought. Darin felt ashamed. At the same time, he couldn't help feeling inspired. It made true love seem like an actual possibility. He took another long slow drink of his beer. Shane rejoined them at the bar. He was visibly excited and spun back and forth on his stool.

"Where's Drew?" Eric asked when he noticed he hadn't returned with Shane.

"He's out behind the bar talking to some broad." He answered motioning behind him with his thumb.

"Remember that girl Nicole Higgins? I think she was two years ahead of us. No, she might have been a senior when we were freshman actually. Anyways, he recognized her and just started talking to her. I don't think he even knows her."

He laughed and twitched his nose sniffing the air. Then, he glanced around the bar a couple of times like he was looking for someone. Darin followed his eyes.

"Do you want to play a game of pool, Shaner?" he asked when they were both looking in that direction.

"Huh? Yea. Sure, I'll play some pool." he had already stood up and was walking quickly toward the table.

"The only thing I can do better than slap a ball to opposite field is land one in a corner pocket." He bragged over his shoulder.

When he looked back his shoulder bumped against a guy telling a story to a couple drunks standing around a small table. It was barely even contact and neither of them spilled a drop of alcohol, but the guy turned with an offended look on his face.

"Why don't you watch where your going there Tonto." He said crudely.

The man was about six foot tall and of medium build. He wore tight work jeans, a white t-shirt, and camouflage hat with a hunting brand stitched across the front. His thick mustache had a red tint to it and made his thin lips almost invisible. If he were a little heavier, he might pass as a member of Eric's family.

Shane had planned to apologize, but hearing the prejudice comment, he decided against it. He looked at the man quickly with wide eyes before taking a few more steps toward the pool table. The man took this as a retreat, so he followed like a tracker follows the blood trail of wounded prey. Trouble was inevitable.

"Hey Chief, don't you speak English? I think you forgot to say you're sorry." He continued to badger.

One of the men from the table, a short, pudgy slob struggling to keep his pants up and eyes open, joined his friend. His face was bright red. He was clearly drunker than the guy Shane had bumped. He had curly hair sticking out from under a cap with an NFL team logo on it. He joined in on the harassment.

"Hey Sitting Bull, I didn't know this bar accepted food stamps." He called out, laughing and nudging his friend for approval.

Shane lost his cool and halted his retreat, turning to face them.

"I didn't know that a man and a sheep could reproduce, but low and behold here you stand." He said angrily.

His face showed no fear. Both men's faces lost all expression, but before they could retort Shane was speaking again.

"If you swampers are finished scrubbing the toilets I'd appreciate it if you went on home. Your stench scares off all the customers."

The man in the camouflage hat pushed Shane hard in the chest. His back struck hard against the pool table. Shane came right back at him. They fell to the ground wrestling for the upper hand in the small open space between the pool table and the other patrons. The man with the curly hair moved into position to attack Shane, but he never got the chance.

Out of nowhere, he was dropped with a hard right haymaker that struck him on his cheek. The fist belonged to Darin. At the same time, Eric pulled the man with the mustache off Shane. He went to throw a punch, but he was hit from the side.

The next twenty or thirty seconds was a blur for everyone. It was impossible for even a sober observer to differentiate between one side and the other. People who frequent small town bars grow used to fights, though, so the mayhem was broken up quickly.

Despite the appearance of a donnybrook, little blood was spilled. The man Darin had punched got the worst of it. The entire left side of his face swelled up like a balloon. His eye was completely shut, and it was already turning purple.

Shane had a little blood coming from his lip and nose. It wasn't serious. He had to forget about any plans of fleeing the scene, for he was being held by a very large man who seemed unimpressed by the entire fiasco.

The cops showed up within minutes. All three boys were led outside where they stood in front of the police spotlight. For Darin, it brought memories of the past summer. This time it felt much different though. He didn't feel the overwhelming regret. In fact, the more he thought about everything and tried to piece together the events, the more confident he was that he had done the right thing.

He might get in trouble, but he had stood up for a friend when the chips were down. It is something that everyone assumes they would do, yet when it happens most people lose the will. He felt a swelling of pride. It reminded him of the camaraderie of his football experiences.

Two officers were questioning them for their account of what happened. Darin could not see any of the men they had fought. He assumed they were somewhere getting the same routine. Darin was explaining the events of the story to one of the officers, who recognized him as a former quarterback. When he finished with his story, the officer asked Darin if he was playing ball in college. Darin told him he yes, feeling a little somber at being recognized. Darin wondered how this would affect the consequences. The officer was starting to say something about being a former running back when he was interrupted.

"Hey Jason, I think you better take a look at this."

The second officer was walking toward them with his flashlight on. Darin looked over to see the officer was holding a small plastic bag. It looked like a sandwich bag, but it was maybe an eighth of the size. It took Darin a moment to realize the bag was a quarter full of a white substance. He knew right away what it was. It only took him a second to know where it was found. The second officer said he found it on Shane. The officer named Jason told him to radio it in. He turned back to Darin. This time his face was much graver.

"Is there anything else you want to tell me?"

"I swear to God, I have never done that stuff in my entire life. I have never even seen it in real life before right now."

Darin could feel his voice quivering with fear. Jason shined his flashlight into Darin's eyes, examining his pupils. Then, he lowered his light and stared at him for another moment. He seemed to believe Darin's claim.

"Alright, sit down on the street and don't go anywhere."

Darin did as he was told and the officer walked over to where Shane and Eric were standing on the far side of the car, on the sidewalk outside the bar. A few minutes later, Jason returned to Darin.

"Ok, here's what's going to happen. I'm writing you a ticket for possession of alcohol. I am going to let you off with a warning for the being in the bar because you guys were never carded. As far as the fight goes, it sounds like it was their fault, and no one got seriously hurt. Everyone scraps once in a while."

"We are arresting your friend Mr. Billingsly for possession of narcotic. He may also be charged with intent to distribute. Is there someone you can call for a ride home?"

"Yes."

"Alright, I don't want to ever see your face down here again. You hear me? Even after your twenty-one. Stay away from this kid, Billingsly. You got too much going for you to be making bad decisions and fightin with Indian drug dealers and these worthless drunks."

He ripped the citation off a pad and handed it to Darin. His arrogance was blistering over.

"Ok, thanks, officer."

"I'm serious now. You better learn something tonight. This town has enough trash and scum in it." He looked hard at Darin. He was a real life old fashion hick cop right out of the old west. Darin figured he couldn't be older than late twenties.

"Thanks," was all that he could respond.

After the cops had left, Darin joined Eric on the sidewalk. The crowd had dispersed, and Darin saw that Andrew was sitting on the curb next to where Eric stood. Eric was filling him in on what happened.

"So the guy just started shit for no reason?"

Andrew climbed to his feet speaking with intensity.

"Yes. It was bullshit."

Eric was clearly tired of thinking about the whole ordeal. He looked burned out.

Andrew turned away shaking his head. His fists were tight at his sides. He walked back and forth swearing out loud.

"Should I call Elizabeth?" Darin asked Eric quietly.

He had been completely out of it since seeing the bag of cocaine.

"No, don't worry. Claire's already on her way, unless you want to be with Liz."

"No, that's fine. I just want to go to bed."

Darin's face was pale and hollow. He looked at the ground the entire time.

"This is my fault. I'm such an idiot." Andrew was still pacing.

"There is nothing you could do about it. Shit just happens." Eric answered apathetically.

Andrew said nothing more. He paced back and forth until Claire arrived. Eric explained the situation vaguely to her from the passenger seat on the drive home. Darin and Andrew rode silently in the back.

The spacing of the streetlights created a peculiar setting for Darin as his eyes adjusted to cyclic patterns of darkness broken by short bursts of pinkish light and he watched the still details of Andrew's erect form pushed up against the far door of Claire's father's Buick, staring despondently out the window lost in his own thoughts. Closed businesses and vacant lots rushed by as they approached the edge of town. Darin could still smell the cigarette smoke stuck to his clothes. He closed his eyes and listened to the tires rolling along.

August 23rd, 1999

Eric was wiping his hands on a rag in the driveway when Darin pulled up to the house. Darin was driving a brand new, full size Chevy pickup that still had the dealership plates. He parked it along the curb. Elizabeth sat next to him in the passenger seat.

The truck was midnight blue, and it had that distinctive shine unique to new vehicles. Eric was in the middle of working on the Lumina but forgot what he was doing and shut the hood lightly as Darin climbed out of the truck. Darin smiled at his friend, removing his sunglasses.

"Do you like it?" he asked, failing to maintain modesty. His excitement radiated outward.

"Nope, I always hated thirty thousand dollar, brand new pickups." Eric shot back sarcastically without smiling at his own joke.

He greeted Elizabeth with a friendly smile.

"Well, you may be blind, but at least this one's got the money to treat you right."

This time he joined her in appreciating his humor.

"Too bad, Claire didn't get so lucky." Darin returned, frowning toward the Lumina. "You'd think working all the time you could at least buy something else."

He stood before the car like a doctor stands before a patient that cannot be saved.

"You'd think so..." Eric began, but he left it at that.

"Where's Andrew at?" Darin asked putting his arm around Elizabeth.

"He's inside saying goodbye to my mom. He's pretty much all ready to go I think. I'm not sure though. He's been real weird ever since Friday night." Eric speculated rubbing his hands against each other.

As they spoke, Andrew came out dragging a blue duffle bag behind him. He stopped before the first step but didn't seem to take any notice of the truck or the visitors in the driveway. He closed his eyes, leaned his head back, and drew in a long breath. Darin couldn't be sure if he cracked a slight smile, or maybe it was the light from the late August sun. After a brief moment, Andrew stepped down off the stairs like the hero of a dramatic film might before heading into the big climatic trial.

No one meant to become silent. They couldn't help it. It was as if his charisma was literally as visible on him as the shirt he wore. He whistled when he noticed the new truck.

"Wow, now that right there is a pickup, bro." He smiled while blocking his eyes from the sun with his right hand.

"Yea, I was just telling Eric it's time he trades this old pile in and puts a down payment on one."

They met each other with a well performed handshake. Andrew shot a quick nod at Elizabeth, but he didn't say anything. Darin thought he noticed excitement in her eyes, thought he recognized that old familiar look girls take on with the glance from a new boy. He knew it immediately because it used to be the look she shot him before things became so routine and tired. He felt the jealousy climb in his throat, but he refused to let it out. The look probably only existed in his mind. He maintained his smile, but the look in his eyes betrayed him telling a different story all together.

"Did you talk to Shane?" He asked trying to get his mind off his jealousy.

Andrew's expression grew instantly grave. Maybe it was the reaction Darin had desired.

"Yes. I talked to him today. I guess he had to spend the whole weekend in the clink." He cleared his throat.

"Are you serious? That's harsh. What kind of trouble is he looking at?"

Darin could barely believe it. He was naive to the world of the American justice system.

"He still doesn't know. He has court tomorrow. If he pleads not guilty nothing will happen for a while. Otherwise, they told him he's looking at three years probation maybe a month in jail."

Andrew moved toward his car, leaving his words to soak in. Darin looked at Eric feeling stunned. Eric didn't see him though. He was somewhere far away. Andrew shifted some things around in the trunk of his car to make room for the duffle bag. His trunk was only about half full, but he wanted to keep it well organized, so that nothing would break. He slammed the trunk shut.

"I can't believe he could serve that much time in jail for having so little. I mean I know coke is terrible and I am pissed that he would even be so stupid," Darin started with honest surprise before catching himself. It wasn't the time for a lecture. It was but there were too many intangibles.

"Either way, I thought he'd get a drug possession on his record, some fines, and maybe have to take a class. I mean it was just that tiny little bit in the bag right?"

"He's not exactly the mayor's kid," Andrew cut in, clearly annoyed. "He's been in trouble a couple times already, and he's an Indian, man. You think the cops give a rat's ass if they ruin his future? Hell no. They figure their just getting another lazy Indian off the streets. I guess one of the fucks was real rough with him his mom told me."

Andrew's face grew beat red as he vented. He had veins sticking out of his neck and forehead. He was no longer talking to Darin. He was fending off demons.

"Come on, it's not like they can just make that stuff up. It's all done by the book. Those are just the consequences of having drugs." Darin said.

He didn't know why he felt obliged to disagree with Andrew. Andrew was making it sound as if Shane had done nothing wrong. This was untrue. Shane had taken the chance to use drugs and have them on him in public. Darin thought, hopefully, he would learn his lesson.

"I am telling you. It could have been way worse. Cocaine isn't weed, Drew. That shit kills people and people kill and die over it."

"By the book? Are you really that naive? Do you think he'd serve a day in jail in this town if he were a rich white kid? Imagine if it were you, Darin. Your parent's lawyer would have them apologizing for taking the blow from you by the end of the whole deal."

Andrew shook his head. It took him a moment to regain his composure.

"I'm sorry bro. I shouldn't have said that. It's just a shitty situation all around. I don't mean to take it out on you."

Darin didn't take it personally. The difficulty for Andrew was obvious. This was why it was so impossible. No one had the guts to talk to someone about these things until something bad already took place and by then it is both obvious and hurtful.

When everything had been resolved, Andrew said his goodbye to Darin and told him how proud he was that Darin had come so swiftly to Shane's aid. They hugged and Darin left with Elizabeth. The entire time, not a single word passed between Andrew and Elizabeth, not even a solitary goodbye. As the truck rumbled down the street, Eric brought up this observation in an attempt to get Andrew's mind off of Shane.

"You must have really messed that girl up something crazy for you." He said. He was leaning on his car watching the truck disappear around the corner while he spoke. Andrew put his hands up under his t-shirt, pushing down on the bottom of it from the inside, deep in thought.

"Why do you say that?" He asked glancing up as if worried Darin could hear them.

"She didn't say a single word after you came outside. Come on, try and tell me you didn't see the way she looked at you every time you said anything?"

"Shut up. I haven't said a word to that girl in well over a year. Why in the hell would she be embarrassed to talk to me?" He asked blushing with interest. He had a half smile that he was trying to hide by looking away across the street.

"I don't know," Eric shrugged his big shoulders, smiling at his friend's embarrassment. "Maybe, she was scared to give away her feelings if she said anything. I mean Darin was watching her like a hawk."

"You're crazy. You've been watching too much Opera with your girl."

Andrew started walking very slowly toward his car. His gaze still kept away from his friend. Eric followed him without dropping the subject. He wanted to see if Andrew would give anything away. Besides, it helped him forget about the fact that, knowing Andrew, he wouldn't be seeing his best friend for a long time. It is sad but goodbyes do get easier over time. At least the physical act does.

"Ok, then why wouldn't you say anything to her either? I mean why not a simple hello or goodbye?" He asked prodding for answers.

He knew he wouldn't get the truth out of him, but he also knew certain signs to look for as hints.

"I didn't want Darin to get pissed." Andrew's reply was short and flat.

He knew exactly what his friend was trying to do. He climbed into his car to end the subject. Eric took this as a clear admission of guilt. He walked over and leaned on the open window.

"Alright bro, whatever you say," his face was all smiles. He reached a hand in the window for a last handshake.

"Take care of yourself, man. Strike some guys out for me with that fastball up and in. You know it was our bread and butter."

"That was the punch out. None of these guys can catch me like you could." Andrew smiled turning the engine over.

"You know this is your home, bro. Don't ever get so prideful that you go forgettin that, k?" Eric said with stoic almost father like kindness.

There it was. He was choked up. Maybe some goodbyes never get any easier.

"Alright, I won't. Tell Brother Chane I will mail him some money when I get some k?"

Andrew's face was rock steady once again.

"I don't think you should get in the habit of taking the blame for everything we do." Eric started, but Andrew interrupted him with impatience.

"It was mine."

"It wasn't though, it was no one's fault." Eric spoke with more firmness this time.

"He is a grown man, Drew. He needs to know better."

"No....The coke was mine."

He looked straight forward through the windshield for a moment.

"I brought a bunch back with me. The bag Shane got caught with was all that was left. It should have been me that night. I asked him to hold it when we went to the bathroom to do a bump. He didn't want to. I could see it in his eyes. He didn't want to have it on him, but he did it for me," He brought his eyes up to Eric's. There was a look of determination in them.

"I let him down. I have to make up for it. I told him that today. He told me to make it to the Big Leagues and I promised him I will."

Eric couldn't speak. He had a million things to say. He wanted to ask questions. He wanted to tell Andrew not to worry, but there was no time. There is never enough time during a goodbye. There was never enough time with Andrew.

Andrew put the car in drive too fast. He said a quick love you as the car started to roll. Eric didn't say a word, to him it was the world rolling. Looking back, Eric thought maybe it didn't all happen that fast. Maybe, he couldn't think fast enough.

Once again, he felt like he had left a friend hanging. He had no way to contact Andrew. He should have said something. He should have said anything.

He gave a long sigh. Unfortunately, he already knew this wasn't the last or even the hardest goodbye he would have to make this week. Claire was leaving in a couple days, and it still hadn't fully hit him. He pulled out his cell phone to call her, but didn't dial. Instead, he walked over and sat down on the bottom step of the porch, phone in hand. Looking down at those worn out, wooden stairs beneath his feet, he spoke a quiet plea out loud,

"I don't get it God. It seems like the deck is stacked against me. How is it so easy for others? Why can't I catch just one break, just one time?"

He couldn't remember ever feeling so empty, but there was no reply. The only noise he could hear was a hot, sudden breeze that shook the wind chime above his head. Then he was alone again in the silence of the afternoon.

August 2nd, 2000

It took Andrew a moment to realize someone's arm was on his stomach. He opened his eyes, straining his head to see who the arm belonged to. Everything came back to him in short flashes when he recognized her sleeping face. He craned his head up slowly to avoid waking her. His eyelashes felt caked together. His alarm clock said it was a quarter to eight. His world was spinning.

Andrew couldn't believe it. This was the first time he could ever remember sleeping through the entire night with someone else in the bed, let alone touching him. He was embarrassed and a little upset with himself. He tried to recollect his last coherent memories.

'Not my game.' He thought with a frown.

He licked at his filmy teeth, looked at her again. She was a very attractive girl, but sleeping she was even more beautiful. She had an enchanting peaceful appearance that seemed to calm Andrew deep down in his chest. She looked like something straight out of a fairytale. A single clumped lock came down over her eye and curled back away from her face beneath her ear. He watched her for several minutes, enjoying the soft rhythm of her breathing. The soft rhythm of morning made his hangover more reminder than pain.

As soon as he was fully awake, his senses repaid him for the assault he had unleashed upon his skinny self a few hours earlier. Carefully, he climbed out from under her arm, rolling out of bed quiet as a cat as he had done a hundred times before. He dug around in a heap of clothes next to the bed until he found a pair of shorts. Being quiet for overnight company was new. He pulled them on, checking to see if his sleeping guest had stirred. Then he left the room, and made his way down the hall toward the front of the apartment. Scully was sitting at the small island in the center of the kitchen. He looked up from his paper when Andrew's movement caught his attention.

"Morning, Casanova. I see you let this one stay the night." He said in his high pitch nasal drone.

"Yeah, I guess I got drunker than I thought."

Andrew yawned stretching out his entire length. He walked slowly across the kitchen slapping his bare feet on the cool linoleum floor no longer cautious. His drinking from the night before really started setting in. He felt distant from his body and could swear his head was about to float straight off his neck any moment. The churning in his stomach reminded him, as it has a million before him, why it was always in the middle hours of the morning that men swore off drinking forever. The only benefit of such mornings was that it spread the pain evenly across his body, away from his elbow.

Andrew's return to baseball hadn't exactly turned out as planned. In fact, it seemed like the worst scenario possible was coming true. He was told during spring training to take it easy. He was told that recovery was a slow process. Andrew didn't do things slow. He couldn't.

Asking Andrew to go out and throw at sixty percent was like asking a fox to chase rabbits at half speed. It wasn't in his genetics. He threw well in his first simulated outings but not well enough for him. He threw in the bullpen every chance he could. Finally, he was allowed to throw to live hitters, fastballs only. The first three hitters all laced torches off him. He asked the coaches to throw two more batters, his promise to Shane looming in the back of his mind. On a 1-2 count to the next batter he faced, something in his elbow gave, and it was all he could do to keep from collapsing.

It was the most excruciating pain he had ever felt. He told teammates he was alright, trying to fake a smile. He walked slowly off the field with his head held high, not knowing he would never return. Sent back to the Rookie Club to rehabilitate, some doctor told him not to throw further than forty feet and not at all for six to eight weeks.

Coach Scully invited him to stay at his apartment for as long as he needed. Andrew got a job at a sporting goods store working part time. All his baseball money had been spent. He did exactly as the doctors told him, but his arm didn't heal. Scully tried his hardest to shed positive light on the subject, but he could see Andrew growing discouraged, distant, animalistic. The natural glow Andrew possessed slowly dulled and diminished day by day.

The two became very close, and Scully began having enormous impact on Andrew. He showed Andrew there was more to life than baseball, encouraging him to chase his dreams and take risks while he was still young. Andrew started taking a great interest toward acting. Often, particularly over beers, he would talk to anyone who would listen for hours about his plans to move to California. In his mind, it was only a matter of time. He had to elevate quickly or he felt it would be too late. Too late for what he didn't know.

Andrew grabbed a glass out of the cupboard and filled it with water from the faucet. He threw his head back and drank the entire thing in one gulp before filling it again. The dryness didn't go away. Only time could beat such pulsing. He breathed deeply preparing for another gulp.

"You got any Advil left?" He asked.

"Nope, I think you took the last of them the other day. I will get some more when I get groceries." Scully answered turning the pages of his newspaper.

"Oh," Andrew couldn't help feeling like an idiot. "My bad."

"No big deal, so you going to tell me a little about the young lady who was making all that racket at four this morning?"

Scully folded his paper in half and placed it on the table, turning his attention to his young tenant. Andrew started to laugh, but it echoed through his pulsing skull.

"Her name is Monique. She works at the little restaurant across the street from my work. I go in there a lot on my lunch breaks. I've hung out with her a couple times, but this is the first time we've really done anything."

He stopped to finish off the second glass of water. This one in three gulps. Not a cure but it sure tasted good, washing away morning breath and sin.

"Ok, but why is she the first that hasn't magically vanished before dawn?" Scully continued prying.

He smiled a sly smile that made him look like a feline of some sorts. All he needed were the whiskers.

"I don't know," Andrew paused momentarily. His usually quick wit with Scully was being held hostage deep in his stomach by six hours worth of hard drinking.

"She didn't drive here, and I guess neither of us had money for a cab."

He sat down next to Scully on a stool and started picking the leftover bacon off of his plate, swirling it in the left over syrup before shoveling it in his mouth.

"Wow, I would give anything for a breakfast burrito right now." He exclaimed in a voice that expressed he was still a bit drunk. The night before was still flashing on and off in his memory. Reality and dream slow danced in the fog.

"Nope, you're not getting off that easy. I know your tricks." Scully said, not letting Andrew distract him.

"Tell me a little about this Monique."

Andrew looked at him through bloodshot eyes without smiling. He rubbed his face for a moment trying to decide what could or should be reported. It was still so damn early.

"She's a brunette. She's got a killer body, and she's got big full lips." He started with a sigh, though his voice showed no interest in his words.

"Blah, Blah, Blah," Scully interrupted him.

He took his plate to the sink, rinsed it, and placed it in the open dishwasher.

"You're describing every girl you bring home."

"I want to know about her. I don't want you to describe her."

Andrew paused again, but this time a slight smile crept over his face while he thought about her. He sighed again, but this time he was reeling back.

"Well, she's got an infectious laugh. It's kinda deep which is amazing for how small she is. I don't even know where it comes from. We like a lot of the same music. She's a big Springsteen fan. She is stubborn just like me. She will challenge me on any opinion I give, but if I state something to be fact she will never dispute its truth. I can't understand it. I really can't understand her."

"Let me see, what else. She's got a wild side and isn't afraid of a little trouble."

The way Scully was listening to him suddenly made Andrew realize he was giving away too much. He tried not to blush, but he could feel his cheeks turning crimson.

"You like this girl don't you?"

Scully's voice sounded giddy like an eighth grade girl at a slumber party.

"No! I mean I like her, but its nothing like that. I'm moving to California soon. The last thing I need is a girlfriend." Andrew tried to play it off without sounding discovered.

"Alright, but you better work on your acting skills before you move because that was terrible." Scully joked.

They both had a good laugh.

"I guess I do kinda feel something there though. It's just that she's always got this far away look in her eyes like she knows she was meant for big things or something." Andrew said mostly to himself. Apparently, it was something he had been trying to put his finger on for a while.

"Sounds like you two were really meant for each other." Scully smirked again picking his newspaper back up.

Andrew wasn't listening.

He couldn't stop wondering if he really was feeling something for this girl. He tried to tell himself it was nothing. He was drunk still that was all. The feelings would wear thin.

Freshness always wore off. He felt his stomach growl. He needed some breakfast before he could sort all this out. He went back down the hall to his room and was still deciding whether or not he would wake her when Monique opened her eyes.

She sat up blinking her eyes hard to figure out her surroundings. Her long brown hair was frizzed up on the right side in a sort of inverted afro. The same loose lock bounced as the morning sun touched it with light. She was wearing one of Andrew's old, worn out t-shirts that advertised a marathon back home. The fabric of the shirt had worn thin and revealed her stunning body. After a few seconds of analyzing the surrounding environment, she seemed to be certain she wasn't dreaming. She squinted up at Andrew standing in the door way.

"What time is it?" She asked in a parched, but still feminine, somehow seductive voice.

"It's almost nine. I got a craving for some pancakes. Would you like to go to breakfast?" He asked speaking quickly, marveling at how appealing she made that old shirt look even with her makeup, or what was left of it, all rubbed off.

"No, I better get home. I have to work today." She said scanning the cluttered floor for her belongings.

"Alright," Andrew said relieved.

He wasn't sure where to go from here though.

"I had fun last night." He said bluntly to fill the awkward moment.

"Yea...Me too." Monique answered still squinting one eye.

Her voice held a beautiful rasp to it. She pulled her pants on then turned her attention to finding her shoes.

"Well, I'll see you around I'm sure." Andrew said.

He regretted his goodbye before it had even fully came out, yet he had to say something. He couldn't just walk away after, 'I had fun last night.' He wished he had taken the time to think of something better, so he turned without looking to see her expression or waiting to walk her out. He went out the back door leaving a girl that was swimming in his mind alone in his room in Scully's apartment at nine a.m. on a Saturday.

August 4th, 2000

I just don't get why the sudden change," Eric muttered, trying his hardest to keep from losing his temper.

"I was all for going to church. I mean I agree that it added great direction to my life. I don't see how it wasn't enough for you. We were both raised in Catholic families. Hell, the entire county is Catholic."

"You went three times, Eric. In how long? A year?"

"I've already told you. I am not going to argue with you about it. You're free to keep going to the same church or not go to church at all. I don't care. All I am asking is that you give this a chance." Claire recited.

She was in the bathroom taking off her makeup. Eric was sitting on the bed watching her through the open bathroom door.

"It's not normal that's why. I mean they don't even drink booze." Eric pouted.

"Oh no. How could anyone possibly live without getting drunk? How on earth would we make complete fools of ourselves without alcohol?" Claire hissed cynically. As she turned off the bathroom light, she went on.

"It's not like anyone is going to brainwash you or force you to do anything. I am not asking you to change your life, just come listen. If you don't agree with the ideas that are expressed, you know I won't push my beliefs on you."

"That is what they do, baby. They brainwash people." Eric begged slapping the bed.

She sat down on the bed next to him, pulling his hand into her lap. He knew that face. He saw precisely what she was trying to do, but he wasn't strong enough to do anything about it. He made the sour face he always made when he knew he couldn't get his way. Claire's face smiled gently. She leaned over, slowly kissing his neck. He could feel his face loosen. Something twitched in his jeans.

"What about sex? Are you gonna stop having sex?" He asked with timid curiosity.

He wasn't sure he even wanted to hear the answer. Claire snorted slightly, looking into her boyfriend's eyes.

"Well, you do realize Catholics shouldn't be having premarital sex either?" She smiled.

"I guess all beliefs have some personal adjustments to be made."

They pulled each other in close and began kissing deeply. Eric laid her on the bed beneath him and began to rub his hands up under her pajama top.

Everything was different with them since she returned from Portland. They no longer argued. They rarely even disagreed. The time apart had taught them both to appreciate being together. An understanding for each other's needs had developed through their all night phone calls while they were apart. Somehow, without any words, the couple had truly learned the meaning of compromise. They had grown up and grown together over the phone lines that spanned great distance. The passion surpassed even their first months of dating. Eric stopped kissing for a moment, pulling his head back to look at Claire's face. He ran his fingers through her hair, catching his racing breath.

"Alright, I'll go with you. *Once.* I'm telling you now though they better not try to force me to do any crazy cult shit. I ain't about to drink no Kool-Aid."

His words made Claire's eyes light up. She laughed.

"You're the best baby. I promise I won't make you do anything you don't want to," She said giddily.

Then, she paused for a moment smiling.

"You will be wearing a tie though."

Eric rolled his eyes. Claire pulled him back to her. She unbuttoned his jeans and slid her hand down into his boxers, and Eric would have gladly worn a chicken suit as long as she didn't stop.

August 5th, 2000

Darin walked across the beach violently attempting to shake the water out of his ear. He could feel the salt water in his eyes, but he knew it was a small price to pay. A beach like this made it difficult not to long for residency near the ocean. Now, if only he could convince his girlfriend to join him in enjoying the water, everything would be perfect.

Elizabeth was laid out on a blanket in the same spot as when he left. The dark sunglasses she wore made it impossible for Darin to realize whether or not she was even awake. The question was quickly resolved when water dripping off his wet trunks landed on her stomach. She squealed in surprise and shot him her best evil look, clearly annoyed at being stirred.

"Are you going to lay here all day?" Darin asked firmly but with an apologetic smile. "You should come out and play in the water with me. It's warm I promise."

Elizabeth gave a quick yawn.

"I'm tanning. I told you I will get in the water in a little bit." She said in her delicate falsetto.

"You said that over an hour ago. I didn't pay for us to come down here to tan. You can tan back home." Darin said with intentional harshness.

"Ok."

"I am getting pretty good at surfing. I think I will be able to ride a wave by the end of the day." Darin said, paying no attention to the fact that she was trying to pout.

Darin had flown them to San Diego two days earlier for their anniversary. They were staying in a beautiful hotel, and the weather was perfect, but Elizabeth wasn't having as much fun as she expected. Darin had been increasingly impatient with her the entire summer, and she had hoped this weekend would be a chance for him to forget everything that was stressing him out. Figuring a break from working out and every single thought being entirely dedicated to football might help him relax, she anticipated the trip with excitement, but the entire trip Dain had been even more verbally abusive than ever. He was very keen with her and rarely asked for her input on anything.

Right from the start, the trip was completely planned out. It didn't matter what she thought about it. Finally, she could take it no more and demanded they do something she was interested in. This meant shopping. Darin ceded to the demand on their second afternoon but not before a twenty minute argument that left them both upset.

They drove a rental car down to one of San Diego's trendy shopping districts, where Darin proceeded to sulk like a spoiled child the entire time, tailing her around maintaining a minimum distance of ten feet between them. It ended up being a waste of three hours, for she didn't even try anything on and the two of them returned to the hotel without speaking. The shopping trip led to another overblown argument followed by eventual fierce, passionate make-up sex.

Early this morning, Darin woke his girlfriend up and proceeded to rush her through getting ready, leaving them on the verge of being right back where they started from the previous afternoon. It was only through the perseverance of Elizabeth's patience and a few well timed compliments to Darin's credit that the two of them made it down to the beach without any blood-shed, where the early afternoon sunshine, beautiful boardwalk galleries, and soothing surf eased the morning's tension. They were able to stake claims to an ideal spot on the yet to be crowded beach.

Finding a nice spot had Darin in particularly high spirits and he tickled and kissed Elizabeth's gorgeous beach body to the chagrin of passing admirers. It wasn't long before his excitement turned to impatience though, and he set off to rent a surfboard. He insisted that Elizabeth join him in the water but was satisfied to leave her to tan in the face of only slight resistance. However, as the surfing proved more difficult than originally anticipated, he grew bored and frustrated. This led him back to fetch her.

Too relaxed to argue, Elizabeth decided a little swim might be a lot of fun and willingly followed him to the water. He was right about the water being very pleasant. They swam around for a while, splashing each other, racing the tide, and diving through the crashing waves. When they returned to their spot on the beach, Elizabeth's mood was much more optimistic. She was feeling cuddly, so she started kissing Darin playfully. She toyed with him until she could tell he was growing too excited then stopped before she found herself in trouble.

"Save some of that for tonight, big boy," she said trying to make her voice sound erotic.

A girl walking by caught her attention.

"I want to get a tattoo."

Darin smirked at her, unsure if she was being serious.

"Why would you want to do a stupid thing like that?"

"I think they are beautiful. I want to get a butterfly on my lower back." She said twirling the tiny blond hairs below Darin's belly button with her fingers.

"That would look trashy, Liz." Darin said. He spoke unemotionally in a plain, conversational tone.

"I wouldn't get like a huge one. I just want a small one. I have thought about exactly what I want for a long time."

"Are you being serious? That is ridiculous. You would have to find a new boyfriend. Those things are permanent." Darin scolded, yet he refrained from raising his voice. It frightened him to realize how sober she was about the idea.

"You would seriously break up with me if I got a tattoo?"

Elizabeth could feel her defiance growing. She wanted to push the subject because she rarely had the courage to stand up for herself. She thought about all the times she had taken his verbal abuse.

"I guess we'll never have to worry about it," he said kissing her.

She pulled away.

"Why's that?" She asked trying to keep her momentum rolling. Darin could see she was building herself up for something. He rarely saw this in her, so he knew he would have to be clever.

"I'm sorry baby. I shouldn't have said that. It's just that I love you so much. I would hate for you to do anything you would regret. I think you should think it over."

Again he ended his sentence by moving in for a soft kiss, sweeping her arms out from under her so that he was lying on top of her. It was a calculated move. Elizabeth didn't want to give in so easily, but she knew if she tried to draw him out on it, she would appear to be the instigator of the argument that was sure to follow. She was upset with the way it ended. He had let her win, but she didn't feel like she gained anything.

"I have an idea. Let's go ride that roller coaster down the boardwalk you were so excited to ride."

Elizabeth smiled. She was too easy. She knew she would forget about the entire thing before the night was over. She was already losing ground.

"Ok." She agreed with a soft smile. They picked up all their things, and she hugged him tight before they moved down the beach. Self consciously, she felt that she was being difficult. Darin treated her better than any other boyfriend would, she told herself. Some boys could never be boyfriends.

'After all, life isn't a fairytale.' She thought.

As their sandal clad feet moved from the hot sand to the hard concrete, Darin threw his right arm around her. He looked around to make sure everyone could see him with his beautiful girl. He knew he would win. He always won.

August 13th, 2000

Eric drove over to Shane's house directly from work. He had been meaning to make the trip for a while. Try as he may, he couldn't give himself a good reason why he had been distancing himself from his friend. Walking up to the apartment, he could feel his heart quicken ever so slightly. He wondered how he could possibly be nervous to see his good friend as he gave his usual three hard raps on the door. There wasn't a sound to be heard from inside. He waited for about a minute listening intently for footsteps approaching the door, yet no one answered. He knocked a second three raps and was turning to leave when the door opened wide.

Shane was standing there with one eye open in his underwear. A noticeable gut had been packed on above his waistband since the last time Eric had seen him. The rest of him was still skinny Shane. His chest had as much hair on it as the day he was born. The pooch made Eric happy, for he had put on more than a few pounds since he dropped out of college. Shane looked like he just woke up, but this didn't surprise Eric at all.

"What's up sleepy head? Did I disturb you from your beauty rest?" Eric tried to hide his anxiety though he could feel the dryness scratching in his throat.

"What's up Eric?"

Shane looked at him like he was a random solicitor. Eric couldn't think of the last time Shane had called him Eric. His nerves tightened further still.

"Oh, not a whole lot really. I've been working a lot...been really busy." He could feel himself trying too hard. Stopping in midsentence, he tried to rethink his next move. Then, he swallowed hard and tried to start again, "Look, I know that I haven't been there..."

Shane didn't let him finish.

"Hey. I understand. Come in man. I'm sorry. I'm just blasted."

Eric sat down on the couch and tried to start conversation about a few different things. Nothing seemed to fit right. He could feel himself rubbing his hands on his thighs. Shane sat down at the kitchen table where he preceded to take hits from a small metal pipe. Everything they talked about felt hollow. It was the conversation total strangers will carry on when they find themselves stuck together to avoid the silence. Those guys from high school you see when you come home that you know but never missed type conversations.

"I've just been laying low man. I smoke a lot of weed. I rarely leave the house except to play hoops. My parole officer is getting me a job though. He says I need to work. I guess I could use some cash."

Shane spoke and looked in every regard as a broken man. It seemed to Eric that he had aged years in the few months since they had last spoken.

"How much longer before you're off probation?"

"More than two years."

He tapped the pipe lightly on the table to empty its contents then brushed the ash into a small pile. Reaching into a plastic sack from his pocket, he reloaded the bowl with trance like concentration. Eric tried to watch the TV while Shane worked. They talk for about an hour with Eric remaining glued to his spot on the couch, and Shane trying his hardest to smoke the entire time. It seemed that Eric was the reason he was smoking.

Noting this, Eric tried to talk about his job. He even went on about Claire wanting to pursue 'Mormonism' as he called it. The old Shane would have jumped on the chance to make wise cracks about a friend's girlfriend, but today, he didn't seem remotely interested. He was tired and distant. Finally, Eric was running out of things to talk about and resorted to asking pointless questions, many of which he already knew the answer to, simply to keep the pulse from flat lining.

Shane eventually became so high that he wasn't even using real words anymore. He would just grunt, nod, or shrug. It was like speaking to a mute. Determined to stay until he had closed the rift that was growing between them or at the very least forced Shane to vent a little frustration, Eric felt he was failing miserably. All his efforts seemed hopeless. The smoke clouding the room combined with the already stained odor of cigarettes made Eric feel both nauseous and depressed

"I better get going." Eric finally forfeited with a deep breath. "I haven't had any dinner yet, and I'm starving."

It was an honest excuse, though it wouldn't make him feel any better. The ten steps from the couch to the door seemed to be the longest, loneliest walk Eric had ever taken. Shane didn't say goodbye. He simply gave a slight flip of his hand to show he was still breathing. Eric felt a cold shudder throughout his body as he closed to door behind him. The taste of failure lumped in his throat along with the stench of weed that stuck to his clothes and hair.

He no longer felt responsible; he could see that Shane was in a downward spiral, and there was nothing he could do to help until Shane decided he wanted help. Unfortunately, Eric had an unyielding feeling it was too late. It was twenty after seven on a warm dry evening, yet Eric still felt cold shivers as he walked to his car in a state of despondent melancholy. The broken old neighborhood seemed to revel in his sorrow.

August 14th, 2000

The small bell above the door chimed as Andrew entered the restaurant. It was a small-family run business, consisting of a small square room with eight or ten tables, a counter in the back, and a kitchen visible only through the plastic window of the door behind the register. The walls were creatively decorated with an Italian theme. There were cut outs in the shape of Italy, an Italian flag, and photographs and paintings of famous landmarks. A little cheesy maybe but a very American effort.

Andrew scanned the room, but he didn't see what he was looking for. The object he desired was actually a woman, and not just any woman but one in particular. Maybe she wasn't a woman. Maybe she was just a girl. He wasn't sure yet, but he was determined to find out.

He hadn't been able to get her off his mind for two weeks. Doing his best to avoid eating at her work or drinking at bars he knew she frequented, he figured it would all go away. But it only grew worse. Half delusional from lack of sleep and figuring it was better than constantly fantasizing about his best friend's girlfriend, a haggard Andrew finally decided he ought to at least find out a little more about her. For as long as he could remember, this habit of becoming absolutely infatuated with some beautiful young girl only to intently search out the smallest flaw in her and blow it completely out of proportion soon after had been Andrew's forte.

It started in the seventh grade when he told everyone he would one day marry a little black haired angel named Joanna Croswell. She was in his social studies class and sat one seat in front of him and to his left. This led to an inability to concentrate in the classroom, and he nearly flunked the subject. Luckily, his classroom pranks and day-dreamy answers were humorous to his teacher, Ms. Furlong, and she took leniency on his test scores, chalking it all up to the difficulties of puberty. Still, it was only through pursuing Joanna constantly, albeit shyly, that he finally able to accomplish his greatest dream.

It was during a time in his life when his greatest thrill was sneaking out at night, and he carefully planned out the details of a late night rendez-vous. Typically, all sneaking out was done from Darin's, for Eric's parents lived out in the valley far from all the action. The fact that Darin's mother was so strict only made the challenge that much more exciting.

The boys would wait until after midnight before creeping out the back door, across the lawn, and over the backyard fence. It was not uncommon for any number of things to go wrong during the escape, whether it was a dog barking, motion lamps turning on, or one of the boy's pants catching on the top of the fence – very common in Eric's case. Years later, they would agree it would have been easier to simply walk out the front door which was a farther distance from Darin's parent's bedroom, but because they had gotten away with it once out the back, they stuck with that formula for two whole summers and were never caught.

One night, Darin and Andrew were alone, and they walked over three miles, which was perfectly normal for them at thirteen, to reach a girl's house where Joanna was staying. The girls snuck out of a bedroom window, and the four of them walked to a park nearby. In a time before any of them had succumb to the siren song of alcohol, the thrill was unmatched. Pulses raced and adrenalin was a natural aphrodisiac to any overly self conscious, know it all adolescent.

Everything came easy that night, far from the ever watchful judging eyes of their peers. Joanna was all that Andrew had imagined and more. The two of them held hands and eventually wandered off from Darin and the other girl. It was at 4:08 a.m. beneath the cool metal of a jungle gym that all Andrew's dreams came true. He kissed his one true love and swore up and down that it would last forever to his exhausted companion throughout their long trek home.

The romance lasted until basketball season when Andrew decided her ears were too small. The next time he spoke to her face to face would be in a drunken stupor at a house party junior year. Every crush thereafter resulted in a similarly quick, similarly shallow end. It may well have been that half the reason he didn't want to see Monique all that time was because he wanted this feeling to last. The sensations of fear, nervousness, and anxiety were uncommon for Andrew, so the butterflies became a pleasant change of pace. All the thinking and worrying were enjoyable during the lonely evenings away from home. The upset stomach and constant tossing at night were a stoic thrill to his idealist nature.

But he figured he couldn't move to California still wondering, so he sacked up and walked to the restaurant after work that afternoon. His palms were sweating and he itched everywhere. He loved the pressure. There was nothing like the threat of failure and embarrassment to motivate the unchallenged.

The restaurant was pretty dead. It was nearly silent. Only the faint and soothing sound of metal on metal could be heard from somewhere nearby. A small dark complexioned man with a mustache was cleaning one of the tables near him.

"Monique isn't working today by any chance is she?" Andrew asked trying to find a place to put his hands. He was ready to leave before the man even realized he was being spoken to.

As he was about to spin and flee, the man turned to him.

"Yes. Monique is at break now."

The man spoke with a choppy accent that Andrew didn't recognize. It wasn't Spanish. He figured it must be Italian, though this was only a guess. Andrew thought he might have been happier if she wasn't working. Waiting wasn't exactly something he had planned for.

"Oh. Do you know what time she will be back?" he asked in preparation again, positioning his body to make a hasty escape.

The man looked at him as if he had said something ridiculous.

"She in the back. She on break." he said speaking louder as if increased volume might help Andrew to understand.

Andrew wasn't sure how to respond. He stood idol trying to calculate his next move. The man pointed his hand toward the back, making a face that clearly showed he took Andrew to be somewhat slow. Figuring he had come too far to turn back now, Andrew walked toward the door to the kitchen. He tried to plan what he would say. He needed a reason to explain why he was there. Unfortunately, he walked faster than he could think.

He pushed open the thin plastic door, entering a kitchen much different from what he expected. There was a man cooking something that smelled delicious and salty on a large grill straight in front of him and a metal bench on the right hand wall that he took to be a prep table. In the back corner, Monique sat on a bucket eating french fries.

She was wearing headphones, swaying to the rhythm of whatever music was playing. She noticed him as he advanced toward her. The look she gave upon recognizing him made Andrew question who was more frightened by this unusual meeting. The question seemed to be answered by how quickly she recovered from her initial reaction.

She smiled brightly. Seeing her smile, Andrew felt his heart beat even harder. Not since Elizabeth had any girl made him react this way. Unknowingly, he was already searching her for a flaw, something to not like. She did look plain in her white work uniform, mostly because he always envisioned her in his head dressed up the way she had been the night they slept together. He stopped in front of her not sure if he should start speaking, for she still wore her head phones.

"Hi there." She said smiling. She spoke loudly trying to compensate for the music of the headphones.

Andrew motioned toward his ears to remind her.

"Oh crap." She cursed, blushing as she removed them awkwardly, allowing them to dangle from her neck.

"Hey, I was just grabbing a bite, and I figured I would see if you were working." Andrew stammered stuffing his hands into the pockets of his jeans.

"That's cool." Monique replied grinning enthusiastically.

Andrew was scanning her to find something that would turn him off. She seemed oblivious to his search.

"So what have you been up to?"

She didn't give away great curiosity with her question. It was more likely she wanted to put the pressure back on him in this unexpected predicament. Andrew couldn't help focusing all his attention on a crooked tooth he spotted in her smile. He was feeling better already, easing him into his usual well planned out angles with women. He spoke shortly of the things that consumed his time, focusing only on the events that she would find interesting and embellishing on them. When he had ended a well articulated pitch, he painted on one of his well practiced swooning smiles.

He knew he had said enough. All he had left to do was ask questions and pretend to listen now, and he felt confident he would have a nice little piece of action on the side until his departure to California. The sight of her headphones reminded him quickly of her love for music. He decided it was as good a place to start as any.

"I'm sorry I interrupted you from your song. It looked like you were pretty caught up there." He said, shifting the attention toward her, then asked, "What are you listening to?"

He took on the role of a hunter already holding the unknowing prey in his scope. She gave an embarrassed laugh.

"Oh, a little Skynyrd. You know you can listen to every song a thousand times, but no matter what they just keep getting better every time."

Andrew's jaw dropped.

"I guess I just really feel an association with the lifestyle they sing about." She continued.

It was too much for Andrew. He could feel his legs buckle. It took all his strength to keep from falling over.

"Wow, my friends back home wouldn't believe it if I told them a girl said that unrehearsed."

He tried to sound cool, but he could feel his cheeks blush. His own voice sounded foreign to him.

"You have the cutest laugh when your nervous. Did anybody ever tell you that?" She continued without missing a beat, almost like she said it intentionally trying to make him more uncomfortable.

The tables had turned, and she seemed to enjoy watching him struggle. Maybe she was exacting revenge for some hard feelings from the other night. He wanted to tell her it wasn't the way it seemed, but she spoke first.

"Look, I hope you're not all worried about the other night," She began.

He was glad she brought it up first. This way he could get an idea of how upset she was about it. If he played his cards right, he might even get another one-nighter out of the deal. He held his breath while she finished.

"I didn't mean to lead you on. I wasn't looking for anything serious. I was just horny. I never do anything like that. Don't worry though. You didn't do anything wrong. You're actually not that bad."

She gave a crooked smile biting her lower lip. Apparently she had a number of smiles in her repertoire. Then, she dipped a few fries in ketchup and took another bite.

Andrew could not believe his ears. He could see the flank crushing his front line and he tried to hold his position, but his archers were already exposed. He told her it was alright but not before stumbling over several early attempts. They spoke for a couple more minutes, but Andrew was defeated. He had lost control. It was unbelievable; nothing like this ever happened to him. He left the restaurant more confused about his feelings than when he had walked in. His life had become one big question mark ever since his career had been cut short, yet this was something entirely more complex.

No doors existed with this girl. Everything was jagged edges and abrupt dead ends. Monique was adding the single certainty to his turbulent life. All he knew was that he wanted this girl with everything he possessed. Andrew decided right then and there, standing outside the little shopping center trying to catch his breath. No matter what the cost, he would make that girl his.

August 20th, 2000

Lying on the floor in the living room doing sit ups, his feet under the couch, Darin was audibly straining when the phone rang. Quickly, he bounced up to answer it. All day, it had felt like he was walking on air.

The coach's poll had come out the night before, and Darin's team was an early favorite to win the conference. More importantly, he had been picked as a preseason All American. Immediately, stress and doubt began brewing beneath his excitement, and soon, he was overcome by the feeling he wasn't working hard enough. He decided he had to step up his regiment.

The truth was he had been working out, throwing, and watching film all summer like a man possessed. He was working so hard at football that he told his parents he had to quit the part time job he had taken for the summer at a fitness club. His dedication was borderline obsessive.

Aside from their trip to San Diego, he rarely found time for Elizabeth. The few free moments he did find to fit her into his schedule he all but demanded that she drop everything she was doing to spend time with him. Such ambition can blind a man to the other loves in his life.

Around her, he would talk almost solely about his future, the upcoming season and his plans after graduation. Elizabeth always had a central role in these dreams, but her input on what that role might involve was rarely asked for. He was entirely consumed with success, and in his eyes, she was content to share in his accomplishments.

In reality, the weight of his growing shadow was crushing her a tiny bit at a time. The weeks since their trip had been particularly difficult. It wasn't as if she considered leaving him; she had long since convinced herself that he was the greatest thing that would ever happen to her. She cried less, but she was lonely in the early hours of the morning and the last moments before sleep. The more she put up with the more he would pile on. Patterns formed and habits were never easy to break.

Not that it was all bad. He still did thoughtful things for her, every goal achieved for him brought her flowers, jewelry, and limo rides to dinner. He still held firmly to be committed to one woman, though he would often remind her with subtle hints about girls he felt sure he could be with or tell her how girls were constantly flirting with him. She didn't doubt that he loved her.

She was merely no longer a priority, no longer the priority. She was another goal that Darin conquered in his path to glory. She was getting older in the same small town of her birth and had needs that he wasn't fulfilling. It seemed only a matter of time before the dam was sure to burst.

Her imagination often turned to Andrew during the rough spells. Though she realized he was far too wild and rare to ever settle down, it was impossible not to imagine 'what if.' She had seen the results of that type of untamed energy after it grew old and burned out in her own family tree. Her uncles were wild hunters, eternal bachelors that closed down bars well into their forties. This was not what she wanted. Such fantasies of Andrew caused her guilt which worked in Darin's favor, even if he was blind to her unhappiness. Some are merely dreamers. Besides, her family loved Darin, his culture, and his charm.

"Hello?"

Darin pressed the receiver to his skull trying to decide which of his teammates was calling about the news.

"Hi, handsome."

Elizabeth's voice coming across the line disappointed him entirely.

"Hello, my little angel," he said masking his disappointment.

"How is your day going little one?"

"It's been pretty long, but I am almost off. All I have thought about all day is you and me driving through the mountains. I have had enough with people today. I can't wait to be far away from the nearest signs of civilization."

Darin had to think a moment before he knew what she was talking about. With all the day's excitement, he had totally forgotten his promise to take her for a long drive tonight. However, in light of the situation, he felt that she would understand.

"Guess what angel! We are picked to win the conference this year!!" He practically shouted before giving her a chance to guess.

"That's great. I am so excited for you." She said sincerely excited. "Wow, you must be in a good mood today."

This was joyous news to Elizabeth, but at the same time, she wondered why he would not have called her to share it earlier. She quickly reminded herself it was all part of being a guy.

"It's pretty amazing. I have been a nervous wreck though. It is a lot of pressure you know? I have been working out like crazy all day. I can't let my team down."

He spoke like an experienced politician.

"I jogged five or six miles this morning, read over a bunch of different offenses, and worked on this new agility program all before lunch."

"I guess you might be needing this ride as bad as me then." She said trying to sound proud of his list of accomplishments for the day.

"Well that's just it," his voice lowered in both volume and tone. "I still have a lot left to do. I don't think I will be able to take you for that drive tonight."

He could hear her exhale, which he had learned to recognize as disappointment, but couldn't help asking, "You understand right, baby?"

Another sigh. Not a good sign.

One night over beers, Eric and Darin had discussed at length the many ways their girlfriends expressed their feelings without saying a single word. Passive aggressive warfare seemed to be imbedded in small town women's DNA, lying dormant and developing until the sheer overwhelming power of their vagina was no longer enough to control the hairier sex. This typically happened during their first serious post high school relationship. There was so much to talk about on the phenomenon that the two wound up having to break it up into categories like body language, behavioral changes, looks, etc. The exhale had been one they both agreed was universal for female disappointment.

"I still want to go. I was hoping we could do it this weekend?"

He knew he was already a ways up shit creek without a paddle. The least he could do was wiggle with the current.

"K."

It was yet another sign that things were looking pretty bleak.

Women unlike men have the ability to say one thing while meaning an entirely different thing even in a fit of blind rage. It is interesting too. Men will piss, moan, and swear. They will let everyone know exactly how they are feeling when they are disappointed or angry. Women are the masters of conserving energy. Eventually, men tire themselves out and concede without even realizing it.

In this instance, it might not have been too late for him to slip a few punches and let the bout go to decision. He could have bit the bullet and tried to make up for it later, but testosterone was pumping too hard through his veins. He ignored all the scouting reports and prior knowledge he had on his opponent and dove head first into uncharted waters without a life preserve.

"I don't see how you can be mad at me about this." He peppered into the receiver, his teeth grinding at the end of his sentence.

His first mistake.

"I'm not mad." Elizabeth maintained with poker like presence, saying one thing while leaving her voice to say something entirely different. Darin was now a coyote in a snare. The more the animal struggles the tighter the trap becomes.

"I can tell you are. You're being selfish."

Mistake number two.

He could feel the word roll off his tongue into the phone. It was a fumbled snap. He pulled his hands out a little early. He wanted it back halfway through. Maybe if he had dropped the -ish off the end, a miracle would lead her toward selfless. He could turn the fight around, compliment her on her unbridled understanding. It didn't happen that way. Instead, he put his head down, bulling forward. It was all Elizabeth needed. She was drawn into a predation state. A shark sensing blood.

"I'm being selfish? I'm being selfish?" She repeated it, not only to let her momentum build, but also wanting him to feel his mistake strike him hard like being run over after throwing a pick.

"Darin, we do what you want to do. We talk about you or subjects that involve you, and that's only if I call you, of course, because you're too busy to call me even once. And, we hang out when you decide you're bored enough or tired enough or horny enough to give me the time of day. You know what? I guess I am selfish. I need to stop thinking so much about myself and more about you. When was the last time you drove over here to hang out, or we went out with my friends? Wait, here's a little harder one. When was the last time you asked my opinion on anything?"

She only paused long enough to catch her breath.

"You're a bastard. You call me selfish for wanting something that can be ours and not just yours. I'm sorry I wanted you to follow through on one promise to me, but I guess I was just being selfish."

That was the farthest she made it before she lost rationality. She tried to continue speaking, but it was impossible through her sobs and profanity. The last thing Darin heard was a violent shriek then the phone clicked.

"Hello?" he asked already knowing there would be no response. "Elizabeth?"

He set the phone down trying to steady his thoughts. He wanted to call her back. He wanted to make things right. He didn't. He told himself there was no way to talk things out with her in that state.

'I will let her calm down,' he thought.

The truth was he knew she was right. It hurt his pride. If he called her back, than he would be giving up control. There was far too much on his plate to risk losing control right now. Arrogance can appear to be harmless in itself. It is always the behaviors that accompany the love of one's self that truly make it such a character flaw. It was likely that her words would never sink in. He would do his best to work things out, promise her this time everything would be different.

Things were definitely going to be different between them, for a while, but then everything was sure to grow stale again. Relationships can grow dangerously routine if they aren't nurtured properly from the start.

It's like building a sky scraper knowing that the beams on the third floor couldn't support the weight of the finished structure through severe incidence of storm. No matter how perfect the appearance from the outside, the longer the mistake is ignored, the greater the disaster waiting to happen. Yet, maybe the arrogant architect has too much on the line to heed advice, so up and up it grows. Until Darin was willing to compromise, their relationship was no different than that skyscraper. Unless Darin could admit that he needed changing, not the relationship, there would be no hope for the couple.

August 26th, 2000

Ten minutes after noon. Eric had finished up with an exhaust instillation and was starving, so he decided to walk over to the pizza parlor across the street from the shop. The smell of grease filled his nostrils as he pulled open the heavy glass door. The restaurant was in an ideal location, nestled amongst the small businesses and auto shops that ran along West Hilton Avenue. It was always a popular lunch spot for blue collared boys especially on Thursday because there was a five dollar buffet that day.

To beat the rush, Eric would usually try to take his break a little earlier than when he packed a lunch from home. Today he hit the middle of the lunch rush. There were the usual familiar faces and he was able to dive right into line. Skipping by the salad bar, he piled a heaping slice of lasagna on his plate and was checking out the pizza choices when he noticed a couple of painters wolfing down as many plates as they could fit on the small, cheese and oil smeared table some eight feet beyond the buffet table's end. Both of them were dressed in white overalls, each with their own unique splatters of paint and caulk. One of them, a kid named Dave, called him over to join them.

Dave was a few years older than Eric. He was very tall and thin with one of those long faces that made him constantly appear sad. His big droopy eyes only added to his depressed appearance. Eric had graduated with his younger brother and known Dave since the fifth grade. Every time Eric saw Dave the first thing that came to his mind was the memory of watching him be one punched by some cowboy at the carnival when Eric was still in middle school. Dave didn't cry, but he didn't make any effort to fight back either. He just sat there bleeding from his lip in semiconscious daze. Today was no different, though Eric didn't dwell on it long. Losing a fight in small town America typically brought with it this type of notoriety for anyone that would otherwise have remained nameless.

He knew the other painter too, yet he couldn't seem to remember from where. He was an older guy with thin brown hair that was graying on the sides. He had a full beard which was well kept and appeared to have been recently trimmed. This second man didn't introduce himself. He seemed to know well who Eric was, making Eric feel worse for not fitting a name to his face. Name recollection had never been Eric's strongest skill.

Each of them made a couple quick anecdotes about working for a living then hunger took priority. As they ate, they spoke very little. Fifteen minutes later, after two more trips through the buffet line, Eric's hunger was subsiding and he sat contemplating whether or not a second slice of dessert pizza was a good idea, when someone slapped him on the shoulder.

"There you are you sneaking son of a bitch."

A dingy, bearded cretin straight out of a John Steinbeck novel stood beside Eric's table. He spoke with a heavy wheeze through cigarette stained teeth, where there were any teeth. "Where the hell you been hiding?"

The sudden jolt answered Eric's dessert question, as heartburn immediately crept up into his chest. His friend Weston had a way of ruining a guy's appetite. The smell of stale B O made Eric's nostrils twitch. His skin was sunless and flaky with psoriasis.

"I've been working." He said leaning back in his chair. "You ever heard of it?"

Pressing his chin down, he pounded the sword of his fist to his chest trying to burp.

"What's wrong man? Too many bread sticks? Damn, Eric, you're starting to get a little soft around the edges."

Weston looked around the table for a laugh but ended up going on without so much as a smile, "I guess that must be what happens when you get hitched huh? By the way, am I gonna get invited to the wedding cuz I still haven't seen anything in the mail?"

"What the hell are you blabbering about?" Eric asked with shock. "Just because I don't still chase wool down at the high school like you doesn't mean I'm a family man, yet."

"And the fats just insulating all the muscle I got beneath it." He added with a wink toward Dave.

"Well, I hope you're gonna use some of that to insulate your house." Weston laughed, again without support from Eric's lunch company. Apparently, these boys weren't big fans of Weston.

"We need you to come play in the state softball tourney next weekend. We have a couple guys that can't make it and without nine guys we have to forfeit. Can you still haul that piano around the bases?"

Oh I don't think so." Eric answered. "Don't get me wrong. I'll whoop you in a footrace till the day I perish, but I am too busy right now."

A long weekend of drinking with the boys did sound appealing. Eric tried to picture himself trotting the bases in glory, but all he imagined was the type of foolish trouble that always accompanied a small town weekend event and the excuses to gather drunken fools from around the state that led to it.

"Come on. If you're worried about the religious consequences, it's ok. Even Mormons are allowed to have some recreation. Besides, we need a designated driver."

Eric felt flustered a little as the hairs on his arms stood up.

"What the hell? Are you drinking on the job, boy?" He asked, trying to sound as backwoods as possible. "You know damn well I'm not Mormon."

"Not yet." Weston teased. "But I heard Claire's been talking anyone who will listen's ear off about all that Salt Lake mumbo jumbo. If the owner's turned, it's only a matter of time before the mutt follows."

Once again, he made it clear he was baiting Eric. Eric was upset, but he wasn't about to lose his temper over it. He was more embarrassed. Who the hell was Claire talking to?

"No. She just picked some of that shit up from her family over in Portland. She'll get over it. She didn't even go this week. I think she's starting to realize how stupid it all is." He said through bites of the pizza he had decided moments earlier not to eat.

The older painter was occupied with something else, leaving only Weston and Dave for him to convince. Still, it felt like a million judging eyes were burning a hole right through him.

"You know what? I do need a good weekend of boozing it up with the boys. Besides, I need to show all you skinny little girls how to hit a real line drive."

"Now that's more like it." The vagabond looking grease ball squealed slapping Eric on the back again with a crusty hand.

He was pleased at manipulating Eric so easily. The two had been friends in high school, but Weston had never been popular and had worshipped Eric and Andrew, constantly risking his own neck in attempts to entertain them. If Eric came to play, everyone would be grateful to Weston for persuading him.

"Alright, I am gonna call you on Monday or Tuesday to give you all the details. I think a couple of us are gonna pull campers down, so you got a place to stay. If Claire is coming, I know where there's a couple real cheap motels down there. Classy though, HBO and shit."

Eric was pleased too. It was time for him to stop going through the motions. This was a chance to start living a little. He couldn't remember the last time he'd gone wild. All he did was work, and he deserved a weekend off. He was actually looking forward to making a few bad decisions. There was a puzzled look on the old painter's face, but Eric didn't pay him any attention. Cracking a last joke to Dave, he paid his check, said goodbye, and headed back to the shop feeling pretty good.

He wondered what Claire would think. She probably wouldn't want to come, but it was impossible to know for sure. The truth of the matter was she was pretty set on this whole religious change, and the issue had been causing Eric quite a bit of stress lately. Work kept him busy six days a week, but Sundays the shop was closed, so he felt compelled to cram as much leisure into it as possible. Growing up with Catholic grandparents, Eric was no stranger to Sunday morning mass, but Claire was beginning to spend half the afternoon at church as well. Lately, she refused to go anywhere or do anything outside the house on Sunday. This drove Eric crazy.

The past Saturday, after another exhausting week at work, Eric finally broke down and pleaded his case. Claire asked him why he couldn't start taking Saturdays off which led to a stand off. Eric rarely used his silent stubbornness against Claire, so after a few hours of it, she realized how adamant he was on the subject.

She caved in, and they followed a long night of love making by sleeping in late, going out for lunch, and then to the movie theater. It was only upon crawling into bed Sunday night that Eric realized Claire's compromise left him in the vulnerable position of owing her. Tip toeing around the subject, he thanked her for spending the day with him and apologized that she had missed church. In the darkness, her answer stung him.

"It's alright, honey. Next month, we are putting on a Fall BBQ, and I thought it would be nice if you would put together some activities for the teenagers." She had said innocently.

Eric swallowed hard but didn't respond, knowing damn well he was stuck like a speared carp.

Weston had stumbled upon this open sore unbeknownst, but it had already been nagging constantly at Eric under the surface. He half jogged, half waddled back across the street, the contents of his full stomach already making that familiar journey toward his bowels. One of his coworkers was standing out front smoking a cigarette. Eric bummed one.

It had become a strange routine for him to have a cigarette most days after lunch. It was strange because he didn't remember the first day he had started doing it, and he never thought about why he did it either. Growing up, Eric had never been a smoker, except for a few rare occasions while drinking, which made his habit even more of an oddity. It was only that one a day. The rest of the day passed without the slightest thought of nicotine.

He was disgusted when others smoked in public places, though he didn't think of smoking as bad or good. He had never bought a pack in his life. It became a regular habit of asking whoever was out front to borrow one. As sometimes happens, Eric lost interest about halfway through the smoke, but not wanting to offend his fellow smoker, he puffed it down a little further before tossing it aside. Before he'd punched back in, the owner of the garage startled him with his raspy voice.

"You're supposed to call your girlfriend. She says it's an emergency."

A statement like this is usually never as bad as it sounds. Eric wasn't worried. He figured either she was being over dramatic to make sure he would call, or his boss had misread the urgency of the circumstances. He walked back outside to grab his phone out of the car. He was about to dial when he noticed that he had half a dozen missed calls. Every one was from Claire. A lump formed in his throat while he waited for her to pick up. She didn't answer. He was about to hang up when he heard the first words of her answering service, stopping him in his tracks.

It was Claire's voice, "If this is Eric, I need you to come to my house immediately when you get this message."

He was still waiting for further explanation when he heard the beep. He couldn't understand it. Her voice sounded solemn almost poetic. He wondered what kind of emergency would leave her time to change her message and concluded it couldn't be an injury. This eased his concern some, but his curiosity increased ten fold.

He went in, explained everything vaguely to his boss, apologized, and whipped his car out of the parking lot. Had he forgotten something? The entire drive over he continued to call her. Anniversary, birthday, or an important favor she asked? He called again - still no answer.

'She better not be trying to be cute,' he thought, but Claire knew how much Eric hated to miss work.

It had to be something serious. His throat was dry and still tasted of cigarette. He had not drunk anything since he smoked. Obviously, there was no time for that now.

He pulled into her driveway, but her car wasn't there. Now things were getting a little too strange. Eric slammed his door shut and hurried into the house. The door was unlocked which wasn't uncommon. He called out a few times; receiving no answer, he began to search the residence for any clues of trouble. He was opening the door to Claire's room when he heard the front door open. He spun and moved his big body swiftly back that direction and entered the front hall to find Claire standing in the entryway.

She was completely still, looking at Eric with longing eyes. She tried to smile, yet Eric could tell she was fighting back tears. Everything about her told the story of a million emotions trying to escape her beautiful little figure. He had forgotten something. As to what, he was at a loss.

"Claire?" Eric asked trying to pull her back from where ever she was.

"What is it babe?"

His voice was both apologetic and confused. A million terrible possibilities were running through his head all at once. She looked down one more time, searching for that added strength. Eric could see now he was about to get something very heavy. He tightened up. He couldn't let her down. No matter what it was, he had to catch it before it crushed her under the weight that was clearly sitting squarely on her fragile shoulders.

"Babe...what is it?" He asked one more time, this time with more supportive undertones.

"I'm pregnant." She said before the large alligator tears started slowly down her cheeks.

She didn't sob or cry out. Regardless of all the possibilities running through Eric's mind five seconds earlier, there is no possible way to prepare for those two words. He would remember the moment forever. Though, he would never be able to recall or even describe the feeling. His brain scrambled, consuming itself in a tidal wave of self doubt, panic, joy, and curiosity, but there was no time for any of that. He felt everything grow distant and his knees weaken. It only lasted a second or two. Two hundred and thirty pounds pushing on jolted knees can be devastating. Something primordial deep inside the recesses of his mind instinctively awoke to take control of his overloaded senses. One voice was heard clearly in his head. He knew what he had to do. Without waiting to hear her thoughts or plans, without another second's hesitation, Eric made a life changing choice, a decision to forget about being young, wild, or free. The clarity, strength, and conviction in his voice surprised even himself as he spoke the words. He had no idea where the courage came from.

"I am gonna be a daddy?"

It was squeaked out but adorable coming from that big teddy-bear. The two locked eyes. Eric smiled, yet it was much more than a smile. It was a solemn vow that everything was going to be alright. Claire could hear the promise that smile spoke. It was more than she could handle. She lost control, crying for joy. She wasn't ready to have a child, but she wouldn't be alone.

Upon discovering she was pregnant, Claire had already decided to have the baby. Preparing to tell Eric, it was impossible to see a positive reaction. They were so young. Finally, she had decided in the best case scenario his first reaction would be to ask her if she would keep the baby. Best case.

Never could she have imagined the words he spoke. Nor would she ever forget those words. Those words committed their lives for eternity no matter what should come to pass. It seems strange because the pregnancy was obviously the biggest event in either of their young lives, yet it was that sentence that truly impacted their lives forever.

Eric had found the strength he always longed for in times of crisis. He proved to be the man he always feared he was not. Claire discovered how much more love can mean in actions rather than words.

Eric would later say he had been looking at life all wrong. He could only think of his rotten luck because he was looking for happiness to come from all the wrong places. He would say this was the Lord's way of helping him see the life that was passing before his very eyes while he stared longingly into the distance. Another favorite he liked to use was the Lord dropped him into the icy waters of life to wake him from his stupor. It was his choice to sink or swim.

No matter what he said about that day or most things from that point forth, it usually involved faith. He no longer wished to search for answers to his religious questions. Now, he was satisfied believing there were many things man had no right questioning. He grew up overnight. He finally chose a path.

August 1st, 2001

The old car could be heard limping and moaning into the drive from inside the apartment. Being accustomed to such racket, Eric didn't think much of it. It was a minute later when he heard a loud knock on the door in a familiar rhythmic fashion that he realized who it must be. He felt a wave of youthful enthusiasm rush to his heart as he heaved himself up out of his chair. He was within arm length of grabbing the handle when the door shot open from the outside.

A long haired, bony young man entered the room with a loud yell. Despite his slim appearance, Andrew proved he still had the same hidden strength by lifting Eric off his feet in a powerful bear hug. This was no easy task. Eric had gained more weight in the past year. He hovered somewhere close to two hundred and sixty pounds. He feared his friend would hurt his back in all the excitement, but Andrew seemed oblivious to the strain.

Andrew's new look made him almost unrecognizable physically. Eric had never seen him with anything other than short hair. His hair was now close to his shoulder and wavy. There was a greasy shine to it, and it made his face appear even thinner. He was also sporting a goatee or what Eric took to be a try at one. It was fairly sparse, but judging by the length of the few hairs no one had mentioned this fact to him. They greeted each other happily, each feeling a little more complete with his friend in proximity. Once the formalities were behind them, they started in on each other.

"I see California already got a hold of you huh, hippie?" Eric said with a chuckle, giving a mock peace sign and already knowing what comment was certain to come in retaliation.

"I guess so. You know I wasn't aware that being a fat ass was one of the requirements of becoming a father." Andrew returned with his well known grin.

"Jesus bro, first Claire has a baby and now you? You look to be at least six or seven months along."

"Well now you know, so don't get caught hanging around the fridge or I might mistake you for a slice of lunch meat you skinny little girl." Eric spoke with a child-like pleasure he hadn't used in a long time.

His son had been born several months early, and it had direct consequences on Eric. He was a nervous wreck all the time. Church, work, and eating became his outlets to rid his mind of worry. It wasn't long before he was abusing them. He had become a workaholic, adding two nights a week bartending to his full time job at the garage.

Claire was too caught up with the baby and planning the wedding to really see the effects that working so much were having on him. His coworkers and friends could see a man that was growing old much too fast. Every meal went down like it would be his last.

"Alright, enough about you already. Where is the little guy?" Andrew asked glancing around as if expecting the child to appear from thin air.

"Claire took him to the doctor. He has to go to checkups a lot because he was born so early." Eric said a little embarrassed.

"Always got to be early, just like his daddy." Andrew said trying to relax his big friend. "I can't wait to see him. I hope he got all his looks from Claire and not the freakin' Adam's family you come from."

"He sure don't look anything like me. I've even told Claire I'm expected some child support from the mailman." He joked.

They both had a good laugh. Eric told Andrew to make himself at home. He told him he would have to sleep on the couch because there were only the two bedrooms. Then, he tried asking about California, but Andrew would have none of it.

"Forget about all that. I'm home. Right now everything is about you and Claire." He said throwing his hair back and slapping his hand at the air. "So how come you kids decided to move the wedding up?"

"Well, the only reason we were planning to wait was so Claire didn't look all pregnant for the wedding. I guess since Nate was born early, and she already lost what little weight she gained, it just made sense to have a summer wedding. We both wanted it outside." He paused for a moment searching for other reasons.

"And you know how Claire is. She was upset about having a child out of wedlock anyways, so she wants to repent for this sin by getting past it as soon as possible."

"Oh that's right, I forgot you two are straight up Latter Day Saints now." Andrew said not sure yet how he wanted to treat the issue.

Eric seemed to flinch. It was a clear sign that he had been hoping to avoid the subject as long as possible. Deep down it was a relief that his new religion had come up so early, so he could hear his friend's opinions on it without fearing the subject come up at a less opportune or less sober moment. Eric searched the dark shag carpet for stains while he spoke in a well rehearsed monotone.

"Yes, I have found my path. I am not saying it is the right choice for everyone, and I choose to follow my own beliefs, so I will not go on a mission or try to change the way others worship. However, I have found peace thanks to the church and our great members."

His voice was sad and stern like a priest giving the final rights before a certain death. He glanced in Andrew's direction without actually looking directly at him, trying to get a read.

"But, it is tough with everyone being Catholic. My grandparents were pretty hurt that the wedding won't take place at the Cathedral."

Andrew nodded his head in understanding. Eric knew Andrew didn't believe in organized Christianity, but he had always been very spiritual in his own way. Never once had he passed judgment in the religious arguments that Darin so loved to instigate. Somewhere in the quiet mystery behind those fierce eyes something inspirational and eternally knowing slept and Eric always wondered what it would lead to. Right then, he was happy to see a look of total acceptance and understanding in his best friend's face.

"Faith next to family is the most important thing in a man's life." Andrew said quietly. "You have both. I know they will carry you far in this world. Everything will work out fine."

He bowed his head for a moment letting his eyes nearly close. Eric spoke the words over in his head noting the reference to family. He was still trying to choose his next words when Andrew suddenly came back to life. His face brightened and his eyes regained that confident gleam. They were the same powerful eyes set in an older face.

"So am I in charge of this whole shindig?" He asked raising an eyebrow the way he used to whenever he had trouble brewing on his mind.

"Claire and her parents are actually doing most of the work, but I mean you're the best man. Of course, you will have some opinion in everything that..." Eric started absentmindedly.

"No, dumbass, I don't mean the wedding," Andrew interrupted shaking his head the way someone does when a dog or child that doesn't know any better does something wrong.

"As long as there's free booze, I could give a shit about the wedding. No offense. I mean am I in charge of the bachelor party?"

Eric's cheeks turned a shade of crimson. He hadn't even thought about a having a bachelor party. Knowing it would be completely impossible to talk Andrew out of the idea, he decided to try to at least try to keep the ball in the park.

"Yea, I guess we could go down to the bar and have a couple of beers one night." He said, picturing it all in his head. And quick as that, the last chance for resistance slipped past.

"Ok good, I will throw something together. I can't promise any miracles though on short notice."

Andrew licked his lips.

"Nothing out of control though." Eric said plainly.

He was aware Andrew's partying probably hadn't cut back like his own in the past year. Andrew wrinkled his eyebrows preparing to respond when Claire opened the door. She was carrying Nathan gently in her arms. His face was nuzzled against her. Andrew was shocked at how thin she was for having a baby four months earlier. His amazement didn't last long though, for Nathan turned his head as they entered the house to look right at Andrew.

His heart skipped a beat. Nathan was absolutely beautiful. Tired and awkward he shook his lip at the air. Andrew stood swiftly, all his hair falling in front of his face. Without taking his eyes off the baby, he whispered an almost inaudible hello to Claire. She smiled softly at him.

"Hello, Andrew. You don't have to whisper. He's wide awake." She said in her gentle manner.

"He is very handsome. Congratulations." Andrew said still whispering to keep himself from screaming. He showed a proud grin. Then shot one at the father.

"Here hold him." She said handing him delicately to the skinny man that stood nearly quivering before her.

"Go see Uncle Andrew."

Claire helped Andrew to get the baby into the right position. He started to fuss, so she told him to bounce him a little bit. Then, with her hands free, she leaned over to kiss Eric.

"Hey momma. What the Doc say?" He asked making room for Claire to sit down on his lap. She smiled, and they both watched Andrew treat their son like a prize antique.

"Everything is ship shape. He is gaining weight and in perfect health."

"Too bad the same can't be said about your dad huh?" Andrew whispered to the child he bounced on his shoulder.

"Hey, don't make fun of my sugar daddy." Claire mock scolded him. Eric leaned forward kissing her on the cheek.

"Thanks momma."

The couple rocked back and forth in the recliner, watching Andrew continue to bounce his entire body gently with the baby held close to his chest.

"Your good with him," Claire pointed out. "I think you're ready for one of your own."

Andrew looked up with fright in his eyes. After a moment, he laughed it off, but it was clear the idea had hit him unexpectedly.

"Someday when I grow up a little, we will talk about kids." he said turning his attention back to Nathan.

"We?" Claire asked with emphasis. The cue jogged Eric's memory too.

"I totally forgot about that." He said rubbing his hands together with excitement. "Enough dancing around it, tell us about your girlfriend and California, long hair."

Andrew laughed, handing the child back to Claire very gently.

"Ok." He said drawing in a long breath.

"I have a girlfriend. Her name is Monique." He began, trying to sound dull.

He didn't want to get into a lot of questions about his life because that would mean he actually had to think about it, so he intentionally avoided details or signs of personal attachment. Unfortunately, the simple fact that he had a real girlfriend or even someone he described as such was a monumental occurrence for those who were familiar with his relationship habits or lack there of.

"She must be some catch. I bet she's tall, blonde and has big tits huh?" Claire teased him.

"Yeah and she must be able to suck the chrome right off a bumper." Eric chimed in.

The couple spent so much time in solitude it was amazing to watch the way they interacted with others. They were like children who have been kept inside too long and finally let out to play.

"Actually." He paused.

"She has brown hair, but her tits are pretty large."

Andrew played along now, seeing the entertainment it was providing for his hosts.

"No, she is an amazing girl. She's smart, motivated, and has a great sense of humor. You'd really like her."

He scratched at the back of his neck. It was awkward feeling obliged to talk her up, but he wanted so badly for approval.

"How did she talk you into moving to California?" Claire asked.

The baby began to cry out. She moved him toward her lap to breast feed him. Andrew looked away quickly feeling ashamed to see her breasts even though they were very comfortable with each other. It made him lose his train of thought.

"Yea, she treats me right." he said not sure if he had crossed some invisible line of etiquette. Claire seeing what had happened repeated her question again.

"No, actually, moving to California was something I was planning to do for a while. I want to be an actor. She had a friend going to school down there that helped us find a cheap place to live."

"You're gonna be an actor? You meet any movie stars down there yet or what?" Eric asked continuing the interrogation.

"No, we are actually living in a little college town right now. I have to save up a lot of money before I can afford to live in LA. Living in California is really expensive."

Andrew was starting to loosen up more, feeling at home again. He began pacing back and forth in front of the door without realizing it.

"We are renting one bedroom in a three bedroom house, and you're not gonna believe this. We pay three hundred and seventy five bucks a month." He said this last sentence very slow emphasizing every word.

Andrew was a fantastic story teller, and he knew exactly how to draw the audience in with a combination of tone, hand gestures, and articulation. It was working too. Both Eric and Claire were hanging on every word.

"You're shitting me!" Eric exclaimed.

He sat up almost knocking Claire to the ground. She knew how talk of money got him particularly excited, so she moved to the couch Andrew had vacated.

"Why don't you guys find somewhere else?"

"That is cheap. We are getting cut a deal because it's a personal home. A one bedroom apartment might cost us closer to eight or nine hundred." Andrew came back quickly.

He had led Eric right to that question, so he was already prepared to answer it.

"That is absurd," Eric said completely perplexed and almost angry.

"How the hell can anyone afford to live down there?"

"I have no idea, but if you ask people down there they act like it's the only place in the world. They don't even think prices like that are unreasonable,"

Andrew couldn't believe how good it felt to finally be talking to someone who could relate to his opinions. It was an outlet for all of the differences he found between California and home. He thought about such things constantly, but people who didn't share his background couldn't understand his view point.

He went on sharing California experiences for over an hour. His stories were compelling and hilarious. He explained that Monique had wanted to come up, but she had only recently landed a new job, making it impossible to take time off. Claire wondered if he was going to wear a path out of the carpet where he paced.

Eventually, Nathan fell asleep, and after Claire put him down, she went to the store to get some beers knowing Andrew would appreciate it. They never kept alcohol in the house of course, but she was smart enough to let Eric drink whenever he wished. She knew forbidding it would only make it a great problem because Eric was so hard headed. Instead, she would use subtler techniques. She figured it was like training a puppy. She gave him rewards when he avoided alcohol and would show clear disappointment when he drank without ever actually saying that either was because of the alcohol.

Of course, it didn't take Eric long to notice this behavior, but he couldn't exactly argue about it. He had no choice but to play along, and over time he drank less and less. It wasn't all bad. The less he drank the less he missed drinking, and after Nathan's birth, he quit completely.

It made the few times he did drink seem more special. Sometimes, drinking made him feel like an outlaw. Not only that, it lowered his tolerance levels to the point where he could get drunk for cheap. Feeling it unnecessary to explain all this to Andrew or risk hurting his feelings, Eric realized this was an opportunity to drink in front of Claire without punishment, so he drank one beer slowly while they reminisced about old times. It was the greatest beer he ever remembered tasting.

Andrew on the other hand finished off the remainder of a six pack without flinching. When the beer was gone, he didn't want the ride to stop just yet. He decided to go out on the town.

"Well I guess I have blabbed on for long enough. I think Claire's getting tired of me too," He said with a wink.

"I better go check on my old stomping grounds. Make sure the Natives haven't gotten restless while Chief's been away."

Claire told him how to pull out the couch and where to find blankets when he returned. He graciously thanked her for allowing him to stay with them, and left with a quick wave. After the door closed behind him, Eric stood up to stretch himself out, crushed his can, and took it into the kitchen to throw it away. Now that Andrew was gone, he was glad he decided to drink only one beer. This way he still might be able to get a little squeeze in before bed. The smile on Claire's face when he came back in the living room reinforced this hope.

"Alright sugar plum, let's hit the sack." he said picking her up off the couch. She kissed him on the neck, and he couldn't remember ever feeling so content.

August 4th, 2001

"Let me guess. He's not here is he?" Andrew asked Shane's mom as soon as she opened the door. She smiled showing her blue teeth, stained from years of daily smoking, then gave a crackled half laugh half cough.

"He was home for a couple of hours yesterday, and I gave him the number you left. He told me he was going to call you. He's never home anymore. He hasn't slept here in over a week I bet."

She didn't seem too interested. She raised her cigarette to her lip for a long drag. Andrew assumed she had some daytime talk show she had better get back to, so he didn't leave a message this time. He kissed her on the cheek and walked back to the street. Climbing in his car, he started the engine and leaned back in the seat. His stay had been pretty uneventful so far. Eric and Claire had become forty year old Mormons overnight, Shane was nowhere to be found, he'd called Darin a couple times but nobody answered or returned calls.

He had expected the bar scene to be the way he remembered it from his previous visits. A bunch of old friends from high school and everyone excited to see him, but the bars had either been full of strangers or completely dead. He was getting bored, and that usually meant he was sure to find trouble. He decided he better check out the park real quick before driving back to Eric's.

The park was only a few minute's drive from Shane's neighborhood. Pulling around the corner, Andrew found a five on five game being played on the main court. Most of the participants were Indians. He couldn't tell if Shane was playing or not.

He pulled up behind the picnic tables, parking the Lincoln beside an old Nissan pickup with a tattered Native Pride sticker in the rear window. The sounds of whistling, whooping and accents brought back fond memories of coming to this park. The boys had been playing pickup games here since middle school. Those memories were filling his thoughts when he heard a familiar voice. Apparently, Shane had schooled someone and felt like he was fouled in the process, for he was really letting this guy hear it.

"I'm not your sister. You're gonna have to slap me a lot harder than that to shut me up, and even then you can't stop it," he was chirping.

"I've been making you look bad at this park for four years. You'd think you'd a stopped showin up. You must be one broke bitch, or I'm sure you would have bought a gun by now and put yourself out of your misery."

Everyone listening had a good laugh. Andrew couldn't help but join in. The excitement of seeing his friend sent a warm shiver through his body.

Shane was shirtless, still built like he was seventeen, and glistening with sweat. His hair was buzzed very short. Other than a new tattoo of a basketball with arrows shot through it on his shoulder and a little beer gut, he looked exactly the same as he did in high school. He was guarding the man with the ball, still talking trash when Andrew couldn't contain himself any longer.

"Hey mouthpiece, why don't you shut up and play the game." he called out cupping his hands to his mouth to amplify his voice.

Shane stopped for a moment, allowing his opponent the opening he needed to drive past him. He ended up dishing it to an open man under the basket when someone stepped up to stop his dribble. Shane didn't notice. He was smiling from ear to ear.

"Speaking of poor bastards, this guy can't even afford a ten dollar haircut." He said walking off the court to greet Andrew.

They embraced each other tightly. The reunion was cut short though. Indians have no tolerance for anything that interferes with their basketball. The game didn't pause for him. Less than a full minute passed before people were bitching for him to get back in the game.

"Sorry bro, we've got no subs today." he said knowing Andrew understood Native law as well as anyone.

"Well, I guess now we got one. Come on let's show these fools how it's done. That is if you still remember how to play." He said with a smile.

Andrew was wearing jeans, but even if he had boots on it wouldn't have taken much convincing for him to play. He was always up for basketball, playing with Shane only made it that much better. He was the sub, so he stretched out a little waiting for someone to need a breather. Some of the guys eyed him, but a few seemed to remember him from long ago even with all his added hair. It wasn't long before a guy on the shirts team told him to come in. Shane was bringing the ball up, so Andrew told a younger kid he would guard him. Shane smiled.

"Well let's see if that baseball team has been keeping you in any kind of shape." he said, pushing the ball smoothly back and forth between his legs then behind his back.

"I'm done with ball, but I don't have to be in shape to swat you." He said bending down into a good defensive position.

He focused in on Shane's waist.

"You only got two moves in your bag of tricks anyways."

"I don't know about that. I've been playing a lot of ball since you left, so don't feel embarrassed. Just try and stay on your feet."

Shane faked right before coming back to his original position.

"Same weak crossover." Andrew said without smiling, the competitive side coming out in him.

From the corner of his eye, he caught a pick coming on his left side. He glanced quickly. Shane was gone like a strike of lightning. Andrew rolled off the pick, but Shane wasn't going to the basket. He pulled up and drained a jumper from about twelve feet out. He stood still as a statue in his follow through for a moment.

"Uh oh, I'm feeling that touch today boys."

He shot a quick look at Andrew and shrugged.

Without a response, Andrew jogged up the court. He posted himself beside the bottom of the key where a bigger guy came down to guard him. The guy was an Indian with short hair that was probably buzzed about a month before and allowed to grow. The guy had a bunch of tattoos. Andrew didn't take the time to see what any of them were.

He cut hard out to the three point line asking for the ball. When he got it, he pulled up to shoot, but he didn't feel it. He decided to dish it off to the younger kid that was originally guarding Shane. The kid tried to take it baseline but wound up missing a lay up. Shane's team pulled down the rebound and passed it quickly down court.

Andrew ran down to stop the ball, but the ball handler dished it past him to Shane who picked up an easy lay up. Now, he was really feeling it. He started talking trash directly at Andrew. Shane never held back either. Andrew could feel himself losing his composure. He hustled back down court. This time no one even passed him the ball, and it got stolen from an older guy trying to shake too much.

"Damn, this game was actually close before you got in here man. Maybe we should have one of the girls over here fill in for you." Shane called to Andrew, showing off some impressive dribbling skills.

Again, a guy tried to set a pick on Andrew's left, but this time Shane faked right then switched direction. He drove the lane with his left. He jumped up hoping to draw a foul down low, but Andrew came from nowhere swatting to ball down court. Shane turned around to see Andrew break. He beat everyone to the loose ball, dribbled it twice, and dunked it with both hands. Everyone was impressed and slapping fives.

The game slowed for a minute. It wasn't everyday this court witnessed a two hand dunk by some long haired white boy in jeans. The ball was inbounded and passed back to Shane. On his third dribble, Andrew picked his pocket and made off again. This time he pulled up at the three point line though and drained it nothing but net. After the shot, he bowed his head, running back down the court with pressed lips. Shane couldn't help but laugh. After all, it was hard to expect anything less from Andrew.

August 7th, 2001

The last remnants of the sun's rays were held tightly in the dust shaken up by slowly passing cars and allowed to linger. From atop a long rotted fencepost, a crow watched and wondered, cawing jealously. The sounds of music and laughter could be heard from the old frontage road nearly two miles away. The evening filled with anticipation and the idea of love which was released to it from the people's smiles. The party was kicked off in the fading beams of this marvelous sun set giving promise to everyone that not only would the reception be a success, but the marriage was destined to last. It was perfect August; an evening in the valley. Not a cloud could be found in the sky, and even the most gentle of leaves sat quietly in the calm cool air.

Claire's parents had rented out the entire campground for the occasion, and there were canopies, a band, an open bar, and even a hundred and twenty-five square foot portable dance floor. When everyone first arrived from the church, the delicious aromas of gristle and BBQ pulled large masses to gather around the biggest tent which had a buffet style setup with a dozen tables scattered around. Just before darkness fell, the band started up, yet the majority of the guests still seemed to be milling around deep in joyful conversations, still pulsating with the halo of doves, swapping stories of the bride, groom, or something totally irrelevant to the festivities.

About a half hour later though, the alcohol was kicking in. It is impossible for people drinking in such great spirits to not start tapping a foot along with the beat. Soon, there was clapping, dancing, and grown men chasing girls around with stars in their eyes looking like middle school children.

Andrew, Shane, and Darin all stood out in their black tuxedos and turquoise vests, yet it didn't stop them from joining in on all the fun. Andrew and Shane had been drinking from silver flasks since long before the ceremony, and they were both out to make the night a memorable one. The bride and groom arrived in a black limo shortly after dark when the band was really starting to find their rhythm. Darin gave a short toast that was sure to pull some votes if he ever decided to pursue a future in local politics. He spoke of Eric's character and his friendship with great articulation, yet he pasted on the perfect amount of sappy wedding humor. There were many tears in the crowd including a few from Andrew. After the speech, the band toned it down for the new couple to have their first dance. While everyone gathered around to take pictures, Andrew approached Darin.

"Hey man, that was a freakin sweet speech you gave," He said, both of them watching the couple along with everyone else.

Andrew shook the ice to swish his whiskey cold.

"Thanks bud." Darin said genuinely.

He sipped champagne from a plastic wine glass.

"Look, I just wanted to say I'm sorry about all the drama the other night," Andrew stammered, getting to his true purpose. He was buzzed and saw no point in beating around the bush.

"Don't worry about it." Darin said.

He was hoping the subject of the bachelor party wouldn't come up, at least not for the night.

"No bro, I am seriously sorry," Andrew went on, ignoring Darin's hint. "Everyone was really drunk. Whatever got said...it was just the alcohol talking."

He was almost whispering by the time he finished speaking.

"I understand. Let's just drop it." Darin said moving toward the other side of the crowd and out of the way of flashing cameras.

He glanced around nervously and extroverted a grin for anyone his eyes found contact with. Andrew couldn't blame him for this reaction. He had promised himself he would avoid the whole matter for a few more days, but the more he drank the more difficult it became to postpone his apology. It was that emotional blur somewhere between drinking all day and being drunk. Patience had been lost or forgotten. He had spoken to Darin several times the night before at the rehearsal dinner, and he could feel the tension that hovered between them. Shane, on the other hand, didn't seem fazed in the slightest. Andrew figured he probably couldn't even remember most of the details.

The first song had ended, and the band went straight into playing a unique rendition of "Runaround Sue". The crowd piled on and around the dance floor. Primal joy gave an unforgettable impression to the chaotic laughter as grandparents and teens all started to wiggle and shake. Andrew watched Shane in the middle of the action flailing his arms around with no rhythm, singing the words off key. He couldn't help but feel a little envious.

Everyone always considered Andrew the crazy daredevil, yet it was Shane that never seemed to let anything get to him. Like the crafty old veteran boxer, who didn't have the greatest abilities, he always slipped the big blows and managed to make it through the round. To go the distance in the fight gave him a chance to win by decision.

That was Shane's life. Everybody seemed to be throwing hay makers but not many were landed. This wasn't the movies though, and for Shane things weren't going to magically fall into place in the final climatic bout.

Growing up, parents never wanted their children hanging out with Shane because they said he was nothing but trouble. At the time, Andrew couldn't exactly argue because they had done plenty of mischievous things. Now, he realized that most of it was childish fun that didn't hurt anyone. Any other kid put in his circumstance would have done the same things or worse. Like the night of the drug bust.

It was a night Andrew thought about often. Shane could have easily wormed his way out of it or softened his punishment at the very least by taking others down with him, but he didn't. There wasn't even a chance, and he was still paying the consequences for that.

Andrew started thinking about all the different times Shane had taken the heat for his friends over the years, including Darin on several occasions. Anyone Shane had ever called a friend knew that the skinny little smart ass would go to war with them without any hesitation or question of what was in it for him. Too bad this meant very little in a society's eyes where people were judged by their wealth, position, class, and skin color. Loyalty and a code of honor were practically null and void.

Andrew stood there watching him dance. He couldn't help it. This young kid, merely twenty one years old, with everyone watching, judging his every move, waiting for the smallest screw up so they could say they saw it coming. Shane had little or no opportunity for a future, yet he danced like he was on top of the world. He danced and lived like he didn't have a care in the world. Watching him twist, jump, and dip brought a big smile to Andrew's face. He was glad to be home. Suddenly, he realized someone was speaking to him. The whisky had set in and he was feeling loose. He turned to the right to see a beautiful, black haired young woman looking at him with a puzzled expression. Makeup hid her true face.

"Andrew....are you there?"

He couldn't remember her name, but for some reason he remembered she was a high pitched screamer during sex that loved to be on top. He almost laughed thinking about it.

"Yea. Sorry, I was just thinking?" he said turning on his charms.

"Oh I'm sorry. Do you want me to leave you alone?" She asked, pleading him, batting her long eyelashes.

"No. Of course not. I was just thinking how beautiful this whole life is. So fragile you know?" He asked still searching for her name.

She smiled but looked confused. Too much to expect, Andrew figured.

"How are you?" He deferred to.

"I am fine. I don't get it. Who is fragile?"

"Oh, I was thinking how lucky Eric is. I sure hope I can find that right lady soon, so I can rescue her on my noble steed and ride off into the sunset." He lied, looking deep into her eyes. It was a lie he wasn't even trying to get away with.

"Oh that is so sweet. I always figured you were the kind of guy who just used girls." she said, trying to hold on to the little protective caution

she still maintained through all the white and flowers, love and entice-
ment.

"I have grown up a lot since high school." Andrew countered back
with.

The young lady bit her lip a moment.

"Do you want to dance?" she finally asked hesitantly.

"I'd love to." Andrew said.

She led him by the hand out to a small opening on the grass off the
dance floor. Noticing her smooth shapely legs sticking out from a short
black skirt, he couldn't help thinking to himself, 'I still got it.'

He let all his thoughts drift away, giving into the power of the alcohol,
the music, and the moment for yet another night. Monique vanished from
his mind. It was a memorable night amongst his truest friends. There was
nothing more he could ask for, and his heart was satisfied for those dark
hours before dawn brought another lonesome day.

AUGUST 11TH, 2001

"Are you serious? What the hell is wrong with my guy?" Andrew screamed his face only inches from the television.

"I swear to God I grab your guy first, but he always ends up chucking me to the mat."

Shane's only answer was a quick, snorting laugh. He pushed a combination of buttons on his controller keeping his eyes glued to the TV.

"No way!" Andrew continued. "That is impossible. How does someone pick up a guy twice his size and do something like that?"

Daylight seeped in through drawn blinds. The sounds of the environment outside drown out by the alternatives created by man and his silicon chips. On the screen, Andrew's character was nearly finished, but Shane showed no signs of taking it easy on him. Finally, Andrew lost his temper. He threw the controller hard on the carpet. Shane was surprised it didn't shatter. With one large swig Andrew finished off his bottle of beer, stood up, and moved toward the kitchen with an angry swagger.

"Once again, the winner and undefeated champion." Shane said putting some finishing touches on his now unmanned opponent.

Andrew came back in the room, twisted the cap off his beer, throwing it harmlessly at Shane who flinched knowing how sour Andrew's temper could be even over something as trivial as a video game.

"Undefeated my ass," Andrew fumed, half jokingly.

"I have seen Darin beat the tar out of you on this game before."

"Yeah well that queer plays way too many video games." Shane said turning the game off. He turned the TV back to cable, picked up his beer, and shadow boxed back to the couch.

"I take it you're still pissed about the other night?" Andrew asked.

I Ie noted it was the first time Shane had made a comment on Darin since the bachelor party, showing that he might be calm enough to vent a little. Shane held grudges with half life of uranium.

"No, I don't care. He's a snobby little rich kid. He always has been and always will be." Shane said washing his words down with a quick tilt of his bottle.

He flipped the channels, searching for a football game, something to drink to. Anything to avoid the current topic would suffice. The events of the now infamous bachelor party were still a little hazy because he was nearly blacked out drunk, yet he was able to distinguish well enough between the drunken emotions and the true feelings.

The trouble all began when Andrew brought a stripper into the back billiard room of the Oasis which he had rented out for the party. This made Eric, in all his new found godliness, feel squeamish. Looking back, Shane blamed this on the fact that Eric had promised his bride-to-be he wouldn't drink. Ironically, she trusted him enough to marry him forever and yet not enough to go out partying one last night with his friends. Whatever the reason, Eric felt uncomfortable, but he didn't want to say anything about it to Andrew, so he did the wrong thing all together by telling Darin instead. Darin's vast experience in leadership didn't necessarily help him in such a fickle matter, leading him to mishandle the problem further by making rude comments and more or less telling the young lady she was a tramp and should get lost. This is where things started taking a turn for the worse.

Unaware of Eric's opinion on the dancer, Andrew and Darin had words, nothing too serious or all that unusual for two such proud men who have known each other so long. The two of them had a strong enough friendship and enough distance between their egos to easily forgive and forget. Unfortunately, the friction that rubbed so brazenly between Shane and Darin was only lubricated by their mutual friend's delicate handling of the two's simultaneous presence. A long night of drinking hard liquor made Shane into a hyena. Seeing a two on one possibility, he moved in for the kill. He approached the two arguing at a corner table away from the action. Even in his drunken state, he remembers hearing Darin call Andrew's behavior immature and typical of someone who always did what he pleased without thinking of others.

Shane couldn't remember his own exact words, but he had been more out to bash Darin than defend Andrew. Unapologetically, he told Darin that at least Andrew wasn't a complete fake. The line that neither Darin nor Andrew would cross with each other disappeared. It was like the two were volatile chemical solutions. No matter how much of one was added to the other, the solution would only get very hot, but adding a touch of the right catalyst would cause a violent explosion. Shane was that catalyst. Darin reacted as if Shane's words had come straight from Andrew's own mouth.

'Of course Andrew never had to be fake,' he replied, 'Andrew didn't care what anyone thought of him.'

Shane laughed at this. Andrew, seeing the two speeding down a dead end road, tried to steer them away from disaster, asking Darin to accompany him for another drink. Darin seemed ready to walk away but not before shooting a quick look back at Shane. Shane met his eyes without fear, and he felt that look of superiority Darin cast. The liquor rolled forth. He couldn't resist it. He pushed further. Starting under his breath, he commented bluntly that, 'it must be better off to not care what anyone thought, for it was pretty clear that even those Darin cared most about liked Andrew more.'

Even though it had already been clearly alluded to, he had gone too far to turn back now, and Shane mentioned that even his own girlfriend had to nearly be beaten away by Andrew with a stick. The words carried monumental force. Andrew remembers feeling as if the room fell instantly silent, even though in reality no one was paying much attention to them. The next few moments seemed to be from a dream. The twisted and contorted beneath his feet as it would in the aftermath of a massive quake. He tried to swallow hard, but the lump in his throat only grew. He felt instantly dry mouthed, sober.

Andrew wanted to strike Shane's words from the air as they left his big mouth in hopes they would disappear into some alternate dimension never to be heard. There was no time though. Darin may have always been the most logical, collected young man around, but he was also strong and gifted with speed. His face never even appeared cross. All of the anger sprang outward into his four limbs. Pushing Shane hard in his chest, Darin sent him sprawling back into the wall. His head struck a framed beer emblem mirror, sending it crashing to the ground and shattering it. The sound was barely audible over the loud music, and heads turned slowly in the dark, smoky bar.

Darin moved like a lion. He was on top of Shane in a split second, pulling his blocking arms away from his face in search of a clean shot. Fortunately, Andrew had been around fighting his entire life. Many fighters will hold back such intense emotion for eternity only letting the rage inside them build in magnitude over time. In such cases, it is best to let them get enough of it out to feel like they have righted whatever wrong was inflicted upon them. This was not the case with Darin. He may dwell on the wound for some time in his quiet brooding way, but he never wished to throw fists.

He was a college graduate, a big name in town, and fighting could only hurt his reputation, regardless of the circumstance. Andrew simply had to separate them long enough for rational thought to regain control of his friend's brain. He dove on top of the pile catching Darin around his chest, rolling them both off of Shane. Darin still probably seeing only red didn't even realize that his opponent had changed. He didn't care. He continued to try to gain position. Andrew had wrestled with friends and teammates his whole life, yet he never recalled anyone with such raw unseen strength. It was as if he were wrestling an alligator in a pool of oil. It was impossible to get a hold of Darin's long frame. Andrew took a hard elbow square on the chin that caused him to see stars for a moment. He was beginning to lose his own cool when a couple of guys pulled them apart. Darin struggled violently. It took several good sized men a few minutes to finally restrain him.

The entire struggle had been quite a show. By the time they both had regained their breathing, they were more embarrassed than angry at how stupid and selfish their actions had been. The party was definitely over. The bartender and the solitary bouncer were already trying to empty the room. The bartender, an old veteran of the business, took charge ordering everyone out with a booming voice. He threatened the police were already on their way. The young bouncer though struggled to maintain some signs of composure. He was a big kid but green. New to the job. This was probably his first taste of chaos. By the look of it, he would never make it in this line of work.

Darin looked around at the corner of the bar. It looked like an old abandoned building after the neighborhood children get done playing in it. He felt a sinking feeling deep in the pit of his stomach. He didn't care in the slightest that the party was over, but the look on Eric's face cut deep. Clearly, he was hurt. While everyone poured quickly toward the doors, Andrew and Darin both tried to apologize to Eric as the bright lights came on in the bar, sobering and exposing to sin.

Eric wasn't interested in hearing anything about the story. The fact they were all asked to leave the bar wasn't a big deal to him. Surprisingly, he felt relieved to be leaving. Try as he may, he couldn't remember what used to seem so fun about being surrounded by other lonely men, pissing away most of the week's pay to drown reality in overpriced depressants under a neon glow. Three of his groomsmen and best friends fighting each other on what was metaphorically his last night to be free with them, however, hurt his pride in ways they couldn't imagine. It was a slap in the face.

He couldn't see it for what it truly was. It wasn't that his friendship meant little to them. On the contrary, it was actually the opposite. The night's violence seemed to stem directly from the impending loss of a key block in the bond that kept their turbulent friendships afloat. The act of his marriage was the official ending to the innocent childhood of their lives. The signs had been there for so long. Ignorance and denial were the only things that stopped them from letting go.

In high school, there had been so many endless dreams and possibilities they would accomplish before growing old. Their youth seemed immortal. Their togetherness felt eternal. Now, each of them was individually reaching the point when young men realize there will be no clear act to tell them it is time to be men. Eric's marriage wasn't causing him to be left behind. He was moving on. Time's effects don't occur drastically every twenty, ten, or even five years. The clock is ticking the hours away at the same rate everyday, changing the world one second at a time. It all happens so suddenly, so constantly, that boys cannot see the signs. They struggle with all their might to maintain the joys and comfortable familiarities of youth. They cling dangerously. Thus, many spend years in a limbo between their idealistic, defiant adolescence and the acceptance of mediocrity and forgotten dreams.

Eric found true love, but it was the unplanned pregnancy that catapulted him quickly into a life in which he no longer needed lofty goals to help him find sleep at night. This event that seemed to crush all his dreamy ambitions became the compass that put his drifting life on course. He began to enjoy the little things, accepting that time passing uneventfully by was a part of life. The fight wasn't proof that his philosophy was wrong. It was proof that his friends would not make the same smooth transition. Their transition would be more jagged, perilous, and perhaps violent.

Andrew was proving this through his actions since the wedding. Originally, his plans were to leave for California the day after the wedding. Drinking had prevented him from that goal. The following day, Eric and Claire left to Hawaii for their honeymoon. They would be gone for twelve days. Eric gave Andrew a key in case he wanted to stay for a couple more days. Having a place to stay and no one to make him feel he was wearing out his welcome, the partying only increased, and he continued to put off his departure. Falling into the same trap as so many before him, his ambitions were forgotten, and the pain of unaccomplished dreams became just another faded scar. Hide it away. Drown it. The few who manage to escape this small sleepy town to chase dreams of greatness usually return planning only to visit. All too often, they find it too easy to come back to the same old routine, same old friends, and same lack of expectations.

Andrew was regressing quickly. If it weren't for Monique's constant pestering telephone calls he would probably give up and become no different from the rest. Anyone can talk about escaping someday or stretch the tales of their short time spent elsewhere, but very few can make it out of a small town for good. Dreamers are often described as hungry. Returning home domesticated the natural predator made him docile and tame. Secure where he was, he began losing that edge. Time lost its urgency. The uncomfortable feeling of no longer being well known or envied is what drove him to desire fame.

In California, his life was harder, forcing him to set deadlines. Time is funny that way. A man can lie on a couch watching television for hours and suddenly wonder how the entire day passed him by. While the man doing a wall sit can wonder how two minutes could possibly last so long. Friends further influence this hunger. Shane had no ambitions or goals, and it was quickly spreading like a disease to Andrew. Besides, he still hadn't spoken to Elizabeth. He couldn't figure out why, but he had been disappointed she wasn't present at the wedding. It didn't make sense though, for surely he wouldn't have spoken to her anyway. Lately, he pictured her pretty face often. He never mentioned this to anyone, secretly hoping it would go away. Still, he wanted to see her. He couldn't figure it out. He was nearing the end of another beer, lost in the mind numbing act of watching television, when his phone rang. Pulling it from his pocket, he checked the number cursing.

"Who is it?" Shane asked.

It was the first signs of life from either of them besides raising a bottle to their lips in twenty minutes.

"It's Monique. She's gonna shit when she finds out I still haven't left."

He rubbed his palm on his jeans trying to plan his words carefully. The phone rang several more times, but he still didn't answer it. The voice mail ended up taking it. Andrew figured he could get an idea of what kind of mood she was in from her message.

"Damn, this girl's really got you by the balls." Shane commented jokingly.

His fear of losing was already surfacing.

"You have no idea." Andrew replied, mostly to himself.

He thought of all the great times with Monique, but it wasn't her face that came to him in the back of his mind.

"What do you do for work down there anyways? I mean how did you get so much time off?" Shane asked.

"I haven't actually got a job yet," Andrew said embarrassed.

"I have some money I saved up over the year, but Monique pays most of the rent. She works as a waitress at some barbeque joint."

"Oh," Shane felt bad for bringing it up. "Well, I guess I see why she might be a little interested in your return."

Andrew laughed. He looked at his phone again.

"I guess I better call her back." He said with a dramatic bellow, climbing to his feet.

He set his empty beer bottle on top of the TV, and Shane could hear what sounded like a very sweet voice answer hello as Andrew walked down the hallway toward the bedrooms. Shane figured Andrew would be leaving soon. He took another long swig off his beer and turned back to the TV. He felt guilty because all along he had been secretly praying that things wouldn't work out. Then Andrew would end up staying.

He couldn't help feeling very alone.

August 23, 2001

The monotonous running of water for Claire's bath was beginning to lull Eric to sleep. The steady rhythm was distant and constant. As he started to drift into dream, the sound of Nathan crying caught his attention. The crying didn't bother or worry him the way it used to. He had become so accustomed to life as a father that he almost needed it. Though he had a great time in Hawaii, he was relieved to be back home, back to work, back to the hectic busy life that he loved. Claire did most of the hard work around the home and with Nathan, but it was being needed that gave him a warm feeling of self satisfaction. There was something strangely spiritual about the routine of hard work day in and day out.

After a quick yawn, Eric climbed out of his chair and lumbered down the hall to the baby's room, dragging his bare feet lazily on the soft carpet. Claire met him halfway. He told her to get in her bath and let daddy handle it, assuring her that he had everything under control. She gave a soft purr and kissed him on the cheek. Eric greeted his cranky son with a silly face and carried Nathan back into the living room.

He held the child across his lap with one of his huge hands behind the babies head and the other near his bottom, rocking him gently up and down. Although he didn't know why it worked, he discovered this trick to calming the baby, and its proven success made it a point of bragging. Being the ever paranoid mother of the new millennium, Claire worried the shaking was some how bad for the child despite Eric's persistent assurances it was harmless. She asked the doctor about it. She asked the doctor about everything. He said that it was fine, but she never mentioned this to Eric of course, for she knew it would only increase his vigilant campaigning for father of the year.

After a few minutes of bouncing, Nathan grew quiet. Eric smiled watching his tiny mouth stretch to yawn. He loved to search the child's face for trait origins. He teased Claire saying Nathan's nose looked an awful lot like the mailman's. This type of inside joking drove their friends insane because Eric laughed as hard the twentieth time he told it as the first.

A few minutes later he returned Nathan to his crib. Looking down at his tiny sleeping body, he felt a swelling of pride that choked him, and he had to blink to keep his eyes from watering. While he was turning to leave the room, something caught his attention. Against the wall near the window, there stood a small dresser covered with different sports memorabilia typical of a child's bedroom. On the top of the dark oak chest, there was a picture frame set between a porcelain football figure and another swinging a bat. The frame stood as the center piece of seemingly organized clutter.

Claire must have added the picture recently. Eric had never noticed it before. He knew the photo well but had never seen it framed. The photo was that old picture of Darin, Shane, Andrew, and Eric taken after the championship game their senior year. They were all shiny from sweat, only Shane still wore his jersey, and the scoreboard could be seen in the background. Each of their young faces was covered with a smile that probably could never be duplicated by any of them ever again. A monumental moment in life captured forever. The photo brought the bachelor party brawl to mind, but he pushed this from his mind quickly. Picking up the frame, he carefully examined the photo's smallest details.

The memories came rushing back to him. He thought of those days often, but looking at the photo, his thoughts weren't of the baseball or any other specific event from the past. He remembered the dreamy boy he was in the photo. All of them had been so bold, so fearless. The future was open and light years away. For a moment he pondered whether he may have wronged or shamed the muscular young man kneeling in front of his three best friends. It was always something he tried to steer clear of.

The past is gone forever, so there is no reason to dwell on it with regret. Strange as it seemed, Eric had rarely paid attention to himself in that old photo, but now that was the only person he seemed to notice. Setting the frame back down softly, he heard the baby give a heavy sigh. It was an instant and divine message straight to his heart. The man he was today hadn't failed or given up on the rebellious ambitions of his youth. The environment he lived in had merely changed, forcing him to make choices.

Either he would adapt as the hands on the clock spun continuously ever onward, or he would be left behind forever lusting for the glories of a time long gone and never to return. It was the common dilemma of all great small town athletes. Experiencing stardom at such a young age can have life long effects on anyone. Darin and Andrew stood on opposite sides of the spectra for the extreme influences of sobering up from a youth of idealistic recognition and praise.

The other day, Eric had read the half page ad Darin took in the newspaper advertising his real estate aspirations with a large photograph of himself dressed like some stock market mogul. In the color photo, Darin wore a black suit with a crimson tie. His hair was pushed back and crystallized hard. He was smiling, but it definitely wasn't anything close to the smile from that old photo. Eric wondered if anything made Darin smile innocently anymore, or if every smile was simply a publicity stunt or political move.

Darin could never stand to see his legacy forgotten, and he would never leave his home town. Nor would he ever be satisfied with any amount of money, awards, or recognition. His scholastic influences promised him happiness was harmoniously intertwined with money and achievement. Thus, he would drive himself from daylight till dark in the pursuit of these things. After all, this is the American dream.

Andrew, on the other hand, fed off the joy he brought to others. In his mind, conclusion, under any circumstance, to his baseball career was a failure and felt the only escape from his apparent failure was to escape far away from the memories that would haunt him. The plague of questions about baseball still came every time he visited home, yet the smiles in response to his presence were shorter lived and less sincere. He needed to find something bigger, more epic to bring home. Andrew lacked any lust for money, but the fame of Hollywood intrigued and enchanted his very soul. If those he cared most about witnessed his face on the movie screen, he believed it would ease their burden. Maybe it could make their lives a little more bearable even for a day or two.

Eric leaned over the crib wishing his friends realized the impact children, and the idea of family can have on the void in one's life. Both of them often spoke of wanting children, but neither of them seemed to speak of fatherhood as a destination or means. Their attitudes were similar in that they seemed to consider children and marriage an inevitable fact of life that came after the achievement of everything else.

Eric had found a very different philosophy. He still wished to open up his own garage, but now he wished to do it because the freedom would be better for his family. Everything was done for the family now. Thinking of how quickly changes were taking place in his life, a far off dreamlike rain set in on his tired mind like the cold sleet of fall.

Finally, Claire walking softly into the room behind him pulled him back down from the clouds. She was wearing a pink silk robe. Small locks of her still wet hair crept out of the towel wrapped around her head, sticking to her temple seductively. She rubbed her pruned hands softly along Eric's forearms to his wrists. He loved the way she smelled after a bath. It was a soft mixture of hot water and lilac.

"What's wrong honey?" She asked, kissing his neck lightly.

"Nothing." He answered almost from another world.

"I haven't heard a peep for half an hour. I was starting to worry." She said moving her cheek to his, so they were both looking down on Nathan's tiny legs kicking in his sleep. Her cheek, still warm, felt comforting against his own.

"I'm fine," he paused, thinking of how important the two people in this very room were to him.

It struck him oddly that so many stumble blindly through life never satisfied. While a fool such as himself some how finds happiness where he wasn't even looking.

"I was just thinking of how rich I am." He said, turning to pull Claire close to him.

She looked up to him, giving a soft purr. He kissed her firmly on her forehead, sliding his rough stained fingers up the sleeves of the robe. She had goose bumps on her arms. They held each other silently in a tight embrace.

"What do you think about lasagna for dinner tonight?" Claire asked guiding Eric back down the hall.

She wrapped her entire hand around his middle and index fingers, pulling him behind her the way a child pulls a parent to an imaginary tea party. He told her it sounded delicious, and his face showed eager hunger while she sat him in his recliner. She kissed him again this time on his lips soft and quick, giving an audible 'mooah'.

He felt his eyes lock on every move of her swaying hips as she moved toward the kitchen. Something about her in that robe was suddenly turning him on. The feeling surprised him. It wasn't like their sex life was dull, but the couple had been together long enough that his love for her was much deeper than the childish lusting it budded from. They used to sit in his room having sex over and over without crawling out of bed for hours, sometimes entire days.

Swallowing hard, he realized how hungry he was. Claire made delicious lasagna. Simply the idea of it made Eric's mouth water. All at once, he realized what was happening, and he couldn't help feeling old. Only an old man could find a woman sexy because of her cooking skills. No it must have been the kiss he thought. Very slowly, the truth came to him. It wasn't that he was past her beautiful looks. There was this more powerful allure to her as a grown and capable woman.

He didn't mean it in an abusive way. It wasn't that he was being a chauvinistic man, trying to use her. She worked as hard as he did all the time, cementing an emotional attachment between them. However, something about sharing the feelings and personal moments of their joint struggles, and the stress of constant burden made him want her physically even more. Rocking gently with his head rested on the chair, he wondered when this phenomenon had begun and why he had never recognized it earlier.

Nearly laughing aloud, he stood up from his chair and walked with purpose into the kitchen. Claire had her back to him pulling a pan from one of the cupboards. Wrapping his arms around her shapely waist, he drew her back to his chest in a firm squeeze, kissing her neck with an open mouth. Before she had time to respond, he untied the belt of her robe allowing it to sag loosely around her tiny frame. She spun around. Her eyes looked up at his in shock.

There was a wild look in his eyes she hadn't seen since the first night in Hawaii. She decided to play ball, but she would be coy about it. As he moved in again, she controlled the kiss by closing the gap between their lips. She gave him a short kiss turning back to her dinner. Just as she expected, he kept trying.

"Alright stop it or your going to starve tonight." she bluffed, hoping her voice wasn't coming across too playful.

"No, if I get too hungry I'll just have to eat you." Eric said kissing her ear.

She giggled and tried to run out of the kitchen. Eric gave chase, catching her and pinning her down on the coach. They both laughed as he tickled her lovingly. He began kissing her first with short pecks, turning the dial up slowly. Finally, she could hold out no longer. She showed her hand, giving a moan and shaking her still wet hair out at the scalp with both hands.

The foreplay heated up, and it wasn't long before they were both naked. His clothes piled on top of her robe in a mound beside the couch. He started out slowly, thrusting deep and covering her with kisses. As the speed increased, Claire lost her inhibitions and grew louder. Things were rapidly approaching climax when Nathan began to crying. Even if they were to let him cry himself back to sleep, a crying baby doesn't have a very positive influence on the libido. Claire pushed Eric off of her and reached for her robe. Eric laid face down on the couch in his own sweat, muttering to himself.

'Maybe not everything about being a father is so terrific' he thought to himself.

August 8th, 2002

The engine roared as the plane lunged before leaving the ground. It was only Eric's second time flying on an airplane. He clutched the arm rest so tightly during take off his hands began to turn purple. The plane was only about half full, and both the window seat and seat across the aisle from him were empty. In the air, he tried desperately to keep his mind off the flight itself, concentrating hard on every heavy breath to prevent hyper-ventilation.

He couldn't sleep, so he tried to read. That didn't work either. All he could think about was the devastating crash he was sure awaited this plane. He prayed continuously to himself, fighting the urges to look out the window. He hadn't expected this type of panic attack. His first flight, for his honeymoon, had gone smoothly. Before boarding the plane to Hawaii, he voiced his fear of flying to Claire, whimpering on the subject for several days. When the morning finally came he was so exhausted from the wedding he fell asleep before take off and slept through the entire flight. Waking up safely on the ground, some how Eric decided he had overcome his fear of flying.

Today, this enormous miscalculation came back to bite him. The night before Claire suggested he take a sleep aid for the flight, but Eric told her not to be silly. The worst possible scenario hadn't seemed nearly this bad at the time.

'Why is my wife always right?' He thought to himself shifting around in his chair obsessively. 'And why can't I ever remember she's always right?' He tugged gently on the short tufts of hair behind his temple over and over.

The stewardess stopped her cart in front of his seat, and he figured she would definitely think he was crazy if he attempted to communicate in his current state of paranoia. He wanted to hide. Regardless of his fears, his pride was still very large, and he was embarrassed to be seen like this.

That is when he saw it. It was sitting silently on the middle shelf of the gray plastic pushcart. It was the Holy Grail; an old friend swooping in when all seemed hopeless.

Eric's eyes locked on. He fought the urge to simply reach out and grab it. The cabin bounced lightly a few times like a diesel truck on a logging road. The plane was hitting a little turbulence. That is what she told him. A little turbulence but nothing big. Eric's nerves were shot. His eyes were glued to the dirty black wheels of the cart, urging it with his mind while it slid carefully forward.

"Can I get you something to drink, sir?"

The stewardess's voice coming over all the buzz of the plane sounded like an angel speaking to a wounded soldier during the most violent battle of a war. Eric smiled what felt like the first smile he could remember. It was a meek, ritual smile. The tiny muscles around his mouth were so foreign to the movements required for smiling it came across looking almost sadistic.

"Jack Daniels, please." He said with urgency.

He used the back of his hand to wipe his lips.

"That will be five dollars, sir. Any soda with that?" The stewardess asked, passing him a napkin and miniature bottle of whisky.

Eric shook his head no. He shifted his weight to his left hip wrestling his billfold from his pocket. He had cashed his check the previous evening, so the wallet was filled with large bills. The smallest note he found was a twenty which he plucked out merrily, passing it on to the woman with one hand and reaching for his prize with the other.

"There's more in it for you if you keep em coming." he said nearly spilling the plastic cup of ice as he snatched it from her unready hand.

The experienced stewardess recognized Eric's dilemma and reached down to grab a second little bottle. Eric beamed his appreciation. The pilot came on the speaker to explain the turbulence. Eric was wrestling the cap off the first little bottle using shaky hands when the pilot explained they would try to find a smoother altitude.

'It's just turbulence huh? No big deal that they are bouncing around like cubes in the blender.' Eric glanced around at the other passengers searching for their reactions to the news. He wondered if this was normal procedure, or perhaps something terrible had happened and the crew simply wanted to keep everyone calm. After all, there was really nothing anyone could do during a plane disaster.

'Stop thinking like that.' He begged. He felt helpless. He went to pour the contents of the bottle into the clear plastic cup then changed his mind. Throwing his head back, he finished it in one swallow, having to suck for the last bit from the small opening. Already fumbling to open the second bottle, the unfamiliar burn of the alcohol seemed to latch itself onto the back of his throat like a back draft. He drank the second bottle down the same way then went back in search of final drops from the first. Next, he tried to rid his mouth of the fiery after taste by sucking on a piece of ice. His mouth tasted foul from the scorched corn, but without realizing it, his concern was slowly melting away.

A few minutes later the Stewardess walked by, and he handed her another twenty. She smiled understandingly, returning shortly with three little bottles of whisky and a cola. Eric poured the soda into the cup, promising God to never instigate another fight with his wife as long as he lived if he made it through this plane trip alive. After finishing the last of the whisky, he lined the discarded bottles in front of him on his tray table and sipped the cola. A warm feeling formed in the pit of his stomach. Pleased with himself, Eric glanced around the plane appearing rather gluttonous. His euphoria didn't last long, and it was only a few minutes before he began feeling sick.

The absence of booze from his life had destroyed all tolerance for drinking. Straight whisky wasn't exactly the best way to remove the training wheels. The front of his skull began pulsating to some ancient archaic drum beat, and it felt like a herd of small animals danced along to the tune inside his stomach. He loosened the seatbelt hoping to find comfort. The nausea only worsened, so he decided to unbutton his jeans. Pushing his flabby stomach out, he raised his fist to his mouth and swallowed a succession of small belches. This temporarily relieved some of the bloating. He wondered how he had possibly drank so much before he was married.

Closing his eyes, he rested his head back on the seat. A few more belches came up as hiccups, and he relieved a little gas out the other end then fell quickly into a vivid nap only to awake as the plane's landing gear touched down. Often the case with daytime dreams, it took him a while to realize where he was and what was real. The stewardess welcomed the passengers to San Francisco over the speakers, helping to jog Eric's groggy mind. He took a quick second to fully wake up, promised himself to take sleeping tablets on the flight home and leaned over to see out the window.

The sky was overcast with rolling gray clouds casting shadows on the tarmac and surrounding terminals. The weather gave the appearance of early evening, although the stewardess mentioned it being one in the afternoon. The sleepy mood set by the low lying fog was broken by all the activities and movements going on outside the plane. The sight of the men in their navy blue coveralls working brought money to Eric's thoughts.

He had made plans with Andrew a long time ago to come visit for Andrew's birthday, but it was the first time he had asked for time off since his wedding. He hated not working, and he was already beginning to worry himself over finances. His constant obsession of working and saving money was one of the biggest reasons Claire insisted he take this trip, even though she worried about her husband under Andrew's persuasive powers in such a city of sin.

It wasn't that they were particularly hard for money. In fact, they were better off than many in Great Pines. Eric made enough money for them to get by on his salary alone, but Claire continued to work part time to keep from going stir crazy sitting in the house all day. Work had simply become Eric's vice. He didn't drink, chew tobacco, smoke, or gamble anymore, so he became addicted to working. The church was constantly speaking of the idol hands or the idol horse. The words went straight to Eric's heart. Whether he realized it or not, a vacation was exactly what he needed, something to break the routine that was building in his life.

Besides, he had always wanted to visit California, and it had been too long since he had last seen Andrew. The plane finished taxiing, and Eric's shoulders tingled with excitement as a series of dinging sounds informed the passengers it was alright to gather their luggage.

At the baggage claim, Andrew met Eric with a firm hug. He attempted to lift him off his feet but gave up after a short struggle.

"At least I know that wife of yours isn't starving you." he joked with wide eyes.

Andrew gave his friend a quick check from head to toe, noticing his hair line had receded even since the wedding. This probably explained why he wore it buzzed very short. It added to the more refined mature look Eric seemed to have working for him. Despite the gut that seemed to protrude further outward every time Andrew saw him, Eric appeared to be in decent health. His strong barrel shaped arms bulged from the white t-shirt he wore. The same block head sat squarely atop his short neck; the tight weathered skin of his face fit as snug as always.

"I'm glad to see you bro," Andrew voiced still taking him all in.

"I was worried you were going to flake out on me."

"Me?" Eric said raising his brows to mock offense to the comment.

"You know I would never back out of celebrating my best friend's birthday."

In truth, he desperately searched for any excuse to not come, and it was Claire's persuasiveness that forced his hand to take the gamble. Andrew didn't need to know this though.

Eric grabbed his large blue duffle bag by the straps, throwing them over his shoulder. The weight in the bag, which was his football equipment bag from high school, was distributed unevenly, causing him to sway left to right as he followed Andrew toward the parking garage.

"Damn, what did you pack in there?" Andrew asked, walking backwards, so he could watch his friend struggle.

"I didn't know what all to bring." Eric huffed, resting the bag on his hip for a moment to catch his breath. "I figured it would be nice, so I packed mostly shorts, flip flops, sun screen and stuff."

"So, why the huge bag?" Andrew pondered, confused.

"Because last night Claire decided I better throw in some rain stuff in case it gets cold, some snorkeling gear she bought incase we go," he did his best impression of a nagging Claire while he spoke, " then threw in her camera, a birthday gift for you, and a big book of different things to do when visiting San Francisco."

"Man, I really missed you." Andrew cried, and they both broke into laughter.

Andrew stopped in front of a beautiful silver BMW coup, pushed a button in his hand, and opened the trunk. He smiled narcissistically at his friend's gaping jaw.

"Here we are." He bragged, jiggling the keys around noisily.

"Where in the HELL did you get this car?" Eric asked setting his bag down on the concrete without taking Andrew or the car out of his skeptical view.

For a moment, he worried the car might be stolen. His better judgment convinced him Andrew would never do such a thing, but it was impossible to guess how far he might go to make the trip memorable. He decided Andrew must have convinced an employer to borrow his car.

"It's mine. You like it?" Andrew asked casually, lifting the heavy bag into the trunk.

Eric looked down both sides of the parking row nervously. The possibility of the vehicle being stolen returned to his worried mind. Andrew laughed seeing his friend's distress.

"I am kidding," he cackled, moving around to the driver's side of the vehicle.

"Monique just bought it. It's something else huh?"

Eric exhaled looking up toward the heavens. He whispered a quick 'thank God' and climbed into the front passenger seat. As he settled in and Andrew started the car, Eric couldn't help but wonder what this trip would have in store for him.

The seat was set close to the glove box, and he instinctively moved his hand under the seat in search of a lever to move it. In Great Pines, Eric rarely had the opportunity to work on luxury foreign cars like BMW, so he was naturally curious about the vehicle. The interior was gorgeous, but he couldn't find the lever for the life of him.

"Oh here its electric," Andrew said leaning over to help him adjust the seat then added, "I really had you freaked out there for a second."

He snorted. Eric pretended to join in. Andrew whipped the car out of the parking spot and guided it toward the exit. When they were out in the open, Eric carefully observed Andrew close up. The baggage claim, lit only by single rows of florescent lights spaced sparingly on a low ceiling, and the dark parking garage had made it impossible for a true perusing of details. Eric noticed that in natural light Andrew seemed tan and healthy. His hair was buzzed short now, a change for the better in Eric's opinion. His complexion was clear, and he even seemed to have put on a little weight, although, he was still quite thin. Perhaps this Monique was truly impacting him for the better.

Andrew merged the car into an endless stream of speeding traffic, skillfully changing lanes with short flicks of the blinkers. Finding a lane he seemed satisfied with, he immediately rolled his window down. The dense air rushing through the open window made Eric realize how fast they were traveling. He glanced down at the speedometer. It hovered over eighty miles per hour. Eric couldn't help feeling nervous, carefully watching the red Honda a few short feet in front of the car's bumper.

"Relax," Andrew shouted to compete with the open window, "I drive this way all the time."

This did little to aid Eric's stomach already twisted from the whiskey. It was typical Andrew logic. Most people engaged in dangerous activities realize it is only a matter of time before their luck runs out. Andrew always figured anything he could live through once must be safe to continue doing as habit. Eric adjusted his seatbelt, wondering how many wrecks happened on this freeway everyday. He figured the body shops in the area must love all the needless tailgating. Always enough work that way. Andrew, noticing his friend's tension, eased off the gas slightly.

"How's the family?" He asked leaning over to be heard.

"Good. Claire's becoming a really great cook and still working part time at the dentist office. And you should see Nathan. He is growing up so fast. You would barely recognize him."

From Andrew's expression, Eric could tell he was trying to fill in some blanks.

"Why don't you roll up the window?" He yelled.

Andrew nodded.

"Sorry about that." He said when the car suddenly became almost vacuum like.

Eric opened his mouth wide trying to free his ears from the new pressure.

"I try to keep the window down as often as I can. The weather is just so nice. I want to take every advantage of it I can."

He changed his tone before continuing.

"I think the fresh air rushing all that oxygen at a person will make me live longer too."

He stopped to contemplate his hypothesis for a moment, a puzzled expression taking over his face.

"Anyways, you were saying something about Nathan?" he asked returning his attention to Eric. Eric filled him in on everything back home, connecting different subjects and stories with the statement, 'I guess not much else has changed.'

Although, everything he spoke of didn't seem interesting or even noticeable to him, Andrew seemed thoroughly intrigued by all happenings, asked a lot of questions, and wanted all the details. Twenty minutes later, they arrived at a large apartment complex, and Andrew pushed a garage door opener clipped to the driver's visor to open the sliding gate. He parked the car in a numbered spot under a wooden canopy and led Eric toward one of three identical white buildings that sat all in a row. The building's only other color was brown used sparingly on the window trims and the rain gutters that made a border around the flat roof.

Andrew's apartment was on the top floor which was reached by climbing up three stories of granite slab stairs in the corner of the building. At the top of the stairwell, Andrew held the door open for Eric who was lagging behind due to his ridiculous luggage. Eric couldn't seem to find a logical way to carry the bag up the narrow stairs. Either the bag or his body kept striking the metal hand rail that kept him from taking a terrible tumble, so he ended up dragging his bag up the final flight.

Upon entering the hallway, his nose was overcome by a strong unfamiliar odor. It smelt spicy, but there was a sour hint to it that caused his eyes to water. He suspected the scent was culinary, but the smell seemed to be seeped right into the walls. He thought it smelt afoul, but Andrew didn't seem bothered by the smell, leading Eric to conclude the pungent aroma must be common.

Andrew stopped at the fourth door on the left. He grabbed the handle turning his body to face back toward Eric. He folded at the waste with his outstretched hand still on the door knob laughing at Eric's expression.

"That my friend is Indian food." He said opening the door.

"And I don't mean Chippewa Cree."

Eric quickened his steps and hurried into the doorway, holding his breath.

The apartment was small, with a miniature kitchen on the immediate left of the entrance. The kitchen was maybe five feet wide and separated from the living room by a thin wall of cabinets and a counter with a window making it available for use from either room. Aside from the kitchen, which was tiled, the rest of the apartment was floored with dull grey carpeting.

The living room was small, yet the heavily decorated walls made it feel even smaller. The walls were covered with photographs of obscene partying and posters featuring scantily clad, large breasted women suggesting that drinking a particular brand of beer would cause them to fall head over heels for anyone. The wall directly across from where Eric stood had a sliding glass door that opened onto a small balcony, which upon further inspection appeared shoddy and unsafe. There was a standing lamp in the far corner of the room behind a two foot wooden shelf that supported an antique television set. The lamp was the only light fixture in the room, but the shades of the glass door were half open to give the room more visibility from the cloud blotted sun.

There was a worn out card table set up directly under the window into the kitchen with an aluminum folding chair on either side. A long black couch lined the right hand wall of the living room opposite the television set, and in the corner there was a maroon recliner. The extreme length of the couch threw off the desired placement of the recliner which would fit naturally in the corner beside the armrest. This would block off access to the hallway, however, so the recliner sat slightly in front of the couch at an angle. Clearly, there was too much furniture for such a small room. The chair couldn't possibly fully recline without being pulled out into the middle of the room, where it would block two seats on the couch.

The couch was occupied by a black man who was fast asleep. He was tall, and the peculiar couch was well designed for his long limbs which took up every last inch. His hair was cut short and well groomed; his face was clean shaven. He slept in athletic shorts and a pair of sneakers. The shoes were the biggest Eric had ever seen.

"The couch is where you'll sleep. This lazy asshole has his own room." Andrew called out intentionally trying to wake up the man, who was apparently his roommate.

The man opened one blood shot eye to see who disturbed his peace then rolled over a few times contemplating whether or not to return to his slumber. Andrew foiled his plan by making introductions.

"Eric this is my roommate Marcus. Marcus this is my best friend from back home." He beamed with pride.

Marcus labored to a seated position. His breathing was heavy, and he appeared wore out. He made no effort to stand up or even look in Eric's direction. He put out his long arm in silence.

"Nice to meet you." Eric said, shaking his hand.

"Coo." was the only reply Marcus gave, completely dropping the l and replacing it with emphasis on the vowels. Eric was surprised to find Marcus appeared much younger sitting up than he had while sleeping. His face and body suggested he was close to thirty, but he had youthful eyes that told a much different story.

"The bathroom is right here next to our bedroom." Andrew said continuing on with the tour.

"There is only one so be cool on duke etiquette."

He quickly generalized a few problems with the toilet and shower before leading Eric into the bedroom. It was the size of a shoe box. The room's limited volume was filled with a small oak dresser, a queen sized bed, and a brown work desk with an aluminum chair similar to the two in the living room. There was little room left over for the two of them to both fit. Eric wondered how anyone could possibly move around in here. On one wall, there were two full length mirrors that could be slid either direction to access the closet. He pictured Andrew and his girlfriend both trying to get dressed in the morning. The tiny space between the dresser and the end of the bed was the only way to use the mirror or closet, and Eric grew claustrophobic just thinking about his heavy frame trying to lodge in such tight quarters on a daily basis.

"Real mansion you got here." he said smugly.

"Marcus's room is even smaller if you can believe that." Andrew said with a smile. Oddly, Eric detected a certain degree of pride in his voice. Eric glanced quickly to his friend. He stood tall with his head held high.

"How come you didn't tell me your roommate was a huge..." He reached the first syllable of an all too familiar word before Andrew's eyes silenced him.

"Black dude?" Andrew quickly finished for him.

"You never asked." Andrew said through tight lips.

"And it had no relevance."

Eric felt ashamed, but he was taken aback at the same time.

'I'm not even racist,' he thought. There were merely very few blacks back home, and he used the word out of common habit. He didn't mean anything by it. Besides, it wasn't like he'd never heard Andrew use the same phrase or worse dozens of times. It wasn't that he was racist, or at least he never considered himself to be. The more he thought about it the more aware he became of his ignorance. He started to mumble an apology, but Andrew stopped him.

"Don't worry. You didn't know. Just don't do it again." He said flatly.

A short half smile was the only consolation he gave. Clearly, there was something sore there, but Eric was hardly about to poke. He looked around the room in a desperate attempt to end the uncomfortable tension between them, but the plain room offered little solace. Then he noticed above the dresser there were two drawings hung up by gold thumb tacks. The drawings were the only decoration on the otherwise hideously, dingy, whitewashed walls which had yellowed and flaked over the years. He squinted to see them more clearly.

The drawings were done in pencil on plain white paper. The first one was of a unicorn prancing beneath what he suspected to be a rainbow, but he was too far away to be sure. The second one was a fairy wearing a tiara. He moved up to the dresser without taking his eyes off the wall. The sketches were done very lightly, giving him a perfect excuse to avoid Andrew's eyes and his own embarrassment. Upon closer inspection, he was impressed by how well detailed the drawings were. There was also something extremely sad in each of them that came across as very unique.

"Pretty good huh? Monique is really starting to get into drawing. She does mostly fantasy stuff, but she can do people's faces too." Andrew boasted with pride.

The usual cordiality had returned to his voice.

"She quit partying completely about six months ago, and art really helps her stay focused."

"I believe it. Hobbies can really help people stay busy. These are amazing. She should really pursue it further. She could probably make some money."

"That's what I said." Andrew agreed with enthusiasm. "I am trying to convince her to take some art classes at the community college. It's just that her schedule is already so busy. And she loves to draw so much I'd hate to see it become something stressful."

Eric saw an opening to ask Andrew how things were going for him, but before he could speak the words, a bellowing voice from the living room interjected.

"Yo Drew, yo agent guy called your cell wile you was gone. Said he mite a got work, an you should call him ASAP." The voice called lazily, destroying the entire English language in two sentences.

An ecstatic look came over Andrew's face, and he rushed out of the room. Eric was left alone in the room trying to decode Marcus's message. All the excitement pleased him, but he was still embarrassed about his derogative comment, and he wanted to make amends for it. He decided the best approach was to earn Marcus's friendship. He was still scratching his head on the subject when Andrew returned to the doorway. He held a cell phone in his hand and paced the three or four step hallway back and forth anxiously, muttering to himself. Eric couldn't hear his exact words, but he gathered that he was planning out his conversation. Eric couldn't handle being kept in the dark.

"You have an agent?" He asked, leaning against the doorway with his arms folded across his chest.

"Sort of." was the only reply he received as Andrew brought the phone up to his ear.

Eric felt more confused then before and decided he should wait for Andrew to explain when he was ready. It was a lot to ask of Eric. He was very nosey, and something that made Andrew this noticeably concerned had to be interesting. Andrew ducked into the bathroom and closed the door behind him. Eric made his way down the hallway, pausing momentarily near outside the door. The muffled voice inside hid little excitement, but he couldn't insight from the short answers given without hearing the voice on the other end.

He walked to the recliner purposefully, avoiding eye contact with Marcus, who still lay prone on the sofa. He worried that some how Marcus overheard his comments or maybe he could read the guilt written on his face. Either way, Eric was fearful. He sat down and immediately turned his attention to the television.

The room's poor lighting and musty air only added to his weary feelings. Eric was unfamiliar with the program on the screen, and he wished it were something he knew about, preferably something involving sports. Sports and cars always made great ice breakers. The tension continued to knot the pit of his stomach until Marcus began surfing the channels.

Eric leaned forward ever so slightly in his chair, trying to anticipate what the next selection would be. He felt like a contestant on one of those game shows where the fate of all his prize money rests on the spin of a giant colored wheel. Marcus stopped on a popular vindicated sitcom, and Eric glanced toward his hand holding the remote waiting to see if the decision would stand. Eric tried to persuade him by laughing slightly at one of the jokes. The laugh came out as something between a snort and a cough, and Eric regretted committing so early.

The long fingers scanned on. It became a game of chess for several minutes. Finally, Eric knew he had to say something soon or his efforts would be futile and transparent. Luckily, Marcus made it easy for him by punching in the numbers for ESPN and dropping the remote when a baseball game came on. Eric smiled. Now it was only a matter of moments before something worth pumping testosterone about would happen. Then his opponent pulled another fast move on him by rolling back over, pushing his face into the corner of the couch.

'He will do anything to avoid talking to the racist redneck.' Eric thought to himself. Feeling defeated for the time being, he turned back to the game. It was hardly a game. The Orioles were pounding on the A's 7-0.

'Hard to blame a guy for choosing sleep over this one,' Eric figured putting his guard down and leaning back into the big chair.

There was a loud whooping scream from the hall, and he heard the bathroom door open.

"Well boys. I told you not to doubt me when I said my autograph would be worth more than dirt someday." Andrew cried entering the room with a visible hop in his step.

Eric sat forward again nearly coming up to a standing position but deciding against it at the last second. Marcus stirred as well, arching himself up with his arms and squinted back over his shoulder.

"Who was that? What did he say?" Eric stammered impatiently.

"That was this buddy of mine who has a few connections in high places," Andrew grinned.

The light shining in from the window hit him directly making him the solitary bright object in the room.

"He had me give him some audition tapes and stuff a couple weeks back, and he found me two auditions last weekend." Andrew exclaimed, rubbing his hands together.

He took a short breath in trying to pause for effect, but he was too excited.

"Well, it turns out someone liked me a lot, so I am going to be starring in a pilot for a new TV program, and I am going to be modeling for a designer show next month."

He arched his head back and shouted with excitement, clapping his hands. Then, turning to the thin wall that separated him from the kitchen, he drummed off a little tune with his knuckles. Eric was excited too. He always knew Andrew would be a big star, and he thanked the Lord silently for putting things into motion. He wanted to call home and tell Claire, his parents, and everyone else. Andrew was going to put their small town on the map. Eric was riding the wave right there with him.

"We gotta celebrate." Andrew realized.

He turned back to Marcus and Eric with bright eyes. Eric hadn't seen that look in a long time. It was a far away look. It was a look of immortal youth, and that look had the power to spread infectious euphoria to anyone it fell upon. Eric felt a swelling of admiration as Andrew smiled that famous smile.

"I am going to go buy up at the liquor store around the corner. What are you boys drinking?"

AUGUST 9TH, 2002

It was through a sheer, piercing pain that Eric heard the distant and yet familiar sound of his cell phone. The popular jingle he had chosen for a ringtone suddenly didn't seem so clever. He rolled his head over slowly so that he was facing straight upward. With the gentle care an emergency response team might give the victim of a terrible accident, he lifted his head at the neck and tried to see through one eye. His vision danced sporadically, giving the affect of looking out the porthole on a ship at sea during a rough storm. It took him a moment to familiarize himself with his surroundings. The jingle was starting over, yet he still had no idea where the noise came from. He was lying beside the card table in the living room with an Oakland Raiders beach towel covering his lower half.

The ringing ceased. Eric tossed the towel aside and searched his pockets, figuring it was Claire calling to check on him. He remembered speaking with her early in the evening, but he couldn't remember whether or not he had spoken with her again before ending up in his present location. His stomach churned and it felt as though subway trains had been using his head as a tunnel all night.

The phone was discovered lying on the floor behind him. He checked the number on the missed calls screen. The call was not from Claire. It was from his parents. He decided whatever it was it could wait.

Checking the time on his phone, he debated on whether or not he should call Claire. It was still early, and he was in no shape to be reassuring her confidence. He crawled like a wounded man across the room to the couch. The spongy cushions were a big step up from the floor, and he was asleep within a matter of seconds. The night before had been full of laughter, joy, and a wake of empty beer cans and shot glasses. Eric fell into a deep sleep, dreaming sedate, blank dreams.

It was after ten when he woke to the sound of voices in the kitchen. From the sound of it, Andrew and Monique were trying to be discreet by whispering, but Monique seemed to be struggling to keep her voice down. Every time she spoke, her words grew closer and closer to an everyday volume, only with higher pitch from trying to whisper. Eric didn't want to be rude, but given his location it was hard not to eaves drop. They were arguing about the previous night. Monique seemed very upset about Andrew's behavior when the boys came home early that morning. Andrew's defense was that he would clean the house.

"It's not that. You were completely blacked out when you came home last night. You know how worried I get and you didn't even call." She fired on the verge of tears.

"I told you I am sorry. It was a final hurrah. I was celebrating my birthday with my best friend who I haven't seen in a long time." Andrew whispered calmly.

"Every time you say it's the last time. Remember about a month ago when I had to bail Marcus and you out of jail that morning, or the whole incident with that sleazy Teresa. I told you I can't do this anymore. If you want to drink and party, then do it. But don't expect me to stick around."

"Baby, I understand. I already told you this was a one time thing. Besides, you have nothing to be upset about. Nothing even happened last night." Andrew replied.

"Who drove you guys home last night?" Monique asked, stopping him before he could add something cute or funny the way he always did.

"Eric did. He only had a few." Andrew answered without missing a beat.

This of course was news to Eric. He didn't remember driving, but he definitely remembered having more than a few. Up until that moment, he thought Monique must have come to pick them up. He tried to recall the trip home, but nothing could be found in his jumbled soup of a brain. He started to imagine Monique's words coming from his wife's voice. He couldn't even picture how much trouble he would be in if she found out he was drinking and driving. It would be far worse if he came home with an out of state DUI.

He said a silent prayer, laying his head back down on the pillow. They continued to argue, but Eric was no longer paying attention. He was too busy envisioning all the worst case scenarios that could have happened the previous night. It seemed like a great night of drinking.

He had been having a lot of fun as far as he could recall. However, the fact that he might have driven them home on a night he couldn't remember going home was frightening. Going out with the boys for a couple of laughs is never worth going through the whole DUI nightmare again. Then again, a DUI is small potatoes compared with wrecking the vehicle and having anyone injured or killed. He realized Andrew, and most of his friends for that matter, could never see it that way. They never stressed about the negative outcomes because they viewed them as such small possibilities. It was the same reason that, despite all the information and statistics on drinking and driving casualties, people continued to get in their car smashed, night after night, and try to drive home.

Eric knew exactly how Claire would react. She would yell and scream for a while, yet that would be the easy part. It would be the days after the yelling when she was silent that would be hardest to endure. She would look at him with a face of disappointment and not say a word. This, of course, would allow it to fester and boil under Eric's skin. She knew it was the best way to make the guilt really sink in and last, and she had perfected the techniques. Eric decided he had to hide it from her at least until he could piece together what really happened, but first, he had to tend to his poor bladder.

He stood up and stumbled his way toward the bathroom. His motor skills were still dull, and his head pulsed with pain when he stood up as all the blood seemed to rush toward his feet. He leaned one arm on the wall to prevent swaying and tried to aim carefully with his other hand. He still ended up getting piss all over the toilet and spraying some on the floor. After cleaning it up best he could, he returned to the living room, sat down on the couch, and tried to devise a plan of action. His achy body and pounding head filled him with feelings of regret. He promised himself he would never drink again.

"Morning sunshine, how'd you sleep?" Andrew asked with a chipper tone, standing in the small entrance way between the kitchen and the living room.

Eric couldn't believe it. Andrew looked showered and well groomed. His face and eyes showed no signs of drinking. He was wearing a pair of tight jeans and a bright yellow t-shirt that hurt Eric's sensitive eyes. Eric couldn't help thinking Andrew was obviously well-seasoned in the arts of drinking.

"I am going to run over to the store and grab some grub for us. What kinda donuts do you like?"

"I don't care. I would eat leather right now," Eric groaned, catching a whiff of his own foul odor.

"What I really need is a big tall jug of orange juice."

Monique stepped out of the kitchen. She definitely didn't share Andrew's smiling exterior. Her arms were crossed defensively and she looked tired. She stopped only long enough to say a short good morning to Eric before marching to the bedroom. She didn't slam the door behind her, but she closed it hard all the same. Andrew winced slightly at the sound.

"Yea some oj would really hit the spot this morning." He said regaining his poise with a big smile.

"Do you want me to come with you?" Eric offered through bloodshot eyes.

"No, the bakery is right around the corner. I'll be back in five minutes." He said grabbing his keys off the kitchen counter. "Unless you want to go pick stuff out?"

"No, it's alright I think I am gonna catch a shower real quick. I have to sound somewhat sober when I call Claire. My parents called me early this morning for some reason too. I didn't answer it, but I am sure they had some reason to call that early. So I can make some phone calls while you're gone."

"That's weird. I had two missed calls early this morning from back home too. I didn't recognize the first number but the second one was from your dad's cell, and I almost forgot until you said that. You had better give him a call."

After Andrew closed the door behind him, Eric took a moment to enjoy the calm silence of the morning. He loved to take a few minutes to organize his thoughts when he woke up at home, but with all the commotion going on this morning along with the hang over from hell he hadn't been able to really take a few deep breaths. He felt like garbage. His throat was dry. His body felt like he had been in a car accident the night before. Luckily, that was not the case. He told himself again to remember the way he felt at that very moment. It could be a valuable tool the next time he debated drinking. He started thinking about the offhand remark Andrew made about the unknown number.

He lumbered into the kitchen, found one of the few clean glasses in the bare cupboards, filled it from the faucet and drank the entire glass in one drink. Swallowing hard a few times, he decided he better call his parents first. He dialed the number, but he only got the answering machine. He brought up his house number, but he didn't push send. His own smell only reminded him of how hung over he was, so he jumped in the shower, hoping it would some how improve his abilities to reason.

Knowing Claire couldn't possibly smell the alcohol on him over the phone didn't stop him from spraying cologne and brushing his teeth all the same. He figured it was better to cover all his bases just in case. Coming out of the bathroom, he was greeted by the sweet, greasy smell of fresh donuts. It was a smell from his youth, reminding him of mornings growing up when one of the parents or coaches would buy donuts after a baseball or football game.

Andrew had everything out on the old card table. He was sitting in the recliner watching TV and smacking his lips on a bite of maple bar. Grabbing a napkin from the large stack beside the box, Eric found a glazed donut to fit his fancy. There were also some small paper cups and a plastic jug of orange juice. Eric filled his cup three times before finishing his donut.

There were close to a dozen donuts left, so Eric decided it wouldn't hurt if he had another one. This time he wanted something a little more interesting. His selection was one with jelly filling and rainbow sprinkles. On his first bite, some of the jelly dripped down onto his chin. He wiped it away with one of the napkins. When he went to discard the napkin onto the far side of the table he noticed the small red light on his phone was flashing. He grabbed it off the table, drinking down another shot of orange juice with his free hand.

The light meant he had a voice-mail. There were no new missed calls which meant it was probably left by his parents that morning, and he hadn't noticed it earlier. He called the number for his voice-mailbox, waited through the instructions, and pressed one when told with a sticky finger. He listened nonchalantly as his father's rough voice began to speak. He picked up his donut for another bite, but froze in mid movement toward his mouth as his father's words fell hard on his ear. One word in particular hit him like a rock: the word dead. He dropped the donut, and stood up desperate to clear his lungs. Shock was causing his throat to feel as though it might swell shut.

Could his father be playing a nasty joke? No, he could tell from the compassion in his voice this was serious. Maybe his hang over had caused him to hear the message wrong. He pushed a button on the phone to replay the message just in case, but already he knew he heard everything correctly. Time seemed to freeze. The room started going into a very slow spin. Trying to decide his course of action, he made the mistake of looking toward the recliner. Andrew had an inquisitive look on his face, and upon catching Eric's panicking eyes, he sat forward with his jaw gaping.

"What is it?" he asked quietly, trying not to interrupt.

His attention was glued on Eric, impatient from the worry he read in his friend's expression and body language. Eric couldn't respond. The news was unthinkable. He felt scared. Something beyond mere worry. His emotions were everywhere, and the message was vague. There were many questions he couldn't answer. Questions that Andrew would want answered. How could he possibly soften the blow when he knew so little? Andrew sat wiping his hands nervously on the napkin he had lying in his lap. A half eaten donut balanced delicately on his other thigh. Eric opened his mouth to speak. Individual grains of sand could be counted as they tumbled gently from an hourglass somewhere. As he opened his mouth and began carefully piecing his words one to the next, Monique came around the corner.

She entered the room with anger flushing her face a crimson shade of red. Their words struck the air simultaneously at different pitches like synchronized dancers on two different pages. Only Eric's words, however, reached Andrew's ears. He shot up in a flash. The maple bar fell, frosting side down, on the carpet. He didn't ask a single question. He stared at Eric with a confused look for a moment. Then his eyebrows narrowed down with anger. He brought a closed hand up to his mouth and looked away for a moment. He spoke evenly. Eric shook his head not knowing the answer, not knowing any answers.

Eric glanced at Monique. She stood silently beside the end of the couch. The anger on her face had been replaced with a lost sorrow. The crimson tint had gone pale. Andrew asked another question then a third. Finally, he fell silent knowing that the facts would come in due time.

"We really don't know the details. Let me call Claire before we start to worry too much." Eric tried.

For a moment, Andrew's anger cracked and his face appeared deeply hurt. All at once, he shot from the room without a word. Monique looked at Eric, yet she didn't speak a word. They stood silently, sharing the dead air of the room. After a moment, Andrew's voice could be heard from the bedroom. Similar to the day before, Eric could hear the short brief sentences on this end of the conversation. He silently prayed for good news, but then there was a loud 'fuck' screamed. It shook Eric to his very foundation and seemed to rattle around inside his soul etching itself forever into his memory. The scream was followed immediately by the sound of something striking the wall very hard. Monique disappeared toward the closed door. Eric sat down on the floor and bowed his head, listening to the continued destruction a few feet away.

He longed to hold his wife and family. He prayed none of this was real. Tears rolled freely down his face onto the carpet below. There was a loud crack he recognized to be Andrew punching a hole in the bedroom door. The sound sickened him because it meant this was really happening. It was true. Shane was in jail. Someone had been killed and Shane was directly linked to the death. He might even stand accused of murder.

August 18th, 2002

The dashed yellow lines between the lanes seemed to blur together as the Mustang charged across the sage covered plains. Distant mountains surrounded the wide valley on all sides and the sound of the custom exhaust broke the calm silence of every new territory it entered. Darin sat behind the wheel, completely passive behind his dark sunglasses. His face was pale. He struggled to maintain his focus, but his mind wondered.

Going out of town on business for a few days hadn't provided the break he was hoping for. He glanced over again at the folded newspaper lying on seat beside him. It was the first time since the incident there was nothing written about Shane on the front page. Not that this was a big surprise. It wasn't everyday something like this happened in Great Pines. The governor had to be pleased that at least the suspect was a Native. That sure made things a little easier. Being born into a membership of the county's elite, Darin knew well the whole deal could easily turn into a witch trial.

It all looked too simple on paper. A strung out Indian carrying a heavy record of prior trouble kills a stand up white youth whose best friend was the sole witness. The prosecutors would play the angle that the boy was a good kid and got mixed up with the wrong crowd. Money would flood into an anti-drug campaign and race relations would hit the skids.

Darin and Shane might have had their differences over the years, but he knew Shane was not the kind of person who could commit murder. He had been following the case religiously. It was beginning to have negative effects on his career, yet he didn't care. Having a friend in trouble can really clear one's perspective. Today was the longest he had gone without hearing any new updates on the case. It was alarming, and he pushed the gas pedal a little bit further toward the floor. The engine opened up as the speedometer climbed smoothly. It was the sort of task the car was made for.

A classic 1968 muscle machine, the car was cherry red, and it was a thing to be admired. Over the past eighteen months, Darin had fully customized and restored the entire car piece by piece. Eric performed the majority of the labor but cost was not an issue for Darin. It had always been his dream to drive this car. Like so many dreams of achievement, however, he never felt fulfilled or satisfied when he finally accomplished it.

In fact, everything he had ever held true about wealth was turning out wrong. He felt like a puzzle with key pieces missing. The more he bought to fill the holes, the emptier he felt. It was a continuing cycle. Shane's problems snapped the regression. Darin felt purpose again in his life. He thought about ways to help constantly. It helped his personal life as well.

Their mutual concerns for Shane bridged the gap growing between Elizabeth and him. He was able to see things from her point of view for the first time in years. It saddened him that something so terrible had to happen to wake him from his selfish funk, but his relationship was improving. They were a team again, striving toward the same goal. He picked up the phone to call her for the third time, but she still didn't answer. He wondered where she could be.

He wanted to hear her voice, wanted to know if anything new had been discovered. He couldn't stand not knowing everything. This constant obsessing had to stop. The trial wouldn't start for at least another five or six months.

Trial. The word made him think of the life and death consequences his friend faced. He couldn't believe it had come to this. It goes to show how terrible drugs really are. In the blink of an eye, they can steal life away and leave other lives shattered forever. Darin lifted his sunglasses to rub his eyes for a moment, trying to estimate how much longer it would take him to reach home. For the tenth time that day, he began going over the case again in his head.

According to Shane's story, he had been staying out at the Gardapee's trailer for a couple days. The brothers had left on Thursday evening to drive to the reservation, and they were supposed to return on Saturday afternoon. The trailer was set on a run down lot of about three acres some five miles out of town. It was accessible from a dirt road off of Highway 9. There were several other homes in the area, but the only other building on that turnoff was a salvage yard about a quarter of a mile east of the trailer. The grass in the field was tall and a solitary cluster of pine trees made the trailer hardly visible from the highway. It was as inconspicuous as it was cheap, which probably attracted its owners. Shane had no money and no car, so he stayed out at the trailer alone.

At the time of his arrest, he tested positive for methamphetamines which he admitted to using for at least a couple days leading up to the incident. He was unable to state any sort of time frame for when the two boys arrived, but the police believed it to be just after one a.m. on Saturday morning. The boys were twenty-one year old, Justin Haines, and nineteen year old Sean Owens. Shane had never met either of them, yet for some reason they would cross paths on that fateful night and a small town would lose its innocence forever.

Haines told investigators he had been robbed of money and personal items by the Gardapee brothers the previous week, and the boys were only coming to retrieve his things. They parked Sean's silver 1990 Ford Ranger in the tall grass about three hundred yards behind the residence. The boys entered the trailer through the only door, which accessed the kitchen to the right and a small living room to the left. This is where the facts run cold.

The only certainty is the two young men entered believing the trailer to be vacant. Instead, they found a man who was deep into a drug binge and hadn't slept for days. The paranoia had surely set in, and it was a recipe for disaster.

Originally, Shane claimed that he heard a noise from the bedroom where he was watching TV and was then attacked by two men wearing ski masks. In the days that followed, he changed his mind, saying he came out to the living room expecting to meet his friends but instead found the two men snooping around in the dark. He said one of them carried a black bag in his hands and the other was digging through a cabinet. He told them to leave and then was rushed by one of the men. Haines version disputes this and claims they were simply trying to adjust their eyes to the dark when Shane attacked out of nowhere. He claims he was dazed and knocked to the floor by a hard blow to the side of the head. It took him a moment to climb back to his feet, but he could hear Owens and the unseen attacker fighting in the kitchen. He said in the darkness he made out his friend being pinned to the floor by the other man. He tried to wrestle him free, but Shane was too strong.

Haines told investigators in the struggle that followed Owens was absent leaving him to believe his friend had fled the trailer. Shane stated that while being assaulted by the two men he was able to grab a small steak knife from the kitchen sink. He said while trying to defend himself he swung the knife around wildly, but he doesn't remember feeling it hit flesh. He remembered everything as a blur. It wasn't until the silhouette of one of the trespassers fleeing outside caught his eye that he realized the other one was injured. Turning on the light, Shane claimed he found the young boy's body, slumped in a pool of blood, motionless from a knife wound to the throat.

Shane told police that he didn't check for a pulse because he was too frightened. The same reason he immediately left the scene without calling 911. Haines claims he saw the knife gleaming in the natural light of the room, so he ran assuming his friend had already done the same. He exited the house and entered the adjacent field without even looking around for the truck. He said he ran for the main road but stayed off it for fear the Gardapees, one of whom he thought was the unidentified wielder of the knife, might come searching in a vehicle.

It wasn't until late Saturday morning that Haines finally made it home. He changed clothes and showered immediately, but he had a large contusion along his left eye and temple. He decided it was best to lay low. It wasn't until early evening that he tried to contact Sean. Owens didn't answer his cell phone. Sean's parents were unaware the two were together that morning, so it wasn't until one of the Gardapees came home to find the body that the police were contacted late that night. Shane was arrested at his mom's apartment Sunday afternoon.

On paper, the prosecutions case was almost too perfect. There were no ski masks found. The suspect clearly fit the stereotype of vagrant junkie. He fled the scene leaving the murder weapon. He was a Native. Most importantly, when he was brought in he had no clear signs of injury. He didn't even have a bruise. This contradicted his story about being attacked first.

Darin figured the prosecutions biggest problem would be getting around the fact that the boys were trespassing. Darin figured a strong defense lawyer could at least work that into a decent manslaughter deal. Unfortunately, Shane couldn't afford any lawyer. He would probably be appointed a very young, green public defender. Likely, this would be a member of the church, someone who would have a hard time truly believing in his client's case. Darin pressed his parents to help provide a lawyer, but they refused, scared their reputation might be smeared by associating with the case.

Besides, Sean Owens came from a rather prestigious family. His parents were members of the country club. His uncle was a former member of the city council. It didn't matter that young Sean had barely graduated high school or been arrested twice for criminal mischief. The papers never mentioned what property it was the boys were searching for that faithful night, but Darin was sure it was drugs or money involved with drugs. Darin was sure Owens wasn't the angel that everyone was making him out to be. Good kids didn't go looking for the Garapee brothers. Good kids shouldn't even know those boys.

Darin squeezed the steering wheel a little bit harder, causing sweat to form along his palm. Suddenly, he hated the invisible patricians that had benefited him for so long. He decided right then and there he would sell off everything he owned to help Shane afford a proper defense. It was the right thing to do, he told himself. What had happened was a terrible tragedy, but who's to say Shane's story wasn't accurate. A faint, sense of hope started to form in Darin's mind. He remembered the words Eric told him the day he returned from his trip. The end of the conversation seemed much more relevant all of a sudden.

They had been discussing the case, and both men were emotionally drained. Darin went into a wildfire rampage blaming the drugs, the Gardapee brothers, Shane's reckless attitude, even the deceased for not being more prepared for criminal behavior. What Eric responded with was what seemed, at the time, to be his usual predestined, religious monologue. He explained that Shane was lost. Life has many paths some righteous and some not, but many people refuse to take any road at all. Eric felt Shane was one of these men, so his soul was forced to wonder blindly because unlike men, souls could not remain stationary.

It wasn't fate or God that put the happenings of that faithful night into action. On the contrary, it was many tiny examples of free will that led to such a bizarre turn of events according to Eric. However, Shane and more than likely both of the boys were addicted to drugs beyond their own control, making it impossible for their free will to be unhindered by this unnatural influence.

Darin argued that these two things contradicted each other. He couldn't understand how free will could possibly coexist with a lack of it. Then Eric said something very quietly. Darin pictured the solemn look on his friends face when he had spoke, "then you have never been addicted to something."

Starting to turn red, Darin had maintained that someone of strong will could overcome addiction. Addiction was an excuse, a crutch. Eric had agreed but added that it was impossible to overcome addiction until one realizes there is an addiction. Again, Darin disagreed. Eric finished by stating that in his understanding of God, man had free will, but he gained this and other freedoms at a price. Included in this price were a mortal life, jealousy, greed, ego, depression and many other things which weren't relevant to the conversation. He said that because of free will every living thing instinctively did what was in its own best interest. Of course, what is best for one man is not necessarily best for another, leading to a spring like oscillation between happiness and misery. This explained why everyone goes through both ups and downs.

Darin had never heard anything like it. He did not believe in God just the same as he did not believe in ghosts or anything else that couldn't be proven to him, yet this theory seemed logical from a faith based standpoint. He asked if this was the teachings of the Mormon Church. Eric answered no, saying he reached this spiritual belief through his own studying. He said there was a great deal of the Church's teaching that he agreed with, but it was the differences between the teachings he grew up with and the teachings his family now followed that led him to seek his own truths. Organized religion was fine, but it was just too definite. There was black or white with no gray. This meant it became difficult to use in gray areas like Shane's current situation.

Darin still didn't understand how all this applied to Shane or related to addiction. Eric carefully tried to articulate by using his earlier spring example, claiming that sometimes it takes something terrible to stretch a spring that was motionless.

Darin's temper boiled. He felt stupid for not seeing through the guise earlier. This was another 'see the good in every bad' speech. He stood up to leave, trying hard to refrain from taking his anger out on his good friend.

At the door, he turned only long enough to ask why it was this God fellow always seemed to choose the minorities, the poor, or someone already up to his eyeballs in hardships like Shane when he wanted to make man suffer. Why couldn't it ever be the beautiful, the powerful, or the rich? He slammed the door behind him before having a chance to hear Eric's answer. Eric hung his head, whispering to himself with a heavy sigh, "Because they are often the only ones strong enough to survive and honestly learn from such hardship."

August 27th, 2002

Marcus could have easily been mistaken for a zombie sitting motionless on the couch watching the television through bloodshot eyes. The smoky haze of the room glimmered in the brilliant horizontal beams of the late afternoon sun shining through the open curtains of the balcony's glass doors. A fly buzzing around the room caught his attention. He tried to follow it as it approached his position in a spiraling flight path. He swatted with the back of his hand hoping to discourage the insect from having any ideas of landing on him. It was hot enough already, and he didn't need the added annoyance.

Late August in northern California can be brutal without air conditioning. Living on the top floor of a populated apartment building didn't make matters any more enjoyable. The sun beat down hard on the building all day, and all the heat rose to sit dormant and grow stale in their apartment. It became a miserable, arid hell.

The fly circled around and around sensing Marcus's salty sweat. Finally, it seemed to take the hint after a few close swats and landed on the television screen to rub his legs together in preparation of a new plan. The truce seemed fair to Marcus, and he returned his attention to the program. He was tired, but the heat made it too uncomfortable to fall asleep, so he sat there brewing in discomfort.

Then, the door swung open startling him from his stupor. Andrew entered the apartment with the same faraway look he'd had for the past two weeks. He closed the door behind him and went directly for the fridge. Marcus could hear his roommate moving some things around, knowing exactly what he was looking for. The rustling stopped. There was a short moment of silence followed by the snap of a can opening.

'Here we go again.' Marcus thought. Andrew came out of the kitchen with his head already tilted back. Marcus made room on the couch for him as he approached, but he changed his mind halfway and made his way toward his bedroom. Marcus laid his head back in defeat. He knew he had a responsibility to be there for a friend during rough times, but he didn't know if he could drink another night. 'I'd like to tell this Indian brotha he owes me a new liver.' He thought already feeling the heartburn.

Ever since the news of Shane's incarceration, Marcus had watched his good friend run the entire spectrum of human emotion. In fact, he could probably write a breakthrough book on human behavior from what he witnessed in these short weeks. The first couple days, Andrew was just plain angry. He hated the world and everything in it, yet his shy friend that was visiting helped him cope a little and at least prevented the destruction of the entire neighborhood.

After Eric left, Andrew became sad and apathetic. He blamed himself for not only his Indian friend, but for the plight of the entire Native American culture and everything else that prevented a perfect utopian society of world peace. Finally, he reached his current state, denial, which had lasted the longest.

He would go to work in the morning without a word to anyone, come home directly after, and immediately dedicate all his attention to forgetting everything. This clearing of the mind was accomplished with a heavy dose of all beverages containing alcohol, a steady flow of marijuana, and topped off with the occasional random pills he could get his hands on. Still, no matter how intoxicated he became he wouldn't mention the problem. Through all the stages he tuned Monique completely out.

She tried to ignore it, to be there for him, but the harder she tried the more he pushed her away. The last straw broke a few nights earlier when she came home to find Marcus and Andrew playing Twister with four half naked, barely legal bimbos. She pulled him aside. She told him enough was enough. If he needed help she would help him find it, but this behavior had to stop. In the spewing nonsense of an attempted excuse that followed, Andrew called her Elizabeth not once but twice. The second time his words came out something like, "Elizabeth you know you're the only girl I've ever loved."

This led to a disastrous fight, the police showed up, and she moved out early the next morning while Andrew was at work. Andrew never mentioned anything to his roommate, and Marcus knew better than to ask. It was one more pain Andrew would crumple up tight in his stomach, hold in, and allow to continue swelling. Marcus knew it was only a matter of time before something burst, but he watched silently while Andrew's behavior spun out of control without check. Marcus decided he would say something soon, and he started trying to imagine how his words would be received.

Andrew reentered the room. He was shirtless; beads of sweat clung to his skinny frame. Despite all the drinking and lack of formal exercise, Andrew kept the same athletic build he'd always had.

"Man, I think it's hotter in this hell-hole than it is outside." He said, scratching at his scalp with one hand then raising his beer to his lips with the other.

He finished it off, setting the empty can, still beading with condensation, onto the card table. The table was Monique's and the couch was too, but she either didn't have the means to transport furniture, didn't have room for it where she was, or didn't care enough to come get it. Marcus was thankful regardless, he had grown quite attached to the old sofa.

"I don't think I can stand this forsaken heat." Andrew continued.

Marcus only nodded in agreement. Andrew returned to the fridge for another beer.

"You want a beer bro?" he called from the kitchen.

Marcus thought hard, practicing to be polite in his refrain, but the heat proved to be too much.

"Aight."

Andrew reappeared, handing him a can. It felt cold in Marcus's hand, and he had to admit that first taste was refreshing, but a cold soda might have had the same effect. Andrew remained standing beside the edge of the couch, gazing out the glass doors. The fly buzzed around him curiously. In one motion, Andrew closed his hand around the hovering fly in midair and dropped the silent remains to the carpet without hesitation.

"Let's get outta here for a while." Andrew said still staring intently at nothing in particular.

"Let's go down to the Pub over here on 11ᵗʰ and let this place cool down a bit."

If he would have continued looking elsewhere, Marcus may have been able to decline. He might have been able to suggest they both take a night off the way he had practiced or at least claim he didn't have the money. A million excuses existed to not drink. Andrew's eyes met his own with the invitation, however, and none came to mind. Those eyes could be very convincing.

Cold Suds Pub was a small, typical dive bar. The wooden sign that hung over the door perpendicular to the street had no lights on it, making the neon beer lights in the two front windows the only way to distinguish it at night as a watering hole. The bar still drew pretty decent crowds on the weekends and had a number of loyal regulars.

The bartender and owner of the joint was a squat little man who appeared to be in his early sixties named Nicholas. His strong jaw protruded out from his saggy, deeply worn face, telling a faded tale of the bright youth he once was, and his eyes were so sunk-in and cautious it was difficult for even his closest friends to guess their color. He had a large head which always wore a Cold Suds baseball cap set ever so slightly on top of, and his Pop-eye shaped forearms were covered in grey hair that matched his side burns. His voice bellowed deep with the slightest remains of an accent which sounded Eastern European, and he was always entertaining guests with his jokes and anecdotes.

Inside the bar, there were four wooden booths along the far wall across from the bar. The booths sat in the dark except for an orange glow from the classic jukebox in the back corner. The old tune maker was the pride of the bar and its patrons. The bar top ran along the opposite wall with about fifteen or twenty stools pulled up to it. Except for Friday and Saturday nights, Nicholas was the only bartender, so patrons were often forced to wait for him to finish one of his tall tales before receiving another drink. Most came for the stories and social environment anyways and were never impatient.

Between the bar and the booths, there was an open space on the tiled floor for customers to dance or flirt, for there was always music blaring out of the jukebox. The space was probably less than eight square feet, yet it worked perfectly for its purpose, allowing a few couples to dance without feeling alone or on stage the way a big empty dance floor did. More than one gentleman had closed the deal with a young lady over the years dancing on those dirty, checkered tiles.

Marcus and Andrew took two stools on the far end of the bar close to the bathrooms and ordered a couple drinks. Marcus was somewhat of a usual at the establishment. Nicholas had grown fond of him, and he would usually pay for a couple of his drinks over the course of the night. The old man recognized his skinny Caucasian companion as well; Andrew had been involved in an altercation at the bar a couple months prior that had been resolved before any blows were thrown. Nicholas couldn't help noticing the young man's eyes when he dropped off their first round. There was a deep burning fire in those eyes unmatched by anything he had seen before. After years of bartending, Nicholas picked up an uncanny ability to read people, and something about Andrew worried him. The kid was always polite and usually pretty quiet, but Nicholas couldn't shake the feeling there was a wild animal lurking behind those eyes, always ready to pounce.

The old bar keep spoke with Marcus briefly. His friend sat by silently. Finally, Nicholas moved on to tend other customers. Marcus tried to open Andrew up while they emptied their first drinks. After a couple more rounds, Andrew was loosening up, and he started conversing more freely.

"How's work, blood?" Marcus asked him, seeing the conversation was improving Andrew's mood.

"It's ok. I am just really burned out on it. You know?" Andrew responded. The alcohol, glazing his words, began to show through.

"Yea I hear dat." Marcus said, nodding his head in enthusiastic agreement. "What else you gonna do though? Everybody gotta work and ain't nobody like it."

"That's just it. There is something I've wanted to do, but I can barely afford to get by as it is. I don't know how I would ever be able to pursue it." Andrew said.

He held his glass in both hands absent-mindedly tilting it away from him, so the small amount of liquid left in it climbed nearly to the rim of the glass.

"What's dat?" Marcus asked.

"Oh it's nothing really. I'll never find time to do it anyways. Maybe I'll do it if I move back home."

Marcus wanted to know more, but Nicholas interrupted.

"Another round for you boys?" He asked with only half a grin. The question hadn't even registered in Marcus's brain before Andrew responded.

"Yeah we'll have one more round. How about two tall shots of Jager each and a pint of PBR to wash em down." He said.

Nicholas shot a questioning glance in Marcus's direction, but Marcus was quick to avoid it. The old barkeep put on a fake smile and turned to retrieve the order.

"So ya been thinkin bout movin back?" Marcus asked returning to the previous topic.

Andrew didn't answer. He sat there twirling the wet coaster on the bar with his pointer finger. After a moment, he glanced over his shoulder to scan two young couples flirting near the jukebox. Tom Petty was singing his story about a girl named Mary Jane. The song reminded Andrew of better days.

When Andrew turned back toward him, Marcus noticed he was smiling. It wasn't the beaten smile of late either. It was the charismatic, confident smile of old. Seeing true happiness on his friend's face again, Marcus couldn't help but smile too.

"Last night, I woke up in the middle of the night." Andrew began, still smiling warmly.

"I was pretty drunk still, but I had to piss real bad so I got up. When I finished, I started to get the spins a little, so I stepped out on the balcony for some fresh air."

He paused for a moment to wipe the corners of his mouth with his finger and thumb. He was about to go on, but Nicholas interrupted again dropping off the drinks. Andrew shot him a wink in appreciation and returned to his story.

"Well, there was a full moon out last night. It was great too. There was this cool orange tint to it, and it was so huge it seemed like it was only a couple miles out of reach."

The joy in his voice was clearly audible now, and Marcus listened intently.

"So, I'm leaning against the ledge, staring at the moon, thinking about all the crazy shit that has been bugging me, and all of a sudden I notice there are no stars in the sky." He paused intentionally for effect.

"I mean it's a crystal clear night, and I can't see one star anywhere. It was unbelievable." He said, shaking his head.

Marcus waited for him to go on, but he didn't.

"Das it? Das ya story?" He finally muttered, figuring there must be more to his friend's sudden transcendence to bliss.

"You see, that's just it." Andrew said putting his palms out and shrugging his shoulders. He laughed. "Back home, people would see significance in that."

Marcus was confused, yet he was excited to hear his friend's laughter. He decided not to push the issue. Knowing Andrew, he would explain himself if and when he was ready. He was wondering what it was he hoped to pursue, but Andrew lifted his first shot.

"To hell with the past, to living for today, and to friendships that last a lifetime." He offered stoically.

"Amen to dat, bra."

They touched glasses, and each tossed a shot back. Marcus was chasing his drink with a mouthful of beer, but Andrew snapped his lips together in an 'ah' and picked up the second shot. This time his face was stern and tight. His eyes began to look dangerous once more.

"This one is to my brother, Shane. A better man and truer friend I've never known."

Again, they repeated the whole process. Marcus was feeling high before the shots, so it didn't take long for the added effects to set in. He sipped slowly at his beer, monitoring Andrew carefully. Andrew's body language began slipping back to a morose dejection with the mention of his friend, so Marcus decided it was now or never. He dove in not knowing where his words might lead. His love for Andrew refused to let him watch his friend slide backwards now that he was finally showing positive signs of acceptance.

"Man, I know dis nigga wuz yo boy, but he made his own decisions, hear?" He spoke, faking confidence. His eyes peered out from beneath the brim of the baseball cap he wore pulled down low.

"Where he is now is a result of his own actions."

Marcus was pleased with his words considering the circumstances; mostly, he was glad he finally spoke up. Surprisingly to him, Andrew seemed very open to discussion of the topic, although, they had not spoken a word about it up to this point.

"Not entirely true." Andrew replied calmly. "A man's decisions and actions are shaped by a unique combination of factors including his environment, education, mental capacity, culture, beliefs, and desires to name a few."

He leaned forward to position himself more erectly on his bar stool. Clearly, this was something he had put a great deal of thought into.

"Brother Chane comes from a long line of screw ups and gypsy-types. He has been constantly reminded of it and seen it with his own eyes his whole life. His father's been in prison most of his life, and his mom loves him, but she is hardly a capable or fully engaged mother. If that weren't enough, he was born into a race that has faced greater prejudice and prosecution than any other. You of all people should understand that stereotyping and racism can all but assume you will be a failure or a criminal. It's the same as the rich get richer. The poor and unlucky only get screwed."

He was gone now. No longer sitting on a bar stool in some run down hole in the wall, Andrew was somewhere else preaching his tribulations on the caste system of American society.

"Indians are even worse off though. Other minorities at least have their own people to support them and push them to break free and find success. Some of the Indians back home do the opposite. They try to hold each other back. If one of them starts to escape the turmoil, then they talk trash and doubt him at every turn. Sometimes an athletic or academic Indian will be pulled back and discouraged by his or her own family."

"Why in da hell would they do dat?" Marcus said, struggling to maintain focus amid his stupor.

"I don't know, but it's true in a lot of cases. A good example is basketball players. Over the years, there have been some great Native basketball players, but not once do you see one playing for a major division one school on TV. Coaches won't recruit them because the drop out rate is too high."

"Damn, nigga. It's all news to me. I hear Indian and I think veggie patty." Marcus couldn't help but laugh at his own joke.

"Yeah, well I knew all of it, and I swore I wouldn't let it happen to Shane. I swore I would protect him."

He was beginning to trail off again. He broke a plastic bar sword in half then continued breaking the two halves into smaller pieces.

"You know they say da Lord has a plan for everyone. Maybe dis all happen for a reason?" Marcus tried returning to the graveness of the conversation.

His attention was starting to wonder now, and a group of young ladies occupying one of the booths were distracting him. He made eye contact with one of the girls and smiled at her, chewing on a straw.

"That's bullshit." Andrew cursed, snapping a piece of green plastic that struck Marcus in chin.

He was rambling on too fast to notice though.

"I used to buy into all that shit too. Where did it get me? Nowhere. There is no God. There I said it. And you know what? It feels good. It's all a lie. You know what else? My buddy Darin, he don't believe in God. Hell, he don't believe in nothing, and he's got everything. I mean if it's such a sin then how does that work? This guy's got money. He's got fancy cars and clothes, and his girlfriend is gorgeous." He paused only long enough for a breath.

"He's got Elizabeth... No, there is no God, or good people like Shaner would be rewarded not punished."

"Naw, you gotta look at da big picture." Marcus chimed in.

He loved a good drunken philosophy talk, so he was starting to really enjoy this even though he was only paying attention to maybe three quarters of what was being said.

"Dat shit happens, and then years later some historian brotha looks back and realize why it all happen."

"That stuff is all crap too. Anyone can look back at events that already happened and see things the way they want to see them. Like when they say famous generals or kings won these amazing battles that ended up changing an entire war. Or someone will say the pope or some religious leader made some monumental decision that altered the path of millions of men. The truth is one man can never have that much effect. Some victorious battle might have won the war, but if this person or that person would have run instead of fought then the other side would have won the battle and the same thing could be said. It just happened to work out that way. There are millions of people in the world, and every single one has free will. So, how is it possible that one person's decisions change the world?"

Marcus finally stopped listening all together, and Andrew spoke only to himself. Marcus couldn't imagine trying to follow his friend's argument completely sober, so it all sounded like gibberish to him in his present haze. The females near the jukebox were now the center of his attention, yet Andrew rolled on.

"I could walk out the door of this bar and turn left or right. It is completely up to me, so if I turn right arbitrarily and see an alien then it was just dumb luck. That wouldn't stop historians from saying my decision to turn right led to the discovery of UFO's."

He stopped, apparently confused by his own logic, but after finishing his beer he persisted none the less.

"I don't know where I was going with that. My point is that fate didn't put Shane in that trailer that night to test his fortitude. It was just dumb luck, and anyone else might have acted in the same way he did. Shit, I would have killed them both."

Reaching his conclusion faster than he had planned, Andrew let out a belch, stood up, and laid a stack of cash on the bar next to the empty shot glasses.

"Let's get outta here. I'm starving." He said, trying unsuccessfully to drain a few last drops of foam from his empty beer mug.

"Why da rush, blood?" Marcus asked, chewing on his straw.

The young ladies at the booth were aware of his glances now, and they had begun sending flirting looks back in the direction of the bar.

"Les sit down wit deez gals and see where da night leads."

Andrew turned, noticing the women for the first time.

"You're gonna have to fly solo on this mission, Maverick." He replied. "I'm pretty beat, and I don't think I could help you much tonight anyways. Besides, if I'm going to stay down here I need to start concentrating on keeping my job, so I better get some sleep."

"Can't you start tomorra?" Marcus asked smugly. "I mean ain't you already drunk tonight?"

"You know what?" Andrew started.

A clouded look covered his face momentarily then faded.

"I think I'm going to go home and call Monique. I want to try and work things out."

He gave a broad grin, supporting his response. Marcus heard the words, but his patients had run out. He could see the girls were growing bored. He couldn't let them leave. He suspected it was only drunken ideals anyways, and he was confident whatever Andrew was talking about would be forgotten by the morning. He tried one last time to convince him to stay, but there was no changing Andrew's mind once it had been made up.

"Aite partna, I'll wake you up tonight if I bring more than one home. Ya hur?" He said grinning.

With that, Marcus glided smoothly over to the booth. As he was exiting the bar, Andrew turned around one last time to see his roommate already charming the ladies with his arm wrapped around one's shoulders. He thought one last second about staying, but he decided if he kept drinking it would only lead to trouble. He stepped outside onto the dark, silent sidewalk and briskly started for home. The evening air was calm and cool. It was a refreshing break from the loud, muggy atmosphere in the bar.

Andrew took a deep breath as his long strides carried him swiftly toward the apartment. He could smell the mixed aroma of the wet grass and flowers as the sprinklers hummed their steady flow. Andrew's thoughts turned to the future for the first time since Eric's visit. His steps felt light, and he was proud of himself for his decision to leave the bar on his own terms.

'Who knows,' he thought to himself. 'Maybe this will be the beginning of something.'

As he turned the corner, he didn't notice another man cross the street and fall silently into stride behind him. Less than two blocks from the gate to his apartment, the street lamps became infrequent, leaving large shadows between their dim white glows. Andrew continued along briskly, oblivious to the danger closing in behind him. He was alone with his thoughts. As he reached his left hand into his pocket in search of his keys, the voice startled him. Only slightly at first, it didn't sound like the voice of a mugger. It wasn't rough enough.

"Give me your fucking wallet." The voice said, greased with heavy Spanish.

Andrew turned to find a man about his own size, holding a five inch blade. The man was within two feet and held the knife out to Andrew's chest. The blade was held up and angled out, so it rested about six or eight inches from Andrew's throat when he turned.

Fear may or may not have struck. If it did it only lasted for an instant. Andrew didn't even think. It was all instincts. Even drunk, Andrew was superior in quickness and athleticism. The mugger obviously hadn't considered the possibility of resistance.

In one fluid motion, Andrew turned to see the knife and pounced like a predator on the arm holding it with all his weight. The surprised man tried to maintain his grip by bringing his other arm over, and, although he was strong, the knife was lost in the dark grass. The two men went to the ground with their legs hitting the concrete sidewalk while their upper halves landed in the damp lawn. The mugger was quite strong. He managed to grasp Andrew in a headlock, but it was only momentarily. He panicked, making the mistake of turning his attention toward finding the knife. Andrew slipped his hold, pinned him to the ground, striking him with a series of fists to the head and knees to the torso. Andrew lost himself in the moment, forgetting everything except survival.

The scuffle lasted for some time and eventually attracted a few witnesses from around the corner. By the time anyone was close enough to distinguish what was happening, it no longer resembled a fight in any way. Andrew had climbed to his feet and was stomping the guy with his boots. The man appeared to be unconscious or nearly so. Still, Andrew didn't let up. All his rage sprung free from within, and he was beyond all rationality. He was striking the man with hard quick kicks saying over and over,

"You wanna try and rob me in my own fucking neighborhood? We let you come to this fucking country you Spic fuck and don't you ever forget that shit."

It took several men to finally restrain him, and it wasn't clear if they stopped him in time. There was little left to recognize the mugger. All that remained was a mangled pile of flesh covered in stained red cloth and soaked in a pool of blood. The cops arrived to find Andrew covered in blood, still screaming racial epithets so lost in his rage that most of his sentences were either unrecognizable or made no sense. He was out of control. The officers had little option but to haul him in.

An hour later, Andrew sat in one of the small holding cells, covered in dried blood, starting to draw a small audience among his peers. Most of them, first time visitors, were drunks or petty criminals and figured this newcomer must have killed a few people to have all that blood from his ears to his socks, yet it was the violent storm behind his eyes that made them all truly nervous. Those eyes seemed to suck the light right out of the room.

Calm now, he sat silently trying to remember any real details of the night. There was little he could recall, but he knew he had definitely beaten someone up pretty good. His buzz was worn off now, and a headache was quickly replacing it. He hung his head, checking out his cut up, swollen hands. His heart echoed hollow from within.

He decided right then and there what he would do. He had to go home. It was his only chance to start over with a clean slate. He pictured being someone else. He pictured being merely another face in the crowd. That is what he wanted but would never have. He pictured himself finding steady work, marrying a nice girl, and raising children. He could coach football in his spare time and go fishing with Eric on the weekends.

It was nearly dawn when he finally laid his head back on the stiff cot. His arms and legs stopped twitching and his fists relaxed. He closed his eyes, and he could smell the future of his dreams. Something told him happiness would always lie just beyond his outstretched fingers. So be it. At home, he would always have people that loved him, always have someone that depended on him. It had been a very long couple weeks, but the blizzard seemed nearly over, and he faded off into a thankless sleep.

August 2nd, 2003

It was Sunday, one of those early August afternoons when a person can actually feel jealous of himself for being able to enjoy such pristine weather. The birds chirped their finest melodies, the sprinklers churned along a steady chorus, and the smell of the pine trees floated down into the valley on a gentle breeze. The air was warm without being hot. The grass was crisp without feeling dry, maintaining that perfect coolness even through the midday sun. Cars sat silent and stationary along the curb as people opted to walk instead. There was no existence of rush. The word hurry was extinct.

It was nearing supper time, but the sun wouldn't set for hours. There was a baseball game on the television in Eric and Claire's front room, but no one was watching it. Claire was in the kitchen chopping vegetables while Eric sat in his recliner watching Nathan entertain himself with a tape measure. It took the toddler a few minutes to figure out how the tool worked, but he was quite pleased with himself when he pulled it out about eight inches and let it go. Now, he was trying to test its limits, dragging the yellow tape with him while he walked away from the silver box which dispensed it so endlessly. It kept slipping from his hand, and he looked confused but remained determined. He would waddle back over slowly to start his experiment all over again, managing to pull it slightly further each time.

Eric couldn't help feeling pleased, seeing the first sprouting signs of a good work ethic growing in his young son.

'He definitely gets it from my side.' He thought smirking to himself.

He was calm and worry-free, feeling he had accomplished enough for the day. It was great to be relaxing on a Sunday. Lately, he had started working randomly on the days that started with 'S' again. Finally, Claire insisted that he not pick up extra hours on Sundays for religious reasons and because she felt it was the only way to guarantee having him around once in a while. Eric had been resistant at first, but he eventually complied with her request. No more Sunday's would be spent under the hood of a car.

It had been over two years now, and he was becoming used to having the weekends off. He would usually still wake up early, not wanting to waste the day away in bed, as he liked to put it, but he no longer found himself over thinking or feeling regretful when he wasn't busy all the time. Naturally, there were days he found himself pacing or stressing too much, but for the most part it wasn't a habit. He mostly did chores around the house and ran errands, but occasionally he treated himself and went fishing or took a long drive through the hills with no destination.

Mostly, he tried to avoid thinking. He was discovering the older he grew the more he tried to elude pondering life's questions, for the more negativity came through when he did it. When he was a kid, there was nothing to worry about. The future was exactly that. The days after high school were so busy with the pregnancy, the wedding, and the baby that all he could do was fight to stay caught up. There was no time for guilt or regret. There was no time for tomorrow when it was a challenge to get through today. After Nathan was born, Eric had turned to religion for his guidance more than ever but having two different religions under the same roof made even that difficult. Eventually, he began to open his mind to spirituality more and more. Claire didn't need to know though. It would only worry her.

Everything Eric had known and loved, everything he was certain of began to change with Shane's arrest. The closer the case drew to trial the more difficulties Eric had finding answers. Now, there was something different. It wasn't that something was missing. He knew he couldn't ask for more, especially in light of everything that had happened. Nevertheless, he constantly felt idle.

Knowing it was probably sinful, he questioned everything he had ever felt confident about. It was a crisis of faith, yet he didn't recognize it as such. He hid his feelings from Claire, but his mind constantly churned on self doubt. He tried to mention his thoughts to Andrew on several occasions but found only passive acceptance. It was difficult to share anything of that sort because the two had never spoken of such things before and because Andrew refused to dig up the past.

Even the fact that he was facing assault charges and failing to follow court orders to stay in California until his trial were only learned by Eric through the grapevine. When asked about what had happened Andrew was quick to change the subject. Eric couldn't understand what Andrew had expected when he came home. There was this constant disappointment about him. It was like he thought his arrival would be like the second coming or something. Eric couldn't forget his friend's sheepish grin that first morning he arrived home.

There had been a knock at his door about quarter after five in the morning. It was in late November, during the first healthy snow of the approaching winter. Eric had been eating pancakes, and he was startled to think anyone was coming over so early, when it must have been about ten degrees and still dark out. He opened the door to find a worn out, disheveled Andrew. He was noticeably thinner than usual, and his body odor was too strong for the cold to kill off. They spoke briefly. Eric had said very little. The entire meeting was a lot to take in at such an early hour, and Andrew had not exactly called ahead.

He said he was planning to work a little construction until he saved up some money, and he hoped to do a little coaching as well. Everything was planned out, but this was not unusual for one of his speeches. Eric figured he would ask for a little money and would have had no problem loaning a little, but Andrew didn't ask for any. He asked if he could sleep on the couch for a day or two while he looked for a place, promising it wouldn't be any longer than a few days. Eric told him it wouldn't be any trouble. Andrew thanked him, gave him a short but affectionate hug, told him it was great to be home and breathing the fresh air then departed as suddenly as he had arrived.

All day, Eric had thought about what implications his friend's return might have, and he expected to find Andrew at his house when he arrived home from work. But when he arrived home, Andrew wasn't there. Claire said she hadn't seen or heard from him, and he never showed up or answered his phone all night. Eric discovered the next day he had found a trailer out by the lake and paid cash for it on the spot. It was on the other side of the bridge some five miles outside of the county lines, so the price had been fair. Still, he couldn't help but wonder where Andrew had dug up that sort of cash, considering his saving habits.

Over the next couple months, Eric saw little of his friend. Occasionally, they would speak on the phone or he might stop by the house to say hello, but for the most part Andrew remained distant. Darin mentioned seeing him a handful of times here or there during regular working hours, so it seemed he was only working sporadically if at all. Other than that, Andrew's habits remained unknown, but this didn't stop Eric from feeling something was sure to come of his return. A small stone thrown in a large body of water seems insignificant, yet in time, the ripples continue to grow outward. More often than not, only reaching the shore can end the disturbance.

Then in July, Shane's trial began, and the entire town was consumed with gossip and opinions. The reality once again set in as the case unfolded in the small packed courtroom. Somehow, it all seemed like a movie or a dream before, but every time the courthouse went silent for the judge's entrance it really hit home how much was at stake. The three young men became close again, finding themselves spending hours on end together, either at the courthouse or the small diner across the street.

Each of them was a complete wreck, but their upbringing and love for Shane forced them to maintain a tightlipped handle on their fears and doubts. Individually, they all found a different role to play, acting on the instincts that came naturally from their unique personality. Darin took the leadership role, and he always maintained the reality of the situation while struggling to keep a positive outlook. Eric was, as always, the level head and keeper of the peace, particularly when things looked dire. Andrew settled for being the utility man and filling in gaps. He was a determined cheerleader, constantly pushing Shane's attributes on the general public. He was a back door attorney, analyzing the motivation behind every move Shane's lawyer made despite Darin's constant assurance he had hired one of the best.

Andrew also took responsibility for drinking up the sorrows of all three men, commonly closing down the bars and sleeping in his car in parking lots downtown. These habits were definitely starting to take a toll on his health. His skin was pale and always clammy in appearance, his thick head of hair was noticeably thinning, and he began coughing up some of the foulest looking garbage imaginable on a regular basis. Clearly, for Andrew there was more on the line in that courtroom than anyone except for Shane and perhaps the family of the deceased.

The truth was that a deal was already in the works to reduce the charges to mitigated homicide. The offer had been on the table originally, but Shane's lawyer, had refused it. Now in light of new evidence that was being kept very quiet, he was encouraging Shane to take a second look at his options. Darin had mentioned this possibility to both his friends before the trial began, but Andrew had reacted with such hostility to the possibility that any of this could be Shane's fault that he decided to only tell Eric of the most recent turn of events, asking him not to mention anything to Andrew until they knew more.

Eric realized that if Shane agreed then time in prison was imminent. He also realized that time in prison can have drastic effects on a man's life, but it sure beat the possibility of being found guilty of murder and facing a possible life sentence. He sat in his chair trying to keep it all from his mind. Either way, it seemed a long and difficult road to choose, but he felt there were others, far more knowledgeable at these matters, working on Shane's behalf to help him make the best decision. Eric could only pray and hope for the best. Though he couldn't figure out why, the face he kept seeing in his worried mind was Andrew's and not Shane's. This had been the case for days, even as Shane's future hung in the balance.

Eric stared out the window a long moment thankful for the little things that make a beautiful sunny day so enjoyable. He scratched his dry, rugged knuckles across his lips blankly. A sudden cry from Nathan snapped him out of his day dream. The youngster must have had his finger pinched by the tape measure. Daddy picked him up and bounced him on his knee for a few minutes until he was alright. Eric figured the tape measure might not be the safest toy for a toddler, but the real world was hardly sterile. Around here, there was little point in sheltering a child, for adolescents have a tendency to grow up fast in small towns. Nathan giggled looking up at his dad. Eric wiped the tears from his son's cheeks, wondering if the boy even remembered why it hurt.

August 5th, 2003

"Six years with parole eligibilities," Darin said, trying to sound positive and steady the way he had rehearsed. "He may serve as few as three."

Unknowingly, his right knee twitched steadily. He had planned to pause before adding in the minimum sentence possibility, yet it didn't come out that way. He sat stiffly, his posture tilting him slightly forward in the worn wooden chair, so his spine remained free of the backrest. His eyes tried to hold eye contact with the four men sitting at the table around him, but he found scanning between them hesitantly to be the only compromise he was able to perform, keeping his body tense and straight while watching the air deflate out of his companions. The temperature of the room increased a few degrees.

He was only the messenger. The decisions were beyond his grasp, but he knew the bearer of bad news can easily be viewed as the first scouts of an enemy's campaign. Coach Dugal, who sat directly across the round table from Darin cleared his throat deeply as if preparing to speak, but Andrew beat him to it.

"So, now what do we do?"

He raised his eyes to the others revealing his frustrations with a nasty scowl. Deep beneath those brilliant blue eyes something lurked that was unfamiliar to anyone. It was fear, and it was a fear that had grown and festered long enough that even Andrew could no longer hide its existence. A great deal could be explained by the presence of this new emotion. The daring are unpredictable for that very reason, but if fear enters the equation the unquestioned confidence begins to wane. When Andrew received no answer after a few short moments, he turned his attention directly to Darin.

"What are our other options?" The words were scratchy and baritone like he was struggling to choke them out.

"Well," Darin sighed deeply, "the other option is to continue with the trial, depending on the outcome and other stipulations I think he would be granted a couple different appeals, but the point here is that this is a great deal and Shane needs…"

"Great deal?" Andrew cut in pounding his hand hard on the table and drawing the attention of the few other guests scattered throughout the diner.

"For some reason, spending six years in prison doesn't sound all that fucking peachy to me,"

He stopped himself and adjusted his baseball cap several times before leaving it set back on his head with the bill pointed upward and slightly to the left, giving a clear view of his eyes as they began to tear up. He went on very slowly and almost inaudibly,

"Someone breaks into your home, threatens your safety, but in this world defending yourself makes you the criminal."

The words were not directed to his fellow companions. There was another short moment of silence.

"I am sorry. I didn't mean it was a great deal." Darin said leaving his eyes glued to the table this time. He felt terrible for his choice of words. "But, it's the best deal we have."

In the sorrowful stillness that followed these words, Coach Dugal tried to rest a comforting hand on Andrew's shoulder. As he touched him, however, Andrew slid his chair back. The metal legs screeching the tile floor made an eerie noise. He stood up and hastened for the door, choking back audible sobs. He leaned both palms on the glass door, stopped only long enough to scream a loud curse, then stormed out. The diner became a graveyard. Fearful looks covered the guest's faces. Everyone left at the table remained seated.

"He just needs to blow off a little steam." Eric said, speaking for the first time since they entered the diner nearly a half hour earlier. His voice was scratchy but he remained strong for his now vacant brother.

After a few minutes, the patrons of the restaurant seemed to forget the disturbance and low conversations resumed. When the food arrived at the table, nobody ate more than a few bites. They sipped their coffee and tried to discuss other topics, but it was a difficult farce to carry out. Eventually, everyone left except Darin, opting to be lonely and depressed rather than continue to publicly sulk. In this town, a man had to appear strong above all else, so many things were continually locked away.

Darin sat alone for several minutes sipping coffee and feeling that he had let everyone down. He was fully aware things would return to normal within a couple months, and he had known all along Shane would serve prison time. Still, somewhere in the back of his mind, the hero left in him had hoped he could find a way to save the day. He saw now how arrogant and self centered this had been, for subconsciously, he was hoping to promote his own self interests. He tried to convince himself that this was not the case, but he was disgusted that he was thinking of himself yet again. He dropped a ten on the table as tip, finished his coffee, and made his way to the exit.

Outside, he was walking down the sidewalk toward his car when he heard someone calling his name. He looked up to see Jason, the police officer he had befriended during the night of the bar brawl, walking across the street toward him. Although Darin was in no mood to speak to anyone, it was in his nature to at least be polite. The two shook hands, and Darin tried to pin on a fake smile. They exchanged the normal formalities, and Darin was about to drop the line that he was in a real hurry when Jason brought up Shane.

"So, I see that Indian you used to run with is in hot water again." He said, pressing his lips together as if speaking down to him all of a sudden.

"Yeah..." Darin replied, feeling his disgust turning into anger.

It was the last thing he wanted to talk about, but Jason went on without noticing how he balked from the topic.

"I knew that kid was nothing but trouble from the beginning. I wish we could lock em all up as soon as they step off the reservation." He said in perfect dehumanizing generalities.

Darin could feel his fists tightening, so he shoved them both into his pockets.

"That little squaw is getting lucky though." He went on unaware.

"They cut him a deal, so he'll probably only serve three years or so. It is bullshit how many advantages Uncle Sam gives them prairie niggers." He said, sneering as he spoke.

Darin wanted to hit him so bad he could taste it. He envisioned it and almost let one fly. Then he tried to remain level headed by speaking loudly,

"Yes, I heard about a possible deal in the works." He nearly shouted.

"Yeah? Well, its official now." Jason said placing a thumb in his belt and snapping it outward, causing the leather to make a popping sound. He eyed Darin like it was all a big conspiracy.

"He agreed to it about an hour ago. Pretty sad if you ask me, letting a murderer back out on the streets could end up being a decision we'll all regret. The next time it might be someone you love. Who knows."

Darin could handle no more. He excused himself, explaining something dire came up.

"Is everything ok?" Jason asked, trying to look heroic and professional.

"Yes, thank you." Darin said, avoiding eye contact so as not to reveal the hatred in his eyes.

"Alright, it was good to see you and you take care now." The officer said suspiciously.

"Thank you and same to you, Jason." Darin replied pulling his car keys from his pocket and spinning around on his heels in one fluid motion.

He sped home, chastising himself mentally for being a coward in such situations. Tears blurred his vision as he slammed his fists on the steering wheel. Upon entering the house, he dropped his keys on the chest in the entrance hall and headed directly to the living room. He slumped himself down on the sofa, turned on the television, and began surfing for anything to calm his mood. He gave up quickly, however, and began pacing back and forth across the room instead; dwelling on his anger until he was on the verge of an eruption. He did not realize it, but this was the first time he had let his anger take control since before the case had begun. He went to the cabinet and poured himself a stout shot of whiskey. As he was sitting back down, Elizabeth entered the room with a smile.

"Hi honey. I thought I heard you come in. How are you holding up?" She asked very supportively.

"Not that well. I just found out Shane agreed to the plea bargain. Now, he has given up his rights to any appeals." Darin said with a long sip from his glass.

"Oh I am sorry honey, but that is good isn't it. I mean didn't you say yourself this deal was the best option he had." She spoke softly, combining sympathy with honest concern.

"Shit, I thought so...But now, I don't know."

His voice was completely defeated, but his anger was only tranquilized. It was far from gone.

"I just wish there was some other way." He finished and returned to the cabinet for another drink.

Elizabeth made her way to his side. She grabbed him gently around the waste, so she could pull herself in for a hug.

"Honey, you did everything you could do. Sometimes people have to pay the consequences for their own actions." She said soothingly, stroking her fingers gently on his neck and behind his ear.

Perhaps if she had used Shane's name instead of saying people, Darin could have suppressed his anger longer, but it was more likely the combination of the climactic situation, the racist cop, and the fact that he had held too much in for far too long that made his explosion inevitable. Whatever the case, the stress finally won out, and the flood waters came pouring down the canyon of Darin's nervous system in the form of a major blowout.

"Five years in prison isn't a fucking consequence. It's a major chunk of your life. If Shane can even return to any sort of normalcy after spending that much time without any rights or freedoms, then he will be ahead of eighty percent of his peers." He shouted as he pulled away from her.

"A much more likely scenario will involve psychological issues upon reentering society that he will have a two month window in which he tries to find a job before becoming chemically dependant again. Of course, no one in this racist world is going to hire an Indian felon, especially not in this town."

Elizabeth, feeling she was directly being accused, instinctively fired back.

"I have been as supportive toward Shane as anyone, but I can't blame people for being hesitant to hire him. He hasn't had the best track record with working, and it would hurt business if customers were scared away."

"You are just another bigot." Darin screamed. "Get out of my house."

"You son of a bitch don't ever call me racist. It has nothing to do with that and you know that. You're just upset right now, and you aren't seeing things clearly."

"I think I am finally seeing things clearly. I bet if I wasn't white or if I was poor you'd be all for pushing me toward the gallows too."

"Stop that shit right now. You don't mean that. Just stop before you say something you will regret." Elizabeth screamed, pleadingly. She was crying hysterically now and trying to hold him, but he continued to push her away.

"I mean every word I say. I am over you. Get out of my house and never come back you gold digging bitch." She reached for him again, and, as she scratched his face, he did something he had never done before.

He shoved her. He pushed her hard into the cabinet and she fell to the floor in silence. All at once, Darin realized he had gone too far. There may well have been time to make emends, yet he made no effort. Instead, he threw his glass hard against the far wall shattering it everywhere, and he stormed out of the house, speeding off with no destination. Quick as that, the first in a devastating chain of events following Shane's trial rocked the small town of Great Pines.

August 9th, 2003

It was early morning, and the sounds of the day were beginning to fill the air. Cars were starting off to work, dogs were barking at joggers and bikers through chain-link fences and front-room windows, and the first sounds of construction work were grinding and rumbling into full swing. Although the sun had been up for a couple hours already, an overcast sky gave the impression it was much earlier. The forecast didn't call for a high chance of rain, but moisture could definitely be smelt in the dense summer air.

Andrew parked in a downtown public lot and turned off his engine, but he didn't climb out right away. He rubbed his eyes and forehead trying to convince his hangover to take the morning off. He was aware he probably still reeked of alcohol, for he could still taste the booze on his belches. He didn't care though. He had put off his purpose this morning for too long already. He reached in the glove box to grab a small bottle he had left there for just such occasions.

"Hair of the dog." He said aloud before throwing back a long pull. He wiped his face one last time and stepped out of the vehicle. The parking lot was positioned along one edge of a small public park. The trees in the park provided adequate shade on the lot for a good part of the morning, keeping cars parked there all day from becoming too sun drenched.

As Andrew made his way through the park, he watched a couple youngsters wrestle in the grass while an elderly gentleman, presumably a grandparent, sat on a park bench and read the paper a dozen or so yards away. Andrew smiled, remembering a wrestling experience of his own in this very park some years back. Due to a serious hangover and a dose of strong anxiety, he couldn't recall the events that led to the dust up, but he was positive it had been pointless and not worth the hassle. He was still searching for the facts of that fight while he crossed the street to his destination, a large old brick building with beautiful stone columns and a gothic cathedral like roof. It had once been the county courthouse, but since the new one had been finished some years earlier, it was now serving as the city jail.

Andrew remembered the last time he had been here, during high school, when Erik's father had been doing some work on the renovations. He needed to get his signature for an academic probation progress form. Those youthful memories of anticipation and excitement to be able to walk around the jailhouse came rushing back to him. He had hoped to see prisoners being guided around in chains or even a riot. Unfortunately, the reality of the visit had been uneventful. Except for the buzz of power tools, the building had been rather quiet, and he had left disappointed. The only men he had seen that day were construction workers and a few snub looking older men in hand me down suits.

This morning, his mind was too caught up to hope for something memorable to occur. He made his way to the clerk's office, and after explaining his visit and signing a few forms, he was led to a small conference room. There were three tables in the room that ran perpendicular to the door with a few squat wooden chairs and aluminum folding chairs scattered throughout the room. There were no windows in the room and, again to Andrew's disappointment, no one way mirror. In fact, the walls, like the rest of the room, were quite plain. The room was painted a hideous pale green, perfectly square, and stuffy even on this cool morning. Apparently, this room had been skipped over during the last renovation.

Andrew paced the room for a few moments, attempting to organize his thoughts, but several minutes passed, so he eventually sat down to wait. He tried to convince himself that he wasn't nervous, yet he hadn't been so fidgety since he first met Monique. Finally, the door swung open to reveal a tired, balding man in his fifties with a several year old pooch hanging over his belt, the gravity of which visually effected the man's posture. Everything about the man's appearance signaled contempt or at least a general lassitude for his job. The man cast an unconcerned look at Andrew before stepping out of view a moment to escort Shane into the room.

Shane's face lit up when he saw Andrew. His face which had been clean shaven for court had gained a few patches of fuzz which only made his baby face look younger. He wore a baggy jumpsuit. His hands were cuffed in front of him. Andrew stood up to hug him, but the guard stepped into the small space between the old friends, making things awkward and cramped. The smell of the old man's tangy aftershave convinced Andrew to step back a moment. The guard removed Shane's handcuffs, nodded in response to Shane's thanks, then shuffled out of the room, closing the door behind him.

Left alone, they hugged and exchanged insults about each other's physiques and appearances trying to sidestep any feelings of discomfort. The first few moments proved difficult in finding a comfort zone. Even the hug seemed too careful. This marked the first time the two had been alone together since Eric's wedding. The tensions had nothing to do with mistrust or fear of judgment from either side. Friends so close with such a strong bond and understanding for each other never doubt each other's unyielding love. Andrew had waited too long to pay a visit. The two had spoken a few short moments at the courthouse in the presence of Erik and Shane's mother, but something kept Andrew from coming to visit here. The longer he stayed away the more difficult it had become.

It wasn't until the paper printed the news that Shane had been sentenced to prison time that Andrew decided he had to visit. The following day, Shane had several visitors come, but Andrew was not one of them. This surprised Shane, and he asked about Andrew's absence that day for the first time. There was no ill will in his heart, but he was scheduled for transfer to the State penitentiary in Boonsville the following week, and he desperately wanted to see his friend before it was too late. Later that evening, Erik had found Andrew passed out in the crimson rays of setting sun sprawled out on the porch of his trailer. He had spent the night out at the lake trying to sober him up, explaining the importance of making the visit not only to Shane but for Andrew himself. Now, two days later, the two sat quietly across a table from each other both on the verge of tears no longer able to slip reality's grasp.

"Happy Birthday, bro." Shane finally said to break the silence of the room.

He spoke genuinely, though there was a look of guilt in his body language.

"Thanks Brother Chane." Andrew responded with a half hearted laugh.

"I totally forgot. You'll probably be the only one who remembers."

Then there was silence again. The heat of the room made Andrew's throat dry, and he swallowed hard.

"Do you remember that time we got all hammered and shot the hell out of this place with Daryl Westin's paintball guns?" He asked, glancing back and forth from his hands folded across his lap and Shane sitting in front of him in that damn jump suit.

"Yea, I remember you kept humming the theme song to Superman while we were walking down here, and Erik was getting so mad about that." Shane said, clearly finding comfort in reminiscing.

"Oh yeah, I forgot about that. He was just scared." Andrew said with a laugh.

His mind wasn't taking him back down memory lane, though. The jump suit made it impossible for him to think about anything except the drear of the present. Andrew had always been the one who lived in the moment. It had always been part of his blessing. Now, it appeared to be a curse.

Shane and Erik had always been the ones who remembered every minute detail from past exploits and adventures. Darin's greatest concerns were always of the future. Andrew could only manage to live in the moment. That's who they are and how they were raised.

Andrew could only see today no matter what he did. Coach Scully claimed the reason Andrew was so good on the mound was his ability to completely forget his previous outing, or even the previous pitch. At the moment, all Andrew could see was the jump suit. Shane, loosened up a little now, was starting into another funny story from years ago. Andrew tried returning his smiles, but he didn't hear a word.

"I'm sorry bro." He interrupted.

The smile disappeared from Shane's face, and he discontinued his story, trading it for a quizzical look.

"For what?" He asked cautiously.

"For everything." Andrew said, trying not to crack.

His face started to prune up as he continued.

"I just know if I wouldn't have failed then none of this would have ever happened. I left you high and dry."

This time it was Shane who interrupted. His voice wasn't choked up like Andrew's, however. His voice was determined, speaking sternly.

"Don't give me any of that bullshit." He barked. "I am so tired of hearing all the fucking reasons why shit happens."

He stood up. As he did, his voice lost some of its grit, and he became much more sorrowful in his body language.

"It's either God's will or it was because of my race or environment. Or maybe, it was the meth that took me over and made me a crazy murdering lunatic." He stood behind the chair leaning on it; the crimson color disappearing from his face.

"It's all a bunch of bullshit." He continued, looking over his hands now.

"I killed someone, bro. I mean it was an accident. I didn't do it on purpose, and he was in the wrong place at the wrong time. But, I killed a young kid who wasn't even a quarter of the way through his life. I killed someone who had parents, family, and friends that loved him."

He looked back up at Andrew who was crying now, but there were no tears in Shane's eyes. He seemed determined to finish what he wanted to say. He had put a lot of thought into this, but this was the first time he had truly spoke his heart unhindered.

"No matter why it happened, I did it. Can't you see, man? So, I will spend a few years in prison. I am alive. He isn't. And there is no turning that around."

He moved to a corner of the room and sat down on the floor.

"I wanted to see you because you were the one guy who could always make me forget about everything and just laugh, even if it was only for a few minutes." He confessed.

This struck Andrew directly in the heart. He wiped his eyes off and thought a moment to himself. When he opened his mouth to speak, he had no idea what was about to come out. He didn't want to let the silence last another moment.

"You remember how we used to always joke about moving up to Alaska to work on the fishing boats?" He asked hoarsely, his eyes still misty and his face contorted to fight the sniffling.

Shane looked up at him and nodded, wondering where he was going with it.

"And do you remember how we always used to say one of us would surely end up dying up there?" He continued.

"But, at least it would be a good story." Shane chimed in, smirking slightly.

"Exactly." Andrew answered without returning the smile.

"Well, I sure hope you didn't fake this whole ordeal just to make me die alone up there."

Before the final words were even out of his mouth, Andrew felt ashamed it was the best he had been able to come up with.

Shane's smile disappeared; his brow creased with a perplexed look. Andrew knew better than to apologize, so he held his gaze. It lasted maybe five seconds, but a million thoughts went through both of their heads in those brief moments. It was Shane that caved first. He started with a slight chuckle shaking his head side to side, but a few minutes later the two were sitting in the corner punching each other in the shoulder and laughing until it hurt.

"Wow, you must be almost as drunk as you smell if that was the best joke you could come up with." Shane exclaimed a few minutes later.

"No, I haven't been in a bar all day."

"What are you waiting for? It must be about ten in the morning by now, and a guy can hardly drink all day if he doesn't start in the morning." Shane chimed back sarcastically.

"I know, but I think I've worn out my welcome at most of the places in town. They all want money in exchange for their goods and services. All I have to offer is wisdom and good company."

"Oh, I can imagine your company has been just grand lately too."

Fifteen minutes later, the guard opened the door to find them sitting in the same corner laughing and wrestling around. The guard noted that time was up, but the boys were determined not to be rushed in their valediction. They each realized this would likely be the last time they would see one another for several years, but neither of them even hinted at sorrow, instead locking the pain in those deep pits that hard-luck, blue-collared kids find at a young age. They smiled, cracked a couple last jokes at the other's expense, and hugged as if they would be playing in a pick up game together the next day. Andrew walked straight out the door and into the park without even a glance at the world around him. His mind was void of thought. A numbing sensation took control.

Anyone who has ever had a loved one sent to prison knows how difficult it can be to climb that hill back to normalcy. The slightest stumble and one can find themselves right back down at the bottom, only a little dirtier and growing tired. Without help, one might decide it's where they belong and stop trying all together. For Andrew, he didn't even look uphill. He climbed in his car and started to drink, not a single tear left in his eyes.

That afternoon Darin, Eric, and some of Andrew's other friends tried getting a hold of him to wish him a happy birthday. He was no where to be found. No one was aware of his morning visit with Shane. Eric worried, knowing how the depression was building up, and those feelings weren't things Andrew was particularly used to. Finally, he decided to take a ride out to the lake to check on him. There was no one there, so Eric said a little prayer to himself, hopped back in his car, and headed back into town. On his way home, he decided to drive by a couple of bars and check for Andrew's car. One of the spots was a tavern on the north end of town.

The place was called the Oasis. It was one of Andrew's favorites; the spot the great bachelor party debacle had taken place. It was pretty large as far as bars go. The type of place that almost never seems packed because of all the open room. There were a few pool tables, a little corner stage plenty big enough for a band, though the closest thing to occupy it these days was a DJ who did karaoke on Wednesday and Friday nights, and a good sized dance floor. There was a limited item menu, mostly burgers and such. The family that opened it still owned it, although there were plenty of tough times for the establishment along the way.

Originally, the bar was located a ways out of town. The last stop before 12th Street becomes the Lake Road, it was the original party destination for weekenders heading to the lake. But it wasn't long before a bar opened up out at the lake and then another restaurant and lounge along the way.

Everyone figured progress would certainly spell doom for the Oasis. If only it weren't so big. Big bars were tough to keep open. Somehow though, it survived for years on its regulars, fisherman, boaters, and the occasional curious wonderer finding himself on the north end of town.

Eventually, a string of developments extended the town further north. Subdivisions began to spring up all around the area. A little plaza with an all you can eat buffet, a gas station, and a drug store was built a mile further north than the bar. People were building everywhere, and homes were common all the way to the lake. The Oasis was hardly out of the way any longer. In fact, it was now the one or two drink stop after work for a lot of the newer homes in the area. Like anything else that still remained from the old days, the Oasis had found a way to survive by any means necessary.

Eric didn't pull into the dirt lot that looped around the bar on both sides. He slowed down, scanning the lot for the familiar 1988 Lincoln Continental. There was no sign of it, and he was almost past the south end of the bar when he thought he saw a familiar vehicle. He had to glance back over his shoulder through the rear passenger side window now, for he was past the lot, but he could almost swear the silver Dodge Durango parked where the lot disappears behind the bar was Elizabeth's. He strained to read the license plates, which would read DDYSGRL, yet he had to turn back quickly when he realized he was veering into the other lane.

The SUV was a common make and color, so he figured it must have been someone else's. Eric couldn't imagine what Elizabeth would be doing all the way over here when she rarely drank, and the Oasis wasn't exactly her friends' type of crowd. He must have been mistaken. Still, he couldn't shake the thought from his head as he checked out two other bars, though they were out of the way from his usual route home. He didn't even know why it mattered to him.

'Why should I care if Elizabeth is at the Oasis?' he asked himself. 'That probably wasn't even her Dodge,' he thought, trying to ease his mind.

'Besides, there could be a million reasons why she would be there.'

But despite all his best efforts, he could only think of one. It seemed a little too coincidental that her car would be parked way in the back, at a bar that Andrew frequented, on his birthday which Eric knew she was aware of, for he remembered Andrew opening a card from Darin and her, in her writing, during his last visit. Eric knew it was wrong to be imagining the worst with no evidence, but he couldn't shake the thoughts from his mind. He sped the last two miles home, hoping to find comfort from his worried mind in the presence of his wife and son. Unfortunately, all he found was a note on the counter.

Claire was shopping for shoes. She wouldn't be home for another hour or two. Ordinarily, Eric loved having a little quiet time alone at the house to watch television or relax and think. This, however, was not one of those times. Eric slouched down into his recliner, picturing only the worst possible scenarios. He told himself Andrew would never cross that line, yet he couldn't help feeling Andrew wasn't exactly himself lately. He pictured a war raging in Andrew's soul. Every drink he took was another advantage to the devil within. His iron will and gritty toughness wouldn't save him this time. Eric knew that if he did fall it would not be a steady downward spiral. No, there was nothing patient about Andrew. If he crashed it could only be the same as when he soared, majestically, legendary and instantaneous.

Eric picked up the paper and began reading the first article to catch his eye, hoping to find anything to keep his mind off the sorrow that was swallowing the people he loved. The article was titled 'Losing Our Town'. He read it absentmindedly, scanning over the words but too distracted to link together the ideas conveyed by the writer. He just couldn't stop picturing Andrew and Elizabeth being at that bar together. Since Shane's sentencing, Eric's faith had taken on a pessimistic character that had been buried somewhere deep inside of him since his marriage. He doubted the positive possibilities. He saw this mostly for what it was, a cheerless mind locked in gloom. There was something different this time, for no good could be seen from a destitute drunken Andrew meeting up with his best friend's girl whom he always held on a pedestal beyond his reach.

Eric's eyes continued to read on about how many of the last mom and pop merchants in the downtown area were being forced to shut down due to their losing battles with the chain and discount franchises. At the same time, he wondered how far a desperate Andrew might go to find himself on top again. Even if nothing happened at all, it would take a single rumor to reach Darin for a total catastrophic meltdown. Eric knew he had better think of something and fast or he was going to lose everything he loved and held sacred outside his immediate family. His mind churned frantically for glimmers of hope, paying little attention to the words his eyes rolled across.

The author ended his article with a plea for help. Dramatically, he wrote that everyone must do what they can because it wasn't only the local color and flavor that Great Pines was losing; it was the small town itself, with all its charm and grace, which was dying. According to this journalist, the citizens of Great Pines were losing a war to themselves against urban consumerism. There was a growing disregard for the history and heritage that makes small towns so special and unique. As Eric's eyes read the words, he gave a defeated sigh, and like so many times before, wondered what ever happened to the carefree days of old.

AUGUST 15TH, 2003

Darin was in his den working at his desk when the doorbell rang. His mind was anywhere but on the papers laid out neatly in small stacks in front of him, and although he put his pen down hard with irritation at the interruption, he was glad for the excuse to move around a little. The truth was after his blowout with Elizabeth he hadn't been able to think straight. He didn't eat, didn't sleep, and couldn't work. He laid awake at night playing every detail over again and again in his mind. His health was deteriorating and he looked terrible. He couldn't convince himself that reality had spiraled out of control so easily. It all seemed so dream-like still.

Even the events following the fight were only remembered with foggy clarity. After he had stormed out of the house, he had driven over to the football stadium. There was no particular reason for his destination. It may well have been the ocean for all he knew. He had just started driving, and that was where he ended up. The length of the rustic stadium runs perpendicular to several through streets, making it a widely found dead end on the east-side of town. Without contemplating his destination, he parked his car along the visitor's end of the stadium, hopped the fence at a familiar spot, and made his way down onto the track.

He was so blinded by rage that he didn't even take in his surroundings or reminisce any of his past glories on this very field. His skin felt hot under the afternoon sun, and his well-tailored slacks and designer shirt clung to his perspiring back and legs. This marked the first time he was down on the field level since that last fateful loss senior year. In the west end zone, he kicked out of his shoes and, hopping on one leg then the other, pulled his socks off.

The field, which sat dormant all summer, was already being prepared for the approaching season. The grass, which would be trampled and smashed by high school students from around the state in the fall, was shaggy, healthy, and full. The sprinklers were set to water automatically around dawn and dusk, but the hot sun beat down on the field mercilessly the remainder of the day, leaving the grass dry, almost sharp beneath Darin's bare feet.

He wiggled his toes a moment all the same, remembering the time he had taken Elizabeth down on the field late one summer night. They had chased each other around in their bare feet laughing and flirting. It seemed like ages ago. His heart beat hard in his chest as he began to realize how far he had crossed the line this time. He was angry at himself, but he was angry at Elizabeth too. He was angry with everyone and everything. Mostly, he was just angry.

He started to run, lightly at first. But, it wasn't long before he was sprinting hard for the opposite end zone. He wasn't hoping for anything. It was nice to be headed toward some destination. When he reached the goal line, he ran back. It felt good. Ignoring the throbbing pulse in the front of his head, he ran hard. It wasn't long before he was sucking hard for air, but the hot midday air hardly made for a rewarding breath. His body was lathered with perspiration. His eyes burned as the hot, salty sweat poured down his face. Still, he kept running. His sides began to ache and his legs grew numb, but he ran on and on. Finally his body could take no more, collapsing just shy of the original end zone where his shoes and socks lay sprawled across the grass. His head still ached as he laid out spread eagle in the grass, sucking hard for air, but his mind could only hear his pulse pounding. The hot grass stuck to his face and body making him itch, yet he couldn't move. He had yet to catch his breath when he started cursing softly to himself. His efforts had failed. He was still angry, and his problems had gone nowhere.

A few hours later, he had snuck quietly back into the house. Elizabeth's car was gone, but he walked through the house like he was walking over eggshells all the same. A short inspection had shown only a few of her things to be missing; nothing in the home had been broken or abused, leaving Darin to hope she was staying at her mom's for a day or two to blow off a little steam.

He hadn't seen or heard from her since. Her curling iron still sat dormant on the counter in the master bath.

He knew the doorbell wasn't her. She wasn't one to ring the doorbell and wait. Then again, he could be wrong. The couple didn't exactly have a lot of experience on such full scale conflict. He began to feel nervous as he started to think it might well be Elizabeth. He had been expecting her to return that first night or the following morning with guns blazing and a chip on her shoulder, yet as the hours turned into days without any sign of her, he prayed for even a phone call.

He thought a great deal about how that call might go. He could almost hear her voice, quiet and somber, drawing him in by using silence as a weapon to strike guilt. He would be at her mercy, of course, feeling terrible, and her sorrow would only break him down further. She would be patient, waiting for the right moment to unleash all her frustrations. Scarcely a moment into his big apologetic monologue, she would attack with fangs bearing, expressing an unmistakable point that disrespecting her was not going to happen again period. The more he thought on it the more he realized the threatening phone call might be his safest first step toward making up. Even with this knowledge, he had continued to put off calling around to find her.

Now, rapidly approaching the door, his heart fluttered as he pictured her, face red with fury, as she chewed him out hysterically before she was only repeating herself then giving in to primal urges of punching, kicking, and biting him until she wore herself out. He put one hand on the brass knob and started to take a deep breath, opening the door while still inhaling. His eyes were shocked to fall on a grizzled Andrew where his brain had already painted Elizabeth to be standing.

Andrew wore a tank top, exposing his tan, lanky shoulders to the bright sun. Darin let his breath out naturally, trying not to tip his eager surprise. Andrew, noticing the shock in Darin's expression, simply figured it was directed toward the unannounced visit. He wore a conniving smile, and instead of hello, he gave the more familiar 'hey bro'. Darin, though disappointed by his surprise visitor, was already curious about Andrew's intentions, for he knew there were intentions. An enigmatic drifter doesn't just stop by one afternoon out of the blue, regardless of how close of friend he is.

"Andrew, what's up?" he asked, returning his friend's smile.

"Nothing much, are ya busy?" Andrew asked, from worn out, hollow eyes.

"Not at all, come on in."

Darin turned and led the way through the house to the air conditioned living room. He was about to offer a drink, but thinking better of it, he took a seat on the sofa. Andrew sat down a good distance away, choosing the arm chair situated in the far corner of the long room. It didn't mean much to Darin. He was well accustomed to Andrew's eccentric ways, and it hardly meant anything was amiss.

"Ooh, it's sure nice an cool in here huh?" Andrew said adjusting his cap.

"Yes, the AC was a big selling point for keeping this home."

"Keeping it?" Andrew asked, confused.

"Well, I had three homes I was selling when Liz and I started talking about moving in together, but it came down to this one or the place I sold over on the Boulevard."

"And you picked this one, gotcha." Andrew finished the explanation, nodding his head. He was slouching forward, giving the impression he had more to say. Trying to avoid the 'how are you and Elizabeth' question, Darin continued,

"I liked this location better, and I had an offer on the other place well over market value. In the end, business is business I guess." He said trying to bore Andrew into a new topic.

"So, business is booming then I take it?" Andrew asked.

Darin knew Andrew well enough to suspect he was being baited, but he figured he was better off to get to the bottom of the visit rather than risk an uncomfortable inquisition.

"We have been getting by. Everyone is waiting for the bubble to burst though."

He played along. Andrew either lost his nerve or didn't feel confident about the timing because he lowered his head and adjusted his cap a second time without probing further.

This cat and mouse style small talk continued a while without any hint from Andrew about the purpose of his presence. Darin figured it must be something serious. It wasn't like Andrew to dance around his intentions this long. If he were in need of money, he would have gone to Eric first. Darin remembered that Eric said he hadn't seen Andrew in days, so unless it was a great deal of money, it had to be something else.

The two volleyed on, Darin's mouth growing dry with anticipation. Finally, he offered Andrew a drink, hoping it would expedite a little courage or at least a slip of the tongue to the point of an insinuation of sorts. Andrew agreed to a beer. Darin went to the fridge to retrieve it, pouring himself a glass of cranberry juice as well. During these short moments while Darin was in the kitchen, Andrew tried to muster up the courage to speak his mind. His anxiety was visible when Darin handed him the cold bottle. Darin returned to his spot on the sofa feeling uneasy. He turned the TV on and flipped it to a baseball game.

The sudden disappearance of Andrew's usual cool demeanor together with Darin's own diffidence created panic in his imagination. Suddenly, he knew exactly what it was Andrew could not say.

'He is going to tell me Elizabeth turned to him after the blowout.' He thought, sipping awkwardly at his juice.

'My God, how could I be so blind? He has come here to confess he held and consoled her...or kissed her...or slept with her.'

His mind raced at the speed of light. The images appeared from all sides. His jealousy grew exponentially, making him feel faint. He tried to put the breaks on, but the blood pulsed onward into his temples, making his head throb. He tried to mask his contempt, fearing Andrew might lose his courage to come clean.

'Just say it you son of a bitch.' He thought to himself.

Meanwhile, Andrew remained oblivious to the storm swirling within his friend's psyche. He was battling his own images of denial while trying to select his words carefully. The silence was torture for both of them. Finally after a long slow swig, Andrew decided it was now or never.

"You know we've been friends a long time, bro." He said, lifting his head to meet Darin's terrified expression.

'Stupid,' Andrew thought. 'Who says that?'

He was so caught up in his purpose that he was oblivious to Darin's sheer coldness. The words hit Darin like a brick to the skull. Nothing had been confessed, yet he was already on the verge of a total collapse.

"I should have never come down on you about Shaner's sentence. God knows, you did more than anybody to help him out. I guess..." he paused to wipe his brow then went on.

"I guess I always pictured everything turning out a lot different when we were younger. While I was in California, I always felt like nothing would ever change here, and I would come back one day to find everyone and everything the way it was the day I left."

Andrew spoke straight from his heart. He wasn't complaining. His voice was low, but it carried a stable tone. He hung his head again, scratching aimlessly at the back of his strong, red neck.

"Then when Eric got married, I just figured we would all follow suit, be happy, and someday each have healthy, happy families."

Darin hung tightly to every word, listening for the first syllable of her name.

"I guess you were always right. If I hadn't always been so damn self centered, none of this would have happened."

Typically, Darin would have responded with sympathetic disagreement, assuring him that there was nothing that could have been done to prevent such unfortunate circumstances, but all he felt was rage and jealousy burning in the primal pits of his being. He wanted to release his fury the way he had in this very room a week earlier. He pictured the battle in his mind. Once and for all, he could find out how tough this seemingly untouchable man really was.

Andrew continued on, but the words fell on deaf ears as his companion struggled with the inner demons threatening to tear him apart. It took several moments for him to realize Andrew had asked a question and fretfully awaited a response. He replayed the past few moments back again, trying to recall what had been asked of him, only to come up empty. The silence may have confused him some what, but by Andrew's appearance, every second was far more agonizing. Without letting his guard down, Darin snapped boldly,

"Say again?"

The retort struck Andrew like a slap in the face. He regained his poker face quickly though, showing little pain.

"It's no big deal, I can scrape it together some how. I am embarrassed I even asked." He began muttering to save face then, rising to his feet, he added,

"Like I said before, I was asking expressly as a business opportunity, and this has nothing to do with our friendship. I hope you take it the same way."

He was back tracking so quickly that he was halfway out of the room before Darin recovered from his stupor. He felt terrible. His insecurities had blinded him with doubt and jealousy. Andrew was tossing the beer bottle in the can marked recyclables, in Elizabeth's elegant hand writing, when Darin caught up to him.

"I am so sorry, Drew. I have had a ton on my mind lately, and I guess I was just spacing out a second there. I don't know what is wrong with me. I'm not myself. I really didn't even catch what you were saying."

He said trying to look apologetic without losing face entirely. It was a business habit from too many insincere apologies. Andrew noticed it, yet he wasn't offended, knowing Darin too well to expect anything else. It had taken a great deal of humility to muster his courage for this visit, and now, his ego begged him not to ask a second time. He tried convincing his pride again that it was a necessity for reaching his goal.

"I came to ask you for some money to fund a project I am working on." He said plainly, skipping the effort at coming across professionally he had been striving for on his first effort.

"I can't really say what it involves just yet, but I think, if done correctly, we could see strong returns in a year or so."

He looked straight into Darin's eyes as only he could in such a humbling moment.

Darin had a difficult time returning the respect. He rubbed the back of his fingers lightly against his unshaven chin. He could only consider the proposal half heartedly. The majority of his brain, still burned out from the tension, was thankful that his nightmares were not confirmed.

August 21st, 2003

Fall arrived early, and Eric felt the wind's chill bite as he stepped out of the car. He zipped his work jacket up about three quarters of the way, regretting that he hadn't worn his hooded sweatshirt instead. The neon lights of the county fair lit up the fading evening sky with a hypnotic dazzle of blinking, colored bulbs. Eric grinned giddily at the distant sounds. Though he was embarrassed by it, Eric always held a special love for the annual festival.

Growing up, he looked forward all summer long to the familiar sights, sounds, and smells of the dingy carnival and all that came with it. He helped Claire load a bundled up Nathan into his stroller, feeling rushed by all his childlike anticipation. He missed the fair the past two summers, marking the first time he had missed the fair since his parents first introduced him to the sub par world of entertainment when he was just four years old. In 2001, he missed it because of the honeymoon, and last year, he hadn't gone in light of the sorrowful events of that summer.

Claire didn't mind the absence. She never liked the fair or the filth that seemed to come with it, but she endured it because she knew how happy it made Eric. Every year, the fair was set up slightly different, in hopes of deceiving the townsfolk into feeling there were new attractions. In reality, nothing changed much.

All the same, Eric was excited for Nathan's first fair. Claire smiled lovingly at story after story about the fairs of Eric's past while she pushed Nathan across the dusty lot toward the gated entrance. She had heard nearly every story a half dozen times or more over the years, yet she loved seeing her husband's joy while he floated on air like he was sixteen again. The young couple was overcome with joy at Nathan's behavior strolling down the grass alleys between the tents and rides. The looks of curiosity and amusement on his face were priceless, and Claire was able to get four or five great photos within the first ten minutes of walking.

Eric, on the other hand, needed a little more babysitting. He spent fifteen dollars on each of the first two games he played and, still prize-less, was beginning to take on a look of desperation. He was being finagled in by another greasy looking vagabond, who was convincing him how easy it was to land a softball into a slanted wicker basket, when Claire stepped in.

"Can we go grab a snack, hun?" She asked coyly.

"Yea baby, just let me win you one of these big stuffed tigers first." Eric replied without turning around then asked the reptilian looking man about having a practice throw.

"I am hungry now though." Claire pouted, refusing to watch the charades continue.

This time Eric turned to her. He knew he was treading into dangerous territory.

"Baby, this will take five seconds. Don't you want a big stuffed animal?" he asked pleadingly.

"No, I want something sweet. We can come back before we leave." she continued, holding her ground.

The carnie teased Eric that he better listen to his woman. Eric pulled a wad of bills from his pocket in search of a five.

"Are you serious?" Claire huffed.

"These games are rigged honey. Do you see a single person walking around with one of those big tigers?"

Eric glanced around a little, feeling embarrassed.

"Doesn't that seem a little strange considering it's the main prize at about three of these games?"

Eric smiled at her sheepishly. The vendor tried one last time to cut a deal, offering extra throws, but Eric was already putting his money away.

He was more than a little embarrassed at having his wife scold him in public, but he enjoyed the fair too much to ruin it with an argument he would end up losing anyway. He put his big arm around his wife's shoulder and squeezed her tightly for a moment, hoping she would understand his annoyance. He then grabbed the stroller with both hands and headed back the way they had came at a brisk walk.

"Let's go get a sweet for my sweet." He called over his shoulder without looking back.

His lips were pursed tightly. He was proud of himself for taking the higher road, but he already decided if she pushed a little harder he would bite back. Reading her husband's body language, Claire was already one step ahead, remaining silent on the walk to the food trailers. She knew there was nothing to worry about. This wasn't serious. She waited until Eric had chosen a vender and was waiting in line before coming up behind him, putting her slender arms around his waste, and standing on her tip toes so she could kiss him on his neck. He tried to remain stoic. The relationship had already seen this act so many times it was merely a formality. She decided it was safe to play cute again.

"Can I have a caramel apple, hun?" She asked with pleading eyes.

She needed little effort to capture the innocence of a child. Claire had a youthful elegant beauty that required no makeup and she rarely wore anything beyond lip gloss. Her high cheekbones and olive eyes gave her the look of Russian royalty.

Eric caught her look, remaining impassive as possible. She blinked her gorgeous eyelashes repeatedly at him, pouting her thin bottom lip. He cracked, grinning with a noticeable blush. He leaned down and kissed her pale lips, feeling victorious. Hugging her tightly, he said a silent prayer for helping him avoid conflict.

Everything felt great. He bought Claire a caramel apple and himself a corndog and a bag of cotton candy. They walked down the gravel road parallel to the fence to the far corner of the fairgrounds where all the livestock barns were. The two large barns along with three smaller tin exhibition buildings were the only permanent structures on the lot, aside from the rodeo grandstands directly behind them and the public bathrooms near the entrance gate. The buildings were set up in a logical rectangular fashion with a large courtyard in the middle. The courtyard included a number of picnic tables and benches ideal for men to rest at while their wives shopped for worthless junk or cheap trinkets that had no place in the home. The right hand side of the courtyard was blocked off by a three foot tall orange plastic fence running between the two original barns. Both barns were worn with faded red paints contrasting from years of remodeling efforts constantly defeated by the effects of hard winters and sun.

The beer garden and the rodeo grounds lay on the far side. This was new for Eric, who always remembered his dad and friends piled in around the courtyard getting tuned up, loud, and obnoxious. He remembered one year Darin and him had smoked their first cigarette on the back side of the last exhibition building. The exhibition buildings still held a faint metallic shine. They were less then a decade old and a constant reminder of change in the wake of progress across from the antique barns. It took them half a book of matches to light the smoke, and they took turns leaning back into the semi circular grooves in the outer wall of the shop-like metal building taking drags.

They felt so brave lighting it up, taking those first couple puffs, listening to all the excitement in the courtyard behind them, daring someone to come catch them in the act, so the story would be immortalized. It never happened, and Darin got sick alone since Eric hadn't been inhaling. A few years later, the rush was all about scoring beer and drinking it from fountain cups right out in the courtyard with the adults all around. It was a ridiculous idea, drinking beer right out in public at seventeen, but it had always been this way, so a lot of people let it slide.

The sheriff's department deputies prowled around the area all the same.

Of course, it wasn't only the cops the boys had to look out for. There were parents, teachers, even family friends that could all catch them. Everyone knows everyone at a small town fair. Maybe not enough to stop and have a conversation with but plenty enough to bust them.

It is like red carpet entertainment for eighty percent of this country. Teens can't resist the temptations of fame. Every year a bunch would be caught, ruining the end of their summers. Then the very next year, everyone would try it again. Eric figured that it probably explained the beer garden fence. He wondered why it hadn't existed years before. Not that he regretted the way things had been, but a lot of his friends would have never been kicked off the football team if the initiative had been taken while he was in school. He joked about it to Claire between monstrous gobs of cotton candy.

"Just another sign of how resistant to change people are in this town." Claire said as she reached out to wipe mustard off the corners of Eric's mouth and chin.

She hated mustard and scrunched her nose at the yellow stain left on the napkin before tossing it in a waste basket and shaking her head, grossed out.

"That and the Zipper." Eric gurgled over a mouthful of cotton candy.

He laughed alone at his own joke. Claire was busy cleaning her hands with baby wipes. Eric felt a rumbling in his stomach. He checked out the remainder of his cotton candy. There was less than a third of the bag left. He debated trying to finish it off but decided against it, stuffing the last of the bag into the pouch behind Nathan's stroller. The last thing he wanted was to get heartburn before boarding the rides. He remained seated on the wooden bench staring with alert wonder at all the glittering, spinning machinery, fond memories twinkling in his eye when a familiar voice startled him.

"Eric, my main man. How the hell are ya?"

The voice came from a short squat man in a worn Carhartt jacket that was unzipped to reveal a pair of paint stained, duck bib overalls. The speaker had dirty blonde hair which was thinning noticeably along the scalp and a thick reddish blonde goatee which didn't appear to receive a whole lot of attention to grooming. He stood along side the bench, hands at his sides, weight shifted to one leg, as if not sure how to appear comfortable while standing stationary and empty handed.

Eric recognized him right away. His name was Chuck Leskar. He was three or four years older than Eric, but he had always been one of those senior guys who showed up to every freshman or sophomore party. He was a pretty good kid in high school. The majority of his time was spent out in the shop trying to make his old Cheyenne sound a little louder or look a little trashier. Whether or not it had been his intention, the silver pickup and its three inch lift would be how most of his school peers would forever remember him if they remembered him at all.

Chuck worked at an auto parts store all through school and always had a little money in his pocket. He didn't mind throwing it around to impress the younger girls either, especially Elizabeth. Everyone knew he had a huge crush on her, and Darin hated when he would buy her things but never spoke of it to Chuck. Darin always considered it stupid to fight over a female or so he said.

"Hey Chuck, I haven't been too bad. How bout yourself?" Eric said, standing to shake Chuck's hand.

As they each concentrated to ensure a firm grip, Eric sized him up unintentionally the way old acquaintances often do.

"Oh, just working a lot and drinking even more." He answered with a smile, showing off a row of crooked, dirty teeth caked with tobacco grains and yellow film.

"Sounds good, you still roofing for Bob Westin?" Eric asked, trying not to stare in disgust.

"You mean Frank Liberman, and no, I just finished my electrician apprenticeship. I am working for Central Electric." He claimed pointing at a blue logo embroidered into the breast of his jacket with evident pride.

"Really, a union guy huh?" Eric said conveying his knowledge.

"Yep, it's the way to go. We are really steam rolling too. I just finished on that new resort they are building over in Red Lakes, and next week I start a big job up in Watsonville."

"You guys are getting jobs way up there huh?"

"Not usually. We work mostly out of the central part of the state, but this is a three or four million dollar job, so we jumped all over it." He said spitting a well practiced spray onto the dirt near his left boot. Evidently, this was one of his current highlights.

"What are they building up there that big, a train station or something?"

"No, it's a county hospital."

Two middle school aged kids ran alongside them yelling spastically. One of them was chasing the other one, cursing him for some misdoing. The other remained a few short steps ahead of him laughing fearfully. It reminded Eric of the fun yet to be had. He turned to Claire who remained seated on the bench. She was playing half heartedly with Nathan, visibly bored.

He sped the rest of the conversation toward its inevitable end, told Chuck it was great seeing him, and wished him good luck. Grabbing

Claire's hand, his mind was already on the Gravitron when the sound waves of Chuck's closing remark reached his ear, tightening his sternum.

"Have you talked to Andrew in the last couple days?"

The words sounded distant over the crowds of high pitched adolescent voices struggling with the advances of puberty, giving the question an ominous reverberation.

"No, I haven't seen him in a couple weeks." Eric admitted honestly.

The last time he had physically seen him had been that afternoon he sobered him up and told him to get his butt over and visit Shane. They had spoken on the phone since, yet anytime his name came up Eric tensed a little. Like the proud father of a hooligan son, he loved to hear from him but knew trouble was probably close behind. After hearing Darin's story about the bizarre visit, Eric had been expecting to receive a visit of his own though it never happened.

"Oh, I was going to ask you how he was doing. I saw him a few nights ago down at the Barn, and I heard he got into a pretty good scrap with the Gardapees after I called it a night."

Eric shifted his weight, scrunching his toes up in his haggard work boots. The astonishment in his wife's expression only confirmed what he thought he heard.

"Who said that?" He asked bluntly.

"Cindy Aimes told me about it the next day, but I was just in there last night, and people were still talking about it." He exclaimed. "I guess it got pretty nasty."

He spoke with a bluntness that showed he felt detached from the story. For him, it was no different than gossiping about something happening in Hollywood entertainment. Everyone busts out their best gossip at picnics and fairs. The worn skin around his temples smoothed easily when he frowned insincerely.

The concern in Eric's eyes only brought more pleasure to his demeanor. His joy didn't come from the pain caused to others as much as the fact that his words carried weight. His story was important. Someone wanted to listen to him speak.

"Which Gardapee?" Eric asked.

The anxiety balling in the bottom of his throat was detectable in his voice.

"Both of em." Chuck nearly shouted, widening his eyes to show the tiny intricate veins funneling the white sclera into a very faint crimson that contrasted harshly with his distinct blue iris.

Eric's curiosity turned quickly into a storm of panic, and every moment new emotion pushed the storm closer to becoming a devastating twister spinning out of control. He felt a small spot on his back shoulder begin to spasm lightly on and off. He tried to focus on it to calm his anger and concern. Chuck could see the pigment disappear from Eric's face. He slumped his shoulders a little and tried to spit, but his mouth was dry.

He was suddenly aware that if he didn't choose his next words carefully he might be on the wrong end of a large, well reputed right fist. He looked to Claire, but she was watching her husband trying to gage his thoughts. She held his arm very lightly, carefully. Her right hand rubbed slowly up and down his left soothingly.

"I guess he ended up getting roughed up a little," Chuck continued, too ignorant to know what else to do. His voice far from the unabashed 'so did you hear' tone it had began the conversation with.

He reached in his pocket for his can of confidence, hoping a little chew would help his composure. He pushed a pinch into the side of his lip smoothly and wiped his finger on his pant leg. Eric remained somewhere far away yet appeared to be waiting for more.

"Just a few battle scars though." Chuck finished his thought aloud.

"It could have been a lot worse messing with them fucking spear chuckers. They just assume kill ya. Their whole families in the pen anyway, wouldn't be no worse off."

His voice trailed off, and he spit again to fill in the silence.

"Yea," Eric finally responded. "I guess you're probably right."

He pulled out his phone and started away without another word. He dialed up Andrew, wishing he had more information. He thought about Chuck's last words, thinking the Gardapees might very well be the lucky ones if there wasn't a second violent run in with Andrew.

AUGUST 3RD, 2004

It didn't take Darin long to find which field he was looking for. Eric's booming baritone echoed across the entire complex. Capp Fields were built in the late 1970's as part of a huge renovation project by the city. Until that time, there were two softball fields in town, located on a couple lonely lots situated inside the remains of a dried swamp pit along the debris scattered, grassy hills that ran a half mile east of the high school. The lots required little bulldozing, making the location a logical choice. But due partly to the poor condition of the facilities and partly to lack of maintenance, softball had little drawing power. The school's softball program was in shambles, and it was only a matter of time before enough people blamed the facilities and forced the city to take action. The renovation plans were meant to fix up the current fields and hire a groundskeeper that would be paid by the city.

Tucker Capps, a local entrepreneur and softball enthusiast, volunteered to match the city's donations, seeing a state of the art softball complex as a great way to create revenue for local businesses. He owned a gas and grocery a mile further east of the fields and he knew it would take six or eight fields to draw the large tournaments that lasted through the summer and all the visitors that came with them.

Nearly a million additional dollars were raised through donations, and Capps was able to create the largest complex in the state. Capp Fields opened in 1977. It was a source of great pride for the community. The new facilities were set up in two large squares of four fields each. The backstop of each field was built on a given corner of the square, so all four fields could share common outfield. Although fences were often brought in for tournaments, there were no fences during the regular season because high school softball and adult softball required different dimensions.

Between the two squares was a large grass park with a few spruce trees, a playground area, and a trailer used for concessions and any administrative needs. There were blue port-a-potties scattered throughout the grounds, but because of the way light beer was consumed during league play, it was fairly acceptable to urinate any place that was unobservable from two sides. It wasn't long before the sport took on a major following in town.

Starting in the spring and running through the entire summer, divisions ranging from coed recreational through men's 'A' league fast-pitch enjoyed the well kept fields from dinner until long after dark on weekdays and virtually the entire weekend. Eric and Andrew played for a new team named the Grave Robbers. They were in class 'C' slow-pitch, the second highest slow-pitch division holding by far the most participating teams. Eric started the new-found squad after numerous disputes with his previous class 'D' team, the Long Ballers, over how serious the team should be.

Eric was a young, devoted father and loving husband, and a hyper-competitive recreational athlete. He wanted to win at any cost. He even went as far as to suggest a no drinking rule during the first game with his new team, but the entire team threatened mutiny, so instead, he asked that everyone at least wait until the game began to crack the first cold one. All the same, he brought a cooler of sports drinks to every game in hopes of swaying his teammates toward the thrills of sobriety.

Darin had forgotten to ask what color uniforms they would be wearing, but he heard Eric barking out rah rah from field five. The Grave Diggers were in the field, and the sight of a fired up Eric pitching was enough to make Darin laugh aloud. They wore black jerseys with neon green lettering and numbers. Everyone wore a jersey along with sweatpants or shorts except Eric, who wore tight white baseball pants with black pin-stripes that were anything but flattering.

He looked like a veteran of the game twice his age; his hefty figure stuffed into full uniform and his sweat stained old Wrangler hat pulled down snuggling on his scalp. He had heavily recruited Darin to the team all spring, but Darin was too busy to commit the time, knowing it would cause a fight if he joined half heartedly. In truth, Darin was a little intimidated of going out unseasoned and looking bad, even if it was to be expected at first. But seeing his friend's out there having so much fun, he longed to take part in the game.

He climbed onto the third row of bleachers behind the screen as a skinny, pigeon toed, hatless batter, sporting a long mane of frizzled brown hair torched a line drive into right center. Darin's eyes followed the path of the ball as velocity and gravity carried it downward toward a geometrically determined spot of grass in the gap. It was definitely a double, more likely a triple if pigeon toes could run. But suddenly, the outstretched glove of the centerfielder destroyed the smooth trajectory, snagging the ball from a nearly perpendicular route and sliding on his chest another four feet to a stop.

Despite the less than graceful landing, the catch was perfect. The glove came up and everyone, including the opposing team, cheered in amazement. Andrew lifted his head, tufts of grass hanging from his chin. The right fielder helped him to his feet, and he tossed the ball toward the mound as they jogged in laughing together. Grass stains were visible across the front of his black top. Darin tasted bitter jealousy on the back of his tongue. He stood clapping and whistling, but everyone was too busy mobbing Andrew near the dugout to notice his presence.

When all the excitement died down, Darin made his way over to the dugout. He remained quiet, waiting for someone to initiate conversation. His body language made it clear he was feeling less than confident, an outsider trying to share in on the team's thrilling wave of momentum. He knew everyone on the team, of course. He had snubbed many of them in high school or bossed them around on the grid iron. Now, he couldn't help longing for that camaraderie and flattery that came with being depended on by peers.

It wasn't that he had any enemies here. Everyone greeted him with a smile and high five, but his role was unnecessary out of uniform. So, despite all his athletic accomplishments from high school and college, he felt like an average Joe standing beside these roofers and plumbers, most of whom never even started a high school game in any sport. He tried to appear unshaken, cool, and confident. The bravado felt see through. He was about to return to his seat in the bleachers when the sight of one smile lifted his spirits.

"Well, well, well, if it isn't Donald Trump coming down to check on his community works effort." Andrew said, a large chew in his lip forcing the words out the side of his mouth.

Despite the joke, Darin quickly felt more at ease. He knew the best compliment Andrew gave was a rag.

"No, I'm down here scouting for the Yanks," he replied.

"I was told the Grave Diggers have one hell of a centerfielder."

"Well, you can go back and tell Steinbrenner to suck an egg, cuz it will be a cold day in Hell before I give up my leadoff." Eric chimed in from the field side of the fence.

He was in the on deck circle huffing and puffing with a weighted bat.

"Leadoff huh? That's surprising. I would have figured you'd have yourself batting in that slot, Coach." Darin said, leaning his head through the opening in the fence. Eric laughed but still took offense to the knock on his speed.

"I might have had enough depth to juggle things around more if I hadn't lost one of my top draft picks to an endorsement deal that forced him to hang up his spikes."

"I guess sometimes a guy has to make sacrifices to do what's best for his career." Darin chimed in retort, ducking his head back to hug Andrew.

"It's alright. The guy was a little too flashy for our team concept. He probably would have ended up being a distraction. Besides, I don't think he had the guts to play hurt."

Eric's remark aimed at revenge for the speed rag. Darin pretended not to hear it. He congratulated Andrew on his catch. Andrew smiled confidently, attributing everything to luck.

He looked amazing.

Darin didn't know what it was, but since spring Andrew really seemed to be his old self again. He was lean and muscular, his skin tanned and his hair cropped in a short fade. He had regained that glow that made him so unique. He was laying sheet rock for a local company from nine to five and bartending out at the lake a couple nights a week.

Darin had yet to receive any payments on the money he loaned Andrew the previous summer, but he wasn't that worried about it. Still, nearly a year had passed since he loaned out the money, and he knew he had to bring it up sooner or later. He figured Andrew had to be making a few bucks, yet he hadn't made any huge purchases Darin knew about and couldn't be spending anymore at the bars than he had been when he was unemployed. So, he started wondering where all the money went. It was the last thing on his mind at the moment, though, and when Andrew told him to stick around because they were all going out for a couple drinks after the game, Darin agreed to tag along.

"What inning is it anyways?" Darin asked.

"It's the fifth. We play seven, so it's almost over."

"What's the score?"

"We are up 8-5, but we need to get a few here because this is one of the best teams we have played." Andrew said with a personalized blend of casual confidence and veteran intensity.

It was like everything out of his mouth was a famous and well quoted movie scene. His Charisma shined like a force-field. All of a sudden, Eric laced a base knock right back up the middle, and Darin made his way back to the stands for a better view. The next hitter parachuted a little Texas leaguer over the short stops head, but Eric didn't read it well and the left fielder hosed him by a step. Comments about unhooking everything from a plow to a piano rang out from his own dugout. Darin couldn't help but laugh. Andrew shot a thick gob of tobacco through the backstop and remained seated and steady.

The seventh batter tripled to score one, and it looked like the Grave Diggers were about to blow the game wide open. The momentum stalled, however, when the next batter tattooed a line drive down the line that the third baseman caught protecting his face. The runner had taken off on contact, ending the inning in a double play. In sports as in life, momentum could be a funny and often short lived advantage.

While the Grave Diggers took the field, Darin spread his arms out on the row behind him and looked about. The glare from the fading sun forced him to shade his eyes. He was amazed to be the only fan in the stands on such a beautiful evening. It wasn't like he expected the place to be packed like game seven of the World Series, yet he couldn't imagine that not a single guy on either team would have a girlfriend, parent, friend, or child sitting in the grandstands. He noticed that the opposing team did have a small gathering of fans, mostly significant others by the look of it, sitting in lawn chairs down the first base line past the dugout.

It didn't make sense to sit down there though because it was hard to see the whole field. Darin couldn't help frowning at his deliberation that this was a typical woman move. They would rather sit close to the dugout where they can keep vigilant eye on their men and smother his last gasps of privacy than sit where they could see the game. Of course, this brought Elizabeth to mind.

Darin and Liz had been back together since the beginning of the year, but the reunion was far from fairytale. With the exception of a few over the top romantic gestures and a seldom flickering of their teenage passion, their relationship was like a rain out in the first game of a double header. Their hearts were no longer in it hundred percent. They stuck around like the boys of summer merely waiting out of obligation to see if the second game could be salvaged. But, the forecast looked bleak. Keeping them together was a memory that what they once felt was the highlight of their young lives. The amber of love lingered hot somewhere hidden beneath the cool ashes.

Darin knew in his heart it was his own fault. He was well aware that if he compromised a little more everything might not feel so jaded. Then, the exact type of moments when he could show humility, remorse, or even just responsibility arose, only to find him dawn a cloak of detached self righteousness all over again. The problem was definitely him, but it is always easier to describe incompatibilities in terms of others than the face in the mirror. A mirror's truth can be altered depending on light.

Many people envied Darin because he was effortlessly successful, compatible in any social environment, and talented at controlling the variables. The problem with Elizabeth was she knew the real Darin, not the Darin Bard he went to such painstaking efforts to be. She knew who he actually was, faults and all. She knew he was human, and her presence only reinforced his own vulnerability.

He found himself wondering, as he often did, whether or not it would be easier to live without her and erase all the wrongs reflected in her eyes or the much harder task of changing himself and not just going through the motions. While pondering this fate, he became so lost in thought he didn't notice his concentrated scowl was focused hard on a newcomer to the bleachers. It wasn't until her nervous glances took on somewhat of a terrified lip quiver that he realized he was no longer alone.

"Sorry." He murmured sheepishly, though after he felt even creepier.

"It's ok. You seemed a little lost in thought." She replied with an air of superiority. There was no forgiveness in her voice.

Darin realized she felt he was gawking at her in longing. His surprise became embarrassment. He turned back to the field, still taking her in with subtle, patient glances. She was definitely a beautiful girl: long, smooth, tan legs crossed at the knee, a tight black tank-top complementing a decent cup size and thin figure. She had long straight brown hair, long batty eyelashes, and full, gorgeous lips. Trying to play it cool, he felt his embarrassment turn toward contempt. Somewhere miles away, the sweet ping of contact told of a ball striking the sweet spot.

Normally, this sound would capture Darin's complete attention, but he only pretended to watch the runners circle the bases. His real interest was how she reacted. Only, she didn't react. A three run triple down the first base line didn't even spark her attention. Her eyes remained focused outward toward the field, but she showed no signs of stimulation. Her neck never moved her eyes one way or the other. The heel of her right flip flop could be heard slapping the bleachers over and over as she twitched her leg impatiently.

The next batter slapped a chopper toward third. It was sure to be a close play, but she glanced down at her nails as the runner beat the throw by a step. Stranger yet, her detachment didn't annoy Darin. It only made him more interested. This behavior continued for sometime with Darin never making any attempt to break the ice, his lust growing by the minute.

The Grave Diggers went down in order in the bottom of the sixth, and it wasn't until a two run double in the top of the seventh that Darin realized that not only had the Diggers blown the lead, but they were now trailing by three and down to their final outs.

Eric appeared to be on the verge of a total mental break down. He was swearing at everyone to 'get it together', kicking the ground, and making faces that would make even the gothic middle school crowd jealous. His teammates ignored him best they could, but their silence spoke volumes.

The mystery girl's cell phone rang, and as she answered it, Darin strained to listen in. Her voice was high pitched, very peppy. Her nasal giggle and choice in vocabulary brought two obvious questions to Darin's mind that had been blinded before by fantasy. How old was this girl? And, what was she doing at this game?

A livid Eric's screams of strung together, vulgar expletives, caused Darin to lose his train of thought. The entire team showed clear frustration coming off the field down three and in need of a massive rally, a miracle, or both. Eric didn't mention the latter. He simply tried to annoy the other team into submission with non stop supportive rally clichés. It wasn't until he was silenced by the five hitter popping the first pitch up to the third baseman that he decided it was time for a 911 call to his maker. The line must have been busy, for the next hitter grounded out to short, leaving two down and the seven, eight, and nine hitters due up.

Eric's holiness turned to hate. He wanted to throw something. Nathan's now famous temper tantrums came to Darin's thoughts. Eric didn't lose it yet though. He stared out at the field with hopelessness chiseled in his face.

The only positive voice from the Digger dugout was Andrew. His voice held the same tone and encouragement it had while playing catch before the game. It wasn't loud or forced. It was his regular conversational voice. He was stretching out along the fence, same as always, fully expecting to come up with two out and three weak hitters before him, watching with the eager intensity that only exists in the tiny minority of truly gifted players. Everyone else slumped around the dugout had already started on the post game drinking with abject, self pity, though most of them over did their disappointment mostly because Eric made the game feel that serious.

The heavy chunk batting snuck a seeing-eye single through the five-hole, and everyone cheered out of obligation. The eight hitter swung and whiffed the first pitch, seemingly squeezing the last remnants of air out of the Diggers' sail. Then, he hit the very next pitch right at the right fielder.

Eric threw his clipboard in disgust, forgetting one of the fundamental rules of slow pitch softball: always hide the weakest link in right. This was a quality team, so their weakest link wasn't as obvious as some. The Digger's only had two left handed hitters and really hadn't hit any fly balls to right, so the derelict looking hayseed that drifted, and drifted, and drifted before letting the ball fall just out of reach, shocked everyone.

Unfortunately, the exploited right fielder shocked the base runner more than anyone. He had been standing stone still between first and second watching the can of corn fall. By the time the ball hit the ground, the centerfielder, well aware of the skeletons in his own team's closet, picked it up quickly, almost throwing the lead runner out at third.

"Come on. Where's the third base coach when you need him?" Darin heckled from the stands.

The girl turned to him with a confused look, missing the joke completely. Darin smiled at her but was unable to read her response. Meanwhile, the game was placed in the hands of the number nine hitter, Ben Colridge. Colridge had never been much of an athlete, definitely not the ideal guy a coach dreams of coming up when the game is on the line, but he had always been tight with Eric and Darin. A class clown back in school, Colridge was the type of guy who wouldn't flinch to rebel against even the most hard laced teachers yet couldn't think of a clever thing to say to a girl for the life of him. Darin wouldn't be surprised if he was stepping into the box still a virgin to this day.

As he made his way around the umpire, Darin took a good long look at his face. He didn't look any different than he had in high school, or middle school for that matter. He was of average height and weight, had average brown hair, and the type of young face that would get him carded well into his thirties. He was one hundred percent Joe Shmoe Middle American white guy. Nothing about him hinted at how he would handle this huge at bat.

The simple fact he wore no glasses puzzled Darin. He had known Ben since they were placed on the same basketball team in sixth grade. Coincidentally, the last sports team Ben probably participated on until the Grave Diggers. All that time, Darin couldn't remember a single time he had seen Ben without glasses. Now, he stood a few short steps from the batter's box taking a deep breath with Andrew on deck, nipping at the bit for his chance to swing. It was up to Colridge, not to pulverize the heroic double into the gap, or even get a hit for that matter. All Colridge had to do was not get out, extend the inning by any means necessary. Darin hoped his old friend had switched over to contact lenses.

"Wait for your pitch. You don't have to swing at the first one unless its there. Just wait for your pitch." Eric drilled, verging on a stroke.

Colridge nodded his head like a bobble-head doll. He looked like a little leaguer, his wide eyes, desperate for guidance, locked on Eric, his nervous hands squeezing the bat grip until his knuckles whitened. The first pitch floated in. Colridge, on the advice of his coach, took it. Strike one.

Darin chuckled to himself, thinking how umpiring slow pitch was a lot like flipping coins. In situations like these, the umpire is praying that the pitcher put it over the plate and the hitter swing. The last thing the umpire needs is to make borderline calls with two outs in the final frame when everyone has a few cans of courage in them. For twelve bucks a game, it's not really worth pissing off either team of buzzed up, testosterone filled, bricklayers. It's only a matter of time before every softball umpire discovers that no call is ever the right call. So, it came as no surprise to hear a horde of pissed off Grave Diggers make their dissenting opinions clear, along with more than a personal opinion or two about the umpire's sexual orientation.

Most of these men lived their day to day lives cycling through monotonous routines of manual labor and bills. From Darin's position, he could see unidentified fingers clung tightly to the chain link separating the dugout from the field of play. Pressed up to the screen as close as possible, peering through the diamond shaped openings between the wires, the players watched, sick with anticipation.

Some hung their heads, so foreign to the lucky breaks in life that they knew Ben would fail. They couldn't watch it happen again. The second pitch tumbled in low. As Colridge prepared to swing, the umpire stepped out from behind the catcher and barked,

"Illegal."

Dozens simultaneously released their breaths. A player can still swing at an illegal pitch, but in this situation it froze everyone stiffer than an early winter storm. Colridge stepped out, trying to compose himself. He looked down to Eric for reassurance, but his coach's anxious appearance did little to calm him. He was alone on an island. He had joined the team for the social benefits, yet all he could think of was how lonely it would feel to blow the game. He unstrapped and restrapped the Velcro on his batting gloves, whispering a low prayer under his breath.

One last time, he searched around for a supportive face. This time he noticed Andrew in the on deck circle behind him. Something instantly struck him as odd. Whereas everyone else looked so rigid and eager, watching closely with anticipation, Andrew seemed completely unaware of the current situation's magnitude. In fact, he didn't even notice Ben's pleading eyes turned on him. He was stretching out a little, swinging a weighted bat back and forth loosely. His eyes went from something on the ground in front of him, to the opposing dugout, passing Ben's stare with only an impassive nod. Just a game those eyes seemed to say.

Seeing this attitude from Andrew had amazing effects on Ben Colridge. Suddenly, a burden slid from his shoulders. His brain realized this moment would not be the end of his world. He stepped into the box, still nervous, but far less so. He concentrated hard on the next pitch, and grounded it right between to third basemen's quivering legs. He couldn't remember ever feeling so fulfilled as he did when his foot touched first base. He jumped up and down, pumping his fist, and transforming instantly from the scared lonely batter he had been moments before into a confident veteran who had come through in the clutch.

"Come on Drew, everyone's a hitter. Keep it going here, kid." He shouted, no longer really caring about the game's outcome.

He had never had that sort of competitive fire. He was only thankful he hadn't been the scapegoat.

Darin, on the other hand, hungered for the competition so bad it hurt. He had been standing up and down throughout the past two at bats. Finally, he forgot all about impressing the mystery girl and went to stand beside the end of the dugout where the left handed batter's box would face him directly. He rubbed his sweating palms together until they squeaked and then wiped them on his shirt. He stretched his neck to each side, tuning out all the screams and shouts.

Andrew dug into the box. He had ice water running through his veins. A coyote's grin rested on his lips confidently. Darin figured the pitcher would hand him the non-intentional, intentional walk simply trying to make him swing at bad pitch. It might work too. Andrew had to be hungry to end it with one swing. He wouldn't take a walk easily. The shortstop, who seemed to be the coach of the team, turned around and motioned for his outfielders to back up. They moved back four or five steps and stopped.

Darin shook his head knowing it wouldn't be enough. Next, he turned his attention to the pitcher, who was huffing air hard. Sweat glistened from his face and arms, and his shirt was saturated with it. He was clearly pissing his pants like a Catholic choir girl in Compton. Darin hoped he wasn't stupid enough to go after Andrew. If he was, he better back his outfielders into the adjacent fields or the next county.

It was because the bases were loaded. Even with a few runs to gamble with, no one wants to walk in a run. It made Darin mad that such an exciting game was being tossed by boneheads that simply didn't understand the strategy of the game. The pitcher tossed the ball up, while Darin continued huffing and puffing to himself.

'It's our precious male egos that blind us to the limits of our abilities and blind us of our weaknesses,' Darin thought, angrily biting his lip.

The ball reached its peak then began tumbling and turning its way back down. Darin hated the pitcher for his ignorance. If there were fences, maybe they would rethink the whole situation. He was wondering how no one on the team had the good sense to at least talk things over with the bases loaded in the ninth when Andrew popped his hips, uncoiling like an industrial spring. He turned on the ball and drove an absolute laser beam into the infield of the unused field three, where it finally rolled to a stop along the backstop.

The ball was hit so hard and traveled so fast it could have been mistaken for a golf ball being crushed by a titanium driver. The Digger's came unhinged. Eric was screaming like a banshee, spinning his arm in a windmill motion so hard it threatened to fly out of socket. The shortstop sprinted out into right field trying to set up the long double cut, but with the exception of the right and center fielders racing for the ball, the rest of his teammates moped around, realizing it was all over but the hand shakes.

Darin didn't move. He stood gaping in awe at one of the most purely beautiful things he had ever seen. The moment washed over him like a pristine morning fog, snaking down from the hillside to reveal the mighty sun in its daily climb over the tallest pines. It was as if the sands in the hour glass were falling one grain at a time and only he could see the unique shine and brilliance of each microscopic ancient stone. Watching his best friend toss the bat aside nonchalantly and go into a sprint that was so natural and so graceful it had to be divine, Darin finally admitted to himself that Andrew was beyond the physical laws and realities that governed other mortals. And as he rounded second, traveling at cheetah-like speeds though the ball was still miles away, Darin felt his eyes swell with tears knowing somehow in his heart that he would never witness anything this beautiful ever again.

For the first time in years and without even realizing it, Darin thanked the God he had so much trouble believing in. He felt no envy, no grudges of the past, nor needs for the future. He felt only tranquility, and though he couldn't possibly capture it with words or recreate the feeling again, momentarily, he knew the incomprehensible satisfaction he had always worked so hard to reach. It was only a softball game, yet it was so much more. And as Andrew rounded third, high-fived his hyperventilating coach, and trotted into a mob of hysterical and still unbelieving Grave Diggers at home plate, Darin shook the chain link on the backstop until his fingers nearly bled, yelling and screaming with as much joy as anyone in that dog pile.

He stood witness as these washed up 'has-beens' and dirty 'never-will-bes' returned to the glorious forms of their bold and fearless youths. These mangy dogs that had seen so few wishes come true that they finally pawned them off cheaply in exchange for the wishes and dreams of a reality television world or a cheap bourbon buzz, suddenly remembered how great it felt to truly live. Maybe, the secret of life was visible right there in the dog pile. Maybe, the secret of life was to never worry about the secret of life. Darin wasn't naïve enough to think this moment would magically lead him to eternal happiness or even fix his problems. What it did do was make him happy, and for once that was enough for him.

"I still can't believe that ending." Eric chomped over a mouthful of thin crust pizza.

He glowed brightly in the moment, looking around him at his dirt clad, sweat soaked teammates floating over their chairs still in ecstasy. He thought of high school and all the countless times that a big Wrangler win had given hope to the hopeless, light to the lost or confused, and confidence to boys becoming men. He knew it was Andrew's gifts that had given this used up old town a reason to come together.

In a town where the cycle of parents passing down shattered dreams and acceptance of the mundane had gone on so long that those dreams, suffocating quietly in the night, passed away unmissed, Andrew had taken the collective burden upon his teenage shoulders and united them as a community once more. His homerun today may not have been as monumental or far reaching as those championship banners, but to those whose spirits it lifted it was a shining moment of immortality that would never be forgotten.

As he poured a mound of parmesan on his next bite, Eric noticed Andrew and Darin playing an arcade game across the dining room. They were laughing, and Eric couldn't remember ever seeing Darin so carefree. After the mayhem at home-plate had cleared, Darin had come to Eric in an elated state and rushed his excited words into a stuttering mess. Eric had nearly died laughing. He knew that no one hated to show vulnerability more than Darin, so seeing him spew out his emotions like an uncorked bottle of the bubbly was quite a treat. It was particularly special because Darin had always gone to great lengths to remain grounded whenever Andrew played the hero.

It was not that Darin wasn't congratulatory or excited. He was too proud to give into worshipping. But, this time he was on the outside looking in, and Eric was convinced it had been a profound revelation for his stoic friend. This allowed him to see the feat for more than its grandeur and truly appreciate how it infected those around it with a nirvana like high. This was great for Andrew as well. The exposure of Darin's dormant inner youth had to feed Andrew's own often troubled soul symbiotically.

Eric wasn't the only one watching the two handsome young men slapping the buttons and jamming the joysticks across the room. The beautiful young fan from the game who Andrew had introduced to everyone as, Ginger, watched with keen interest, going great lengths to maintain a look of boredom and disinterest despite all the drinking and yelling men around vying for her attention. Every time Andrew would turn his smiling face from the game for a moment, she would pout her lips and shoot him the same looks of desire that fell unnoticed upon her legs and tight, young body by the twenty or so other men in the pub.

Eric guessed she couldn't be much older than eighteen, but he didn't question what Andrew saw in her. She was magazine gorgeous and obviously very interested in him. Still, he couldn't help wishing his passionate friend would stop picking girls from the same mold. This one appeared the most plastic yet. Eric felt bad suddenly, realizing he was passing judgment. She seemed nice enough. Besides, he didn't even know if it was serious or not. He was merely being overprotective.

When Andrew's life was this peaceful, it was hard to let go. Eric couldn't imagine what it must be like to be the one square peg in a world of round holes. Eric wondered if Andrew even realized how different he was. He wondered if Andrew ever wished he were someone normal, someone who could live totally in this world, instead of drifting between this one and another.

"Eat that shit you punk-ass bitch." Darin shouted surprising nearly everyone present with his vocabulary.

Eric chuckled to himself and stuffed another huge bite of pizza in his gaping mouth.

"What can I say? You always were the martial arts master." Andrew replied in his best Asian accent.

"Thank you for the brutal reminder, master sensei."

The game ended, the two of them returned to the table, but Andrew made no approach at his lonely female friend. Instead he made a wise crack thanking Eric for saving some pizza for everyone else, picked up his glass of beer, and turned his attention to the karaoke stage, where the first brave singer was grabbing the microphone stand.

The singer was one of about eight or ten patrons in the pub who weren't with the softball party. He was probably in his late teens or early twenties and wore a grey hooded sweatshirt with a black track cleat printed across the chest. He was smiling at a table near the stage where a guy and a girl about his age couldn't sit still due to a vicious case of the giggles. Apparently, they had dared him to take the stage, and an educated guess said this was outside any of their normal comfort zones.

His courage was definitely diminishing exponentially as the first few notes of 'Hotel California' came out of the large speakers in the corner of the dining room, and his voice betrayed him momentarily as he sang,

"On a dark desert highway…"

But, it wasn't long before everyone in the room was singing along with him, and he took comfort in the company. All together, the room made the youngster look pretty wise for his song selection. Everyone clapped loudly when the song ended, and the greasy, aged hippy DJ thanked him for breaking the ice with a gracious nod before asking who would follow the lead.

Eric laughed to himself and grunted, "An-Drew, An-Drew."

Andrew turned to him with a look that said shut it. It was too late. Within moments, ten or fifteen people were chanting loudly, "AN-DREW, AN-DREW." His face turned crimson and he sat down in the nearest chair shaking his head, but the audience wouldn't take no for an answer.

"Come on, Drew." Some called.

"We want to hear the hero sing." A voice shouted, and the chanting continued.

It wasn't long before they were banging the tables in anticipation. Finally, a blushing Andrew rose to his feet in acceptance of the challenge. Everyone cheered and whistled as he made his way up to the DJ's table and began paging through the binder of songs. He made his decision quickly, whispered a few words to the DJ, who laughed, then whispered something back.

Andrew pulled the microphone out of its slot on the stand and turned to face his audience. His eyes were no longer fierce. He peered out into the crowd timidly. Then, clearing his throat a smile that pulled back on one cheek transformed him from a sheep into a fox.

"I think you'll like this one." He said flatly with a hint of shyness.

A sea of cheers responded, as a steady guitar strum poured out of the speakers, crashing down on the room like the waves of the ocean.

"Lazy yellow moon coming up tonight, shining through the trees..." He sang in perfect twang and harmony over the whistling and howling of the thrilled bunch of misfits that comprised his audience. They were banging on the tables and growing rambunctious with glee.

Andrew didn't only have the voice; he had the attitude, the rhythm, and the choreography to work the room into a frenzied mob. This definitely wasn't his first ride on the karaoke rodeo, though he would later claim it was his soberest. By the time he rolled into the chorus, he was lying across a table cooing,

"Spend the whole night through, feels so good to be with you," into Ginger's adoring eyes.

She was eating it up too, but then again, half the males in the room were probably feeling desire for him by this point. His charisma was flooding the room with sexual energy, and although it had always made Eric nervous when Andrew went so far over the top, he was hooting and hollering louder than anyone. And as Andrew climbed on top of Ginger, giving her his best effort at a lap dance, and belted out the chorus one last time, there wasn't a patron in the pub that wasn't belting it out with him joyously.

It was impossible to know the song ended, for the bar had come unglued. The trickle down effect of the performance was the ordering of three or four more pitchers of golden elixir.

Challengers, full of gusto and liquid courage tasting of the night's epic feel, crowded around the DJ's table thumbing madly in search of that magic song that could win them the crown. Over the next hour or so, there were some pretty worthy performances, but nothing that could surpass Andrew's.

It was after twelve when the DJ finally packed up his stuff, and the room started to come back down to earth. The crowd started the slow process of debriefing for the upcoming weekend and saying good bye to a special night, knowing from years of experience that this type of night could never be emulated but not wanting to admit that depressing fact. They left much quieter than they had arrived, knowing the alarm clock would call early tomorrow. The bartender and the busboy were cleaning up the physical evidence of the celebration while Darin and Andrew finished off the last pitcher, while Eric and Ginger watched, fighting off sleep.

Darin and Andrew had filled their glasses as often as any, so they were rambling on and on about any subject either happened to form a complete sentence on. Finally, Eric could wait politely no more.

"Alright, I have to go to bed." He yawned, looking like a big grizzly.

His hat was laid worn out and creased before him and he slapped at his matted bangs with his thick, dry fingers.

"Who needs a ride home?"

"Don't worry about it, bro." Andrew replied with a grin, apparently finding something funny.

"Ginger hasn't been drinking. She will give us a ride home."

Eric was too tired to argue. He shot her a tired glance to see if she vetoed, but she only smiled, so he said his goodbyes and made his way out into the cool night air, smiling as he reflected on the victory that now seemed like text book history. After Eric left, Ginger went to the restroom, leaving the two buzzed up blabbermouths alone at the table. Andrew seemed content to spend the moment staring at the half empty glass held loosely in his left hand, but Darin had been waiting for this opportunity all night.

"So what's up with this little fox?" He asked immediately, nodding toward the restrooms with a look that was itchier than a frat boy at four a.m.

"You tapping that or what?"

Andrew glanced around slowly, as if he had no idea what 'little fox' his friend spoke of.

"Who? Ginger?" He asked innocently. "No, we are just friends."

The smile on his face conflicted with his response, prompting Darin to probe further.

"Come on tell me the truth. I bet she's something else huh?" He pushed.

Andrew laughed a little, seeing the desire in his friend's blood shot eyes.

"Yea, I bet she probably is." He agreed, before adding, "But I doubt I will ever find out. I don't think she is interested in me in that way."

Darin knew he was being bated, but the booze and the lust drove him further.

"You're so full of shit." He snapped.

Then he paused, nearly choking on his laughter.

He tried to take another sip from his glass, but the laughter came back, and beer went up his nose. They both had a good laugh at this, and Ginger was slapping her flip flops back toward the table when Darin half whispered,

"You're the luckiest prick I ever seen with girls. I would give anything to sleep with that girl."

Ginger didn't hear a word but noticed his face as she sat back down.

"What?" she asked, giving her best look of innocent oblivion, blinking her eyes for extra kick. Her efforts were clearly successful with Darin who melted with yearning, but when she turned to Andrew, he was staring across the table with a checked out expression.

"Are you ready to go?" she asked, trying even harder to lock him into her seductive trance, but he remained unscathed and unnoticing. She looked back across the table at Darin, who still watched her entirely, unaware of Andrew's gaze. She began to wonder what had transpired while she was in the restroom, immediately hoping it would lead to a dispute over her. She flashed her eyes at Darin, who bit the hook and ran upstream.

"So when are you gonna let me drive your car?" She asked while digging an ice cube from the empty glass in front of her.

"Ha," Darin laughed then added with only the slightest conviction, "No girl drives my car, even if she drives me."

"Well, I'm not ever gonna drive you, but I will drive that car soon. I'm a good driver." She complained, too tired from the long night to maintain the seductress approach.

"What about your ex?" Andrew suddenly sputtered. He watched Darin's jaw clench and his mood shift as he turned his full attention away from Ginger, before going on, "Did she ever get to drive the Stang?"

Darin huddled himself quickly, trying to regain his poise.

"She's driven it before," he said, steadfast, his balls clanging like steel. He wasn't blaming the alcohol or excusing it, but he saw the inquiry as a brush back, high and tight, and for the same reason, he dug right back in and prepared for another one.

"So, she is your ex then?" Andrew retaliated, dropping the twelve to six and catching the black for a strike the way only he was able to after a high hard one.

In Darin's mind, all the events that made this day such a unique and wonderful one melted away. He crawled into his respective corner and prepared to defend himself until he could mount some sort of an offensive.

"We are working on things." He said then narrowed his eyes as if to ask, 'What of it?'

Andrew flinched at the cold response, sipped down the last of his glass, and leaned forward with his forearms on the table. Darin watched him carefully, unsure of what to expect next. Andrew sat quietly, seemingly considering his next move, knowing he had already crossed over the line. Ginger reached into her glass again, stirring ice cubes around the cylindrical walls, making an unsteady clacking noise. She knew nothing of her two companions history or relationship, but she suspected from the ex talk that the two had chased the same girl before. She loved drama with a passion, and she only wished there was a better audience present to see them fight over her.

The truth of the matter was that neither Andrew nor Darin even realized Ginger was still present. Darin became solely consumed with protecting his pride, and Andrew merely wanted to make his point without injuring their friendship. Realizing too late that this was neither the time nor the place, Andrew bit his tongue. Finally, after several agonizing seconds of nothing but ice cubes rattling against each other, Darin decided his best bet was to simply change the subject, and he was about to bring up how late it was, when the busboy dropped a sugar caddy, and it shattered on the floor.

It was a small diversion, but it worked the same way poking a hole in the plastic covering on a microwave dinner does. The tension seeped out slowly, but eased all the same.

"Let's get out of here." Darin finally suggested in a voice hoarse from the beer and emotion.

Then, he watched Andrew, drunk and worn out, struggle to a standing position, a sliver of the hero he was only a few hours early, and it made him think of Shane, sitting in a musty cell somewhere, lonely. All he could think of at that moment was how much he hated alcohol and drugs and the problems they led to. The three of them walked out to the car in silence. Each of them too tired to reach out, too alone to start an exchanging of words.

Ginger drove a Rav-4. It was one of two cars left in the parking lot, and despite everything, Darin couldn't help but imagine Ginger and himself messing around in the spacious backseat as he climbed in behind the driver's seat. He felt slimy for even thinking that, and turned to stare out the window as she pulled the little truck out onto an empty, dimly lit 8th Ave.

The ride may have gone smoothly if the two boys were left to sulk in silence, but Ginger wouldn't think of it. She put in a CD, and turned the volume up on some poppy eighty's song. Naturally, this only further agitated the inebriated. Who knows, that may have been her intention. Either way, the seismograph readings from back at the bar were only a warning of the coming quake. The music only seemed to add to the stress grinding the two plates against each other. The first song was followed by an even more annoying one, but this time Ginger turned the volume down low enough to ask Andrew a question.

"Do you have work tomorrow, or could I come over for a little bit tonight?"

This cute, honest question set off the epicenter.

Before Andrew had time to answer, Darin lashed out.

"I know this might be a bad time to ask," He started, strictly for that reason, "But, when can you pay me back that money I loaned you?"

He was leaning to his right from behind the driver's seat, so he had a clear look at Andrew's face in the blue glow of the stereo light. Knowing he was being particularly spiteful, he expected to see absolute hatred and anger in Andrew's reaction. He craved it. He wanted to recreate what he had felt in the bar. What he saw was something totally unexpected.

Andrew's face showed no anger. He looked Darin right in the eyes, and his face wore the saddest most defeated look Darin had ever seen. Maybe it was the tint of the pale blue shadowing his features, or the sweat and dirt from the game, or all the alcohol and being beat tired, but none of this could explain why his eyes looked so hollow and defeated.

All those times Darin had been jealous of his accomplishments or the ease of Andrew's accolades vanished. Looking in to those eyes in the haunting blue glow, he realized how different their lives were. Those eyes that he had either avoided or ignored for arrogant reasons for so many years told the tale of a man who would never be understood and to some extent would always be alone. Looking into Andrew's eyes was like looking into an ancient warrior's world, and despite that warrior's noble ways, there was no place for him in this world, so he was forced to exist on the outskirts between assimilation and misunderstanding.

To Darin, this profound epiphany seemed to take minutes, but in real time, he could only hold eye contact for three or four seconds. There was something spiritual about those eyes. He shifted his gaze quickly to the stereo, his own character too deeply ingrained in him to let his conscience blow it on sympathy. The clock on the face read 12:52. It was late. He had been drinking.

There had to be a logical explanation for everything. Spirituality was only what the uneducated masses used to explain coincidence and stave off depression, he told himself. It is a figment of the imagination. He had far too much schooling to give in to hocus pocus now.

"Sorry man, I will pay you as soon as I can." Andrew replied.

"It's ok. There is no hurry." Darin replied, happy to say anything that would snap his chain of thought.

He was starting to feel nauseas. He cracked his window to get some air.

"No, I feel terrible about that whole thing. I should have paid you back by now." Andrew said scratching at his chin. "I will give you at least some of it when I get paid this week." He promised, pride nullifying the sorrow that had covered his face.

"What do you owe him money for?" Ginger chimed in, annoying Darin more with every word.

Andrew didn't answer, reminding Darin that he still didn't know either. This only annoyed him further. He pondered momentarily what could possibly be so secretive without being illegal.

Why didn't Andrew simply tell him? He felt he deserved at least that. They were only blocks from Darin's house, and Andrew was repeating directions to Ginger for the third or forth time.

"No, I need to go to Capp. I left my car there." Darin gurgled from his position slumped against the door.

Andrew glanced back at him over his left shoulder, but he didn't shake his head or roll his eyes. He had been there too many times.

"No, we are already by your house. You can get your car in the morning." He assured him, speaking gently like a third grade teacher would to a disappointed student.

"I have to be to work early though." Darin complained weakly, his voice stammering off as he began keeping his eyes closed for long moments between blinks.

"You'll have to call Eric or have Bethel give you a ride." Andrew told him, carefully again.

If he had called her Beth, it would have slid right by him, but Darin had never heard anyone call Elizabeth Bethel except her immediate family. Dark thoughts pushed him back into a seated position. He stared at the small square of Andrew's hair visible through the gap made between the seat and the headrest. Conspiracy filled his mind. He knew it was all too plausible. He fell silent, deep in thought.

The car pulled to a stop in front of his empty driveway. Andrew turned with a faint, tired smile and offered a hand to Darin. In Darin's worked up mind, he was sure the smile was due to the fact that Elizabeth's car wasn't parked and waiting. He slapped the hand, hiding his rage deep within as he climbed out of the car. He could hear Ginger's high squeaky, "bye, nice to meet you," muffled by her half open window, but he didn't turn. He strode with determination to his door.

As he closed the door behind him, and the RAV-4 pulled away, Ginger commented, "Your friend is really weird."

Andrew said nothing. He ejected the CD, turned up the radio, and stared through the windshield at the road ahead.

Later that morning, Darin laid awake in bed thinking about the unfortunate ending to one of the most entertaining and memorable nights he had experienced since before Shane's trial. As he slowly sobered up in the darkness of his room, the details of the previous night continued to fall into different light as they tend to do when one simply thinks off a buzz. The more he allowed himself to think about the events rationally the more he realized it was his own insecurities that led him to always jump to conclusions. He knew that he was in a peculiar dilemma, knowing that he loved Elizabeth with such intense passion but, at the same time, unsure of how he could ever possibly live happily and content with the joys he possessed without constantly craving more.

Around that same time, Andrew sat on his sofa in front of a muted television infomercial. Ginger was laid out across the sofa, her head on his lap, and a Budweiser blanket wrapped around her sleeping body. She had tried unsuccessfully to snap him from his funk, but when he couldn't be convinced to come to bed and responded only, 'yes', 'nothing', and 'fine' to everything, she eventually gave up and fell asleep. In the short time she had known him, she was already accustomed to Andrew's moody silence, particularly when he drank, and she decided it was best to wait until he thawed a little rather than cause a scene. Unbeknownst to her, the Andrew that she had met and known in the past month was rapidly vanishing as the wild beast within once more began to stir from its slumber.

August 6th, 2004

Andrew awoke with a start to the sound of tires crunching gravel. He sucked the spit that lingered in his mouth and took in his surroundings for a moment. He had fallen asleep in his old arm chair, and his neck and back were already regretting it. He stretched out a moment before remembering the sound of a vehicle. Listening carefully, he heard brakes squeaking ever so slightly. He grabbed his jeans off the sofa and hopped over to the window while pulling them on at the same time.

Peering through the half open blinds, he watched two officers climb out of a Crown Vic and slam their doors simultaneously behind them. He couldn't help but smile at the idea that they might actually practice that at an academy somewhere. He gave himself another quick stretch, hacked up a mouth full of phlegm, and spit it in an empty beer can as he headed for the door.

Opening the door, he was forced to shade his eyes with cupped hand. He guessed it must have been nearing noon already. A high, bright sun lit the lake beautifully, but all he could see was the glare off the white Vic and the two well pressed officers walking up his drive; their aviators giving them a stern, old-school look.

"Afternoon, Andrew." The driver called in a gruff drawl, confirming Andrew's premonitions on the time of day.

Andrew recognized Sheriff Briggs immediately. The sheriff was a long standing political face of Lodge Pole County. He stood around six foot three, yet his naturally thick, country frame made even tall men looked dwarfed beside him. Everything about him represented law and order. The immaculately trimmed silver hair showing beneath his patrol cap was the only clue to his true age, which was probably close to sixty. His handsome face had changed little over the years, still youthful and snug skinned. Traces of gold gleamed in his fierce smile. He had been a tremendous three sport athlete in his prep days, playing a little semi-pro baseball before a stint in Korea ended his career and eventually led him to his passion for law enforcement. Andrew had never known any other sheriff in Lodge Pole County.

Briggs was very active in the community and a huge Wrangler's fan. During the second championship season, the Sheriff had personally shown up to a big party bust to pardon several baseball players from possessions that would have definitely cost them their eligibility. Shane and Andrew had both been present.

The story became hot gossip that summer. Some even whispered that the breach in protocol would cost him in the election. Then, the Wranglers went on to win another state title, and the move appeared to only further solidify another landslide victory. Small towns love winning. Sheriff Briggs loved his small town and the power his position wielded.

It was probably for this reason that he had always been particularly kind to Andrew over the years. But as he returned the sheriff's smile and gave a tired salute, Andrew couldn't help feeling more than a little nervous, knowing he was far from the high school hero Briggs had let off the hook for a underage drinking. He had a pretty good idea what prompted the visit, and he silently clung to the hope that the sheriff still had a soft spot in his heart for alumni, for it was clear from the second officer's stern frown that there would be little compassion behind his dark shades.

He couldn't recall his name, but Andrew recognized him from different places, different times. None of them were pleasant memories. He dug through his hung over brain for a name, but all he could remember was that he had been a talented wrestler years ago. As he strained to make out the name on the little rectangular plate pinned to his chest, Andrew couldn't help but imagine this was the type of guy who went into law enforcement just to kick people's asses.

Andrew estimated him to be around five nine, very small walking alongside the sheriff. He figured more than a few drunks had probably taken his undersized stature for granted before catching a night stick to the dome and a few hard kicks to the ribs for good measure. The officer removed his sunglasses to reveal stone cold brown eyes that complemented his scowl perfectly.

He had smooth features, a small nose, full eyebrows and lips, and wore blocked off side burns at the base of his ears. Andrew recognized him now as the stereotypical cop that every girl dreams of being pulled over by and every guy dreams of knocking the shit out of. He shot the officer a similar salute to the one he had given the sheriff; this only succeeded in further hardening his expression.

"Sheriff Briggs, what brings you all the way out here?" Andrew asked, still eyeing the younger officer, whose name he now read to be Rocklin. Sgt. Rocklin.

"Well, we were hoping to ask you a few questions actually." Briggs replied.

He spoke with an easy mannerism, then, as if it were an after thought,

"If you have a couple minutes?"

"Of course," Andrew smiled, dragging his right hand down across his right eye and rubbing the corner of it with his finger.

"You boys like to come in for a cup of coffee?" He yawned.

The sheriff seemed willing to consider it, but Rocklin shot a disapproving look, and Briggs conceded.

"Thanks, but no thanks." He replied with his photogenic smile.

Andrew was pleased with this answer, as he neither wanted the police seeing all the paraphernalia he had lying around his trailer nor did he have coffee or even a coffee maker for that matter. It seemed like something a guy should ask cops.

"Look, if this is about me dropping my pants the other night at the Cattle Crossing, I apologize, but I was piss drunk and figured it was all in good fun. I mean the place was practically empty." He confessed with a grin, dancing the fine line between confidence and fear.

The sheriff gave a half chuckle and thumbed at his cap. Rocklin remained hard as a rock.

"Nope, we ain't got no complaint with you having a little fun down at the bars, Andrew." The sheriff started, "We were actually wondering about a friend of yours that was seen in town a couple of months back."

With that he too removed his glasses, to unveil the kind dull grey-blue eyes of a grandfather.

"Well hell sheriff, I have a couple friends." Andrew answered, scratching at the back of his greasy mane.

"We are looking for an African American male of medium build, standing well over six feet tall." Rocklin cut in sharply, reading from a small notepad in his right hand.

"Marcus? What about him? He's a great guy, one of my best friends. He was my roommate for a while when I was living in California." Andrew challenged back.

He had a quizzical look now, and he was really starting to dislike Rocklin's drill sergeant act.

"Kid was an athlete, sheriff. Played a year at Cal before he got hurt and lost his scholarship."

"Was he in town visiting you this spring?" The sheriff asked, his voice much firmer than before.

"Yes, he came up a week in March or April I think it was."

"And did he stay with you during his trip?"

"Yea." Andrew responded.

He was about to ask a question of his own, but the sheriff continued.

"The whole trip?" He asked, broadening his legs beneath him without slouching his posture.

"Yes." Andrew repeated.

"What's this all about, sheriff?"

Briggs didn't answer. Instead, he continued with more questions of his own.

"You say he stayed for a week?" He asked raising a brow, "Do you remember exactly how many days?"

Then, without waiting for a response, he went on.

"What was the purpose of his visit?"

This time, Andrew didn't rapid fire any responses. He scratched his head again checking under his nail at the dried scalp he picked off. When he did answer, he took his time, trying to choose his words carefully, as he was starting to realize the gravity of the visit.

"Hell fellas, I just woke up from a long night of drinking. I really can't tell you if it was five, six, or seven days, but as far as the point of his visit, I am pretty sure he came up here to visit me. I highly doubt he was looking for a job or thinking about changing climates." Andrew said, coolly.

"Now, I have answered a full barreled barrage of questions, and I wonder if you fine officers of the peace could let me in on why Marcus would be wanted in this great county of ours?"

Again, he was patronizing.

"Who said he was wanted?" Rocklin fired, crunching gravel under his boot as he shifted his weight forward. His eyes narrowed as they homed in on Andrew's; a rattler trying to stare down a cobra.

"I guess I did." Andrew mumbled through clenched teeth.

He rubbed hard on his index knuckle with his thumb, trying hard to avoid tightening his left hand into a fist.

"Sorry, I guess I must have jumped to conclusions. I just have a hard time seeing you boys coming all the way out here to ask me a bunch of questions about Marcus if your only desire was to send him a state visitor's brochure."

His words were answered only by more hard looks. Andrew drew a deep, nasal breath. He was smart enough to know he shouldn't push it and angry enough not to apologize, so he stalled in silence. A slight breeze shifted dust through the air, making him squint. Finally, the sheriff tipped his hand.

"Around the same time your friend came to visit you, David and Jonathan Gardapee turned up missing." He said, carefully watching Andrew for even the slightest twitch.

"Now, its probably just coincidence, but we have to follow all leads."

Andrew waited, but the sheriff said nothing more.

"I don't get it. What in the hell would connect the Gardapees to Marcus?" He asked. "And, how do you even know they are missing? They are probably up on the reservation cooking up meth or raping middle school girls."

"Their grandmother reported them missing in April. She said they hadn't answered the phone in over a week. We didn't become concerned about it until last week when Billy's truck was found in an old abandoned dump in some ghost town thirty miles from the state's southern border."

He paused a moment, then continued, "The truck was beyond the dump road, piled up in the entrance of a caved in mine of some sort. A local man found it while hunting rabbits."

"Everything about it points to foul play." Rocklin chimed in.

"We have since tracked down friends and family of the boys on tribal land, and no one has seen either of them since late March."

Again, Andrew made sure the officers had finished before responding.

"Ok, so a couple of low life drug dealers turn up missing, so its only too easy to pin it on the first black man that has set foot in town in five years?"

"Don't try and make this out to be about race, Mr. Main." Rocklin fired.

"He isn't even the primary suspect."

"Why is he a suspect at all?"

Rocklin turned to the sheriff in search of approval, but the sheriff only made a slight grimace up toward the wispy clouds floating high in the bright blue sky.

"Andrew, it is a well known fact that you aren't best of friends with those boys, and I know you're not alone, but we are just checking out all possibilities." Briggs said evenly.

His thin lips were dry and cracked under the midday sun.

"No one is accusing anyone of anything."

Andrew read from Rocklin's face, still locked on the sheriff, that there was definitely more to it. He knew if anyone were going to leak information it would be this youngster, itchy to bust some heads.

"They are the scum of society, and if they are missing, they sure aren't missed by me. I will admit that. I am not telling you men how to do your jobs, but I can't help but feel that if they were killed, it would be a blessing to us all."

Andrew spoke with his arms folded across his chest. His hip was leaned against the worn out rail of the deck, and his stare was locked on the lake in the distance. He spoke with passion. Then he let his instincts take over. He turned straight to Rocklin and asked, "I guess I still don't see what any of this has to do with Marcus?"

He challenged Rocklin with a firm gaze, knowing it would be too much for him not to brag his trump card. He was right. Rocklin didn't even look to his superior this time, as he spoke with the self-importance of the only kid in class to have his dog at show and tell,

"Your friend Marcus was overhead mentioning the Gardapees at the Oasis, and a little further investigating led us to discover he had also been asking about where he might score a large amount of pot."

He couldn't help but smile smugly. Andrew caught sight of his yellow, chew stained teeth and could no longer blame him for frowning all the time.

The sheriff shot Rocklin a look of stern criticism for a long moment. When he turned back to Andrew he appeared more than a little flustered. Andrew smiled, which only seemed to further annoy the sheriff. Clearly, he hadn't planned to leak so much information.

"Sheriff, I can't speak as to whether or not Marcus smokes weed, but I will say that this town is infamous for rumors, and the fact that a rumor was started about the big, scary black man can hardly be the basis for suspecting my friend to be involved in the disappearance of two men he had never met. As for me, I fight my own battles."

Before either of the officers could speak again, Andrew saw his chance, quickly slamming the door on their questions.

"All I can tell you is that he was here for a week. We went out to a couple bars, went bowling and fishing, and he was definitely well noticed everywhere he went. So if there is nothing else, it's my day off, and I would really like to catch up on my sleep."

Rocklin flamed up wanting blood, yet the sheriff just tipped his cap a little.

"Thank you much, Andrew. We'll be seeing you around."

With that, he gave his strapping smile, his big teeth glimmering like a movie star's, and headed back to the car. Andrew gave a quick nod to Rocklin, who still stood his ground glaring hard, then pulled open the screen door. He could barely keep his hands from punching a cupboard as he pulled a plastic cup from his dish rack, filled it from the faucet, and downed it in one guzzle nearly choking himself.

He held his breath a moment, for he couldn't help but notice it was a long time before the tires could be heard backing down the drive. Setting the cup down on the counter, he wiped the water from his cheeks and tried to pull his thoughts together. Try as he might, though, all he could see was Rocklin, his cold lifeless eyes, and uncompromising scowl. He couldn't shake the feeling that this was not the last he would see of that arrogant prick.

August 8th, 2004

Shane wiped the sweat from his face only to have more flood from his scalp to replace it. His heart still pulsed hard against his sternum. His thighs and feet both burned. He knew his legs would get sore if he didn't stretch. Who was he kidding? A guy doesn't sit down and stretch in a dump like this.

He looked around the room at the plain, dull concrete walls and matching sullen faces. Seated on a metal bench attached to a metal table up against a wall in the recreation room, there wasn't a whole lot of scenery for one to gaze upon. Usually, Shane hated the time spent here as much if not more than any other time he'd spent serving his penance to the state, but after some basketball, it had its advantages. Sure it wasn't fresh air by any means. At least it was wide open, though. A guy had a chance to catch his breath.

Shane hated the cell time after activities worst of all. Dozens of stinky, sweaty cons wheezing on the same stagnant air made his entire hall almost unbearable. That's why the guards did it. It had to be he figured, especially after the particularly intense contests.

They see a bunch of deadbeat Indians running around having a good time. No sir, that's not what they are here for. Send those drum-beaters back to their cells, back to the tepees as they liked to call that section of the prison since practically the entire corridor was Native inmates. Shane would ignore the supposed punishment, pace the couple steps back and forth and think about how he could have played better. It was his way of killing time.

Not today though. Today, he sat with arms laid out flat across the cool surface of the table. He rotated his ankles trying to stretch his calves. Across the room, a few guys were playing cards quietly, other than that most everyone was doing their own thing. Some read, some doodled or sketched depending on ability, others stared dumbly at the walls or nodded off. The prisoners always spent some time alone after fitness hour. Sure, most wanted to chat it up a little or talk trash about a game, but the silence was a sort of unspoken show of gratitude for the outdoor privileges.

Shane didn't mind. He had made a few of friends. He even had two cousins here, but he was well aware that too much socializing only brought negative attention on oneself. He laid his forehead down on the table, still breathing deeply through his nose. The cool surface felt great on his hot skin. He closed his eyes and was starting to doze off when the sound of mail call shook him to attention. He waited patiently, aware that wishing usually led to disappointment in all things prison. The orderly called his name. He raised his hand quickly, trying hard to appear impassive while joy sprang in his spine. The guard slapped the envelope on the table and moved on.

Shane picked it up for an inspection and was thoroughly excited to see Andrew's name. He had received a letter from each of his friends, yet this was the second letter from Andrew, and in a way, it marked the first true letter of correspondence, since it was practically required for his closest friends to at least write him a letter while their guilt and pain were still fresh. These first letters were merely a formality and were all broad and impersonal; for, it was not often any of these people had sat down to write a close friend in prison, making it difficult to sound well practiced or comfortable with the task.

Shane's mother, on the other hand, had been writing to friends and family in the clink for years. She wrote Shane twice a week. Her letters were short but straight to the point. In her very first letter, she asked if she could move his TV into her room. That was simply the way she was.

Andrew's first letter was much different. It was carefully worded. Andrew wrote as if Shane wasn't aware he was in prison. Shane wrote him back thanking him for taking the time to write and regretting that he couldn't send a postcard, but unfortunately, he hadn't found one that could capture the true beauty of his new place of residence.

He hoped his message would be clear. He wanted a letter from the real Andrew not some anonymous church patron worried about saving his soul before it was too late.

Shane opened the envelope carefully. There was no hurry. He knew this letter was the only thing he had to look forward to all day. It was written on notebook paper, crisply folded, and read as follows:

> *BrotherChane,*
>
> *How's it hanging? Short and shriveled I bet. I am glad to hear you're getting a little B-Ball in. Hopefully, your opponents will see how poorly you cross over and decide against making you their wife. Just kidding. I hope I didn't go too far with that one, but I know you can take care of yourself. It's pretty boring around here without you. All these damn law abiding friends of ours are all grown up. They don't have time to drink or raise a little hell and they sure as hell don't want to play wingman on a Friday night. I guess that's life though. Everything changes, and the more you try to resist that change the faster it happens. Shit man I remember when we used to sit around eating cheese sticks and talking about who had the dirtiest arm in the Bigs. Now, everyone only eats salad and shit because they are watching their weight, and Darin wants to talk subdivisions and Eric yaps on and on about some History Channel special on the dark ages. I don't know. I guess I just need to keep up with the bills and give up on my dreams like everybody else.*
>
> *What the hell am I crying about? I'm sorry man. Things really aren't all that bad. I have been spending a lot of time with this new girl. Her name is Ginger. You got to meet this broad. She's gorgeous. Drives me completely bonkers sometimes with her ranting and complaining, but she's great really. What about you? Any new ladies I should know about? Ha ha I am kidding again. Anyways, you take care of yourself in there. You hear? The two of us are going to get out of here when you're out. We'll head down to San Diego. It's like*

paradise down there. Sun all year round. Just let that be what keeps you together when shit gets tough. Keep your mind on the future, the sun, and the beach.

By the way, I want you to know I took care of everything. You don't need to worry about any of that bullshit anymore. It's over. Write me back soon.

Andrew (Big Sexy)

Shane read the last few lines again. What did he mean by it's over? What was over? Try as he may, he couldn't figure it out. It should not have really worried him, yet he couldn't stop thinking about it.

All that night he thought about the letter. He tried to imagine this chick, Ginger. She must really be something for Andrew to actually admit interest. He also thought about how down Andrew seemed in much of the letter. Mostly, he thought about those two words: it's over. Andrew hadn't said he was taking care of everything; he said he took care of everything. What problem did he think he had solved? And, what was the bullshit he thought Shane was worrying about? He thought about it and thought about it, but none of his theories seemed to convince him of anything.

Finally, he decided he was probably looking too far into it, but before he drifted off to sleep, he couldn't help thinking Andrew had done something rash. There was no way around it. Whatever it was, it would just have to remain a mystery, for Shane had no room to be worrying about vague letters. It was enough work trying to remain positive. The next morning, his concerns for Andrew were little more than a dream like memory. He had his own problems, and with enough of those pushing to control the majority of his weary mind, he never even questioned his friend when he finally wrote back.

August 12th, 2004

The sound of his cell phone awakened Eric from his sleep. It didn't take much. He had always been a light sleeper. Fatherhood only increased his sleeping woes. He rolled over and silenced the ringer quickly, hoping to not wake Claire but knowing it already had. He checked the bright screen with squinted eyes. It was Andrew.

The alarm clock on Claire's side of the bed read 1:08 in red. He sent the call through to voicemail and rolled back over. The last thing he needed was a drunk dial conversation tonight. He had been irritable all day. Estimates on fixing up his new shop had been much higher than he expected, and it seemed there were new unforeseen costs lurking around every corner. He decided it would be easier to do the work himself. The problem was his time was already stretched thin. He tried to remind himself that the only reason he could afford the shop was the fact it was a fixer upper, but this did little to cheer him.

He had purchased the building nearly four months earlier, and with the mortgage interest already rolling, he needed to open the doors soon. Progress was slow, however. Eric had fallen for the old welding warehouse as the perfect place to call his own largely due to its location, space, and price. The building was cosmetically lacking to say the least, particularly from the outside, but it sat squarely on Industrial Blvd between a truck stop and Do It Today Hardware. Eric knew these were places men frequented. Also, the place was spacious for the price. Three garage doors already hung on the east entrance, and the vast warehouse had sung nothing but growth opportunity in Eric's little ears.

The problem was Eric knew very little about running a business. He fixed cars, and he worked hard. These were the primary tools he had to offer. Finally, he acted on impulse for the first time in his life and moved one step closer to achieving his life's dream of running his own shop. Since that day, however, every time he set foot on the property he saw only more overhead and more setbacks. Realizing it had already been four months, he nearly gave himself a panic attack at how much work was yet to be done before the place could even open for business.

Sometimes, the stress would leave him woozy and he would have to sit down to regain his breath. Earlier that night, a long talk with his wife after dinner had really helped to ease his worried mind, but that could only last so long. He had known it was going to be a tough, treacherous path, so he prayed for guidance and grace every step of the way, yet he knew praying can only get a guy so far. He knew he would have to reach down deep and put his back into it.

The phone vibrated on the surface of his night stand. Andrew must have left a voicemail. Eric rolled over once more, turning the phone onto silent mode since Andrew could be quite persistent some nights. Returning his head to his pillow, Eric tried to fall back asleep but his mind could only picture his huge empty shop followed by debt, upon debt, foreclosure, and eventual bankruptcy.

He rolled onto his side, peering through the shadows to make out his wife's face. Even in the dark, she was the most beautiful woman he had ever laid eyes upon. The thin moonlight of the early morning slipped through the drawn shades just enough to make out her long eyelashes. He smiled, realizing, as long as she stood beside him, he could never fail. Closing his eyes again, he began drifting off.

Suddenly, the house phone pulsed from its cradle on Claire's dresser, and in a flash, she rolled over, grabbed it, and shoved it hard into Eric who, fearfully, covered up in defense. Then, she rolled back over without missing a beat. Eric, still a little frightened by the speed of everything that had transpired, pushed 'talk' before the third ring, kicked off the covers, and moved quickly for the door. It was easy for him to get out of the room without turning on the light because his eyes were already adjusted to the dark. He moved down the hallway and into the living room before finally asking, "Hello?" in a hoarse, unrehearsed voice with more than a little annoyance in his tone. There was no response, so he repeated himself; this time in a forced hybrid of a whisper and a demand.

"She's hurt," replied a choked up voice. "She's hurt real bad."

Andrew spoke with a detached, almost lost meandering to his words. Almost like each word was causing significant pain in his wind pipe.

"What's wrong, Drew? What happened? Are you ok?" Eric fired, no longer careful about his volume. He forced himself to pause as adrenaline pumped him instantly alert.

"She's hurt." The voice repeated, quietly.

Then asked, "How could this happen?"

"Who's hurt, Drew? Don't worry. Everything is going to be alright. Just take your time." Eric addressed, pacing back and forth across the living room. The phone clenched tightly in his left hand.

"Just take your time, and tell me what happened."

Andrew could be heard on the other end sniffing hard at a running nose.

"We were just driving along, and the fucking deer came out of nowhere." He said unsteadily, his words jumping back and forth between moans and creaks. He was on the verge of tears.

"Where are you now, bro?" Eric interrupted, trying to discern only the crucial information rather than an emotional account of the story that would only replay it all over again in Andrew's mind.

"At the hospital." Andrew responded, his voice gathering resolve, only to collapse again with his next words, "Ginger is in the ER, Eric. She smashed into the windshield, and she is in real bad shape."

"Was she," Eric began to ask but thought better of it, "Is she conscience?"

"There was blood and glass everywhere, Eric, and the screams. Why the fuck would this happen?"

Andrew's anger blended itself in with his sorrow as he spoke.

"She will be ok, buddy. Alright? I promise you." Eric said with his best consoling effort. He turned to find a frightened Claire, standing in the hallway, one hand over her mouth, her eyes frantic with concern.

"I'll be right there, ok? You just keep yourself together. I'm on my way."

"Thanks, Eric," was Andrew's timid reply, then, "I didn't know who else to call."

When Eric arrived at the hospital, he found Andrew standing with his back against the wall and his head hung down in a hallway of the emergency ward. Andrew didn't smile when he met him, but his eyes did show a flash of gratitude, as if in a familiar face he found comfort. The rest of him, however, was in pretty rough shape. His shirt was torn and stained with blood. His face was a pale yellow; his lips were dry and cracked. He had a pretty decent sized goose egg along his scalp, but otherwise, looked intact.

Eric tried to get the facts straight at first, but Andrew was still somewhere else. After a few minutes, he was able to get his shaken friend to take a seat while he went to get some coffee.

There was no coffee machine to be found, so he returned with two bottles of water instead, handed one to Andrew, and pulled a chair down the hall to sit across from him.

"So are her parents here?" Eric finally asked.

Andrew stared directly through him like a ghost, his eye lids bouncing around wildly.

"They're in Vegas." He wheezed.

"Jesus, we have to get a hold of them, Drew." Eric said, setting his water bottle alongside his chair.

"The cops are trying to find them already." Andrew assured him.

He unscrewed the cap of his water bottle and took a long drink, squeezing the sides, and letting a small stream drizzle down his chin and onto his mangled shirt.

"The cops are here right now?"

As he asked, Eric looked down the hall in both directions as if he wouldn't have noticed police officers standing down either end of the vacant, white hallway.

"They were."

Andrew clenched at the hair along his scalp, leaving a greasy cal-lick sticking up.

"Did they ask you any questions?" Eric asked again, fearing that a breathalyzer would probably mean serious jail time in an injury accident, or worse, it could mean negligent homicide if Ginger was as badly injured as Andrew led on.

"Only whether or not I was driving and whether or not she was drinking." Andrew mumbled with some effort.

"So, she was driving?" Eric asked, continuing to gather data. Andrew nodded.

"Was she drinking?"

"We weren't drinking. Neither of us was drinking." Andrew growled with sudden intensity.

"It's like I told you before. We went to the late movie, and afterwards, we sat in the car and talked for a while."

It seemed he was mistaking Eric for an officer that had questioned him earlier.

"She was giving me a ride home, and this damn deer came out of nowhere. I swear it wanted to get hit, but Ginger swerved, and we went off the road."

Despite his wavering state, Eric believed he was not drunk. He was shaken up, but he didn't smell of booze.

"When I came to my senses, my leg hurt pretty bad. My first instinct was to get out of the car. Everything was happening in slow motion."

Eric knew by every tremble and change in his friend's voice that he was reliving the entire episode that very moment.

"Then, then, I saw her," and with that the gates that had held back so many pent up sorrows through out this young man's tough life could hold on no longer, and small tears began to roll down Andrew's cheeks.

"There was so much blood. She was hurt so bad."

Eric moved over to his friend, on the verge of tears himself, and leaned over his chair, hugging him with their heads leaned together. Andrew only continued to sob for a minute or two, but Eric held him the entire time. Finally, Andrew pulled away to wipe his eyes, and Eric returned to his chair, staring at the ground for fear of embarrassing his friend. This went on for several minutes. The sound of Andrew clearing his throat was the only disharmony to total silence. A couple of nurses scurried through the hall careful to keep their eyes on the clipboards they carried. Otherwise, the hallway remained deserted.

Eric wanted to find out which room Ginger was in. He was surprised no one had come to tell them any updates on her condition. He also continued expecting a police officer, but none came. It was only the two of them and this enormous burden alone in the sterile hallway.

"Has anyone come to tell you her condition or if she is being operated on?" Eric finally asked, seeing that Andrew was more alert now and seemed to be looking around with the same questions.

"No, I came in and told the lady at the entrance who I was. She told me that I needed to fill out some paperwork, and they would take a look at me, so I told her I was fine and that I wanted to know how Ginger was. She told me the ambulance had brought her in and I could wait in this hall." Andrew said, his voice showing a great deal more composure than before.

"The two of you didn't come here together?" Eric asked with confusion.

"No, when they loaded her into the ambulance, I told them I was fine, so they left, and I rode with Jeff or Jim, the guy that found us."

Eric was still confused. Andrew explained that this man had been out at the lake night fishing, but he had forgotten to bring tippet, so when he broke his line, he decided the heck with it and headed home early. Luckily for Andrew and Ginger he was driving along the lonely road just after they rolled down the embankment. He called 911, crawled down the hill, and was able to help Andrew move Ginger up to the highway. Not a single other car drove by the entire time.

"God truly works in mysterious ways." Eric said about the improbable aid. Andrew clenched up suddenly. His expression turned dark; his eyes narrowed.

"God?" he blurted angrily. "Fuck God."

Eric looked at him sternly. The two had never spoken crossly on the point of religion. Eric knew Andrew was not a pious churchgoer, but he had always been respectful about other's beliefs and even quite spiritual at times. In fact, Andrew had always been one of Eric's greatest supporters against Darin's atheistic bigotry.

"I only meant that I am glad you two were found so quickly." Eric retracted, knowing that this was a difficult time for Andrew and not wanting to add to the strain.

"I am sick and tired of hearing about God's master plan and all his mysterious ways." Andrew went on rampaging.

"God's plan starves people, throws my best friend in prison, and tells a deer to stand in the middle of the road simply to hurt two people in love. What is that? I was doing so good, bro. I was finally getting somewhere in life. You tell me," then before Eric could respond, "What is he just jealous? Is he bored and has nothing better to do? Tell me! No, I'll tell you."

He moved close to Eric with rage in his eyes.

"Next time you talk to God tell him when Andrew Main sees him, he is going to kick his all knowing teeth down his holier than thou throat."

Eric repressed his anger because of the situation, but he wasn't above replying,

"You know what happened to Shane isn't yours to just horde. It affected all of us, Andrew. He was doing drugs big time though. You weren't here. You didn't have to watch him become a shell of his old self. I mean yea, what happened was terrible, but at least he didn't kill himself. He is alive, Andrew. He has been given a second chance."

He paused, seeing none of this was having any effect on Andrew's anger.

"You need to come to terms with the past, bro. What is done can't be changed. You can only change the future, and focusing so much on the negatives doesn't help. Negative thoughts will only bring more bad things. It's the law of attraction."

He stood and walked down the hallway to ask the clerk for an update on Ginger's condition before one of them ended up saying something they couldn't take back and might end up regretting forever. Behind him, he heard Andrew kick or throw the chair, yet he didn't look back.

August 18th, 2004

It was another pristine afternoon. The flag sat totally motionless atop the pole in centerfield, the temperature was dead locked at eighty-five degrees, and the sun shined down on the field as though it had been created solely for the purpose of incubating baseball in the dimensions locked between these two chalk lines. The skies above were crystal clear aside from one peculiar, grey cumulonimbus cloud formation starting to peak over the hills to the north of town. Darin couldn't help but notice it. It seemed to know it was out of place, so it just hovered beyond the horizon, watching the game unfold from a distance.

It was the top of the third, and a young southpaw was finishing his warm up pitches while a pair of batters tried to time him with practice swings from the on deck area. The lefty was a tall, thin reed. His appearance reminded Darin of another Wrangler hurler from the not so distant past, though his mound presence was anything but Andrew like. This kid was a laborer. He lacked Andrew's confident grace. In two innings, he had already thrown at least thirty pitches despite only having one base runner to his name. He worked long counts, paced the hill a lot, and always maintained a stern grimace. It was like, aside from the opposing team, he was in a battle against time and heat, two very tough opponents during a game of baseball.

This was the first time the Wranglers had played host to a playoff game since the back to back title seasons, and there wasn't an empty seat to be found. They had a scrappy squad, a bunch of veterans, with great speed. They were the three seed in the conference, so they had drawn the six seeded Bucks. Unfortunately, the six seed in the conference held one of the most highly prized arms to come out of the state in years, a big, strong, ogre by the name of Red Call-Sparrow.

As one might guess by the letters stitched out across the broad back of Red's jersey, he was a Native American. Although, this was also quite clear from his physical appearance. What wasn't quite so clear was how old Red was. He was about six-one and probably weighed about two hundred and thirty pounds. He had the wiry mustache of a seventeen year old and the hands and wind burned features of a thirty five year old.

Red grew up in the tiny map dot of Fort Hill, which was a small outcropping of trailer homes and cattle ranches left over after the army abandoned a fort by the same name some thirty years ago. Fort Hill was forty miles from Jordan, where the Bucks called home. Red's father, Allan, was a hardened third generation rancher that drove Red to and from practice everyday. It was a generous commitment yet so was the commitment made by teams to drive all the way to Jordan. It was in the middle of nowhere and on days that Red pitched the trip was almost futile.

In the past two years, Red had compiled a 17-2 record, including two one hitters and a no hitter. One long standing conference coach finally commented, only half jokingly, that if it wasn't scheduled to be a double header or Red hadn't reached three days rest, it was probably just as easy to forfeit the game and save gas. All too often, even this second circumstance didn't matter. The Buck coaches were known to throw Red fifteen, sixteen, even as many as eighteen innings in a weekend, when the conference schedule was at its thickest. Darin and Eric had heard all the legends and hearsay, and they both knew how much intimidation and exaggeration play a part in high school baseball, but so far, each of them was equally impressed with what they had seen out of this 'hefty Indian.' In two innings, he had already fanned five and the sole blemish to his K-parade was a walk that was caught stealing. Otherwise, he would probably have six.

Every thing about Red screamed dominance. He threw three pitches: a high eighties tailing fastball, a low to mid eighties hard slider, and a completely overpowering, low nineties four-seamer. He wound up slow, coiling demonically like a prairie rattler and then grunted hard upon exertion. Of course, by the time the grunt could be heard, the ball was probably already in the catcher's glove. Even his name, Red Call-Sparrow, sounded like the pseudonym of some mythical pitcher from a time long since past.

On the other side, this Wrangler lefty, Rockel or Bockel guessing from the crackling voice on the outdated PA system, was Call-Sparrow's polar opposite. Where one challenged in, the other nipped that outer third. When the hefty fire-baller climbed the ladder, the skinny lefty took more and more off. Darin hoped the underdog would prevail, at least long enough for some sort of divine intervention or a little dumb luck to take over. A quick glance over at Eric, wiping his big sweaty palms together constantly and popping up out of his seat at every borderline call, told Darin that his friend was pushing for this hope on a whole other level.

'I guess some guys are Wranglers till they die.' He thought watching the veins pulsate in his friend's temples. It made Darin smile. There was something about that small town athlete nostalgia and brotherhood that really spoke of the community. He thought of Nathan as a teen, playing ball for the Wranglers while middle aged versions of Eric, Shane, Andrew, and himself went on and on about the glory days from the grandstands.

This vision was something he wished for but feared might never come to pass. It suddenly seemed odd to him that he could imagine himself meeting foreign dignitaries and living for months at a time on a yacht parked in tropical waters, yet it was difficult to imagine his best friends experiencing such simple pleasures as being together and tamed in a not so distant future. He tried to refocus his attention, but for a split second on the trip from imagination back to reality, his mind paused to consider whether or not another Bard would ever suit up in a Wrangler uniform. The first batter stepped into the box, immediately sending the first pitch he saw over the shortstops glove for a base hit.

"Shit," Eric exclaimed.

Darin scanned around the crowd while the next hitter walked confidently to the plate. He turned his mind away from the future and replaced the armor he cherished so dearly then turned his attention toward his favorite crutch, women. He noticed more than a few good looking females in the front few rows behind the backstop, down and to their right. He fought off any feelings of shame by telling himself that most of them were at least twenty but knowing differently. How could he possibly forget that the larger the crowd, the bigger the game, the closer the high school girls moved to the action and the more skin they revealed.

The crowd cheered as the batter whiffed. The energy in the stadium was overwhelming.

Excitement and anticipation floated in the hot summer air. Darin continued his survey, moving his eyes to the far back corners of the grandstands then working his way back toward their own seats. By the look of things, this year's squad came from pretty decent stock. There were a few trophy looking mothers around. Most of them seemed to be as concerned about their appearances as the high school girls down in front yet tried to show more discretion. Then there were the grandparents and the VFW boys focusing calmly on the game same as they had hundreds of before - every pitch reminding them of a 'you had to be there' tale from the past that had long since strayed from anything close to historical fact. And finally, there were the fathers scattered in small tribes or sitting off alone with their nervous ticks and loving, passionate shouts of encouragement. Praying for their son's happiness while fearing the failure that could crush the child permanently and injure their own pride, their stomachs were constantly knotted with stress.

Darin spotted the sheriff standing in one of the aisles to the right of home plate. He was leaning against the handrail that framed in the central exit. He wore his aviators and a sheriff's department ball cap, but otherwise looked like any other fan in his Wrangler's t-shirt. His eyes were on the game, but he had the usual crowd of important parents and pompous community big wigs sitting all around him laughing at his jokes and hanging on his stories. He was chewing at a toothpick; his big teeth were gleaming in the sun. Suddenly, he turned his head slightly to listen to a fellow old timer. 'Probably telling a war story,' Darin thought. As the sheriff's eyes changed direction, he seemed to catch Darin and Eric in his gaze.

Because of the dark sunglasses, Darin couldn't tell whether or not he had been spotted. He was about to wave just in case when a ball drilled at the third baseman saved him. Everyone's attention was diverted. The three-bagger fielded the ball clean, flipping it toward second in a fluid motion. The crowd rose to its feet. The snap of the first baseman's mitt completed the sequence for a bang-bang double play. The entire place erupted. Errands were going unfinished on this day; nobody was leaving early.

The zeros continued back and forth as the innings moved along. The lefty proved to be just that, using a mix of craftiness, guts, and luck to work himself in and out of jams, while Red continued to mow down batters with increasing velocity and domination. The man-child went with fewer and fewer sliders each inning, grunting harder while looking more and more in control. It was the bottom of the sixth, and he still hadn't given up a hit when the sheriff marched his way slowly, deliberately up the aisle toward Eric and Darin. Darin beamed a quick smile and stood to shake the tall man's hand. He had forgotten how much effort the sheriff put into his handshakes and was caught off guard by his iron grip.

"We sure got us one hell of a ball game here huh, sheriff?" Eric shouted with excitement.

Following Darin's lead, he stood to greet the sheriff, and as they shook hands, Darin couldn't help but think of two grizzlies pawing for dominance at watching each of them arch their arm back in preparation for the great squeeze. Darin fought back a laugh. The sheriff dutifully remained standing firm in the aisle beside the boy's seats, since they were back far enough that no one was sitting directly behind them.

"Yes we do," the sheriff spoke indirectly, his dark lenses directed toward the field.

Darin had forgotten how tall Briggs was. The man had to be around sixty, but he carried himself with impressive posture and youthful pride.

"I have a feeling this big horse is beginning to tire himself out though."

"We better hope so because that skinny lefty can't keep them off balance much longer." Darin responded lightly.

The sheriff removed a hanky from his pocket and moving it toward his nose answered.

"Oh, I wouldn't count on that. Young Rocklin has three generations of Wrangler pride and tradition pulsing through his veins. He has been waiting for this game a long time."

The sheriff wiped his nose and gave a short blow.

The smile on Darin's face disappeared.

"That kid pitching is Jason Rocklin's brother?" Darin asked.

"Nope, it's his nephew." Briggs responded. "Joey Rocklin, he is the son of Jason's older brother Garrett."

"Garrett Rocklin? How do I know that name?" Eric asked joining in with sudden interest.

"He runs Valley Plumbing and Heating." The sheriff offered.

"Yeah, I think we did some customs on his truck a few years ago. He owns a classic job right?" Eric asked.

Darin listened, keeping his eyes on the game. Red had the hitter down 1-2. Darin knew he would stick with the high heat. These kids were going up intimidated. Stepping in the box scared, a batter has already lost the battle.

"He owns that black fifty-eight Apache short bed."

High heat and the poor kid was a day late, one out.

"I remember it now. That truck is a real thing of beauty."

The next batter was spent in silent observation. Red got behind 2-0 before coming back to carve up another victim on the pay off pitch. Two down in the bottom of the sixth and big Red already had thirteen strike outs. His stuff was overpowering.

The hitter that followed, a little runt with wild hair and the baggiest uniform on either team, hustled to the box. Darin recognized him as the shortstop and leadoff. He was a squat, spunky kid with a lot of energy. He had already made a few spectacular plays with the glove despite being hitless in two at bats. Darin couldn't help thinking of Shane watching him play. Perhaps, he was not alone in making the association.

"I notice Andrew isn't here today." The sheriff observed coolly.

"I tried calling him," Eric said with evident regret, "I guess he just doesn't have that passion for it anymore."

"That's strange because he has been at every home game this month," Briggs said evenly. "I heard through the grapevine he has even been to a few road games."

"Andrew? That really surprises me. I wonder how he has been getting the time off work." Eric said, speaking Darin's thoughts aloud.

"I don't think he is working." The sheriff said without hesitation.

It seemed that he had steered the conversation to this point, but when neither Darin nor Eric continued down that road, he took a timeout as well.

"He has been pretty shaken up since the accident." Eric shrugged without looking over.

"This kid is one of the scrappiest ball players I've seen in all my years." The sheriff said apparently content with planting the seed and leaving it to grow.

The kid fouled a fastball straight back evening the count at 1-1.

"His name is Bobby McElroy." Briggs went on, seeing as he'd already started.

"Hell of a wrestler too."

Meanwhile, Bobby took two more pitches, bringing the count to 2-2. 'Slider down and away,' Darin thought. He was correct, and Bobby fouled a dribbler toward the home dugout. A few cheers of encouragement murmured out of the hometown crowd.

"Tough little son of a bitch." The sheriff said absently, grinding down on what little was left of his frayed toothpick.

"He's coming hard in", Darin predicted aloud, suddenly imagining he was standing in Bobby's place.

Sure enough, Red brought a scorching four seamer up high and slightly in. The ump called it a ball, and the count went full. The next pitch, Red challenged the little hobo looking teenager out over the plate; Bobby fouled it straight back again. He was only missing it by a sliver. He was starting to get his hands around on the heat. Although Darin was feeling a little unsure of his Wrangler pride in the face of discovering their ace pitcher was of the same blood line as the racist prick that instigated his melt down with Elizabeth, he was pulling hard for long haired Bobby McElroy. He wondered if he would ever be told how scrappy his own boy played.

Bobby fouled off another slider. His swings at everything other than a fastball were defensive, barely getting the job done. But, he was battling. The crowd started gathering behind him. In a no hitter, long at bats like this are crucial momentum changers. Red unleashed a hard two seamer. It cut hard down, but caught too much plate and Bobby put solid barrel on it driving a liner the other way. It scooted out of the reach of the untested right fielder's outstretched glove and skipped across the short August grass toward the wall.

"Now watch this boy fly." The sheriff shouted over the frantic cheers rippling through the stands.

His voice lost its careful delivery in his excitement, as the toothpick fell from his lip. And, Bobby did fly. Bobby McElroy and his baggy uniform moved with the effortless beauty of a spooked antelope in full gallop. He lost his helmet rounding second, skated into third still gaining speed, only to be held up by coach Dugal's big paws to the crowd's chagrin. The relay man turned to fire, then, seeing there was no play, trotted the ball toward the mound. The crowd was outraged.

"He would have made it," Eric cried disgusted. "Damn Dugal and his conservative calls."

Darin disagreed. He knew it would have been close. He also knew that making that third out at home not only crushes the crowd's momentum, it saves big Red from his first pressure situation all day.

"Time to test his nerves," The sheriff said leaning in toward Darin's ear.

Apparently, he was thinking the same thing. It was about more than pitch count. If Red was as emotion dependant as advertised, he would throw the next few pitches harder than any he had thrown all game. The crowd was clapping and stomping. A good three quarters of the crowd were on their feet.

If Red was likely to make a mistake, this might well be the time. Dugal called the next batter down the line for a word. The Bucks coach came out on the front steps of the dugout. With a heavy bark, he reminded his team that there were two outs and that the play was at first. It was obvious information even for a baseball novelist, but in the heat of a tense moment, it came as sage wisdom.

Red stared at young Bobby McElroy while he bounced around like a house fly trapped between the window and screen. He went from the full wind up, kicked, and grunted. By the effort and sound, the pitch must have traveled at ninety five miles an hour. It took the catcher's full effort to snag it. The umpire stood up in silence.

The stadium turned up the volume on its frenzy. Everyone was going ballistic regardless of team affiliation. The cheers in support of the Bucks simply muffled into the white noise. The next pitch, Red didn't even glance over at Bobby. He wiped the sweat off his face with the sleeve of his undershirt, took a deep breath, and let fly.

The ball skipped off the front of the plate, past the catcher's sprawling legs, and rolled to the backstop. McElroy soared across the plate and met his teammates on the dugout steps in the blink of an eye. It was 1-0 Wranglers. The Buck's coach hustled out to the mound, showing his youth according to an overjoyed Sheriff Briggs, and looked more unsettled than Red as he tried to calm his big ace.

Whatever he said must have worked though. Red came back and threw two strikes, inducing a weak groundball toward first to end the inning. The crowd gave a slight show of disappointment as the first baseman stepped on the bag, but they were howling and hooting like drunken fools again as the Wrangler's hustled out onto the field.

"A lot of strikes here, Joey." The sheriff hollered with a single clap.

"You know he's only a junior." He added, showing those big pearly whites.

"All together we got five juniors starting and one sophomore. A second run at repeating isn't impossible." He added, shaking his own head as if to agree with himself.

Darin raised a brow, trying to choose his next words carefully. He didn't want to come across negative, but he didn't want to help plan the parade yet either. Turns out, Eric would beat him to the punch.

"They gotta win one before they can repeat." Eric said, cracking a peanut.

He put emphasis on the words one and repeat, but it was the subtle use of they instead of the more inclusive we, which Eric always used when referring to anything involving the Wranglers, that really stood out. He was very discrete to keep his eyes on the game, but Darin felt a swelling of pride that warmed his heart and pumped adrenaline into his veins. There was pride in the fact that what they had done, what they had accomplished, meant something. Whether or not it was done again, or even out done, it would never be lost or underestimated by those who physically experienced it.

Eric used the word they, not to exclude himself from the sheriff's prophecy, only to remind him that it was the twelve or fifteen young men on the field, in the dugout, on the road, at practice, in hotel rooms, on long bus trips, in their free time, and with their hearts, thoughts, and wills that achieved what the community glorified and collectively celebrated, then scrutinized, over analyzed and finally used only for comparison. After it was all said and done, the summers were remembered by statistics, on base percentages, earned run averages, wins and losses, while the sweat, the emotions, and those unbreakable bonds just sort of fade away.

Eric had thought of all this so many times but to hear it so lightly predicted made him angry. He turned to the sheriff and spoke earnestly, "I remember, when I was on the twelve year old all-star team, Andrew dove head first into a gate trying to catch a foul ball. The padlock on the gate put a six inch gash across the top of his head. He was twelve years old, mind you. He said he was fine. His next at bat he struck out on three pitches. It was like he was swinging blind. He admitted to me that he was feeling dizzy but continued telling the coaches he was fine. Looking back, I don't even know why the adults let him keep playing in that game. I suppose they wanted to win even more than the kids."

As Eric spoke, Darin remembered the game. It had been during the District Tournament that year, and they were facing some real tough pitching.

"Well, he came up to bat again in the bottom of the sixth and we were down one. There was one out and nobody on. Everyone at that game knew something was wrong. He stepped in the bucket on his first two swings before stepping out of the box. I was on deck, and I thought he was going to collapse, so I started toward him. Then, he turned to me, pale as a ghost, and I swear to this day, he winked at me. He denies it, but I know what I saw. It was as if he was already aware of the outcome. He stepped back in the box and slapped a slow roller between first and second."

The excitement grew in Eric's voice, and a foul ball slowed the present action on the field, while the umpire called for more baseballs.

"The first step he took out of the box he knew he was going for two. He beat the throw by a miracle or possibly it was a missed call by a surprised and out of position ump. Either way, the next pitch he stole third, and without the coach's permission, he took a huge lead off third, drew a throw and took home when the third baseman returned a high relay to the catcher. Now, this may sound more like stupid aggression than great baseball, but as everyone cheered, he leaned in and told me he was sorry but if he stood out there any longer he was going to throw up. We ended up losing the game the following inning, and afterward, my dad took Andrew to urgent care where the doctor said he had a concussion."

As Eric finished, a Buck's batter slapped a base hit back up the middle. There was one on and one out. The sheriff's eyes and full attention were still on Eric.

"We could sit here and split hairs all day about the toughest and scrappiest players that have or will come around, but Andrew Main is the toughest son of a bitch that ever walked the face of this planet, sheriff, and there is nothing anyone could do or say that could convince me otherwise. We won two state titles through a combination of hard work, die hard love for the game and for each other, and luck, having the toughest guy and the most returning underclassmen played only a small part in the big picture. In baseball, it isn't always the team with the best players that brings home all the hardware." And with that, Eric turned deliberately back to the game.

The Sheriff remained facing Eric momentarily, processing the story in silence. He remained quiet, as another batter smashed a line drive back up the middle. The base runner advanced to third, and just like that, the Wrangler's thin lead was in serious jeopardy. The crowd murmured with quiet fear as Dugal, slowly waddled his bulky mass out toward his waiting lefty. Meanwhile, Eric felt like an ass for the timing of his story, superstitiously feeling partly responsible for the current dilemma.

"This is the fourth time through the lineup now." Darin said impartially. "He needs to switch things up, get these guys off balance again. The last two hitters haven't been fooled a bit."

Darin knew this is where a pitcher could get himself into a real tough spot. Young Joey Rocklin might be tougher than concrete, but he was an off speed pitcher. He needed to use his head, not his guts here. If he tried to let adrenaline get him out of this jam, he might not make it out of this inning. He didn't have the type of over powering stuff a guy like Red could rely on. He needed to use the off speed stuff to get ahead, and take a little bit more off in hitting his spots. It can be one of the most difficult tasks for a young pitcher. When the tension rises and the heart pumps hard, it is nearly impossible to take a little off without telegraphing it. Joey seemed to agree with whatever Dugal had told him, however, and he looked very determined as the big coach paced deliberately back toward the dugout.

The next hitter didn't appear to be a great presence at the plate. He was short but stocky with wrist bands and black stubble on his chin. Eric's first guess was a farm boy. Farm boys always had that wide squat stance, like they were straddling a bull. He looked like he would be more comfortable at a rodeo.

The crowd was growing anxiously loud once more, yet this time the noise was far less steady, at least from the home majority. Joey gave a long stare toward the runner at first and spun a curve ball toward the plate. It broke a little bit too sharply, falling low for a ball. Eric hopelessly wished he had kept his thoughts to himself.

Joey paused and delivered. Another curveball, this time he didn't over throw it, dropping it in for a called strike. Some cheers rose out of the crowd, but most held clenched hands to their lips or rocked silently. Darin couldn't believe Dugal had nobody warming up. He must have a lot of confidence in this kid.

A sudden breeze blew dust up along the front few rows, as Rocklin straddled the rubber. Darin squinted as the wind rattled to the back of the grandstands. He hadn't realized it, but the grey clouds were approaching fast. They still didn't look too intimidating, slightly dark and patchy, but they seemed to be circling. 'That's impossible,' he thought. Joey tried to pick the runner off, but he was able to dive back in time.

"The wind's confusing itself this afternoon." Sheriff mentioned, pulling his cap down a little more.

Darin agreed that something strange was happening. The wind nearly always blew out toward right-field, but it seemed to be circling around. The clouds worked quietly, despite all the tension in the ballpark, continuing to gather increasingly closer to the centerfield flag pole. Joey held a long moment then came toward the plate once more. He tried sneaking a fastball over the outer corner, but it caught the fat portion of the plate.

The farm boy was all over it. He drove a laser into the gap in left center. It might have carried right out of the stadium, but the wind hung it up a little, and it bounced just in front of the wall. The air sank out of the hometown crowd, as the opposing runners charged around the bases. One run scored. The sun disappeared behind the smoky colored clouds. Two runs scored. The batter slid into third safely, and suddenly Eric felt sick to his stomach.

A chunky kid wearing the number thirty-eight followed by a young kid carrying a catcher's mask hustled out of the dugout and down to the pen. The clouds kept creeping in, feeding off all the hysteria, taking advantage of everyone's attention being diverted by the drama unfolding on the field, everyone's attention except Darin's that is. He was keeping track of the events on the field, yet his mind couldn't stop thinking about the clouds. They were so foreboding and so unlike anything he could remember seeing before. Darin was never superstitious, yet something about this particular cloud formation was giving him the chills.

The next batter drove the first pitch he saw, a hanging curve, into left field for a base hit, plating another run. That quick, it was 3-1 Bucks with one out. Dugal signaled his chubby right hander to hurry it up. Rocklin started the following hitter off with a strike before beaming him in the shoulder with an off speed pitch. His rhythm was shattered. If he appeared slightly shaken up after three straight hits, he was now visibly lost. His emotions were showing. Eric felt terrible for him and the team. The shame of his own prideful, self indulgent attitude left him silent and alone. The catcher hustled out to have a word with Rocklin or possibly just buy time, but it didn't work. The next hitter shelled a fastball down the third base line, scoring another run and leaving runners on first and third. Dugal had seen enough, he marched out with his head down, signaling for number thirty-eight before he had even crossed the chalk line.

"Not a very pleasant turn of events." The sheriff said, his words branding into Eric's chest like a scolding iron.

"I will see you boys around." He sighed.

With that, he started down the stairs. He moved slowly through the hordes of silent, broken hearts. His eyes were already focused on the group of board members seated just off the corner of the home dugout. The sheriff had politicking to do.

He only made it a few steps before he turned around and added, "You boys be sure to tell Andrew, Sheriff Briggs says hello." It was a chilly message, and both Eric and Darin felt the compressed frustration behind the words.

"Will do Sheriff." Darin almost squawked through a choked up, dry voice. He knew it was a direct attack for the story Eric told.

Eric didn't say a word. He didn't say goodbye, or smile, or even wave. He locked up for a moment, but as soon as Briggs had made it down the aisle, he spoke directly, "Is he going to blame Andrew for a story that I told?"

His look was wild eyed with concern. He was still sorrowful for his timing, but he was angry at the Sheriff's indirect warning.

"No, he wouldn't do that." Darin replied. "He is just upset about the game that's all."

"I am too." Eric insisted.

The first batter to face the chubby relief pitcher was stepping to the plate. Eric looked over to where Briggs stood. He was talking closely in the ear of one of the team's primary boosters. Eric could all but hear him relaying the tale of Eric's arrogant desires for the Wranglers to fail in their quest for a state title.

"Shit, it was just a story. I want the Wranglers to win as much as anybody." Eric pleaded, honestly.

Darin started to reassure his worried friend that he had done nothing wrong, but the batter smashed a ball deep to left, sending the visiting fans into hysterics. Darin followed the ball as it carried like a missile further up and outward. His peripheral vision picked up the flag pole in centerfield and was amazed to see it blowing straight out. He didn't even have to watch the rest of the ball's flight. Instead, he looked for those clouds. To his surprise, the sky out beyond center was clearing. Most of the clouds were sparse and light. The grey clouds had moved over the grandstands and off down the first base line. They had blown right over the stadium, but now the wind was pushing them back over the field.

The umpire signaled the homerun as Darin noticed the first drops of rain through the nylon backstop. By the time the batter touched home plate and was mobbed by his entire team, the rain was falling steadily, slanting hard toward the home dugout due to the ever changing whims of the wind. For a few moments the entire park seemed to hang in limbo. Nobody could believe what was happening to their beloved Wranglers, and the rain only made things all the more bizarre.

It was only a minute or two before the sun shined through again, and the rain slowed to a misty drizzle then stopped completely.

"Sunshine showers won't last an hour." Eric recited smugly, looking around for signs of what the weather might do next.

Darin sat beside him lost deep in his own rainy thoughts. He was thinking of probabilities. He was thinking about God. Some people only consider religion when it is beneficial for them. Darin usually considered it when improbable occurrences happened. Lately, he found himself taking more and more notice of such improbable events. He knew that although it was highly unlikely to win the lottery, it did happen. What he didn't know was how it was possible that on this particular day, it could rain solely and suddenly on one team, while leaving their opponents bone dry.

He was still stuck on it, when a rainbow appeared out beyond the right field wall. Nobody took much notice though, they were all too sick at the scoreboard in left reading 7-1.

That night, the rain continued to threaten without carrying through, as dark overcast clouds blocked out the starless sky and cold winds howled and groaned. Darin picked up the phone just after dark. He dialed Andrew's number and held his breath, trying to decide what he would say. It is strange when a man has to plan out a conversation with his best friend, yet it happens more often than not as the years slide on. Eventually, men grow up. All too often, they grow distant. Andrew answered on about the third ring, much sooner than Darin was prepared for.

"Hello Andrew. How have you been?" he asked, faking a certain level of comfort. Andrew recognized this immediately.

"Pretty good, buddy. Look, I am really sorry about the money. I promise I am working on it..."

"Relax." Darin cut in. "I'm not calling about the money. I know you will get it."

Then, after a short pause, he added, "I was wondering if you wanted to go grab a beer and some wings or something."

"Ooh, I would love to, bro, but I'm real busy right now. Is there anyway we could do it next weekend?"

Andrew's rushed speech, and the distance in his voice confirmed what Darin had expected.

"Alright, next weekend it is then." Darin said, regretfully. "If you change your mind or just want to talk, you can call me anytime."

"Thanks, bro."

"How is Ginger doing?" Darin asked.

Now, he was hopelessly holding on.

"She is doing better." Andrew said showing signs of life.

"She is pretty banged up. She broke some ribs and her collarbone, and she will have some pretty nasty scars on her head, but her face shouldn't show anything permanent, which is good. I think she will be getting out of the hospital in the next day or two."

He spoke quickly. His voice was free of remorse, as if he were simply stating facts.

"That is good." Darin said. He began scrambling for more to say. He didn't know why, but he felt like he was helping by keeping Andrew on the phone.

"Alright, bro, I better get back to it." Andrew said. "I'll see you soon."

Darin didn't even get a goodbye out before he heard the click on the other end of the line. He worried what 'getting back to it' meant. He poured himself a glass of cranberry juice and went into the den, where he found Liz staring at the TV and concentrating on one of her hour long weekly addictions. He sat down in his recliner and watched her. She made him smile.

"What?" she asked when she noticed him staring at her.

"Nothing," he mumbled, "I was just admiring how beautiful you are."

Now, it was Liz's turn to smile. She stood up and moved over to his chair, where she curled up on his lap.

"You are the most beautiful girl in the world." He whispered down to her, kissing her head.

"Are you trying to get some?" She asked, wrinkling up her nose and squinting playfully at him.

"No." Darin laughed. "But, that doesn't mean I wouldn't take some if you've got extra."

They both laughed, and Darin began to tickle her.

"Stop that." she pleaded, "Seriously, stop it, baby. My show is coming back on."

Darin persisted.

"I'll bite your dick off," she screamed.

"Whoa there crazy." Darin said, finally stopping.

"I am serious. I would do it too." She panted, still trying to regain her breath.

"I know." Darin agreed. "Why do you think I stopped?"

They both laughed again, and Liz leaned up to kiss him.

"You're violent." He told her.

"Well, don't mess with me then."

She turned her attention back to the television. Darin played with her hair, kissing her again.

"I love you, baby." He whispered to her hair.

"I love you too." She replied.

Darin tried to turn his attention to the show, but he never could understand the appeal of reality television. The concept that life had become so boring it was more entertaining to watch talentless actors pretend to live totally amazed him.

He thought about his conversation with Andrew. He had gotten the feeling at the game that the sheriff suspected Andrew was doing drugs, but after everything that Andrew went through with Shane, he couldn't believe it. He had to admit Andrew definitely sounded wired on the phone. He was worried, but there was nothing he could do. He kissed Liz's head again, and though he didn't know why silently asked for God's help.

August 20th, 2004

Shane was tossing and turning, trying to catch a nap, but it was nearly impossible with all the noise this time of afternoon. He hadn't been sleeping well. Over time, he had grown accustom to the schedule of going to sleep early and rising even earlier, but the last week or so, there had been some pretty serious scuffles between some of the Natives and the white inmates. Hatred and racism were boiling, and many of the guards made it clear where their loyalties lied. There were far more Indians, but not one was amongst the guard's ranks. Shane hadn't caught any violence yet, but the constant remarks and threats were growing increasingly difficult to shake off. He wished he could stay in his cell, but that wasn't an option.

The only time he felt alive was during basketball games, though they hadn't been allowed to play for several days because of the lock down. Shane fell into a deep depression. He didn't talk, hardly ate, and had fought off suicidal thoughts. Often, he would feel certain that all was lost and cry silently in his bunk. A letter had arrived a few days earlier from Eric. He was very supportive, but there was so much church and God mumbo jumbo that Shane barely read the whole thing.

'If God is real, he sure as hell don't come visit here,' Shane thought. A lot of the guys Shane met turned to prayer, others turned to hate, most gave up and went through the motions. Shane refused to give up, though the uphill climb only grew tougher everyday. He was paranoid of what might happen if he didn't remain allied with his fellow Natives. The thought of violence or even death was more acceptable than being changed forever. Rapes weren't that common here, but they still happened and Shane was hardly a big guy. He rolled over on his back and stared at the concrete ceiling of his concrete cell. He trembled with fear. He would die before he let anyone violate him.

Finally, he reached under his pillow and removed the other letter he had received. He had waited long enough. It was time to open it. He let out a sigh, bit at his lip, and began tearing at the sealed flap of the envelope. The letter was from Sean Owens's mother. The return address said Mrs. Janine Owens and nothing more. It was written in a graceful print that made Shane want to cry. It was the first and only response to a half dozen apology letters written by Shane addressed to the family starting the second day he had arrived in prison. He had been awaiting this letter for some time. Eventually, he had come to terms with the fact that he wouldn't receive any response. He didn't blame them by any means, but he went on writing the apology letters all the same. He had written another eight or nine that he never even mailed, simply wrote and discarded.

He pulled the single piece of notebook paper from the envelope carefully. Already, he could see the message was short. He figured it probably told him to fuck off and die or simply stop writing. He unfolded the paper, smoothed out the creases, and read the elegant, feminine print carefully. He had expected a negative response. Still, it was difficult to fight back the tears. He read it all the way to the end, wiped his eyes, and laid his head back down on the cot. The voices and hollow noises from his hall muffled off the cold, smooth walls, ricocheting through his head down into his empty soul. He wanted to die. No, he just didn't want to live.

Mr. Billingsly
You are a cold blooded murderer. You stole my only son from this world in the prime of his life. You should not be apologizing to my husband and I for your sins. You should be making your peace with God, for only Jesus can save you now. As far as I am concerned, I feel confident that you will keep Jesus from entering your heart and die a cold miserable man. Prison is no worthy punishment for your crimes. An eternity in Hell awaits those who do

not repent their sins to the Lord. Do not write again. We throw the letters out without reading them anyway.

There was no signature. Shane rose off his cot only to fold the letter back up and return it to the envelope. He placed the letter on top of the stack of others. Then, he climbed back onto his cot, pushed his face down on his pillow and unleashed all the hurt that filled his heart. It took him nearly fifteen minutes to cry himself to sleep.

August 28th, 2004

Eric made his way slowly toward the back corner booth. He held a pitcher of amber colored beer in his right hand, and three glasses stacked together in his left. As he navigated his way through the crowd of pool players, he kept his eye on the contents of the pitcher, which was filled to the very brim, determined not to spill a drop. It was a rarity that he drank even a single beer anymore, yet he had never let go of his passionate love and respect for the sudsy nectar. Even in high school, Eric had always made it a point to finish every last drop of every beer he drank. He was quick to scold those who left wounded soldiers, always giving the same response to their worn out excuses, 'Well, it wouldn't get warm and flat if you tried drinking it in under an hour.' Out of nowhere, a young lady spun away from the pool table to his right directly into his path.

"Right behind," he said kindly, stopping on a dime.

She turned to him embarrassed, but he only smiled a concentrated smile. This wasn't his first time in a bar. He knew accidents can happen. She grinned back at him, thinking he was flirting, but Eric skated around her. Finally, upon reaching his destination, he set the pitcher down gently with only minimal drops sliding over the edge and down the sides to the table below. He handed Darin a glass and released a sigh.

"Thank you, sir." Darin responded unaware of the determination that had gone into the delivery. "I'll get the next one."

"No problem, bro. I am glad you convinced me to come out." Eric responded, sliding into the booth opposite his friend.

"Did you get a hold of Drew?"

"No, he didn't answer." Darin answered, glancing at his phone just in case.

"I don't know why he has that phone. He either never answers it or it's turned off because he hasn't paid the bill."

Darin laughed at this.

"He told me he has been really busy. I can't imagine doing what, but he seemed excited, and it was his idea to meet up tonight. That is why I was surprised he never called you."

"If he said he'll come, he will be here." Eric said.

He took a long sip of beer and tapped his left fingers on the table to the beat of Paint It Black. Darin wasn't quite as sure.

"You know he's changed a lot since he moved back." He said, trying to feel Eric out.

"I mean he's not working, and he says he's always busy. What the hell is he doing all the time?"

"I think about that a lot too, but you can't worry about him. He's a grown man." Eric shrugged, "He will find his way."

Once again, Eric went for a gulp of beer to wash down his words. This time it was a larger pull. Darin hadn't seen Eric drink in a while, so as he watched Eric fill his glass a second time, he decided to share his concern.

"I think that Andrew might be doing speed."

Eric gave him a quizzical look taking it for a joke.

"I had been thinking it was possible for a while, but after the way the Sheriff acted at the game, I really started piecing some of the signs together." Darin went on, reaching for his beer.

"I mean you know he was experimenting with coke way back when, and nobody knows what he was doing down in California. I mean you said it yourself. He was living with that crazy black guy. And with all the emotional stuff he has gone through, it's not that far of a stretch."

Then, realizing he was gossiping because he lacked evidence, he added, "I know he is our best friend, but it's a possibility…I am just worried is all I am saying."

Eric could see and hear Darin's concern. He didn't argue. The thought had obviously crossed his own mind, but like he said, there was little they could do.

"I never said Marcus was crazy." He said without making eye contact.

"What?"

"His black roommate," Eric clarified. "I never said he was crazy."

They drank in silence for a few minutes, observing the room's crowd as it grew loose and the taps poured. Darin pointed out a couple that was arguing up near the bar. A man dressed in a worn ball cap and dirty work clothes was at a loss for words as a young lady in tight jeans and high heels, apparently his girlfriend, chewed him out in a high pitched whine that carried throughout the establishment. Eric laughed, and the mood lightened a little. The first few chords of Alice Cooper's Poison were playing when Eric turned back to Darin and spoke.

"You know Andrew never slept good."

The sentence was random, out of the blue, and drew only a blank look from Darin.

"I think that's why he drank. Because he was always having troubles sleeping, and he slept like a rock whenever he drank," he laughed then added, "Probably because he always drank too much."

"Yes, but if I remember correctly, you used to out drink him more often than not." Darin echoed.

They both had a good laugh at this.

"That's what I am saying," Eric went on, though it had nothing to do with his point.

"I mean he drinks, and he's probably an alcoholic, but he doesn't have that personality type to fall into meth or whatever." He had convinced himself with an argument roughly on these same grounds a week or so earlier, but his thoughts were all muffled up now.

Seeing that concern was starting to wear on his friend's face, Darin decided he didn't want the night to turn into an intervention unless Andrew was showing clear signs of using.

"You used to get so damn wasted. If you wouldn't have met Claire, I don't know what would have happened."

"I have been blessed that's for sure." Eric agreed, crossing himself.

The two spent the next thirty minutes catching up, reliving football glories, and talking absently about where they wanted to be in the future. They were almost finished with their second pitcher when Andrew strolled up to the table grinning.

"Well, well, well, if it isn't my two favorite people in the world." He said sliding in beside Eric.

"Bard," he greeted with a nod.

He then noticed the red hue to Eric's cheeks.

"How you holding up, Preach?"

"Good." Eric replied, shyly. He felt a little embarrassed, but it was only momentary.

"Good," Andrew nodded in agreement.

"Well, we have a gathering of two or more, so I guess that means he's present huh?"

Eric smiled sheepishly, wiping at his mouth with the back of his big hand. He was buzzed but could still tell Andrew was in a particularly pleasant mood. At least he wasn't spouting blaspheme anymore. Darin was more coherent yet came up with the same inference.

"Somebody just got laid." Darin jabbed coyly.

This led to another fit of laughter out of Eric.

"I wish," Andrew laughed and grasped the beer Darin poured him. "No, it's just real nice to be out of the house again."

His words quickly reminded Eric of the alleged drug use, and, despite a look from Darin, he began watching Andrew intently.

"What have you been up to lately anyways? Briggs tells us you have been spending an awful lot of time down at the ball field." Eric blurted.

Darin frowned, seeing the conversation headed straight for an argument.

"Briggs huh?" Andrew asked with a snort.

"That old man really needs a hobby cuz being sheriff just don't seem to keep him busy enough."

Eric only seemed to take this divergent answer as evidence in favor of the accusations.

"Well, maybe..." he started, but Darin was quick to interrupt him.

"What's had you cooped up in the house lately?"

He wasn't sure if this would be taken as nosey, but he figured it had to be better than whatever idiocy Eric was planning to spew. Eric was already visibly drunk. His tolerance must be next to nothing. Andrew beamed at the question.

"Let's just say I am starting a business where I can be my own boss." He said with a wink. Although, this seemed self incriminating, Darin didn't take such gloating as a sign of drug dealing.

Eric, on the other hand, was practically spewing beer out his nose. Darin watched the alarm bells going off in his friend's head and was preparing to interrupt again, when Andrew continued before either could speak.

"It's going to be a surprise though, so no more talk about it. If it works out the way I plan, you will both know about it soon enough. Tonight, we are celebrating our friendship and praying for our buddy Shane who is still hanging tough. Let's not forget."

He raised his glass in a toast, and Eric and Darin were quick to do the same.

"Now," Andrew said putting his glass down after swallowing a large gulp, "Who wants a shot of whisky?"

"No thanks. I am sticking to beer." Darin replied. He hoped Eric would have the good sense to do the same, but he did not.

"I'll take a shot." Eric said putting a mask of courage over his crimson face.

"Alright, I'll be right back." Andrew said.

After he departed for the bar, Darin looked at Eric sternly.

"You really think you need a shot of whiskey, lightweight?" He asked.

"What?" Eric answered with another question.

"We are celebrating. One shot isn't going to kill anybody. Relax a little."

"I can't relax when you're running your mouth like Oprah. Andrew isn't on drugs, so let's just be thankful and drop it until we figure out more ok, Sherlock?"

Eric was confused, seeing as it had been Darin who brought up the drug accusations in the first place, but he was happy to acquit his best friend and agreed with an inebriated thumbs up.

"And ease off the gas on the drinking a little, Turbo. You aren't in high school anymore."

Andrew returned to the table with three shots. He slid one in front of each of his friends and started toasting.

"To health and happiness."

"Whoa, I told you I didn't want a shot." Darin snapped.

Andrew looked at him with shock as if he had heard no such thing.

"Come on. How often do we all get together?" He asked, keeping his shot raised up along side Eric's.

"Better yet, how often do I have anything worth celebrating?"

It was a self critical question that was asked only half in jest. Despite Andrew's mood, it wasn't hard for Eric or Darin to conjure up the broken man he was of late. It was a whole new method of persuasion from Andrew's usual self confident bravado that Darin wasn't prepared for. He looked into Andrew's eyes and raised the shot. Andrew smiled and Eric barked,

"To us!"

Darin was quick to chase the burning liquid with a slug of beer, and he could tell his reactant gag reflex wasn't alone when he saw the look of pure regret written all over Eric's face. Meanwhile, Andrew watched his friends with a loving smile. After that first shot, Andrew made no effort to catch up. It surprised Darin that he found himself pouring yet another beer for himself and two more for Eric, yet Andrew still sipped slowly at his first.

"You need a nipple?" Darin asked him, feeling self conscience.

Andrew laughed but gave no excuse.

"Shane's mom called me today. She said that Shane has a visit day coming up, and she suggested we should go see him." Eric said.

"She said she was trying to get a hold of you, but like everyone else, she couldn't."

Again, Andrew took the words in without response.

"I wonder why Shane didn't mention anything in his letter." Darin said.

He was partly wondering and partly boasting that he was in correspondence with their friend.

"I was wondering that same thing when she told me." Eric exclaimed.

"He probably doesn't want us to think of him in that setting." Andrew shrugged, finally joining in.

"He has a lot of pride, and he doesn't want this to be how me remember him, or maybe, he just doesn't want to deal with a big emotional ordeal, which we all know it would be."

"So you're saying we shouldn't go?" Eric asked.

He thought Andrew would have been excited by the news.

"No, I will definitely go." Andrew said. "I was just explaining why he might not have mentioned it."

This new topic put a damper on the mood again, and the table fell into silent thought for a few moments. The noise of the bar around them made Darin feel like oil in a bucket of water.

"Do you remember that time when you and Shane had us convinced that you had found your dad, and you were going to visit him in some prison in New Mexico or something?" Darin asked. His eyes continued to scan the activities of the room.

"Oklahoma, yeah, I do remember that." Andrew said with a forced chuckle.

"And Shane told you guys that I was moving down there with him after he was paroled. Then, Eric went and told his dad like a little girl."

"Shane said he was a hit man." Eric said in his own defense.

"I was just worried about you."

Even now, Eric's big face showed general concern. Andrew laughed.

"I know you were brother." He said slapping Eric's sturdy shoulder.

"You have always been my guardian angel. I hope you keep praying for me no matter what happens."

"You know I will." Eric blushed.

"Promise?" Andrew asked, finishing off his beer.

He reached for the pitcher, but stopped when he heard a voice from behind the booth.

"You're a real piece of shit you know that, Main?"

The three of them turned to find a grizzled man in a white t-shirt two sizes too small and a worn Budweiser cap that had been faded to a salmon color. He addressed Andrew with a sneer. He was a big fellow with a big shiny belt buckle protruding out between his shirt and jeans.

Behind him, two other cowboy looking fellows appeared equally as ticked off. Darin didn't recognize any of them, but he could tell immediately that they weren't old friends of Andrew's coming over to buy him a beer.

"You just love getting on other guy's girlfriends don't you, you little snake?"

"I have no idea what you're talking about." Andrew started to reply remaining calm, but the man interrupted him.

"You know a girl named Lacy Hepshire. You might not even remember her, but you fucked her, and she's my brother's girlfriend."

"I do know her. She never said anything about a boyfriend." Andrew answered without denying the allegations.

There was no fear in his face, no anxiety in his voice. His expression was deadpan neutral. He knew anger would only encourage a fight, and he was trying to defuse this situation without violence. The fact that the men came over talking instead of swinging was a positive sign.

"Fuck you, pretty boy. You knew. You just didn't care."

The man was trying to appear as intimidating as possible. He had his fists clenched at his side, and his voice was rising in volume. Darin could see that Eric was ready to fight, but he worried about their seated positions, and he really couldn't afford to have yet another blemish on his reputation, especially over something this stupid. He hoped everything could be smoothed out without bloodshed.

"Why isn't your brother here then, asshole?" Eric shouted, prompting the majority of the bar's patrons to take notice of what was taking place.

Darin looked to the front of the bar. The bartender still didn't seem to realize there was a problem. He was busy flirting with a cross legged girl on a bar stool that was likely under age. He couldn't have been much older than twenty-one himself. If things escalated to a fight, it would likely be the first one on his shift.

"Mind your own business, chubby." Someone shouted from behind the belt buckled leader.

"Let's go outside, and I'll show you chubby." Eric said pushing at Andrew to move out of the booth.

His good natured vocabulary lacked the profanity laced insults of the now turbulent crowd, but his anger was obvious. Andrew held him back.

"Listen, whatever happened. I apologize. I will apologize to your brother. I was never aware Lacy had a boyfriend. We were both drunk, and we both knew it was a mistake. It was a one time thing. She is a friend of mine."

The big man saw this as Andrew backing down. The dynamics of the situation changed as Andrew stood to his feet. Eric tried to follow him.

"Sit down Eric." He said his voice suddenly forceful as a jackhammer.

It caught Eric off guard, yet he remained half sitting on the edge of the booth both his legs solid on the ground. The crowd was fired up. They wanted to see a fight. The last thing they wanted was to see this end with a handshake.

"What about you Darin?" Someone shouted.

"You're gonna sit here with this piece of shit."

Darin recognized the speaker but couldn't think of his name.

"This fuck was all over your girlfriend when you two were fighting. They were out at the bars together all the time."

Darin felt hot, but he fought it with all his might.

"Watch your mouth. You're lying, and that shit is going too far." Andrew warned.

The old familiar intensity was building in those piercing eyes. This was the Andrew both Darin and Eric had expected to see when the man in the belt buckle first accused him. Darin had been proud to see his friend's maturity at the situation, but he was now torn between two feelings. Andrew was either pissed because it was a bold faced lie, or he was angry because he was being snitched out.

"You mean you didn't know that."

The speaker, a short, baby faced young man in a bright green polo and a hat he wore backwards, was the only non-hick in the bunch. He was skinny, probably the youngest in the group, but he spoke boldly like any coward will when standing behind others. He started to laugh but would never get that far. In a flash like lightning, Andrew's fist met hard on the kid's temple.

There was no time left to debate. Hell was breaking loose, and Darin didn't need an invitation. The accusations, his reputation, his own feelings that Andrew might need a good thumping, none of it mattered. Instinctively, he shot out of the booth and put his shoulder above the belt buckle of the big talker before anyone else could even throw a punch. Glasses broke, tables crashed, and the voices of shrieking girls and cheering boys sent the room into a chaotic state of emotion.

Everything was pure madness, but in these moments of total anarchy, Darin experienced clarity. Time seemed to crawl to nearly a stand still, and in the midst of fighting, he found himself at peace with his decisions and truly self confident for the first time in a long time. Perhaps, it was the first time he felt this sure of a decision since high school. He had acted on his gut instincts without over analyzing every detail of the decision making process. To his adrenaline filled body, this was athletic competition. When a hard right hook caught him on the ear, it didn't hurt only intensified his concentration.

Only a couple minutes into the fight, patrons began trying to break things up. The same people who had thirsted for blood were quickly nauseated at the sight of it. Darin wasn't so easily persuaded to turn off his competitive instincts as he was his anger. From the corner of his eye, he could see the gentle giant was hardly contemplating the idea of turning the other cheek.

Eric was tangling it up with two cowboys that were only now beginning to realize that their efforts to hurt him with fists alone were futile. Surprisingly enough, it was Andrew that was the first to cease. The kid in the polo was limping away from the mayhem as fast as he could, his face already swollen beyond recognition. Andrew let him flee without pursuit. He busied himself with trying to slow down the Eric juggernaut working its way through the crowd. Finally, everything ended as quickly as it had begun.

Andrew motioned for Darin to follow him as he guided Eric toward the back door. When the three of them reached the pavement of the back alley, Andrew broke into a sprint without explanation. Eric and Darin followed his lead. They dashed across an avenue, through another alleyway, and then veered right down a side street. Darin may have been more excited about the running than the scuffle itself, but it was clear that Eric was struggling to keep any sort of pace.

Eric shouted for Andrew to wait up. Andrew stopped until he was caught up. He explained that it wasn't much further but gave no answer to Eric's question of what *it* was. Andrew turned left on another street and slowed to a fast walk as the street climbed a hill. Eric huffed and puffed yet continued to move. About three-quarters of the way up the hill, Andrew disappeared into a row of bushes that lined the sidewalk. His friends followed him and found their path blocked by a chest high wall. Andrew had already climbed the wall and was walking across the roof of a second wall.

They followed his lead, finding themselves looking down over the dimly lit streets of the area and the twinkling lights of town sprawling out beyond in all directions. It was a beautiful view. All was quiet below aside from the flashing lights of two cop cars alternating between red and blue. The cars were parked along a well lit street, which Darin realized was Grand. A large crowd was gathered outside the bar they had fled, and the sound of muffled voices floated through the still night air.

"We are on top of the parking garage huh?" Eric asked, still huffing for air.

Andrew nodded, but his attention remained fixed on the movement down below.

"I didn't know it was this easy to climb up here." Eric added.

The parking garage was only a couple years old, part of a massive development project to encourage businesses to move beyond the familiarities of downtown.

"Remember when we used to climb this hill and throw water balloons down at cars driving along Nightingale?" Eric asked, searching behind him for familiar landmarks.

He spoke as if they hadn't just been involved in a massive barroom brawl.

"They tore that old bed and breakfast down." Andrew replied. "It used to be just on the other side of that shit over there."

He nodded toward a bulldozer and a trailer labeled with a maroon sign that read Grover Construction. The lot was fenced off. Everything inside the fence had been stripped down to dirt and bare ground, and it looked like a foundation had been dug.

"I bet they still throw water balloons from up here though." Eric continued. "This spot would be way better than the old one."

"Shit." Andrew shouted. His attention was still directed to the happenings outside the bar. "This is gonna be real bad."

"Relax," Darin suggested, trying to calm his friend.

He was checking himself for damages, but in the dark light of night it was nearly impossible. He still had quivers from all the excitement.

"Likely, nothing will come of it. Maybe we won't be welcome back there. At worst, we are charged with disorderly conduct, but I'll fight it if that's the case. They have to arrest you on the spot for something like that."

"That little prick in the polo is Mitch Melvin's kid. They've been out for me since I got back, but this time something will stick."

"Who are they?" Eric asked naïve as a bear.

"Robbie Melvin." Darin said without responding to the question.

"I knew I recognized him from somewhere."

Mitch Melvin was a county judge, and a very powerful man in the state. Robbie was a couple years younger than Darin. They had golfed together when Darin was young. The situation had suddenly become much more stressful. He began to worry, seeing all the worst possible outcomes.

This would definitely be a dire blow to his political future. He remembered Robbie's hurtful words about Liz. The way he had laughed about it. Spoiled little brat always had been a troublemaker. That's what happens when privileged boys, beyond the consequences of local authority, grow up in small towns. Darin's anger branched out. He began feeling angry toward Andrew.

'Why does he always stir up trouble?' he asked himself. He started to wonder whether Robbie's accusations had carried any weight.

"Everything will be fine." Eric reassured.

"You have witnesses to prove that they started the fight."

"Not to say Robbie started it." Darin disagreed. "He was just fueling the fire. I don't even think that little bastard is even old enough to be in a bar."

"It wouldn't matter either way." Andrew sighed. "It's only a matter of time before Rocklin pays me a little visit, and as long as he's alone, he will make sure that I resist."

"What?" Eric asked, more than a little frightened by what Andrew was insinuating. Even for a realist like Darin, openly discussing the strong arm tactics of local law enforcement was pretty intense.

Andrew didn't answer. He kept watching the distant scene intently. Darin hung his head. He had his own worries to think about.

"In Shane's last letter, he told me he's been reading the Bible." Andrew laughed dryly.

"He told me there is some pretty crazy shit written in there. He says he pokes around in it randomly, never reading more than a couple pages in a row, but he says there is a lot of stuff in there that makes a lot of sense."

"It was pretty inspirational to tell you the truth. I couldn't help thinking that he would show up some day as a love spreading, psalm singing, choir boy just like Eric. Hell, I figured if he could do it I could too."

He stopped. Turning his shoulders to face the mountains, his friend's could see that his eyes were strong and clear, though his voice was tired and sorrowful. He was speaking from the heart, but he wasn't looking for sympathy. He was look for absolution.

"I tried so hard guys."

He sighed and went on, "Tonight, I realized we are who we are. No matter how hard I try, I will always fail my friends."

"That isn't true." Eric said.

He was teary eyed, and his voice was choked up. He spoke with that determined voice that a loved one conjures up during the toughest part of a eulogy because the deceased deserves it done right.

"You're a great person. You are the best friend anyone could ever ask for. Sure you've made a couple wrong decisions, everybody does. But damn it, what happened to Shane was not your fault. You've been dragging it around like an anchor for too long. You need to let it go, bro. It's killing you, and it kills me watching it happen."

Andrew listened to his friend with a solemn expression. He kept his chin up and fought against the quiver of his lip.

"As for all the religious and spiritual questions you've been having, the truth is nobody knows, Drew. Nobody knows anything except God. It's all just searching, bro. And I can tell you from my own experience, the closer you think you are to finding the answers, the more questions will come. Look, I'm not telling you what to believe or not believe. Hell, I don't know what I believe these days, but I promise there isn't some clear and simple solution to life's problems out there. I wish there was. It's not that easy."

With this, Eric realized he was rambling off the subject. He was winded, a little foggy, and at a loss, so he turned to Darin, with tears rolling down his cheeks and onto the front of his torn shirt, for help. Darin had been listening closely to all that Eric said. He was still unsure of his own decisions and the consequences related to the fight, but he saw an opportunity to express some fears he had been bottling up for far too long, so he took a deep breath and looked out over the town into the distant night.

"I used to lie in bed and think about all the great memories I have. Baseball trips, hanging out in the locker room before football practice, pick up games in Eric's driveway, whatever they were they all made me smile. I worry about everything, and those memories were always a stress reliever for me. I would think about the good times for a few minutes, and I would start to set future plans and goals in my mind, sort of a routine before sleep. Lately, if those memories pop up, they depress me. I just keep thinking of how those great times keep growing further and further into the past. Anxiety starts to grip me."

He had to glance down to hide his eyes.

"I try to think about the future in a positive context, but I only long for the past more. I tell myself it is not healthy to live in the past. I mean I have so many dreams and big plans for the future, but at night, in the darkness, sometimes I see only gloom," he stops himself there, realizing he isn't helping the situation any.

The truth was that for months in the dark silence before sleep his mind continuously turned to death. It came to him like a premonition, but he fought it. He thought of other things, stresses and deadlines at work, or he took sleep aids, anything to avoid that dark emptiness of the unknown. Anything to escape the end.

Eric was visibly shaken by Darin's candid tale. It wasn't exactly the positive spin he had been hoping for. For Andrew, the reaction was much different. With his uncanny ability to read people, he could see all that Darin was thinking but had not said. He moved over to Darin slowly, stopping with about a foot between them.

"I would never do anything to hurt you." He said softly.

Darin remained impartial for a moment, but his strength couldn't fight off the tremble. Then, there was a sniffle. Finally, he turned to his friend and, as he had wished he had done that night at the falls he replied, "I would do anything to help you. I love you."

It felt weird, but his instincts had led him here and he let them take over once more. The two embraced tightly for a few short seconds each of them sensing this opportunity would never rise again.

"I love you too, bro."

Then, turning to Eric he spoke clearly.

"I am leaving tonight guys. I thank you for everything, but I have to leave."

Neither Eric nor Darin tried to convince him otherwise. They both wiped at their tears. Eric wondered how he would say goodbye, until Andrew made the decision for him, grabbing his big hand and pulling him in for a hug.

"Keep on praying for me, you hear." Andrew whispered, causing Eric to wrench down even harder on his powerful squeeze.

"Whatever happens, just keep on praying."

That was it. There was nothing more. Andrew jogged away from his friends, hopped off the first wall, and disappeared into the darkness. Eric watched him go, weeping like a dateless girl in a prom dress. Darin sat down, crossed his legs, and gazed out into the night, but the night didn't notice them. The heavens didn't change for their situation.

Darin wondered where Andrew would go. He wondered what the future would bring. He gazed thoughtfully out at the moon so far away in the distant night. It was a solitary orange beacon of light peaking out from the clouds in the starless sky. Noticing the way the street lights from town seemed to reflect back off the canvas of the night, Darin realized that if not for his spatial location, more stars would be seen. It wasn't that the stars weren't there or that they shined any less bright only that the observer always believes what is visible to the eye. He realized this, but he worried about other realities that may go unseen due to his faith in observation. He decided to close his eyes to see.

Instantly, he began to see and feel the sounds of the night. He could see the lilac's he smelled. He saw the erratic pattern of the wind as it blew gently against the moist, sticky skin of his face. He concentrated harder, exhausted from the evening's events, fighting to focus his wondering mind. Shortly, he began seeing the past, the faces in the bar, the words and the anger. He saw Eric's present sorrow.

Then, for an instant, he saw a little girl. She was beautiful and bright. It took only a moment for him to recognize Elizabeth when she flashed him that familiar, shy smile. She spun and played on a fresh cut lawn, her doll like features highlighted by the slanting golden rays of a rising sun. She seemed to be calling Darin toward her, but her voice was gentle and distant. She began to run across the grass, continuously inviting him to follow her with that loving smile.

Darin tried to follow but was unable. She continued to dance and play further away. The light of the sun grew blinding. Everything was becoming white. Darin squinted desperate to keep sight of little Liz, calling out for her to come back. Suddenly she stopped and gave him a quizzical look. Only her face was visible in the blinding light. Darin called out, 'Elizabeth.' As her smiling face faded toward white, he realized her eyes were not Elizabeth's yet very familiar still. That's when he finally heard her tiny adorable voice. She wasn't calling Darin. She was calling Daddy. Upon making this distinction, everything went white, and she was gone.

Darin shook with a jolt. His eyes opened to a beautiful crimson sky. His arms were cold, and his shirt and pants were damp. He sat up to find Eric fast asleep nearby, curled up on the roof of the parking lot. His face and arms were dirty from sweat and tears. His huge knuckles were covered in scrapes and had dried blood blotched across them. Darin climbed to his feet with a moan. His back felt stiff and sore from the hard surface of the roof. He had little pieces of gravel lodged into his triceps and forearms. There was a light wind, blowing thick cottony clouds across the golden sky overhead. Darin dug around in his pocket for his cell phone and patted his other pocket for his car keys. The sun was beginning to peer out from beyond Galvin Mountain far to the east.

His phone was blinking to warn him his battery was low. He pushed the menu button to learn it was 5:20. He had three missed calls all from Liz. Seeing her name on the screen, he remembered the little girl from his dream and wondered if it was his daughter. He pushed send and Elizabeth's voice answered on the second ring.

"Hello." Darin answered back.

"Are you alright?" She asked timidly.

Darin remembered the accusations Melvin had made.

"Yes, it's a long story, but I am ok." He sighed.

"I was worried about you," she told him with obvious concern. "A police officer called the house last night."

"Really?" Darin tried to fake surprise.

"Like I said, it's a long story, but I am headed home right now."

There was a short pause on the other end. Clearly, she was expecting a little better explanation for the time being.

"Ok. I love you." She said, partly afraid and partly confused. Her voice was emotional and innocent like a child's.

Darin pictured Melvin and everyone else in town discussing the common knowledge that his girlfriend was sleeping with his best friend. He started to grow angry, but then he remembered the little girl fading to white.

"I love you too, baby." He whispered gently. They both said goodbye.

Darin hung up the phone and ran a dirty hand through his greasy hair wondering what would come of all things. While he was wondering, he squinted toward the sun rising over the panoramic view of the valley and decided it was going to be a beautiful day. He knew he shouldn't, yet he had to smile.

"Eric, get up." He shouted, playfully. "We need to get out of here."

AUGUST 29TH, 2004

Around that same time, Andrew stepped out onto his weathered stoop under that same brilliant transitional sky. He hadn't slept a wink, but he felt more off kilter than worn out. He always loved the dawn. Multiple birds sang and serenaded for his attention, but only the closest and most consistent managed to capture him fully. He didn't know much about birds. He had never really cared, yet he was suddenly curious as to the composer of this particularly long winded and beautiful chirp.

Something haunting echoed through the recesses of his soul, tingling with the elegant song. Andrew thought of all the dawns he had seen with Monique down in California, how they would stay up all night being loud and alone amongst large crowds only to find themselves silently gazing out at a slowly brightening sky in the pleasant company of their own thoughts.

Staying up till sunrise can play some strange tricks on the human body. For Andrew, dawn was bringing on a nagging feeling of longing. Those carefree California nights seemed so far away. It wasn't the time though, for the memories were still fresh. It was something else something far more painful. He remembered Darin's words from the night before. Maybe it was part of growing older. The darkness that haunts children is of invisible and imaginary critters; years later, the darkness loses the mystery, becomes empty and cold, and even more terrifying than ever before.

Andrew climbed into his car feeling alone once again. Loneliness had never bothered him. It had always worked as a useful motivator. He turned the key and the engine sputtered and moaned in response. He tried again and again with the same outcome. He smacked the steering wheel hard with his palm, yet he wasn't angry. In fact, he smiled a little at the irony. Here he was finally running away, and suddenly it seemed the universe that encouraged him so often was now holding him back. He didn't even pop the hood. He climbed out, overwhelmed by the pulling sensation of what he always hoped was destiny, and headed down the drive toward the road.

He had over four hundred dollars in his wallet, durable boots for walking, and a pair of strong legs. He decided wherever it was he belonged he was going to make it there. His thoughts began to wonder as he pictured greatness for himself for the first time in a long while. He was able to see his work become a best selling book instead of just a means to explain to those he loved why he had fallen apart. The words that had nearly killed him in their transfer to paper were now out of his hands, out of his head. This fact gave him freedom from their burden and a sense of accomplishment. To be forgotten was his greatest fear. Forgotten by a father that left or a mother for paradise's eternal sleep. There was strength in his stride that had been missing since that horrible day he first heard the news. He remembered how artificial the problems of his own life seemed after learning his best friend was in such peril. It could have been enlightening. Had he forgotten his duties? Had he over leaped his place? There was no way to know; only his thoughts and this moment which he had been given.

Upon reaching the road, Andrew turned and headed toward town, the birthing of a bright warm day surrounding him. He gave only a short glance back at his place, but in that moment, he realized he had been accepting an existence that wasn't given to him but chosen by him. The run down trailer and the trash that covered the weedy excuse for a lawn only brought him illness now. He had stepped into the role of the broken down and beaten man without even the slightest fight and given up his own emotional independence to feed off another's sorrows.

The birds kept chirping and the gravel crunched under his boots, otherwise, there wasn't a sound to be heard. There was no wind, and the still, warm morning air foretold that it would be a scorcher by noon. His internal dialogue raged forth, grinding every available resource as he tried to distinguish rational thought from pure tugging emotion and pain. Images of success filed through Andrew's weary mind one by one. He pictured himself gloriously once again. Who knows maybe his book would be an inspiration to others. Maybe someone somewhere had felt the way he did or would in a day that had yet to arrive.

It was less than twenty minutes before he reached the bridge. He was making great time. One foot in front of the other seeing only sometimes, hearing only others, but constantly grinding out thoughts. Now and again he might roll his tongue in his mouth but unknowingly.

The temperature seemed to dip down a degree or two as he closed in on the lake. Out over the water and into the canyon, the low, eastern sun glimmered and danced on the water. Andrew couldn't help but stop and stare. This lake was his one true love beyond the human limitations of his friends. For a friend or a lover no matter how special can always change, choose to leave, or be taken, yet the lake was constant and always easy to read. Cold and motionless in the winter when nearly all fades toward death, vibrant and loving during the summer when life is in full swing. Its beauty, unlike the material joys of life, seemed eternal even though some day it like everything else would likely dry up and die. He was glad he would never wake to find it gone.

Andrew didn't reminisce too long. He said a quiet thank you that was more of a goodbye and started across the bridge. There wasn't a car as far as the eye could see in either direction. Ahead the road seemed to dance in waves beckoning him forth; the path so open. The world felt like it belonged to him and him alone. Everything was taking on a positive light. It was a new beginning. This time he would let nothing stand in his way. He would prove that fate did not control the outcome of men. He would prove that a single prayer addressed to God at eighteen years old couldn't tighten the string of a man's whole life. He would prove that a single moment would not define his existence. He began pondering nature and God.

He had long since decided there was no judging God sitting on a throne with a long grey beard waiting to damn his creations for being exactly as he created them. It just made no sense. It was illogical. The Lord he knew in his own soul would not send people influenced by their environment and natural human weaknesses to eternal damnation. Eternity is forever, and a God that could create the beautiful complexity of the Earth, let alone the universe, could never be so shallow.

His mind was weary; he was on the brink of exhaustion. He tried to recall the bible. There wasn't a whole lot he could remember. He inhaled and exhaled as he walked.

Jesus Christ suffered for mankind, but he was born the son of God. He knew his father and learned right and wrong from him. He was crucified, but was he ever truly abandoned? Did he ever abandon? These questions and a million more plagued Andrew's busy and exhausted brain.

Andrew was halfway across the bridge when he reached some ultimate conclusion, and he became overwhelmed with joy and hope, anxiety and fear. He became gripped with the type of adventurous shiver that drives teenage boys to pull crazy stunts that even the most daring and brave of men would not dare. His eyes dilated without realization or change of perception. His arms tingled and his heart pulsed. He looked out at the railing and remembered the head rush that came with doing a flip off the bridge.

He hadn't jumped off the bridge since high school. It had never struck him as odd before that he no longer did such things. It had always seemed like some things were reserved for boys. His brain would not shut up. How could he think all night and not stop with the arrival of a new dawn, a new day? A gentle breeze crept through the scorched grasses of the surrounding prairie.

Forgetting about the money in his pocket, and the fact that he was wearing jeans and boots, he moved to the rail and looked down into the shaded water below. He checked toward town for cars. There were none. From this spot on the bridge, he could no longer hear the birds or the bugs, only the many voices inside his head. As his decision was made, the voices lowered in volume, slowed in their vying to be heard.

Instead of climbing up onto the rail, he backed up a few steps. Deciding a back flip would take a little practice, the first jump he would go for distance like they used to do from the cliffs down in Grady. He smiled to himself, or he smiled to all those absent, ran toward the railing, and stepping one foot onto it, went to catapult himself outward. All at once, the voices fell silent and his mind freed him into a pleasant and wonderful dream.

September 10ᵀᴴ, 2004

Darin was chopping up peppers and onions for fajitas, and he chomped on a piece of gum to prevent himself from tearing up. He had never been much for cooking, but there were a few dishes aside from throwing meat on the barbeque that he could make pretty tasty. Cooking had always been his mother's specialty; naturally, he took on the traditional family mentality. In college, he had played ball with a couple of guys that were real wizards in the kitchen. His other teammates felt blessed to simply share in the meal, but Darin began to see cooking as a useful skill and another attribute to impress people with.

The problem was never an issue of having the time or the energy. It was the cooking itself that always worried him. He wanted everything to be perfect. There were so many steps that needed to be judged by eye that he always felt he was doing something wrong, but he found a certain satisfaction in knowing the meal was self-prepared. Besides, he had been promising Liz his self-proclaimed 'famous' fajitas for nearly a week.

The challenges of several things going on at once were increased by the heavy thoughts weighing on Darin's mind. He had been asked to help coach quarterbacks and receivers for the Wranglers, an opportunity he had long dreamed of. Unfortunately, he didn't think he would be able to dedicate himself fully to the task with his current work schedule. It was a dilemma that had his brain fatigued to the point of exhaustion. The staff was hoping to have an answer by the following day, as two-a-day practices were set to begin on Monday. Earlier that morning, Darin had all but finalized a decision to coach no matter what sacrifices must be made, but now, he had turned a complete one-eighty and was disappointed in himself. He couldn't figure out what it was, but there was this nagging fear that kept him from picking up that phone and accepting the position.

The chicken looked ready and Darin was about to add the veggies. Then there was a steady, business like knock on the front door. Darin was irked by the timing; he was expecting Liz any minute now, and he had hoped to have the table and romantic dial set when she walked in the door. Things had been going very well between them since the incident at the bar. She had not been upset about it. In fact, she seemed to be turned on by the thought of Darin as a bad boy, for their sex life had really started becoming adventurous since that morning Darin came home dirty and scraped up.

She hated fighting with a passion, but the fact that he had fought for his friends without self interest or concern gave him a hero like quality. And even though gossip was flying around town like mosquitoes round a stagnant puddle, nothing legal had come of the incident. The one conclusion left unwritten was that no one had heard from Andrew yet, but this didn't surprise Darin or Eric much. They figured he would send word when he got around to it. Darin turned down the heat on the burners and hollered toward the door, "Coming."

He wiped his hands on the seat of his jeans, spit out the gum, reached out for the doorknob, and shook with a jolt at finding the sheriff's sturdy frame blocking the doorway. He didn't have his aviators on, but he still made a sizable presence, standing erect with his broad shoulders and head blocking out the evening sun behind him and casting a shadowy silhouette over Darin even though they were roughly the same height. The sheriff removed his hat allowing for a better view of his face. His eyes seemed hollowed out and dry. The lines in his face, which usually gave him a distinctive wise appearance, seemed much deeper now, and his skin sagged loose around his jaw line, so that he appeared much older than Darin ever remembered him. He tucked his hat under his arm and wiping his matted hair to one side, spoke first.

"Evening, Darin." He said without smiling or frowning.

"Good evening, Sheriff." Darin finally mustered out after a moment. His voice scratched with surprise. His mind was racing a million miles a second.

"Are you busy? I was hoping to talk with you for a couple of minutes. Mind if I come in?" The sheriff asked.

His words came out rushed and without rhythm. There was definitely something heavy weighing down on him. Darin could see this even in his state of shock.

"No...I mean yes of course, no problem. Come in. Come in." Darin continued to stammer.

Upon entering the house, Briggs immediately commented on the smell, reminding Darin of the fajitas.

"I was just whipping up a little supper," he said, surprising himself at choosing the word supper instead of dinner.

He couldn't recall ever using the term supper unless he was poking fun at Eric.

"Can I grab you anything to drink?" He asked over his shoulder as he rushed toward the safety of the kitchen.

"No thanks, but thank you." He heard.

He leaned both palms on the counter top and tried to regain his composure. After a few quick breaths, he felt prepared for the conversation he knew was coming, poured himself a glass of ice water, and walked back into the den using light steps on steady legs.

The sheriff was sitting on the sofa beside the end table. His hat sat on the coffee table in front of him, and he seemed to be deep in his own thoughts. Again, his apparent age caught Darin's attention with some surprise. Darin took a seat on the recliner across from the sheriff, but he sat forward in it so that his back was unsupported and erect. The sheriff didn't even glance up. He seemed to be carrying on some silent dialogue with himself, so Darin saw the opportunity to go on the offensive.

"So what brings you to visit tonight, Sheriff?" He asked bluffing some upper hand.

This frankness seemed to help the sheriff gain some composure. He pursed his lips a moment, but his face seemed to be gaining its natural color.

"So, I hear the Wrangler's might have added a new member to the coaching staff this season?" Briggs fished.

Darin's mind went to work. He knew this visit was about the fight, but he was surprised to learn that the sheriff would turn to the football card so early.

"It's a possibility, but I can't figure out where I will find time for sleep or life between work and coaching." Darin replied, trying hard to control the conversation.

He had yet to figure out whether the sheriff was buttering him up or trying to pressure him toward an acceptance of the position. Darin was well aware how important football was to the sheriff both personally and politically, but he couldn't see him going as far as to lean on anyone for the sake of the boosters.

"Nothing wrong with staying busy. Sometimes work and a single passion are enough to make a life." The sheriff said offhandedly.

"Yes, but I just bought this house, that damn car out there won't pay for itself, and work has been a little slow lately. I just don't know how I can afford coaching yet."

At this, the sheriff let out a short, deep chuckle then sighed.

"I am going to share a little wisdom with you that I learned a long time ago. You can take it for what you want. All I can say is if you wait until you can afford it in life, you may well never leap."

The confident twinkle returned to his eyes, though he still looked worn down and wore out.

"I believe that." Darin said with a smile. Then, after a pause,

"I guess I just grew up with so many leapers that I grew a little tired of all the splats."

The sheriff didn't laugh at this comment. He didn't even budge, and Darin waited a few moments before continuing on, "The truth is that I will probably take the job. I mean I know it's not a coordinator position, but it will still be a huge challenge, and I don't want to get into it without fully dedicating myself to the job and ensuring those boys a chance to win." He finished speaking his true feelings rather candidly.

"Well, that's good to hear," The sheriff nodded. "It sounds like you have been putting a lot of thought into it, and I know you will make the right decision for you and them boys."

He paused there for a moment, breaking his steady eye contact and glancing toward the floor. Darin caught this immediately. It made him a little uneasy. He realized the formalities were over. They were about to come down to business. Darin sipped at his glass of water and prepared for a mental game of chess. The room suddenly seemed stuffy as the two men once again locked eyes.

"You know I hate to be a bother, but I think I would have a glass of water after all, if you don't mind. My throat's a bit dry." The sheriff stalled.

It was a tactic he was using intentionally, but Darin took it for weakness and uncertainty. This is what the sheriff was hoping for. He knew that if Darin felt confident and on the same level, he would open up without over thinking his responses. Darin returned quickly. He seemed to be holding back a slight smile, though still visibly quite nervous. He returned to his seat, forcing himself to sit back slightly without totally falling into the deep chair.

"Earlier you mentioned leapers. I am curious as to what you meant by that comment." The sheriff began. He shifted his large frame into an upright position similar to Darin's earlier posture.

"I think you know what I mean, Sheriff. We were a wild bunch when we were younger. My entire class seemed destine for early graves, yet it was mostly just reckless youth. Today, many of those same friends amaze me with how much they have matured."

The sheriff wiped a hand across his hair slowly.

"What about Andrew? You know him as well as anyone. How is he getting along these days?"

"Actually, he really seems to have come a long way since everything with Shane. I mean he is just so passionate about his friends, well, about everything really, that he takes things very personally, and it was difficult for him to cope with such a tragedy."

"So you think he felt responsible for what happened to Shane Billlingsly?"

"I am not sure. I suppose in a way yes, but there was obviously nothing he could have done to prevent what happened."

"Clearly." The sheriff agreed with a slight nod.

"Did he ever mention anyone else being to blame?"

"He never really spoke about it to me after that day the plea was reached, but I think he knew deep inside that drugs are becoming a problem around here."

Andrew had never said anything like this to Darin, yet he couldn't help but throw a little personal opinion in as he seemed to be in the driver's seat. Darin always felt there should be more concentration on the meth problem and less on trying to catch high school kids drinking beer and partying. Now seemed like a great chance to speak his mind.

"Really?" This sparked a great deal of interest in Briggs.

"Do you think he might have ever wanted to try and stop the drug problem on his own?"

Darin suddenly noticed he was being baited.

"I don't think so, no. Can I ask what this is all about sheriff?"

"Well, hell you're a grown man," The sheriff said, shifting his weight to the other hip. "I suppose there is no point tip toeing around the facts. Them Gardipee boys that Billingsly ran around with were found murdered."

He paused to gauge Darin's response. Seeming satisfied, he continued,

"Their bodies were found yesterday afternoon by some campers in the Great Basin Wilderness area. They were identified late last night."

Darin was speechless.

"These boys were worked over something nasty. I mean they were unrecognizable to human eyes. I won't go into all the details, but I have to know in all honesty, son. Do you think Andrew might have had anything to do with these boys' death?"

As he asked, he leaned in close to examine the details of Darin's face. His expression wasn't suspicious, only honest with concern.

Darin's gears had been shifting so fast that he nearly choked. He opened his mouth immediately, but the words took a moment to arrive.

"Sheriff, I...I really can't imagine," he stuttered, but then seeing the graveness in the Sheriff's face, his courage rose.

"No. Of course not. Andrew is incapable of anything like that. Drew would never murder anyone."

The Sheriff, seeming to have expected this answer, relaxed a little. Darin couldn't imagine what Briggs had expected him to say but suspected that after years of questioning people he had a pretty good idea when someone was hiding something.

"So where is Andrew?"

The question was meant to sound off handed, but something told Darin that this wasn't the first place the Sheriff had stopped since the bodies had been identified.

"He went back to California I suppose."

"When was the last time you spoke with him?"

"Thursday before last." Darin said honestly.

"The night of the big fight down there at the Tavern?" Briggs pressured, raising a brow.

"Yep." Darin said coolly, biting his tongue. He felt light headed as his face flushed.

"It was his going away party. He said he was going to search out some old flame that still had his heart."

The Sheriff remained still a long moment waiting for some crack to show itself. Finally, he seemed satisfied and climbed to his feet. He didn't say another word about the fight.

"Well, when you hear from him, you tell him he needs to give me a call ASAP, alright now?"

"Will do Sheriff."

"I mean that, son. I can help him."

"I understand."

With that, the Sheriff faked a polite grin, placed his hat on, and headed toward the door. Darin followed him silently, his heart still pounding a mile a minute. At the door, the Sheriff turned back around.

"I spose I'll be seeing you around, coach."

This time his smirk seemed genuine though stern. Darin shook his hand without a word and, after shutting the door behind him, nearly collapsed right where he stood.

OCTOBER 2ND, 2004

Darin was watching film with the offensive coordinator when his cell phone rang. He didn't recognize the area code.

"Hello, this is Darin." He answered.

"Is this Darin Bard?" The voice on the other end said through a Jersey accent.

"Yes."

"Hello Mr. Bard. My name is Zack Carlson. I was hoping you might know the whereabouts of Andrew Main."

"I am afraid I haven't heard from Andrew in over a month. May I ask what this pertains to?"

"Yes of course. See, I am a literary agent, located in Hartford, Connecticut. I was contacted some months back by Mr. Main about a story he had written, and after hearing a synopsis and reading a few sample chapters, I told him that I would see what I could do about getting his manuscript published."

Darin figured this was some type of joke, just the kind of thing Andrew would do after weeks of absence.

"Oh yeah, and what exactly is this story about?" Darin asked, lowering his phone to check out the area code once more.

"You mean you haven't read the book?" The man asked with great surprise.

"I never even knew Andrew write much more than his name."

Darin was growing frustrated.

"Ok, so you're the gambling type. I respect that." The man said with a chuckle.

Darin didn't understand.

"The reason I am calling is that the book is being published by a small company over in Minneapolis, and we need Andrew's signature on a few remaining documents before we can get the ball rolling on this. Unfortunately, I haven't been able to reach Mr. Main for some time, and he left your name as the financial backer of the author. As you are probably well aware, your number is unlisted, and you don't even want to know what I had to go through to get a hold of this number."

Again, the speaker laughed, but this time it was a nervous laugh. Apparently, he wasn't sure what to think of Darin Bard so far. Suddenly it struck Darin that if this were a joke, it was definitely well rehearsed, and there was a very good chance that it wasn't a joke at all.

"Financial backer huh?" He asked, while he planned his next move.

Again, the voice laughed a hearty laugh.

"I know right. Sometimes you have so much money invested out there that you forget where it all goes. So how do you know Mr. Main?"

It was becoming quite evident that this Carlson fellow really wanted to find Andrew soon.

"We've been best friends our whole lives."

This threw Carlson into a whole other world of confusion, but he felt like he was finally getting somewhere.

"Ok, so how do you suppose we go about finding him?" The man asked impatiently.

"I really don't know. He disappeared over a month ago, and nobody has heard from him since." Darin answered, realizing this meant Andrew was still missing.

"Well, this offer won't wait around for him Darin. Can I call you Darin?"

"Sure."

"Does he have a wife, mother, father, brother or sister that I could speak with?"

"No."

"How about an aunt, or a cousin, maybe a roommate?"

"He doesn't have any."

"Damn, does the kid have any family at all?"

"Not really. No."

"Isn't that always the case with these genius writers? I mean it seems like the great ones always come from tragedy."

Darin began to feel that old nagging sorrow return to him. This definitely wasn't a joke.

"Well, here's the deal. I have an offer on the table. It might last a month. It might last a week. It might last through the weekend. I don't know. First time author, small resources publisher, this stuff is hit or miss at best. How about I fax you over the terms of the contract, you read things over, and if we can't get a hold of Andrew then you decide what's best. After all, it's your money."

Darin thought about the offer silently a moment, glancing around the empty hallways outside the PE center. Photos of past champions lined the walls on either side of him. State champions from as far back as the fifties, their smiles captured forever.

"Can you send me a copy of the book too?" Darin finally asked.

"Of course. Give me an email address and I'll send it to you within the next ten minutes. So are we playing ball?"

"Yea, let me give you my fax and email."

After excusing himself from practice that afternoon, Darin called Eric and explained his conversation with the agent. Eric, always the optimist, wasn't suspicious at all. He said that Andrew had never said anything about a book and figured that it must have been the surprise he had mentioned the night of the fight. He told Darin it was no surprise that Andrew couldn't be reached, and he felt Andrew wouldn't have given Darin's name if he didn't trust his opinion.

Eric was overwhelmed with excitement to think that Andrew had written a story, and he wanted to know all about the story. Darin told him he didn't know anything yet and told him he would bring a copy by Eric's house as soon as he could print one off at his home office.

Darin drove home, poured himself a glass of wine and went into the den. Seeing the email from Zack Carlson's office, he grew very nervous but couldn't figure out why. The email connected him to a Word document attachment that was several hundred pages long. Written in normal sized print atop the first page was, 'The Religion of Baseball.' Below that were the words dedicated to and a colon. Darin's eyes scanned down the page, and he nearly dropped his glass as he read the three short dedications. Tears streamed down his cheeks once more, and he realized how hard it was going to be to read this story. The dedications were as follows:

To Shane the loyalist friend a man could have. Without you, I couldn't possibly be me.

To Eric for all your guidance and love. I know we don't appear to be listening, but we hear. Keep shining light upon our paths.

To Darin for taking the chance to make this all possible. I know you want it all, but I hope you learn to see how much you already have.

Printed in the United States
136617LV00004B/2/P